Praise for
THE ENDLESS FRONTIER
Books:

LIFE AMONG ◁ THE ▷ ASTEROIDS

Edited by
Jerry Pournelle with John F. Carr

ACE BOOKS, NEW YORK

LIFE AMONG THE ASTEROIDS

An Ace Book / published by arrangement with
the editors

PRINTING HISTORY
Ace edition / October 1992

ISBN: 0-441-48232-5

PRINTED IN THE UNITED STATES OF AMERICA

10 9 8 7 6 5 4 3 2 1

ACKNOWLEDGMENTS

The stories and essays contained herein are copyrighted as follows:

FOREWORD: THE ENDLESS FRONTIER by Jerry Pournelle appears here for the first time. Published by arrangement with the author's agent, Eleanor Wood, Spectrum Agency. Copyright © 1992 by J.E. Pournelle & Associates.

LIFE AMONG THE ASTEROIDS by Jerry Pournelle appeared first in the July 1975 issue of *Galaxy Science Fiction*. Copyright © 1975 by UPD Publishing Corporation and 1979 by J.E. Pournelle & Associates.

TINKER by Jerry Pournelle was first published by *Galaxy Science Fiction* in the July 1975 issue. Copyright © 1975 by UPD Publishing Corporation and 1977 by J.E. Pournelle & Associates. Published here by arrangement with the author's agent, Eleanor Wood, Spectrum Agency.

TOOL DRESSER'S LAW by Jack Clemons appeared for the first time in the November 1989 issue of *Amazing Stories*. It appears here through permission of the author. Copyright © 1989 TSR and 1991 by Jack Clemons.

THE GRAND TOUR by Charles Sheffield appears here by special permission of the author. The story appeared in the PROJECT SOLAR SAIL collection in 1990. Copyright © 1987 by Davis Publications and 1990 by Charles Sheffield.

INDUSTRIAL REVOLUTION by Poul Anderson was first published in the September 1963 issue of *Analog*. Copyright © 1963 by Street and Smith and 1991 by Poul Anderson.

THOSE PESKY BELTERS AND THEIR TORCHSHIPS by Jerry Pournelle appeared in the May 1974 issue of *Galaxy Science Fiction*. It appears here with permission of the author's agent, Eleanor Wood, Spectrum Agency. Copyright © 1974 by UPD Publishing Corporation and 1991 by J.E. Pournelle & Associates.

CONTENTS

The Endless Frontier

Jerry Pournelle

IN FOURTEEN HUNDRED and ninety two, Columbus sailed the ocean blue, or so we learned when I was in grade school. As I write this it's nearly 1992, five hundred years later. It's also ten years since I put together the first two volumes of this series.

In those heady days we thought that by 1992 we would be well on our way to space. A permanent space station, surely; and more importantly, new ships to give ordinary citizens access to space. After all, why not? It takes the same amount of fuel to fly a pound to Australia as it does to put that pound in orbit. Airlines operate at three times fuel costs. Spacecraft are no more complex than aircraft, indeed are less complicated: surely they can operate at five times fuel costs, meaning that it should cost no more than twice as much to get to orbit as it does to get to Sydney.

A lot happened during the eighties but going to space wasn't part of it. In 1980 I (as chairman of the "kitchen cabinet" group on space policy) told incoming President Reagan that "the statesman who leads mankind permanently to space will be remembered when Isabella the Great is long forgotten." That was heard and understood and for a while it looked as if something revolutionary might be done; but then came the assasination attempt. After that there were the Cold War complexities, and many other things, and the space program was not abandoned by the President, but left to others; and the others simply couldn't get it going.

There were a number of reasons for that. Most don't matter. One thing though: there was money. Not as much as NASA wanted, but more than enough to get the job done, if it had been done properly.

It wasn't. The space program collapsed because it didn't matter how much money was appropriated. NASA won the turf battle. NASA kept complete control over space. Thus the money went to NASA, and NASA, while very good at political turf wars, had become—well, incapable of building and operating space hardware. NASA produced paper; NASA produced good reasons why we didn't have results; NASA produced studies of a space station; NASA produced study after study to explain *Challenger;* but NASA didn't even try to produce low-cost ways to get to orbit.

Why should it? The only way to reduce the costs of space flight would be to turn it over to someone else, and that's hardly in the interest of the NASA officials. Few voluntarily abandon an empire. NASA never did. NASA took a Saturn V, the most powerful machine mankind ever built, a fully operational man-rated rocket, and laid it on its side as a lawn ornament, thus making sure that this monster didn't launch another Skylab to threaten Space Station Freedom.

NASA won the turf wars, and you and I lost access to space.

And yet: the dream isn't dead. It's still possible to build a civilization in space. All those things we said in volumes one and two, all that stuff about industries in space, taking the pollution off the Earth: all that's still true.

It's a dream worth fighting for.

Remember the song? "And the Earth is clean, like a Springtime dream, no factory smokes appear, for we've left the land to the gardener's hand, and they all are orbiting here."

It's all true: we could put most of the high pollution sources into orbit. We can stay rich and not pollute the Earth. We've only to do it.

More. It's still true that ninety percent of the resources easily available to mankind are not on Earth at all. They're out there, on the Moon, and in the asteroids, where it's raining soup, even if we haven't built the soup bowls. And it's still true that some of our best storytellers still dream of those times.

Herewith stories and plain talk about what we could still accomplish in THE ENDLESS FRONTIER.

Jerry Pournelle
Hollywood, Fall 1991

LIFE AMONG
| THE |
ASTEROIDS

Life Among the Asteroids

JERRY POURNELLE

ONE OF SCIENCE fiction's biggest problems is consistency. Whenever we make an assumption, it's not enough simply to leave it at that; to be fair to the reader, the science fiction writer should also see what that assumption does to everything else.

For example: What happens if we get an *economical* space drive?

The problem is more complex than it sounds. In fact, until we have some idea of what *kind* of space drive, there's no answer at all.

As an illustration, let us suppose we have a magical space drive in which we merely turn on an electric motor and "convert rotary acceleration to linear acceleration." Some readers may recall the Dean Drive, which was supposed to do just that.

Incidentally, the Dean Drive wasn't suppressed by big corporations, as I've heard some fans speculate. I am personally acquainted with two men who were given large sums of money by aerospace companies and instructed to buy the drive if they saw any positive results whatever in a demonstration.

After all, if the thing worked, even just a little bit, it would be worth billions. Think what Boeing could do with an anti-gravity machine! But, alas, no demonstration was ever given, although the prospective purchasers had letters of credit just waiting to be signed. Dean wanted money up front before anyone could look at his machine.

However, couldn't we simply assume that it will work and write a story about the resulting space civilization?

No. The discovery of a "Dean Drive" would mean that many fundamental notions we have about physics are dead wrong. It would mean a revolution at least as far-reaching as Einstein's modification of Newton; indeed, it would be a total refutation of Newton. The Third Law states that for every action there is an equal and opposite reaction. A Dean Drive, or anti-gravity machine, is a "reactionless" accelerator, exactly what Newton's Third Law says can't exist.

An anti-gravity device like that would have consequences reaching far beyond space drives, just as $E = mc^2$ affected our lives in ways not very obviously associated with the speed of light.

This doesn't mean that "Dean Drive" systems are impossible, of course. Firmly accepted scientific "laws" have been overthrown before, and will be again. It does mean that looking at their implications is a bigger job than a working writer wants to tackle for a single story, or even novel.

So we narrow the question down: What happens if we have something that gives one gravity acceleration over interplanetary distances at reasonable costs per ton delivered?

Part of that question is easy to answer. When I first started fooling around with this stuff I had to do the calculations with logs and a slide rule; then came the Texas Instruments SR-50 scientific calculator to change my life. Now, of course, everyone has computers. Anyway, I've made up a couple of tables to show what we could do with such a system.

The figures in Table One assume you accelerate halfway, turn end for end, and decelerate the other half, so that you arrive with essentially no velocity. The numbers aren't exact, because I haven't accounted for the velocities of the planets in their orbits— but after all, Pluto is moving about 5 kilometers a second, Mercury about 50, and when you're playing with delta v (the total velocity change is generally referred to as delta v, since it's written that way [Δv] in the rocket equations)—when you have velocity changes like these, who cares about the measly 45 kilometers per second difference between the two? For shorter trips the effect is even less important, of course.

The numbers are a bit startling if you're not familiar with them. Twenty days to Pluto? They won't surprise old-time SF readers, though. A full gravity is pretty hefty acceleration. If you don't bother with turnovers but just blast away, the results are Table Two, and they're even more indicative of what one gee can do.

Of course, long before you've reached light-speed at the end of a year, you'll have run into relativistic effects. We're only concerned with the solar system, though, so we can ignore trips

TIMETABLES FOR
INTRA-SYSTEM TRAVEL
UNDER CONSTANT ACCELERATION

TABLE ONE

TRAVEL TIMES AND DISTANCES
AT ONE GRAVITY ACCELERATION

DISTANCE		TIME (in hours)		VELOCITY CHANGE (delta v)
380,000	(Earth–Moon)	3.5		122 km/sec
1 AU*	(Earth–Mars, Venus, Sun)	68		2,421 km/sec
3 AU	(Earth–Asteroid)	119	(5 days)	4,194 km/sec
9 AU	(Earth–Jupiter, Saturn)	206	(8½ days)	7,265 km/sec
50 AU	(Earth–Pluto)	485	(20 days)	17,123 km/sec

TABLE TWO

HOW FAR CAN WE GO AT ONE GRAVITY?

TIME OF BOOST	VELOCITY REACHED	DISTANCE COVERED
1 hour	35 km/sec	63,500 km
1 day	850 km/sec	¼ AU
1 week	5,930 km/sec	12 AU
1 month	25,000 km/sec	200 AU
1 year	300,000 km/sec (speed of light)	½ light-year

*An AU (Astronomical unit) equals 150 million kilometers, which is the average distance from the Earth to the Sun.

longer than a month and avoid relativity altogether.

Now can we answer the problem of what happens when we have an economical space drive? Wrong. The problem is that last column in Table One. Just how do we expect to get delta v as big as all that?

Let's illustrate. Delta v can be calculated from mass ratio and exhaust velocity. Now you can hardly call a drive *economical* if the mass ratio is much worse than, say, three, which means that if you start with 1,000 tons you'll arrive with 333. What, then, must our exhaust velocity be to make a simple trip from Earth to Mars?

It's horrible. About 2,204 kilometers per second, and what's horrible about that is it corresponds to a temperature of 50 million degrees Kelvin. The interiors of stars are that hot, but nothing else is.

Just how are we going to *contain* a temperature like that?

One answer might be that we'd better learn how; fusion power systems may require it. OK, and the fusion troops are working on the problem. However they solve it, we can be sure it won't be anything small that does the trick.

It's going to take enormous magnetic fields, superconductors, heavy structures, and a great deal more. After all, nothing material can hold a temperature like that without instantly vaporizing, and even containing the magnetic field that holds that kind of energy is no simple job.

Let's assume we can contain fusion reactions, though. We know immediately that energy is going to be no problem for our interplanetary civilization. With plentiful energy we'll find that a number of our other problems vanish.

There won't be many "rare" materials, for example. If they're rare and valuable enough, we'll simply *make* them out of atomic building blocks. Of course it may be cheaper to go find them somewhere, such as on Mars or among the asteroids, but we'll always be up against competition from the transmuters.

Life on Earth, at least among the people of the high-energy civilizations, will change drastically. Pollution will cease to be a problem (unless the fusion plants themselves are polluters, which is unlikely but not impossible). The Affluent Society will be with us and so will regulations and rules, bureaucracy, and all the other niceties of a universal middle class.

All this comes as a result of assuming our space drive. More central to our immediate topic is the fact that the ships will be quite large—*Queen Mary* or supertanker size, not one-man prospector jobs. Someone is going to have to put up a lot of capital to build them, and it's not likely to be the Rolling Stones and their kindly uncle building ships in the backyard.

Only governments or very large international corporations will be in the spaceship-operating business, that's for sure. Thus there have to be profits in interplanetary travel. Not even governments will build more than one of these ships simply for scientific reasons. There's got to be commercial traffic.

Next, there's a technological problem: assuming we have fusion power and a method of getting electricity from it doesn't necessarily give us a space drive. Contrary to the notions of a lot of high school science teachers back in the forties, rockets don't "need air to push against"; but the rocket exhaust certainly does need something on the rocket to push against.

What can that be? Perhaps some kind of magnetic field, but an open-end fusion system is at least two orders of magnitude harder to build than a "simple" system for generating electricity. It's one thing to take 50 million degrees and suck electricity out of it, and quite another to use that as a reaction drive.

Perhaps I'm not sufficiently imaginative, but for all these reasons I decided to shelve the one-g system and design something much simpler. In fact, if we had the electric power generation system, we could build these ships right now.

Ion drive systems solve the "something to push against" problem by shooting charged particles out the back end. The ship is charged, the particles are charged, and they repel each other. You can get very high exhaust velocities, on the order of 200 kilometers per second, with ion systems. They're among the most efficient drives known.

The trouble with present ion drives is that electricity costs weight. As an example, a currently useful system needs about 2,100 kilowatts of power to produce one pound of thrust. Since the power plant weighs on the order of four tons, the total thrust is not one g, but about one ten-thousandth of a gravity.

It works, but it's a little slow getting there. Not as slow as you might think: it would take about 140 days to go a full AU (93 million miles), and your ship would reach the respectable speed of 12 kilometers per second. Still, it's hardly interplanetary rapid transit.

Suppose, though, we had a fusion system to generate the electricity. It would undoubtedly weigh a lot: let's say 1,000 metric tons, or about 2 million pounds, by the time we've put together the fusion system and its support units. We'd still come out ahead, because we'd have lots of power to play with. Assuming exhaust velocities of 200 kilometers per second, which we can get from present-day ion systems, we'd still have quite a ship.

She wouldn't be cheap, but it's not unreasonable to think of her as on a par with modern tankers. She wouldn't be enormously fast: I've worked out the thrust for a ship massing about 100,000 tons with that drive, and she'd get only a hundredth of a g acceleration. Still, a trip from Earth to Ceres would take no more than seventy days, and that includes coasting a good part of the way to save mass.

A worldwide civilization was built around sailing ships and steamers making voyages of weeks to months. There's no reason to believe it couldn't happen in space.

For example: IBS (Interplanetary Boost Ship) *Agamemnon* masses 100,000 tons as she leaves Earth orbit. She carries up to 2,000 passengers with their life-support requirements. Not many of these will be going first class, though; many will be colonists, or even convicts, headed out in steerage under primitive conditions.

Her destination is the asteroid Pallas, which at the moment is 4 AU from Earth, and she carries 20,000 tons of cargo, mostly finished goods, tools, and other high-value items they don't make out in the Belt yet. Her cargo and passengers were sent up to Earth orbit by laser launchers; *Agamemnon* will never set down on anything larger than an asteroid.

She boosts out at 10 cm/sec^2, 1/100 gravity, for about fifteen days, at which time she's reached about 140 km/second. Now she'll coast for forty days, then decelerate for another fifteen. When she arrives at Pallas she'll mass 28,000 tons. The rest has been burned off as fuel and reaction mass. It's a respectable payload, even so.

The reaction mass must be metallic (so that it will ionize), and it ought to have a reasonably low boiling point. Cadmium, for example, would do nicely. Present-day ion systems want cesium, but that's a rare metal—liquid, like mercury—and unlikely to be found among the asteroids, or be cheap enough to use as fuel from Earth.

In a pinch I suppose she could use iron for reaction mass. There's certainly plenty of that in the asteroid belt. But iron boils at high temperature, and running iron vapor through them would probably make an unholy mess out of the ionizing screens. The screens would have to be made of something that won't melt at iron-vapor temperatures. Better, then, to use cadmium if you can get it.

The fuel would be hydrogen, or, more likely, deuterium, which they'll probably call "dee." Dee is "heavy hydrogen," in that it has an extra neutron, and works better for fusion. We can assume that it's available in tens-of-ton quantities in the asteroids. After all, there should be water ice out there, and we've got plenty of power to melt it and take out hydrogen, then separate out the dee.

If it turns out there's no dee in the asteroids it's not a disaster. Shipping dee will become one of the businesses for interplanetary supertankers. There's plenty on Earth.

Thus we have the basis for an economy. Whatever people go to the Belt for, they'll need goods from Earth to keep them alive at first. Later they'll make a lot of their own, and undoubtedly there will be specialization. One flying rock colony will produce water, another steel, and yet another will attract technicians and set up industry. One may even specialize in food production.

Travel times are long but not impossible. They change, depending on when you're going where. It costs money to boost cargo all the way, so bulk stuff like metals and ice may be put in the "pipeline": given enough delta v to put the cargo into a transfer orbit. Anywhere from a year to several years later the cargo will arrive at its destination. If there are steady insertions, the deliveries are quite regular after that first long wait.

Speculators may buy up "futures" in various goods, thus helping capitalize the delivery system.

People wouldn't travel from rock to rock much. Thus each inhabited asteroid will tend to develop its own peculiar culture and mores. On the other hand, they will communicate easily enough. They can receive educational television from more advanced colonies as well as Earth and the Moon. They can exchange both technical and artistic programs, and generally appreciate each other's problems and achievements.

What kind of people will go out there? Remember that life on Earth is likely to be soft, because technologies like these will make Earth relatively wealthy; those going out will be unhappy about something. Bureaucracy, perhaps. Fleeing their spouses. Sent by a judge who wants them off Earth. Adventurers looking to make a fortune. Idealists who want to establish a "truly free society." Fanatics for some cult or another who want to raise their children "properly."

All this begins to sound familiar: something like the colonial period with elements as late as just before World War I.

On the other hand, the "frontier" conditions will be so different from Earth that the Belters may not be too concerned with Earth. What Earth does about them is another story.

Given fusion power, Earth could go either of two ways: fat and happy, ignoring the nuts who want to live on other planets and asteroids—or officious, trying to govern the colonies, and sending up air force or navy ships to enforce edicts set down by bureaucrats who've been outside once for a month and didn't like it.

Obviously there's a story or two in either alternative.

What kind of government will evolve if the rocks are left to themselves?

Well, each might *seek* independence, but they wouldn't necessarily *be* independent. They'd depend entirely too much on commerce. Given the enormous investments required to build the ships that carry that commerce, they'd depend on big monied interests, whether private or government.

The outfits that control the shipping will make most of the rules, then. They might not reach down into the colonies themselves to spell out laws and regulations, but the big decisions will be theirs. If we envision several large competing companies getting into the act, we can envision more room for Belt freedom through exploiting that competition.

The corporations themselves will have to set up some kind of corporate "United Nations," simply because you can't do business without enforcement of contracts, reasonably stable currencies, and the like. Their system may or may not be influenced by pressure from Earth—depending on how much Earth even cares.

There are probably other futures that can be built up from ships of this kind, but this story presents one reasonably consistent picture of life among the asteroids.

I think I might like it.

Tinker

JERRY POURNELLE

"THE TINKER CAME astridin', astridin' over the Strand, with his bullocks—"

"Rollo!"

"Yes, Ma'am." I'd been singing at the top of my lungs, as I do when I've got a difficult piloting job, and I'd forgotten that my wife was in the control cab. I went back to the problem of setting our 16 thousand tons of ship onto the rock.

It wasn't much of a rock. Jefferson is an irregular-shaped asteroid about twice as far out as Earth. It measures maybe 70 kilometers by 50 kilometers, and from far enough away it looks like an old mud brick somebody used for a shotgun target. It has a screwy rotation pattern that's hard to match with, and since I couldn't use the main engines, setting down was a tricky job.

Janet wasn't finished. "Roland Kephart, I've told you about those songs."

"Yeah, sure, Hon." There are two inertial platforms in *Slingshot*, and they were giving me different readings. We were closing faster than I liked.

"It's bad enough that you teach them to the boys. Now the girls are—"

I motioned toward the open intercom switch, and Janet blushed. We fight a lot, but that's our private business.

The attitude jets popped. "Hear this," I said. "I think we're going in too fast. Brace yourselves." The jets popped again, short bursts that stirred up dust storms on the rocky surface below. "But I don't think—"

The ship jolted into place with a loud clang. We hit hard enough to shake things, but none of the red lights came on. "—we'll break

9

anything. Welcome to Jefferson. We're down."

Janet came over and cut off the intercom switch, and we hugged each other for a second. "Made it again," she said, and I grinned.

There wasn't much doubt on the last few trips, but when we first put *Slingshot* together out of the wreckage of two salvaged ships, every time we boosted out there'd been a good chance we'd never set down again. There's a lot that can go wrong in the Belt, and not many ships to rescue you.

I pulled her over to me and kissed her. "Sixteen years," I said. "You don't look a day older."

She didn't, either. She still had dark red hair, same color as when I met her at Elysium Mons Station on Mars, and if she got it out of a bottle she never told me, not that I'd want to know. She was wearing the same thing I was, a skintight body stocking that looked as if it had been sprayed on. The purpose was strictly functional, to keep you alive if *Slinger* sprung a leak, but on her it produced some interesting curves. I let my hands wander to a couple of the more fascinating conic sections, and she snuggled against me.

She put her head close to my ear and whispered breathlessly, "Comm panel's lit."

"Bat puckey." There was a winking orange light, showing an outside call on our hailing frequency. Janet handed me the mike with a wicked grin. "Lock up your wives and hide your daughters, the tinker's come to town," I told it.

"*Slingshot*, this is Freedom Station. Welcome back, Cap'n Rollo."

"Jed?" I asked.

"Who the hell'd you think it was?"

"Anybody. Thought maybe you'd fried yourself in the solar furnace. How are things?" Jed's an old friend. Like a lot of asteroid Port Captains, he's a publican. The owner of the bar nearest the landing area generally gets the job, since there's not enough traffic to make Port Captain a full-time deal. Jed used to be a miner in Pallas, and we'd worked together before I got out of the mining business.

We chatted about our families, but Jed didn't seem as interested as he usually is. I figured business wasn't too good. Unlike most asteroid colonies, Jefferson's independent. There's no big Corporation to pay taxes to, but on the other hand there's no big organization to bail the Jeffersonians out if they get in too deep.

"Got a passenger this trip," I said.

"Yeah? Rockrat?" Jed asked.

"Nope. Just passing through. Oswald Dalquist. Insurance adjustor. He's got some kind of policy settlement to make here, then he's with us to Marsport."

There was a long pause, and I wondered what Jed was thinking about. "I'll be aboard in a little," he said. "Freedom Station out."

Janet frowned. "That was abrupt."

"Sure was." I shrugged and began securing the ship. There wasn't much to do. The big work is shutting down the main engines, and we'd done that a long way out from Jefferson. You don't run an ion engine toward an inhabited rock if you care about your customers.

"Better get the Big'uns to look at the inertial platforms, Hon," I said. "They don't read the same."

"Sure. Hal thinks it's the computer."

"Whatever it is, we better get it fixed." That would be a job for the oldest children. Our family divides nicely into the Big Ones, the Little Ones, and the Baby, with various subgroups and pecking orders that Janet and I don't understand. With nine kids aboard, five ours and four adopted, the system can get confusing. Jan and I find it's easier to let them work out the chain of command for themselves.

I unbuckled from the seat and pushed away. You can't walk on Jefferson, or any of the small rocks. You can't quite swim through the air, either. Locomotion is mostly a matter of jumps.

As I sailed across the cabin a big gray shape sailed up to meet me, and we met in a tangle of arms and claws. I pushed the tomcat away. "Damn it—"

"Can't you do anything without cursing?"

"Blast it, then. I've told you to keep that animal out of the control cab."

"I didn't let him in." She was snappish, and for that matter so was I. We'd spent better than 600 hours cooped up in a small space with just ourselves, the kids, and our passenger, and it was time we had some outside company.

The passenger had made it more difficult. We don't fight much in front of the kids, but with Oswald Dalquist aboard the atmosphere was different from what we're used to. He was always very formal and polite, which meant we had to be, which meant our usual practice of getting the minor irritations over with had been exchanged for bottling them up.

Jan and I had a major fight coming, and the sooner it happened the better it would be for both of us.

Slingshot is built up out of a number of compartments. We add to the ship as we have to—and when we can afford it. I left Jan to finish shutting down and went below to the living quarters. We'd been down fifteen minutes, and the children were loose.

Papers, games, crayons, toys, kids' clothing, and books had all more or less settled on the "down" side. Raquel, a big bluejay the kids picked up somewhere, screamed from a cage mounted on one bulkhead. The compartment smelled of bird droppings.

Two of the kids were watching a TV program beamed out of Marsport. Their technique was to push themselves upward with their arms and float up to the top of the compartment, then float downward again until they caught themselves just before they landed. It took nearly a minute to make a full circuit in Jefferson's weak gravity.

I went over and switched off the set. The program was a western, some horse opera made in the 1940's.

Jennifer and Craig wailed in unison. "That's *educational*, Dad."

They had a point, but we'd been through this before. For kids who've never seen Earth and may never go there, *anything* about Terra can probably be educational, but I wasn't in a mood to argue. "Get this place cleaned up."

"It's Roger's turn. He made the mess." Jennifer, being eight and two years older than Craig, tends to be spokesman and chief petty officer for the Little Ones.

"Get him to help, then. But get cleaned up."

"Yes, sir." They worked sullenly, flinging the clothing into corner bins, putting the books into the clips, and the games into lockers. There really is a place for everything in *Slingshot*, although most of the time you wouldn't know it.

I left them to their work and went down to the next level. My office is on one side of that, balanced by the "passenger suite" which the second oldest boy uses when we don't have paying customers. Oswald Dalquist was just coming out of his cabin.

"Good morning, Captain," he said. In all the time he'd been aboard he'd never called me anything but "Captain," although he accepted Janet's invitation to use her first name. A very formal man, Mr. Oswald Dalquist.

"I'm just going down to reception," I told him. "The Port Captain will be aboard with the Health Officer in a minute. You'd better come down, there will be forms to fill out."

"Certainly. Thank you, Captain." He followed me through the airlock to the level below, which was shops, labs, and the big compartment that serves as a main entryway to *Slingshot*.

Dalquist had been a good passenger, if a little distant. He stayed in his compartment most of the time, did what he was told, and never complained. He had very polished manners, and everything he did was precise, as if he thought out every gesture and word in advance.

I thought of him as a little man, but he wasn't really. I stand about six three, and Dalquist wasn't a lot smaller than me, but he *acted* little. He worked for Butterworth Insurance, which I'd never heard of, and he said he was a claims adjustor, but I thought he was probably an accountant sent out because they didn't want to send anyone more important to a nothing rock like Jefferson.

Still, he'd been around. He didn't talk much about himself, but every now and then he'd let slip a story that showed he'd been on more rocks than most people; and he knew ship routines pretty well. Nobody had to show him things more than once. Since a lot of life support gadgetry in *Slingshot* is Janet's design, or mine, and certainly isn't standard, he had to be pretty sharp to catch on so quick.

He had expensive gear, too. Nothing flashy, but his helmet was one of Goodyear's latest models, his skintight was David Clark's best with "stretch steel" threads woven in with the nylon, and his coveralls were a special design by Ambercrombie and Fitch, with lots of gadget pockets and a self-cleaning low-friction surface. It gave him a pretty natty appearance, rather than the battered look the old rockrats have.

I figured Butterworth Insurance must pay their adjustors more than I thought, or else he had a hell of an expense account.

The entryway is a big compartment. It's filled with nearly everything you can think of: dresses, art objects, gadgets and gizmos, spare parts for air bottles, sewing machines, and anything else Janet or I think we can sell in the way-stops we make with *Slingshot*. Janet calls it the "boutique," and she's been pretty clever about what she buys. It makes a profit, but like everything we do, just barely.

I've heard a lot of stories about tramp ships making a lot of money. Their skippers tell me whenever we meet. Before Jan and

I fixed up *Slingshot* I used to believe them. Now I tell the same stories about fortunes made and lost, but the truth is we haven't seen any fortune.

We could use one. Hal, our oldest, wants to go to Marsport Tech, and that's expensive. Worse, he's just the first of nine. Meanwhile, Barclay's wants the payments kept up on the mortgage they hold on *Slinger*, fuel prices go up all the time, and the big Corporations are making it harder for little one-ship outfits like mine to compete.

We got to the boutique just in time to see two figures bounding like wallabies across the big flat area that serves as Jefferson's landing field. Every time one of the men would hit ground he'd fling up a burst of dust that fell like slow-motion bullets to make tiny craters around his footsteps. The landscape was bleak, nothing but rock and craters, with the big steel airlock entrance to Freedom Port the only thing to remind you that several thousand souls lived here.

We couldn't see it, because the horizon's pretty close on Jefferson, but out beyond the airlock there'd be the usual solar furnaces, big parabolic mirrors to melt down ores. There was also a big trench shimmering just at the horizon: ice. One of Jefferson's main assets is water. About ten thousand years ago Jefferson collided with the head of a comet and a lot of the ice stayed aboard.

The two figures reached *Slingshot* and began the long climb up the ladder to the entrance. They moved fast, and I hit the buttons to open the outer door so they could let themselves in.

Jed was at least twice my age, but like all of us who live in low gravity it's hard to tell just how old that is. He has some wrinkles, but he could pass for fifty. The other guy was a Dr. Stewart, and I didn't know him. There'd been another doctor, about my age, the last time I was in Jefferson, but he'd been a contract man and the Jeffersonians couldn't afford him. Stewart was a young chap, no more than twenty, born in Jefferson back when they called it Grubstake and Blackjack Dan was running the colony. He'd got his training the way most people get an education in the Belt, in front of a TV screen.

The TV classes are all right, but they have their limits. I hoped we wouldn't have any family emergencies here. Janet's a TV Doc, but unlike this Stewart chap she's had a year residency in Marsport General, and she knows the limits of TV training.

We've got a family policy that she doesn't treat the kids for anything serious if there's another doctor around, but between her and a new TV-trained M.D. there wasn't much choice.

"Everybody healthy?" Jed asked.

"Sure." I took out the log and showed where Janet had entered "NO COMMUNICABLE DISEASES" and signed it.

Stewart looked doubtful. "I'm supposed to examine everyone myself . . ."

"For Christ's sake," Jed told him. He pulled on his bristly mustache and glared at the young doc. Stewart glared back. "Well, 'least you can see if they're still warm," Jed conceded. "Cap'n Rollo, you got somebody to take him up while we get the immigration forms taken care of?"

"Sure." I called Pam on the intercom. She's second oldest. When she got to the boutique Jed sent Doctor Stewart up with her. When they were gone he took out a big book of forms.

For some reason every rock wants to know your entire life history before you can get out of your ship. I never have found out what they do with all the information. Dalquist and I began filling out forms while Jed muttered.

"Butterworth Insurance, eh?" Jed asked. "Got much business here?"

Dalquist looked up from the forms. "Very little. Perhaps you can help me. The insured was a Mister Joseph Colella. I will need to find the beneficiary, a Mrs. Barbara Morrison Colella."

"Joe Colella?" I must have sounded surprised because they both looked at me. "I brought Joe and Barbara to Jefferson. Nice people. What happened to him?"

"Death certificate said accident." Jed said it just that way, flat, with no feeling. Then he added, "Signed by Dr. Stewart."

Jed sounded as if he wanted Dalquist to ask him a question, but the insurance man went back to his forms.

When it was obvious that he wasn't going to say anything more, I asked Jed, "Something wrong with the accident?"

Jed shrugged. His lips were tightly drawn. The mood in my ship had definitely changed for the worse, and I was sure Jed had more to say. Why wasn't Dalquist asking questions?

Something else puzzled me. Joe and Barbara were more than just former passengers. They were friends we were looking forward to seeing when we got to Jefferson. I was sure we'd mentioned them several times in front of Dalquist, but he'd never said a word.

We'd taken them to Jefferson about five Earth years before. They were newly married, Joe pushing sixty and Barbara less than half that. He'd just retired as a field agent for Hansen Enterprises, with a big bonus he'd earned in breaking up some kind of insurance scam. They were looking forward to buying into the Jefferson co-op system. I'd seen them every trip since, the last time two years ago, and they were short of ready money like everyone else in Jefferson, but they seemed happy enough.

"Where's Barbara now?" I asked Jed.

"Working for Westinghouse. Johnny Peregrine's office."

"She all right? And the kids?"

Jed shrugged. "Everybody helps out when help's needed. Nobody's rich."

"They put a lot of money into Jefferson stock," I said. "And didn't they have a mining claim?"

"Dividends on Jefferson Corporation stock won't even pay air taxes." Jed sounded more beat down than I'd ever known him. Even when things had looked pretty bad for us in the old days he'd kept all our spirits up with stupid jokes and puns. Not now. "Their claim wasn't much good to start with, and without Joe to work it—"

His voice trailed off as Pam brought Dr. Stewart back into our compartment. Stewart countersigned the log to certify that we were all healthy. "That's it, then," he said. "Ready to go ashore?"

"People waitin' for you in the Doghouse, Captain Rollo," Jed said. "Big meeting."

"I'll just get my hat."

"If there is no objection, I will come too," Dalquist said. "I wonder if a meeting with Mrs. Colella can be arranged?"

"Sure," I told him. "We'll send for her. Doghouse is pretty well the center of things in Jefferson anyway. Have her come for dinner."

"Got nothing good to serve." Jed's voice was gruff with a note of irritated apology.

"We'll see." I gave him a grin and opened the airlock.

There aren't any dogs at the Doghouse. Jed had one when he first came to Jefferson, which is why the name, but dogs don't do very well in low gravs. Like everything else in the Belt, the furniture in Jed's bar is iron and glass except for what's aluminum and titanium. The place is a big cave hollowed out of the rock.

There's no outside view, and the only things to look at are the TV and the customers.

There was a big crowd, as there always is in the Port Captain's place when a ship comes in. More business is done in bars than offices out here, which was why Janet and the kids hadn't come dirtside with me. The crowd can get rough sometimes.

The Doghouse has a big bar running all the way across on the side opposite the entryway from the main corridor. The bar's got a suction surface to hold down anything set on it, but no stools. The rest of the big room has tables and chairs and the tables have little clips to hold drinks and papers in place. There are also little booths around the outside perimeter for privacy. It's a typical layout. You can hold auctions in the big central area and make private deals in the booths.

Drinks are served with covers and straws because when you put anything down fast it sloshes out the top. You can spend years learning to drink beer in low gee if you don't want to sip it through a straw or squirt it out of a bulb.

The place was packed. Most of the customers were miners and shopkeepers, but a couple of tables were taken by company reps. I pointed out Johnny Peregrine to Dalquist. "He'll know how to find Barbara."

Dalquist smiled that tight little accountant's smile of his and went over to Peregrine's table.

There were a lot of others. The most important was Habib al Shamlan, the Iris Company factor. He was sitting with two hard cases, probably company cops.

The Jefferson Corporation people didn't have a table. They were at the bar, and the space between them and the other Company reps was clear, a little island of neutral area in the crowded room.

I'd drawn Jefferson's head honcho. Rhoda Hendrix was Chairman of the Board of the Jefferson Corporation, which made her the closest thing they had to a government. There was a big ugly guy with her. Joe Hornbinder had been around since Blackjack Dan's time. He still dug away at the rocks, hoping to get rich. Most people called him Horny for more than one reason.

It looked like this might be a good day. Everyone stared at us when we came in, but they didn't pay much attention to Dalquist. He was obviously a feather merchant, somebody they might have some fun with later on, and I'd have to watch out for him then, but right now we had important business.

Dalquist talked to Johnny Peregrine for a minute and they seemed to agree on something because Johnny nodded and sent one of his troops out. Dalquist went over into a corner and ordered a drink.

There's a protocol to doing business out here. I had a table all to myself, off to one side of the clear area in the middle, and Jed's boy brought me a big mug of beer with a hinged cap. When I'd had a good slug I took messages out of my pouch and scaled them out to people. Somebody bought me another drink, and there was a general gossip about what was happening around the Belt.

Al Shamlan was impatient. After about a half hour, which is really rushing things for an Arab, he called across, his voice very casual, "And what have you brought us, Captain Kephart?"

I took copies of my manifest out of my pouch and passed them around. Everyone began reading, but Johnny Peregrine gave a big grin at the first item.

"Beef!" Peregrine looked happy: He had 500 workers to feed.

"Nine tons," I agreed.

"Ten francs," Johnny said. "I'll take the whole lot."

"Fifteen," Al Shamlan said.

I took a big glug of beer and relaxed. Jan and I'd taken a chance and won. Suppose somebody had flung a shipment of beef into transfer orbit a couple of years ago? A hundred tons could be arriving any minute, and mine wouldn't be worth anything.

Janet and I can keep track of scheduled ships, and we know pretty well where most of the tramps like us are going, but there's no way to be sure about goods in the pipeline. You can go broke in this racket.

There was more bidding, with some of the storekeepers getting in the act. I stood to make a good profit, but only the big Corporations were bidding on the whole lot. The Jefferson Corporation people hadn't said a word. I'd heard things weren't going too well for them, but this made it certain. If miners have any money, they'll buy beef. Beef tastes like cow. The stuff you can make from algae is nutritious, but at best it's not appetizing, and Jefferson doesn't even have the plant to make textured vegetable proteins—not that TVP is any substitute for the real thing.

Eventually the price got up to where only Iris and Westinghouse were interested in the whole lot and I broke the cargo up, seven tons to the big boys and the rest in small lots. I didn't forget to save out a couple hundred kilos for Jed, and I donated half a ton for the Jefferson city hall people to throw a feed with. The rest went for about thirty francs a kilo.

That would just about pay for the deuterium I burned up coming to Jefferson. There was some other stuff, lightweight items they don't make outside the big rocks like Pallas, and that was all pure profit. I felt pretty good when the auction ended. It was only the preliminaries, of course, and the main event was what would let me make a couple of payments to Barclay's on *Slinger*'s mortgage, but it's a good feeling to know you can't lose money no matter what happens.

There was another round of drinks. Rockrats came over to my table to ask about friends I might have run into. Some of the storekeepers were making new deals, trading around things they'd bought from me. Dalquist came over to sit with me.

"Johnny finding your client for you?" I asked.

He nodded. "Yes. As you suggested, I have invited her to dinner here with us."

"Good enough. Jan and the kids will be in when the business is over."

Johnny Peregrine came over to the table. "Boosting cargo this trip?"

"Sure." The babble in the room faded out. It was time to start the main event.

The launch window to Luna was open and would be for another couple hundred hours. After that, the fuel needed to give cargo pods enough velocity to put them in transfer orbit to the Earth-Moon system would go up to where nobody could afford to send down anything massy.

There's a lot of traffic to Luna. It's cheaper, at the right time, to send ice down from the Belt than it is to carry it up from Earth. Of course the Lunatics have to wait a couple of years for their water to get there, but there's always plenty in the pipeline. Luna buys metals, too, although they don't pay as much as Earth does.

"I think something can be arranged," al Shamlan said.

"Hah!" Hornbinder was listening to us from his place at the bar. He laughed again. "Iris doesn't have any dee for a big shipment. Neither does Westinghouse. You want to boost, you'll deal with us."

I looked at al Shamlan. It's hard to tell what he's thinking, and not a lot easier to read Johnny Peregrine, but they didn't look very happy.

"That true?" I asked.

Hornbinder and Rhoda came over to the table. "Remember, we sent for you," Rhoda said.

"Sure." I had their guarantee in my pouch. Five thousand francs up front, and another five thousand if I got here on time. I'd beaten their deadline by 20 hours, which isn't bad considering how many million kilometers I had to come. "Sounds like you've got a deal in mind."

She grinned. She's a big woman, and as hard as the inside of an asteroid. I knew she had to be sixty, but she had spent most of that time in low gee. There wasn't much cheer in her smile. It looked more like the tomcat does when he's trapped a rat. "Like Horny says, we have all the deuterium. If you want to boost for Iris and Westinghouse, you'll have to deal with us."

"Bloody hell." I wasn't going to do as well out of this trip as I'd thought.

Hornbinder grinned. "How you like it now, you goddam blood-sucker?"

"You mean me?" I asked.

"Fucking A. You come out here and use your goddam ship a hundred hours, and you take more than we get for busting our balls a whole year. Fucking A, I mean you."

I'd forgotten Dalquist was at the table. "If you think boostship captains charge too much, why don't you buy your own ship?" he asked.

"Who the hell are you?" Horny demanded.

Dalquist ignored him. "You don't buy your own ships because you can't afford them. Ship owners have to make enormous investments. If they don't make good profits they won't buy ships, and you won't get your cargo boosted at any price."

He sounded like a professor. He was right, of course, but he talked in a way that I'd heard the older kids use on the Little Ones. It always starts fights in our family and it looked like having the same result here.

"Shut up and sit down, Horny." Rhoda Hendrix was used to being obeyed. Hornbinder glared at Dalquist, but he took a chair. "Now let's talk business," Rhoda said. "Captain, it's simple enough. We'll charter your ship for the next 700 hours."

"That can get expensive."

She looked to al Shamlan and Peregrine. They didn't look very happy. "I think I know how to get our money back."

"There are times when it is best to give in gracefully," al Shamlan said. He looked to Johnny Peregrine and got a nod.

"We are prepared to make a fair agreement with you, Rhoda. After all, you've got to boost your ice. We must send our cargo. It will be much cheaper for all of us if the cargoes go out in one capsule. What are your terms?"

"No deal," Rhoda said. "We'll charter Cap'n Rollo's ship, and you deal with us."

"Don't I get a say in this?" I asked.

"You'll get yours," Hornbinder muttered.

"Fifty thousand," Rhoda said. "Fifty thousand to charter your ship. Plus the ten thousand we promised to get you here."

"That's no more than I'd make boosting your ice," I said. I usually get five percent of cargo value, and the customer furnishes the dee and reaction mass. That ice was worth a couple of million when it arrived at Luna. Jefferson would probably have to sell it before then, but even with discounts, futures in that much water would sell at over a million new francs.

"Seventy thousand, then," Rhoda said.

There was something wrong here. I picked up my beer and took a long swallow. When I put it down, Rhoda was talking again. "Ninety thousand. Plus your ten. An even hundred thousand francs, and you get another one percent of whatever we get for the ice after we sell it."

"A counter offer may be appropriate," al Shamlan said. He was talking to Johnny Peregrine, but he said it loud enough to be sure that everyone else heard him. "Will Westinghouse go halves with Iris on a charter?"

Johnny nodded.

Al Shamlan's smile was deadly. "Charter your ship to *us*, Captain Kephart. One hundred and forty thousand francs, for exclusive use for the next 600 hours. That price includes boosting a cargo capsule, provided that we furnish you the deuterium and reaction mass."

"One fifty. Same deal," Rhoda said.

"One seventy-five."

"Two hundred." Somebody grabbed her shoulder and tried to say something to her, but Rhoda pushed him away. "I know what I'm doing. Two hundred thousand."

Al Shamlan shrugged. "You win. We can wait for the next launch window." He got up from the table. "Coming, Johnny?"

"In a minute." Peregrine had a worried look. "Ms. Hendrix, how do you expect to make a profit? I assure you that we won't pay what you seem to think we will."

"Leave that to me," she said. She still had that look: triumph. The price didn't seem to bother her at all.

"Hum." Al Shamlan made a gesture of bafflement. "One thing, Captain. Before you sign with Rhoda, you might ask to see the money. I would be much surprised if Jefferson Corporation has two hundred thousand." He pushed himself away and sailed across the bar to the corridor door. "You know where to find me if things don't work out, Captain Kephart."

He went out, and his company cops came right after him. After a moment Peregrine and the other Corporation people followed.

I wondered what the hell I'd got myself into this time.

Rhoda Hendrix was trying to be friendly. It didn't really suit her style.

I knew she'd come to Jefferson back when it was called Grubstake and Blackjack Dan was trying to set up an independent colony. Sometime in her first year she'd moved in with him, and pretty soon she was handling all his financial deals. There wasn't any nonsense about freedom and democracy back then. Grubstake was a big opportunity to get rich or get killed, and not much more.

When they found Blackjack Dan outside without a helmet, it turned out that Rhoda was his heir. She was the only one who knew what kind of deals he'd made anyway, so she took over his place. A year later she invented the Jefferson Corporation.

Everybody living on the rock had to buy stock, and she talked a lot about sovereign rights and government by the people. It takes a lot of something to govern a few thousand rockrats, and whatever it is, she had plenty. The idea caught on.

Now things didn't seem to be going too well, and her face showed it when she tried to smile. "Glad that's all settled," she said. "How's Janet?"

"The wife is fine, the kids are fine, the ship's fine, and I'm fine," I said.

She let the phony grin fade out. "OK, if that's the way you want it. Shall we move over to a booth?"

"Why bother? I've got nothing to hide," I told her.

"Watch it," Hornbinder growled.

"And I've had about enough of him," I told Rhoda. "If you've got cargo to boost let's get it boosted."

"In time." She pulled some papers out of her pouch. "First, here's the charter contract."

It was all drawn up in advance. I didn't like it at all. The money was good, but none of this sounded right. "Maybe I should take al Shamlan's advice and—"

"You're not taking the Arabs' advice or their money either," Hornbinder said.

"—and ask to see your money first," I finished.

"Our credit's good," Rhoda said.

"So is mine as long as I keep my payments up. I can't pay off Barclay's with promises." I lifted my beer and flipped the top just enough to suck down a big gulp. Beer's lousy if you have to sip it.

"What can you lose?" Rhoda asked. "OK, so we don't have much cash. We've got a contract for the ice. Ten percent as soon as the Lloyd's man certifies the stuff's in transfer orbit. We'll pay you out of that. We've got the dee, we've got reaction mass, what the hell else do you want?"

"Your radiogram said cash," I reminded her. "I don't even have the retainer you promised. Just paper."

"Things are hard out here." Rhoda nodded to herself. She was thinking just how hard things were. "It's not like the old days. Everything's organized. Big companies. As soon as we get a little ahead, the big outfits move in and cut prices on everything we sell. Outbid us on everything we have to buy. Like your beef."

"Sure," I said. "I'm facing tough competition from the big shipping fleets, too."

"So this time we've got a chance to hold up the big boys," Rhoda said. "Get a little profit. You aren't hurt. You get more than you expected." She looked around to the other miners. There were a lot of people listening to us. "Kephart, all we have to do is get a little ahead, and we can turn this rock into a decent place to live. A place for people, not Corporation clients!" Her voice rose and her eyes flashed. She meant every word, and the others nodded approval.

"You lied to me," I said.

"So what? How are you hurt?" She pushed the contract papers toward me.

"Excuse me." Dalquist hadn't spoken very loudly, and everyone looked at him. "Why is there such a hurry about this?" he asked.

"What the hell's it to you?" Hornbinder demanded.

"You want cash?" Rhoda asked. "All right, I'll give you cash." She took a document out of her pouch and slammed it onto the table. She hit hard enough to raise herself a couple of feet out of her chair. It would have been funny if she wasn't dead serious. Nobody laughed.

"There's a deposit certificate for every goddam cent we have!" she shouted. "You want it? Take it all. Take the savings of every family in Jefferson. Pump us dry. Grind the faces of the poor! But sign that charter!"

"Cause if you don't," Hornbinder said, "your ship won't ever leave this rock. And don't think we can't stop you."

"Easy." I tried to look relaxed, but the sea of faces around me wasn't friendly at all. I didn't want to look at them so I looked at the deposit paper. It was genuine enough: you can't fake the molecular documents Zurich banks use. With the Jefferson Corporation Seal and the right signatures and thumbprints that thing was worth exactly 78,500 francs.

It would be a lot of money if I owned it for myself. It wasn't so much compared to the mortgage on *Slinger*. It was nothing at all for the total assets of a whole community.

"This is our chance to get out from under," Rhoda was saying. She wasn't talking to me. "We can squeeze the goddam Corporation people for a change. All we need is that charter and we've got Westinghouse and the Arabs where we want them!"

Everybody in the bar was shouting now. It looked ugly, and I didn't see any way out.

"OK," I told Rhoda. "Sign over that deposit certificate, and make me out a lien on future assets for the rest. I'll boost your cargo—"

"Boost hell, sign that charter contract," Rhoda said.

"Yeah, I'll do that too. Make out the documents."

"Captain Kephart, is this wise?" Dalquist asked.

"Keep out of this, you little son of a bitch." Horny moved toward Dalquist. "You got no stake in this. Now shut up before I take off the top—"

Dalquist hardly looked up. "Five hundred francs to the first man who coldcocks him," he said carefully. He took his hand out of his pouch, and there was a bill in it.

There was a moment's silence, then four big miners started for Horny.

When it was over, Dalquist was out a thousand, because nobody could decide who got to Hornbinder first.

Even Rhoda was laughing after that was over. The mood changed a little; Hornbinder had never been very popular, and Dalquist was buying for the house. It didn't make any difference about the rest of it, of course. They weren't going to let me off Jefferson without signing that charter contract.

Rhoda sent over to city hall to have the documents made out. When they came I signed, and half the people in the place signed as witnesses. Dalquist didn't like it, but he ended up as a witness too. For better or worse, *Slingshot* was chartered to the Jefferson Corporation for 700 hours.

The surprise came after I'd signed. I asked Rhoda when she'd be ready to boost.

"Don't worry about it. You'll get the capsule when you need it."

"Bloody hell! You couldn't wait to get me to sign—"

"Aww, just relax, Kephart."

"I don't think you understand. You have half a million tons to boost up to what, five, six kilometers a second." I took out my pocket calculator. "Sixteen tons of deuterium and eleven thousand reaction mass. That's a bloody big load. The fuel feed system's got to be built. It's not something I can just strap on and push off—"

"You'll get what you need," Rhoda said. "We'll let you know when it's time to start work."

Jed put us in a private dining room. Janet came in later and I told her about the afternoon. I didn't think she'd like it, but she wasn't as upset as I was.

"We have the money," she said. "And we got a good price on the cargo, and if they ever pay off we'll get more than we expected on the boost charges. If they don't pay up—well, so what?"

"Except that we've got a couple of major companies unhappy, and they'll be here long after Jefferson folds up. Sorry, Jed, but—"

He bristled his mustache. "Could be. I figure on gettin' along with the corporations too. Just in case."

"But what did all that lot mean?" Dalquist asked.

"Beats me." Jed shook his head. "Rhoda's been making noises about how rich we're going to be. New furnace, another power plant, maybe even a ship of our own. Nobody knows how she's planning on doing it."

"Could there have been a big strike?" Dalquist asked. "Iridium, one of the really valuable metals?"

"Don't see how," Jed told him. "Look, Mister, if Rhoda's goin' to bail this place out of the hole the big boys have dug for us, that's great with me. I don't ask questions."

Jed's boy came in. "There's a lady to see you."

Barbara Morrison Colella was a small blonde girl, pug nose, blue eyes. She looks like somebody you'd see on Earthside TV playing a dumb blonde.

Her degrees said "family economics," which I guess on Earth doesn't amount to much. Out here it's a specialty. To keep a family going out here you better know a lot of environment and life-support engineering, something about prices that depend on orbits and launch windows, a lot about how to get food out of rocks—and something about power systems, too.

She was glad enough to see us, especially Janet, but we got another surprise. She looked at Dalquist and said, "Hello, Buck."

"Hello. Surprised, Bobby?"

"No. I knew you'd be along as soon as you heard."

"You know each other, then," I said.

"Yes." Dalquist hadn't moved, but he didn't look like a little man any longer. "How did it happen, Bobby?"

Her face didn't change. She'd lost most of her smile when she saw Dalquist. She looked at the rest of us, and pointed at Jed. "Ask him. He knows more than I do."

"Mr. Anderson?" Dalquist prompted. His tone made it sound as if he'd done this before, and he expected to be answered.

If Jed resented that he didn't show it. "Simple enough. Joe always seemed happy enough when he came in here after his shift—"

Dalquist looked from Jed to Barbara. She nodded.

"—until the last time. That night he got stinking drunk. Kept mutterin' something about 'Not that way. There's got to be another way.' "

"Do you know what that meant?"

"No," Jed said. "But he kept saying it. Then he got really stinking and I sent him home with a couple of the guys he worked with."

"What happened when he got home?" Dalquist asked.

"He never came home, Buck," Barbara said. "I got worried about him, but I couldn't find him. The men he'd left here with said he'd got to feeling better and left them—"

"Damn fools," Jed muttered. "He was right out of it. Nobody should go outside with that much to drink."

"And they found him outside?"

"At the refinery. Helmet busted open. Been dead five, six hours. Held the inquest right in here, at that table al Shamlan was sitting at this afternoon."

"Who held the inquest?" Dalquist asked.

"Rhoda."

"Doesn't make sense," I said.

"No." Janet didn't like it much either. "Barbara, don't you have any idea of what Joe meant? Was he worried about something?"

"Nothing he told me about. He wasn't—we weren't fighting or anything. I'm sure he didn't—"

"Humpf." Dalquist shook his head. "What damned fool suggested suicide?"

"Well," Jed said, "you know how it is. If a man takes on a big load and wanders around outside, it might as well be suicide. Hornbinder said we were doing Barbara a favor, voting it an accident."

Dalquist took papers out of his pouch. "He was right, of course. I wonder if Hornbinder knew that all Hansen employees receive a paid-up insurance policy as one of their retirement benefits?"

"I didn't know it," I said.

Janet was more practical. "How much is it worth?"

"I am not sure of the exact amounts," Dalquist said. "There are trust accounts involved also. Sufficient to get Barbara and the children back to Mars and pay for their living expenses there. Assuming you want to go?"

"I don't know," Barbara said. "Let me think about it. Joe and I came here to get away from the big companies. I don't have to like Rhoda and the city hall crowd to appreciate what we've got in Jefferson. Independence is worth something."

"Indeed," Dalquist said. He wasn't agreeing with her, and suddenly we all knew he and Barbara had been through this argument before. I wondered when.

"Janet, what would you do?" Barbara asked.

Jan shrugged. "Not a fair question. Roland and I made that decision a long time ago. But neither of us is alone." She reached for my hand across the table.

As she'd said, we made our choice. We've had plenty of offers for *Slingshot*, from outfits that would be happy to hire us as crew for *Slinger*. It would mean no more hustle to meet the mortgage payments, and not a lot of change in the way we live—but we wouldn't be our own people anymore. We've never seriously considered taking any of the offers."

"You don't have to be alone," Dalquist said.

"I know, Buck." There was a wistful note in Barbara's voice. They looked at each other for a long time. Then we sat down to dinner.

I was in my office aboard *Slingshot*. Thirty hours had gone by since I'd signed the charter contract, and I still didn't know what I was boosting, or when. It didn't make sense.

Janet refused to worry about it. We'd cabled the money on to Marsport, all of Jefferson's treasury and what we'd got for our cargo, so Barclay's was happy for a while. We had enough deuterium aboard *Slinger* to get where we could buy more. She kept asking what there was to worry about, and I didn't have any answer.

I was still brooding about it when Oswald Dalquist tapped on the door.

I hadn't seen him much since the dinner at the Doghouse, and he didn't look any different, but he wasn't the same man. I suppose the change was in me. You can't think of a man named "Buck" the same way you think of an Oswald.

"Sit down," I said. That was formality, of course. It's no harder to stand than sit in the tiny gravity we felt. "I've been meaning to say something about the way you handled Horny. I don't think I've ever seen anybody do that."

His smile was thin, and I guess it hadn't changed either, but it didn't seem like an accountant's smile anymore. "It's an interesting story, actually," he said. "A long time ago I was in a big colony ship. Long passage, nothing to do. Discovered the other colonists didn't know much about playing poker."

We exchanged grins again.

"I won so much it made me worry that someone would take it away from me, so I hired the biggest man in the bay to watch my back. Sure enough, some chap accused me of cheating, so I called on my big friend—"

"Yeah?"

"And he shouted 'Fifty to the first guy that decks him.' Worked splendidly, although it wasn't precisely what I'd expected when I hired him—"

We had our laugh.

"When are we leaving, Captain Kephart?"

"Beats me. When they get the cargo ready to boost, I guess."

"That might be a long time," Dalquist said.

"What does that mean?"

"I've been asking around. To the best of my knowledge, there are no preparations for boosting a big cargo pod."

"That's stupid," I said. "Well, it's their business. When we go, how many passengers am I going to have?"

His little smile faded entirely. "I wish I knew. You've guessed that Joe Colella and I were old friends. And rivals for the same girl."

"Yeah. I'm wondering why you—hell, we talked about them on the way in. You never let on you'd ever heard of them."

He nodded carefully. "I wanted to be certain. I only knew that Joe was supposed to have died in an accident. He was not the kind of man accidents happen to. Not even out here."

"What is that supposed to mean?"

"Only that Joe Colella was one of the most careful men you will ever meet, and I didn't care to discuss my business with Barbara until I knew more about the situation in Jefferson. Now I'm beginning to wonder—"

"Dad!" Pam was on watch, and she sounded excited. The intercom box said again, "Dad!"

"Right, sweetheart."

"You better come up quick. There's a message coming through. You better hurry."

"MAYDAY MAYDAY MAYDAY." The voice was cold and unemotional, the way they are when they really mean it. It rolled off the tape Pam had made. "MAYDAY MAYDAY MAYDAY. THIS IS PEGASUS LINES BOOSTSHIP *AGAMEMNON* OUTBOUND EARTH TO PALLAS. OUR MAIN ENGINES ARE DISABLED. I SAY AGAIN, MAIN ENGINES DISABLED OUR VELOCITY RELATIVE TO SOL IS ONE FOUR ZERO KILOMETERS PER SECOND, I SAY AGAIN, ONE HUNDRED FORTY KILOMETERS PER SECOND. AUXILIARY POWER IS FAILING. MAIN ENGINES CANNOT BE REPAIRED. PRESENT SHIP MASS IS 54,000 TONS. SEVENTEEN HUNDRED PASSENGERS ABOARD. MAYDAY MAYDAY MAYDAY MAYDAY."

"Lord God." I wasn't really aware that I was talking. The kids had crowded into the control cabin, and we listened as the tape went on to give a string of numbers, the vectors to locate *Agamemnon* precisely. I started to punch them into the plotting tanks, but Pam stopped me.

"I already did that, Dad." She hit the activation switch to bring the screen to life.

It showed a picture of our side of the Solar System, the inner planets and inhabited rocks, along with a block of numbers and a long thin line with a dot at the end to represent *Agamemnon*. Other dots winked on and off: boostships.

We were the only one that stood a prayer of a chance of catching up with *Agamemnon*.

The other screen lit, giving us what the *Register* knew about *Agamemnon*. It didn't look good. She was an enormous old cargo/passenger ship, over thirty years old—and out here that's old indeed. She'd been built for a useful life of half that, and sold off to Pegasus lines when P & L decided she wasn't safe.

Her auxiliary power was furnished by a plutonium pile. If something went wrong with it, there was no way to repair it in space. Without auxiliary power, the life-support systems couldn't function. I was still looking at her specs when the comm panel lit. Local call, Port Captain's frequency.

"Yeah, Jed?" I said.

"You've got the Mayday?"

"Sure. I figure we've got about sixty hours max to fuel up and still let me catch her. I've got to try it, of course."

"Certainly, Captain." The voice was Rhoda's. "I've already sent a crew to start work on the fuel pod. I suggest you work with them to be sure it's right."

"Yeah. They'll have to work damned fast." *Slingshot* doesn't carry anything like the tankage a run like this would need.

"One more thing, Captain," Rhoda said. "Remember that your ship is under exclusive charter to the Jefferson Corporation. We'll make the legal arrangements with Pegasus. You concentrate on getting your ship ready."

"Yeah, OK. Out." I switched the common system to *record*. "Agamemnon, this is cargo tug *Slingshot*. I have your Mayday. Intercept is possible, but I cannot carry sufficient fuel and mass to decelerate your ship. I must vampire your dee and mass, I say again, we must transfer your fuel and reaction mass to my ship.

"We have no facilities for taking your passengers aboard. We will attempt to take your ship in tow and decelerate using your deuterium and reaction mass. Our engines are modified General Electric Model five-niner ion-fusion. Preparations for coming to your assistance are under way. Suggest your crew begin preparations for fuel transfer. Over."

Then I looked around the cabin. Janet and our oldest were ashore. "Pam, you're in charge. Send that, and record the reply. You can start the checklist for boost. I make it about 200 centimeters acceleration, but you'd better check that. Whatever it is, we'll need to secure for it. Also, get in a call to find your mother. God knows where she is."

"Sure, Dad." She looked very serious, and I wasn't worried. Hal's the oldest, but Pam's a lot more thorough.

The *Register* didn't give anywhere near enough data about *Agamemnon*. I could see from the recognition pix that she carried her reaction mass in strap-ons alongside the main hull, rather than in detachable pods right forward the way *Slinger* does. That meant we might have to transfer the whole lot before we could start deceleration.

She had been built as a general-purpose ship, so her hull structure forward was beefy enough to take the thrust of a cargo pod—but how *much* thrust? If we were going to get her down, we'd have to push like hell on her bows, and there was no way to tell if they were strong enough to take it.

I looked over to where Pam was aiming our high-gain antenna for the message to *Agamemnon*. She looked like she'd been doing this all her life, which I guess she had been, but mostly for drills. It gave me a funny feeling to know she'd grown up sometime in the last couple of years and Janet and I hadn't really noticed.

"Pamela, I'm going to need more information on *Agamemnon*," I told her. "The kids had a TV cast out of Marsport, so you ought to be able to get through. Ask for anthing they have on that ship. Structural strength, fuel-handling equipment, everything they've got."

"Yes, sir."

"OK. I'm going ashore to see about the fuel pods. Call me when we get some answers, but if there's nothing important from *Agamemnon* just hang on to it."

"What happens if we can't catch them?" Phillip asked.

Pam and Jennifer were trying to explain it to him as I went down to the lock.

Jed had lunch waiting in the Doghouse. "How's it going?" he asked when I came in.

"Pretty good. Damned good, all things considered." The refinery crew had built up fuel pods for *Slinger* before, so they knew what I needed, but they'd never made one that had to stand up to a full fifth of a gee. A couple of centimeters is hefty acceleration when you boost big cargo, but we'd have to go out at a hundred times that.

"Get the stuff from Marsport?"

"Some of it." I shook my head. The whole operation would be tricky. There wasn't a lot of risk for me, but *Agamemnon* was in big trouble.

"Rhoda's waiting for you. Back room."

"You don't look happy."

Jed shrugged. "Guess she's right, but it's kind of ghoulish."

"What—?"

"Go see."

Rhoda was sitting with a trim chap who wore a clipped mustache. I'd met him before, of course: B. Elton, Esq., the Lloyd's rep in Jefferson. He hated the place and couldn't wait for a transfer.

"I consider this reprehensible," Elton was saying when I came in. "I hate to think you are a party to this, Captain Kephart."

"Party to what?"

"Ms. Hendrix has asked for thirty million francs as salvage fee. Ten million in advance."

I whistled. "That's heavy."

"The ship is worth far more than that," Rhoda said.

"If I can get her down. There are plenty of problems—hell, she may not be fit for more than salvage," I said.

"Then there are the passengers. How much is Lloyd's out if you have to pay off their policies? And lawsuits?" Rhoda had the tomcat's grin again. "We're saving you money, Mr. Elton."

I realized what she was doing. "I don't know how to say this, but it's my ship you're risking."

"You'll be paid well," Rhoda said. "Ten percent of what we get."

That would just about pay off the whole mortgage. It was also a hell of a lot more than the commissioners in Marsport would award for a salvage job.

"We've got heavy expenses up front," Rhoda was saying. "That fuel pod costs like crazy. We're going to miss the launch window to Luna."

"Certainly you deserve reasonable compensation, but—"

"But nothing!" Rhoda's grin was triumphant. "Captain Kephart can't boost without fuel, and we have it all. That fuel goes aboard his ship when you've signed my contract, Elton, and not before."

Elton looked sad and disgusted. "It seems a cheap—"

"Cheap!" Rhoda got up and went to the door. "What the hell do you know about cheap? How goddam many times have we heard you people say there's no such thing as an excess profit? Well, this time *we* got the breaks, Elton, and *we'll* take the excess profits. Think about that."

Out in the bar somebody cheered. Another began singing a tune I'd heard in Jefferson before. Pam says the music is very old, she's heard it on TV casts, but the words fit Jefferson. The chorus goes "THERE'S GONNA BE A GREAT DAY!" and everybody out there shouted it.

"Marsport will never give you that much money," Elton said.

"Sure they will." Rhoda's grin got even wider, if that was possible. "We'll hold on to the cargo until they do—"

"Be damned if I will!" I said.

"Not you at all. I'm sending Mr. Hornbinder to take charge of that. Don't worry, Captain Kephart, I've got you covered. The big boys won't bite you."

"Hornbinder?"

"Sure. You'll have some extra passengers this run—"

"Not him. Not in my ship."

"Sure he's going. You can use some help—"

Like hell. "I don't need any."

She shrugged. "Sorry you feel that way. Just remember, you're under charter." She gave the tomcat grin again and left.

When she was gone Jed came in with beer for me and something else for Elton. They were still singing and cheering in the other room.

"Do you think this is fair?" Elton demanded.

Jed shrugged. "Doesn't matter what I think. Or what Rollo thinks. Determined woman, Rhoda Hendrix."

"You'd have no trouble over ignoring that charter contract," Elton told me. "In fact, we could find a reasonable bonus for you—"

"Forget it." I took the beer from Jed and drank it all. Welding up that fuel pod had been hot work, and I was ready for three more. "Listen to them out there," I said. "Think I want them mad at me? They see this as the end of their troubles."

"Which it could be," Jed said. "With a few million to invest we can make Jefferson into a pretty good place."

Elton wasn't having any. "Lloyd's is not in the business of subsidizing colonies that cannot make a living—"

"So what?" I said. "Rhoda's got the dee and nobody else had enough. She means it, you know."

"There's less than forty hours," Jed reminded him. "I think I'd get on the line to my bosses, was I you."

"Yes." Elton had recovered his polish, but his eyes were narrow. "I'll just do that."

They launched the big fuel pod with strap-on solids, just enough thrust to get it away from the rock so I could catch it and lock on. We had hours to spare, and I took my time matching velocities. Then Hal and I went outside to make sure everything was connected right.

Hornbinder and two friends were aboard against all my protests. They wanted to come out with us, but I wasn't having any. We don't need help from groundpounders. Janet and Pam took them to the galley for coffee while I made my inspection.

Slingshot is basically a strongly built hollow tube with engines at one end and clamps at the other. The cabins are rings around the outside of the tube. We also carry some deuterium and reaction mass strapped on to the main hull, but for big jobs there's not nearly enough room there. Instead, we build a special fuel pod that straps onto the bow. The reaction mass can be lowered through the central tube when we're boosting.

Boost cargo goes on forward of the fuel pod. This time we didn't have any going out, but when we caught up to *Agamemnon* she'd ride there, no different from any other cargo capsule. That was the plan, anyway. Taking another ship in tow isn't precisely common out here.

Everything matched up. Deuterium lines, and the elevator system for handling the mass and getting it into the boiling pots aft; it all fit. Took our time, even after we were sure it was working, while the miners who'd come up with the pod fussed and worried. Eventually I was satisfied and they got to head for home. I was still waiting for a call from Janet.

Just before they were ready to start up she hailed us. She used an open frequency so the miners could hear. "Rollo, I'm afraid those crewmen Rhoda loaned us will have to go home with the others."

"Eh?" One of the miners turned around in the saddle.

"What's the problem, Jan?" I asked.

"It seems Mr. Hornbinder and his friends have very bad stomach problems. It could be quite serious. I think they'd better see

Dr. Stewart as soon as possible."

"Goddam. Rhoda's not going to like this," the foreman said. He maneuvered his little open-frame scooter over to the airlock. Pam brought his friends out and saw they were strapped in.

"Hurry up!" Hornbinder said. "Get moving!"

"Sure, Horny." There was a puzzled note in the foreman's voice. He started up the bike. At maximum thrust it might make a twentieth of a gee. There was no enclosed space, it was just a small chemical rocket with saddles, and you rode it in your suit.

"Goddamit, get moving," Hornbinder was shouting. If there'd been air you might have heard him a klick away. "You can make better time than this!"

I got inside and went up to the control cabin. Jan was grinning.

"Amazing what calomel can do," she said.

"Amazing." We took time off for a quick kiss before I strapped in. I didn't feel much sympathy for Horny, but the other two hadn't been so bad. The one to feel sorry for was whoever had to clean up their suits.

Ship's engines are complicated things. First you take deuterium pellets and zap them with a big laser. The dee fuses to helium. Now you've got far too much hot gas at far too high a temperature, so it goes into an MHD system that cools it and converts the energy into electricity.

Some of that powers the lasers to zap more dee. The rest powers the ion drive system. Take a metal, preferably something with a low boiling point like cesium, but since that's rare out here cadmium generally has to do. Boil it to a vapor. Put the vapor through ionizing screens that you keep charged with power from the fusion system.

Squirt the charged vapor through more charged plates to accelerate it, and you've got a drive. You've also got a charge on your ship, so you need an electron gun to get rid of that.

There are only about nine hundred things to go wrong with the system. Superconductors for the magnetic fields and charge plates: those take cryogenic systems, and *those* have auxiliary systems to keep them going. Nothing's simple, and nothing's small, so out of *Slingshot's* 1600 metric tons, well over a thousand tons is engine.

Now you know why there aren't any space yachts flitting around out here. *Slinger's* one of the smallest ships in commission, and she's bloody big. If Jan and I hadn't happened to hit lucky by being the only possible buyers for a couple of wrecks, and hadn't had friends at Barclay's who thought we might make a go of it, we'd never have owned our own ship.

When I tell people about the engines they don't ask what we do aboard *Slinger* when we're on long passages, but they're only partly right. You *can't* do anything to an engine while it's on. It either works or it doesn't, and all you have to do with it is see it gets fed.

It's when the damned things are shut down that the work starts, and that takes so much time that you make sure you've done everything *else* in the ship when you can't work on the engines. There's a lot of maintenance, as you might guess when you consider that we've got to make everything we need, from air to zweiback. Living in a ship makes you appreciate planets.

Space operations go smooth, or generally they don't go at all. I looked at Jan and we gave each other a quick wink. It's a good luck charm we've developed. Then I hit the keys, and we were off.

It wasn't a long boost to catch up with *Agamemnon*. I spent most of it in the contoured chair in front of the control screens. A fifth of a gee isn't much for dirtsiders, but out here it's ten times what we're used to. Even the cats hate it.

The high gees saved us on high-calcium foods and the drugs we need to keep going in low gravs, and of course we didn't have to put in so much time in the exercise harnesses, but the only one happy about it was Dalquist. He came up to the control cab about an hour out from Jefferson.

"I thought there would be other passengers," he said.

"Really? Barbara made it pretty clear that she wasn't interested in Pallas. Might go to Mars, but—"

"No, I meant Mr. Hornbinder."

"He, uh, seems to have become ill. So did his friends. Happened quite suddenly."

Dalquist frowned. "I wish you hadn't done that."

"Really? Why?"

"It might not have been wise, Captain."

I turned away from the screens to face him. "Look, Mr. Dalquist, I'm not sure what *you're* doing on this trip. I sure didn't need Rhoda's goons along."

"Yes. Well, there's nothing to be done now, in any event."

"Just why are you aboard? I thought you were in a hurry to get back to Marsport—"

"Butterworth interests may be affected, Captain. And I'm in no hurry."

That's all he had to say about it, too, no matter how hard I pressed him on it.

I didn't have time to worry about it. As we boosted I was talking with *Agamemnon*. She passed about half a million kilometers from Jefferson, which is awfully close out here. We'd started boosting before she was abreast of the rock, and now we were chasing her. The idea was to catch up to her just as we matched her velocity. Meanwhile, *Agamemnon*'s crew had their work cut out.

When we were fifty kilometers behind, I cut the engines to minimum power. I didn't dare shut them down entirely. The fusion power system offers no difficulty with restarts, but the ion screens foul when they're cooled. Unless they're cleaned or replaced we can lose as much as half our thrust—and we were going to need every dyne.

We could just make out *Agamemnon* with our telescope. She was too far away to let us see any details. We could see a bright spot of light approaching us, though: Captain Jason Ewert-James and two of his engineering officers. They were using one of *Agamemnon*'s scooters.

There wasn't anything larger aboard. It's not practical to carry lifeboats for the entire crew and passenger list, so they have none at all on the larger boostships. Earth side politicians are forever talking about "requiring" lifeboats on passenger-carrying ships, but they'll never do it. Even if they pass such laws, how could they enforce them? Earth has no cops in space. The U.S. and Soviet air forces keep a few ships, but not enough to make an effective police force, even if anyone out here recognized their jurisdiction—which we don't.

Captain Ewert-James was a typical ship captain. He'd formerly been with one of the big British-Swiss lines, and had to transfer over to Pegasus when his ship was sold out from under him. The larger lines like younger skippers, which I think is a mistake, but they don't ask my advice.

Ewert-James was tall and thin, with a clipped mustache and graying hair. He wore uniform coveralls over his skintights, and in the pocket he carried a large pipe which he lit as soon as he'd asked permission.

"Thank you. Didn't dare smoke aboard *Agamemnon*—"

"Air that short?" I asked.

"No, but some of the passengers think it might be. Wouldn't care to annoy them, you know." His lips twitched just a trifle, something less than a conspirator's grin but more than a deadpan.

We went into the office. Jan came in, making it a bit crowded. I introduced her as physician and chief officer.

"How large a crew do you keep, Captain Kephart?" Ewert-James asked.

"Just us. And the kids. My oldest two are on watch at the moment."

His face didn't change. "Experienced cadets, eh? Well, we'd best be down to it. Mister Haply will show you what we've been able to accomplish."

They'd done quite a lot. There was a lot of expensive alloy bar-stock in the cargo, and somehow they'd got a good bit of it forward and used it to brace up the bows of the ship so she could take the thrust. "Haven't been able to weld it properly, though," Haply said. He was a young third engineer, not too long from being a cadet himself. "We don't have enough power to do welding and run the life support too."

Agamemnon's image was a blur on the screen across from my desk. It looked like a gigantic hydra, or a bullwhip with three short lashes standing out from the handle. The three arms rotated slowly. I pointed to it. "Still got spin on her."

"Yes." Ewert-James was grim. "We've been running the ship with that power. Spin her up with attitude jets and take power off the flywheel motor as she slows down."

I was impressed. Spin is usually given by running a big flywheel with an electric motor. Since any motor is a generator, Ewert-James's people had found a novel way to get some auxiliary power for life-support systems.

"Can you run for a while without doing that?" Jan asked. "It won't be easy transferring reaction mass if you can't." We'd already explained why we didn't want to shut down our engines, and there'd be no way to supply *Agamemnon* with power from *Slingshot* until we were coupled together.

"Certainly. Part of our cargo is LOX. We can run twenty, thirty hours without ship's power. Possibly longer."

"Good." I hit the keys to bring the plot-tank results onto my office screen. "There's what I get," I told them. "Our outside time limit is *Slinger*'s maximum thrust. I'd make that twenty centimeters for this load—"

"Which is more than I'd care to see exerted against the bows, Captain Kephart. Even with our bracing." Ewert-James looked to his engineers. They nodded gravely.

"We can't do less than ten," I reminded them. "Anything much lower and we won't make Pallas at all."

"She'll take ten," Haply said. "I think."

The others nodded agreement. I was sure they'd been over this a hundred times as we were closing.

I looked at the plot again. "At the outside, then, we've got a hundred seventy hours to transfer twenty-five thousand tons of reaction mass. And we can't work steadily because you'll have to spin up *Agamemnon* for power, and I can't stop engines—"

Ewert-James turned up both corners of his mouth at that. It seemed to be the closest thing to a smile he ever gave. "I'd say we best get at it, wouldn't you?"

Agamemnon didn't look much like *Slingshot*. We'd closed to a quarter of a klick, and steadily drew ahead of her; when we were past her we'd turn over and decelerate, dropping behind so that we could do the whole cycle over again.

Some features were the same, of course. The engines were not much larger than *Slingshot*'s, and looked much the same, a big cylinder covered over with tankage and coils, acceleration out-ports at the aft end. A smaller tube ran from the engines forward, but you couldn't see all of it because big rounded reaction mass cannisters covered a portion.

Up forward the arms grew out of another cylinder. They jutted out at equal angles around the hull, three big arms to contain passenger decks and auxiliary systems. The arms could be folded in between the reaction-mass cannisters, and would be when we started boosting.

All told she was over four hundred meters long, and with the hundred-meter arms thrust out she looked like a monstrous hydra slowly spinning in space.

"There doesn't seem to be anything wrong aft," Buck Dalquist said. He studied the ship from the screens, then pulled the tele-scope eyepiece toward himself for a direct look.

"Failure in the superconductor system," I told him. "Broken lines. They can't contain the fusion reaction long enough to get it into the MHD system."

He nodded. "So Captain Ewert-James told me. I've asked for a chance to inspect the damage as soon as it's convenient."

"Eh? Why?"

"Oh, come now, Captain." Dalquist was still looking through the telescope. "Surely you don't believe in Rhoda Hendrix as a good luck charm?"

"But—"

"But nothing." There was no humor in his voice, and when he looked across the cabin at me there was none in his eyes. "She bid far too much for an exclusive charter, after first making certain that you'd be on Jefferson at precisely the proper time. She had bankrupted the corporate treasury to obtain a corner on deuterium. Why else would she do all that if she hadn't expected to collect it back with profit?"

"But—she was going to charge Westinghouse and Iris and the others to boost their cargo. And they had cargo of their own—"

"Did they? We saw no signs of it. And she bid far too much for your charter."

"Damn it, you can't believe that," I said, but I didn't mean it. I remembered the atmosphere back at Jefferson. "You think the whole outfit was in on it?"

He shrugged. "Does it matter?"

The fuel transfer was tough. We couldn't just come alongside and winch the stuff over. At first we caught it on the fly: Agamemnon's crew would fling out hundred-ton cannisters, then use the attitude jets to boost away from them, not far, but just enough to stand clear.

Then I caught them with a bow pod. It wasn't easy. You don't need much closing velocity with a hundred tons before you've got a hell of a lot of energy to worry about. Weightless doesn't mean massless.

We could only transfer about four hundred tons an hour that way. After the first ten-hour stretch I decided it wouldn't work. There were just too many ways for things to go wrong.

"Get rigged for tow," I told Captain Ewert-James. "Once we're hooked up I can feed you power, so you don't have to do that crazy stunt with the spin. I'll start boost at about a tenth of a centimeter. It'll keep the screens hot, and we can winch the fuel pods down."

He was ready to agree. I think watching me try to catch those fuel cannisters, knowing that if I made a mistake his ship was headed for Saturn and beyond, was giving him ulcers.

First he spun her hard to build up power, then slowed the spin to nothing. The long arms folded alongside, so that *Agamemnon* took on a trim shape. Meanwhile I worked around in front of her, turned over and boosted in the direction we were traveling, and turned again.

The dopplers worked fine for a change. We hardly felt the jolt as *Agamemnon* settled nose to nose with us. Her crewmen came out to work the clamps and string lines across to carry power. We were linked, and the rest of the trip was nothing but hard work.

We could still transfer no more than 400 tons an hour, meaning bloody hard work to get the whole 25,000 tons into *Slinger*'s fuel pod, but at least it was all downhill. Each cannister was lowered by winch, then swung into our own fuel-handling system where *Slinger*'s winches took over. Cadmium's heavy: a cube about two meters on a side weighs a hundred tons. It wasn't big, and it didn't *weigh* much in a tenth of a centimeter, but you don't drop the stuff either.

Finally it was finished, and we could start maximum boost: a whole ten centimeters, about a hundredth of a gee. That may not sound like much, but think of the mass involved. *Slinger*'s 1600 tons were nothing, but there was *Agamemnon* too. I worried about the bracing Ewert-James had put in the bows, but nothing happened.

Three hundred hours later we were down at Pallasport. As soon as we touched in my ship was surrounded by Intertel cops.

The room was paneled in real wood. That doesn't sound like much unless you live in the Belt—but think about it: every bit of that paneling was brought across 60 million kilometers.

Pallas hasn't much in the way of gravity, but there's enough to make sitting down worth doing. Besides, it's a habit we don't seem to be able to get out of. There was a big conference table across the middle of the room, and a dozen corporation reps sat at it. It was made of some kind of plastic that looks like wood; not even the Commission brings furniture from Earth.

Deputy Commissioner Ruth Carr sat at a table at the far end, across the big conference table from where I sat in the nominal custody of the Intertel guards. I wasn't happy about being arrested and my ship impounded. Not that it would do me any good to be unhappy . . .

All the big outfits were represented at the conference table. Lloyd's and Pegasus Lines, of course, but there were others— Hansen Enterprises, Westinghouse, Iris, GE, and the rest.

"Definitely sabotage, then?" Commissioner Carr asked. She looked much older than she really was; the black coveralls and cap did that. She'd done a good job of conducting the hearings, though, even sending Captain Ewert-James and his engineers out to get new photographs of the damage to *Agamemnon*'s engines. He passed them up from the witness box, and she handed them to her experts at their place to her right.

They nodded over them.

"I'd say definitely so," Captain Ewert-James was saying. "There was an attempt to lay the charge pattern such that it might be mistaken for meteorite damage. In fact, had not Mr. Dalquist been so insistent on a thorough examination, we might have let it go at that. On close inspection, though, it seems very probable that a series of shaped charges were used."

Ruth Carr nodded to herself. She'd heard me tell about Rhoda's frantic efforts to charter my ship. One of Ewert-James's officers testified that an engineering crewman jumped ship just before *Agamemnon* boosted out of Earth orbit. The Intertel people had dug up the fact that he'd lived on Jefferson two years before, and were trying to track him down now—he'd vanished.

"The only possible beneficiary would be the Jefferson Corporation," Mrs. Carr said. "The concerns most harmed are Lloyd's and Pegasus Lines—"

"And Hansen Enterprises," the Hansen rep said. Ruth Carr looked annoyed but she didn't say anything. I noticed that the big outfits felt free to interrupt her and wondered if they did that with all the Commissioners, or just her because she hadn't been at the job very long.

The Hansen man was an older chap who looked as if he'd done his share of rock mining in his day, but he spoke with a Harvard accent. "There is a strong possibility that the Jefferson Corporation arranged the murder of a retired Hansen employee. As he was insured by a Hansen subsidiary, we are quite concerned."

"Quite right." Mrs. Carr jotted notes on the pad in front of her. She was the only one there I'd seen use note paper. The others whispered into wrist recorders. "Before we hear proposed actions, has anyone an objection to disposing of the matter concerning Captain Kephart?"

Nobody said anything.

"I find that Captain Kephart has acted quite properly, and that the salvage fees should go to his ship."

I realized I'd been holding my breath. Nobody wanted my scalp so far as I knew, and Dalquist had been careful to show I wasn't involved in whatever Rhoda had planned—but still, you never know what'll happen when the big boys have their eye on you. It was a relief to hear her dismiss the whole business, and the salvage fees would pay off a big part of the mortgage. I wouldn't know just how much I'd get until the full Commission back in Marsport acted, but it couldn't come to less than a million francs. Maybe more.

"Now for the matter of the Jefferson Corporation."

"Move that we send sufficient Intertel agents to take possession of the whole damn rock," the Lloyd's man said.

"Second." That was Pegasus Lines.

"Discussion?" Ruth Carr asked.

"Hansen will speak against the motion," the Hansen rep said. "Mr. Dalquist will speak for us."

That surprised hell out of me. I wondered what would happen, and sat quite still, listening. I had no business in there, of course. If there had been some suspicion that I might have been in on Rhoda's scheme I'd never have heard this much, and by rights I ought to have left when she made her ruling, but nobody seemed anxious to throw me out.

"First, let me state the obvious," Dalquist said. "An operation of this size will be costly. The use of naked force against an independent colony, no matter how justified, will have serious repercussions throughout the Belt—"

"Let 'em get away with it and it'll *really* be serious," the Pegasus man said.

"Hansen Enterprises has the floor, Mister Papagorus," Commissioner Carr said.

Dalquist nodded his thanks. "My point is that we should consider alternatives. The proposed action is at least expensive and distasteful, if not positively undesirable."

"We'll concede that," the Lloyd's man said. The others muttered agreement. One of the people representing a whole slew of smaller outfits whispered, "Here comes the Hansen hooker. How's Dalquist going to make a profit from this?"

"I further point out," Dalquist said, "that Jefferson is no more valuable than many other asteroids. True, it has good minerals and water, but no richer resources than other rocks we've not developed. The real value of Jefferson is in its having a working colony and labor force—and it is highly unlikely that they will work very hard for us if we land company police and confiscate their homes."

Everybody was listening now. The chap who'd whispered earlier threw his neighbor an "I told you so" look.

"Secondly. If we take over the Jefferson holdings, the result will be a fight among ourselves over the division of the spoils."

There was another murmur of assent to that. They could all agree that something had to be done, but nobody wanted to let the others have the pie without a cut for himself.

"Finally. It is by no means clear that any large number of Jefferson inhabitants were involved in this conspiracy. Chairman Hendrix, certainly. I could name two or three others. For the rest—who knows?"

"All right," the Lloyd's man said. "You've made your point. If landing Intertel cops on Jefferson isn't advisable, what do we do? I am damned if we'll let them get away clean."

"I suggest that we invest in the Jefferson Corporation," Dalquist said.

The Doghouse hadn't changed. There was a crowd outside in the main room. They were all waiting to hear how rich they'd become. When I came in even Hornbinder smiled at me.

They were getting wild drunk while Dalquist and I met with Rhoda in the back room. She didn't like what he was saying.

"Our syndicate will pay off the damage claims due to Pegasus Lines and Lloyd's," Dalquist told her. "And pay Captain Kephart's salvage fees. In addition, we will invest two million francs for new equipment. In return you will deliver forty percent of the Jefferson Corporation stock to us."

He wasn't being generous. With a forty percent bloc it was a cinch they could find enough more among the rockrats for a majority. Some of them hated everything Rhoda stood for.

"You've got to be crazy," Rhoda said. "Sell out to a goddam syndicate of corporations? We don't want *any* of you here!"

Dalquist's face was grim. "I am trying to remain polite, and it is not easy, Ms. Hendrix. You don't seem to appreciate your position. The corporation representatives have made their decision, and the Commission has ratified it. You will either sell or face something worse."

"I don't recognize any commissions," Rhoda said. "We've always been independent, we're not part of your goddam fascist commission. Christ almighty, you've found us guilty before we even knew there'd be a trial! We weren't even heard!"

"Why should you be? As you say, you're independent. Or have been up to now."

"We'll fight, Dalquist. Those company cops will never get here alive. Even if they do—"

"Oh, come now." Dalquist made an impatient gesture. "Do you really believe we'd take the trouble of sending Intertel police, now that you're warned? Hardly. We'll merely seize all your cargo in the pipeline and see that no ship comes here for any reason. How long will it be before your own people throw you out and come to terms with us?"

That hit her hard. Her eyes narrowed as she thought about it. "I can see you don't live to enjoy what you've done—"

"Nonsense."

I figured it was my turn. "Rhoda, you may not believe this, but I heard him argue them out of sending the cops without any warning at all. They were ready to do it."

The shouts came from the bar as Jed opened the door to see if we wanted anything. "THERE'S GONNA BE A GREAT DAY!"

"Everything all right here?" Jed asked.

"NO!" Rhoda shoved herself away from the table and glared at Dalquist. "Not all right at all! Jed, he's—"

"I know what he's saying, Rhoda," Jed told her. "Cap'n Rollo and I had a long talk with him last night."

"With the result that I'm speaking to you at all," Dalquist said. "Frankly, I'd rather see you dead." His face was a bitter mask of hatred, and the emotionless expression fell away. He hated Rhoda. "You've killed the best friend I ever had, and I find that I need you anyway. Captain Anderson has convinced me that it will be difficult to govern here without you, which is why you'll remain nominally in control after this sale is made."

"No. No sale."

"There will be. Who'll buy from you? Who'll sell to you? This was a unanimous decision. You're not independent, no matter how often you say you are. There's no place for your kind of nationalism out here."

"You bastards. The big boys. You think you can do anything you like to us."

Dalquist recovered his calm as quickly as he'd lost it. I think it was the tone Rhoda used; he didn't want to sound like her. I couldn't tell if I hated him or not.

"We can do whatever we can agree to do," Dalquist said.

"You seem to think the Corporations Commission is some kind of government. It isn't. It's just a means for settling disputes. We've found it more profitable to have rules than to have fights. But we're not without power, and everyone's agreed that you can't be let off after trying what you did."

"So we pay for it," Jed said.

Dalquist shrugged. "There's no government out here. Are you ready to bring Rhoda to trial? Along with all the others involved?"

Jed shook his head. "I doubt that it—"

"And there's the matter of restitution, which you can't make anyway. And you're bankrupt, since you sent no cargo to Luna and the window's closed."

"Just who the hell is this syndicate?" Rhoda demanded.

Dalquist's expression didn't change, but there was a note of triumph in his voice. He'd won, and he knew it. "The major sums are put up by Hansen Enterprises."

"And you'll be here as their rep."

He nodded. "Certainly. I've been with Hansen most of my life, Ms. Hendrix. The company trusts me to look out for its best interests. As I trusted Joe Colella. Until he retired he was my best field agent."

She didn't say anything, but her face was sour.

"You might have got away with this if you hadn't killed Joe," Dalquist said. "But retired or not, he was a Hansen man. As I'm sure you found when he discovered your plan. We take care of our people, Ms. Hendrix. Hansen is a good company.

"For company men." Jed's voice was flat. He looked around the small back room with its bare rock walls, but I think he was seeing through those walls, out through the corridors, beyond to the caves where the rockrats tried to make homes. "A good outfit for company men. But it won't be the same, for us."

Outside they were still singing about the great days coming.

Tool Dresser's Law

JACK CLEMONS

In 1973 Larry Niven and I went out to Hughes
Research Laboratories in Malibu for the first
time. The laser was invented at Hughes, so of
course they do a lot of laser research there.
They're also among the top people in ion-drive
engines, and they've done a lot with advanced
communication concepts.

All that was fascinating, but we went to talk
with Dr. Robert L. Forward, who's known as one
of *the* experts on gravitation. These days Dr. Forward is also an established SF writer with several
published novels. I'd met him because he liked my
story "He Fell Into a Dark Hole" and had been kind
enough to call and tell me so.

Bob Forward is also the inventor of the Forward Mass Detector, a widget that can track a
tank miles away by mass alone. It can't distin-
guish between a tank at a mile and a fly on the
end of the instrument, but if you use two and
triangulate you're safe enough. His detector can
also be lowered into oil wells, or towed behind an
airplane to map mass concentrations below.

After lunch we talked about black holes. Bob
was particularly interested in Stephen Hawking's
then-new notion that tiny black holes might have
been formed during the Big Bang of Creation.
Since at that time it was thought that the Second Law of Thermodynamics demanded that they

never get smaller, there should be holes of all sizes left. Some might be in our solar system.

They would come to rest in the interior of large masses. There might be quite a large one inside the Sun, for example, and even in the Earth and Moon as well. A very large-mass hole, say 10^8 kilograms, would still be very small: about 10^{-19} centimeters radius. An atomic radius is around 10^{-9} centimeters, very large compared to such a hole, so that the hole couldn't eat many atoms a day, and wouldn't grow fast.

Black holes inside the Earth or Sun aren't too useful because they're hard to get at. Bob Forward wanted to go to the asteroids. You search for a rock that weighs far too much for its size. Push the rock aside and there in orbit where the asteroid used to be you'll find a little black hole.

You could do a lot with such a hole: for example, you could wiggle it with magnetic fields to produce gravity waves at precise frequencies. There might be all sizes of holes, even down to a kilogram or two, and each size would have a use.

It sounded marvelous. Larry and I figured there were a dozen stories there. I'd already written my black hole story, and Larry hadn't, so he beat me into print with a thing called "The Hole Man," which won a Hugo. All I got from the trip was a couple of articles and columns.

Well, Larry's story was reprinted in his collection *A Hole in Space*, while the columns I did about little black holes have been forgotten—I hope!

I'm glad I have nothing in print about tiny black holes, because a year later Stephen Hawking proved they can't exist. Oh, they can be formed all right, but they won't be around very long. It seems that black holes aren't really black. They radiate, and left to themselves they get smaller all the time. The Second Law needs modifying.

Hawking points out that Einstein's general relativity, which produces most of the primary equations for black holes, is a classical theory. It doesn't take quantum effects into account.

Hawking corrects this. In quantum theory a length, L, is not fixed. It has an uncertainty or fluctuation on the order of L^0/L, where L^0 is the Planck length 10^{-33} cm.

Since there is uncertainty in the length scale, it follows that the event horizon of the black hole isn't actually fixed. It fluctuates through the uncertainty region.

In fact, the black hole is *fuzzy*, and energy and radiation can tunnel out of the hole to escape forever. It's the same kind of effect as observed in tunnel diodes, where particles appear on the other side of a potential barrier.

Since black holes have no hair, although they do have fuzz, the quantum radiation temperature—that is, the rate at which they radiate—must depend entirely on mass, angular momentum, and charge.

It does, but I'm not going to prove it to you. Hawking uses math that I *can* tool up to follow, but I'm not really keen on Hermetian scalar fields, and I doubt many readers are either.

The first thing to see is that small holes have uninteresting lifetimes. In order for one to be around long enough to use it, the hole must be massive.

Any black holes formed in the Big Bang would be 10^{10} years old now; so if they weren't larger than a small asteroid they're gone already. Worse, that exponential decay rate defeats us even if we find a hole just decayed to an interesting size. It will still vanish too fast for use.

So there went Larry's story, and two I had plotted but hadn't written, and I suspect a lot of other science fiction as well. Sometimes I feel a bit like Alice when she protested, "Things *flow* here so!"

Hawking's paper pretty much rules out black holes in our Solar System, but that doesn't rule out the possibility that there are some lurking in

the space between stars. In "Tool Dresser's Law"
Jack Clemons has a black hole lurking behind
an asteroid about the size of Cuba drop in for
a visit.

The results, needless to say, are spectacular.
But also, lurking behind every catastrophe, is an
opportunity.

WILDCATTER DROPPED ONTO Hawking a month ahead of perihelion. We slammed down after losing a brutal tug of war between
our ship and the singularity that had started when we closed to 60
klicks. I was in the cockpit running a spectrometry survey through
the assayer ay-eye during our final approach. I have flown a lot
of AUs with McRae; he is a damn fine pilot. I looked up from
the display when I heard him curse.

"Jeezus!" he hissed. His face was rigid.

"What is it, Curt?" I asked him. I thought I heard panic in his
voice and it made me edgy.

"We're dropping down one helluva g-cliff," he said. "This baby
could suck the numbers off a coin!"

I twisted in my seat to glance at the forward screen. Hawking
didn't *look* very formidable, just another hunk of gray-brown rock.
I turned back to look at McRae.

"We in any trouble?" I asked.

No answer.

"Curt . . . ?"

No answer. He was staring holes in the readout panel; he had
completely dismissed me.

I don't think he took three breaths in the entire fifteen minutes it took him to keep from augering in. I remember his face
checkerboarded with colored light from the crazy flickering panel
displays. His hand was gripping the stick so tightly that his fingers
were bone white from the knuckles to the nails. We collided, hard,
and Hawking swiped once at us and missed. We bounced about
100 meters before the landing struts slapped the dustless rock
again—and this time dug in.

McRae later liked to brag that he'd had it under control all the
way. But I was there. McRae blew it. He had underestimated the
muscle of that sucker, and I guess the rest of us can be glad he
was a better pilot than judge of character.

Not to say that Hawking was an easy character to judge. Nothing with axes that short should have packed that many gees. We

had all read the reports filed by the IGA several months earlier, just after the singularity was discovered wandering in solar system real estate. Star occultations, apparent albedo, etc., etc., all put Hawking at about the size of Cuba. Large for an asteroid (which is what it looked like) but tiny by planetary standards.

Then the early reports from the Chinese fly-by and the Korean drone lander had come in, followed by the extensive data supplied by the Japanese survey party, made while Hawking was out beyond the Belt. All of them had confirmed the same finding—this baby was *not* what it seemed to be.

Hawking had played a mean game of billiards with Sol's family jewels as it screamed sunward. The goddam planets had *rocked* when Hawking slid by them. Mars lost Phobos and Deimos permanently; they're out there now, trying to solve the *n*-body problem by trial and error.

The Moon got nudged pretty hard when the singularity intersected Earth's orbit. I heard that it played hell with the Terries: weather, agriculture, tides, even the length of the day. Several million killed; Paris turned into a beach-front city. Earth was damn lucky to be as far away from Hawking as it was when it passed.

Konstantine Station got tossed like a jackstraw—luckily, I wasn't home at the time. Lots of injuries and a couple of deaths and several months of correcting burns to get back to L-5.

Yeah, the crew of *Wildcatter* had heard all about Hawking, long before we had caught up with it inside Venus' orbit. All of that info was in our *heads* during that final approach, but we were staring at something that our *intuition* told us was no big deal. Then Hawking had cast its vote, and we were suddenly on a slip-sliding trajectory *down* at over 0.8 gees. Son of a bitch, that was a scary landing.

I don't know how well a full-auto system would have handled the landing. We all spent a lot of time kicking *that* one around during lounge time afterward.

"This is bullshit!" was Cal Bartley's summary then. "Goddam Snyder and his goddam credit pinching nearly bought it for us." Cal always had an irritating habit of being loudmouthed when he was skittish.

Chan Singh shook his head violently.

"And that's *your* bullshit, Bartley," he said. "Full-autos are out of the question on spec ships and you know it."

"Flock ass, Singh!" Cal handled language like a bouncer. "Old Man Snyder has more money than God. He could outfit this tub like the *Constitution* if he cared more for his crew than what lines his pockets."

"Hey, I'm no cheerleader for Snyder," Chan said. "But if he did things the way you say he should, we'd all be working for table scraps. He got rich because he *understands* this business, and you'll get rich working for him for the same reason."

"That's easy for you, Singh," Cal shot back. "You've made yours."

"And I did it working the Old Man's way," Chan said.

"You were always a bootlicker for Snyder, Chan," Lou Williams threw in. "The Old Man's a goddam horse's ass, and this trip proves it. We're each paying a month's expenses, and we'll probably all wind up dead to boot—and for what? So that egomaniac can get his name in the history books trying to bronco-bust this worthless rock."

"Goddam right," Cal added. "We've got a fortune waiting for us on Titan, and Snyder's got us out here mucking around like *scientists*, for God's sake."

None of the crew, me included, were very happy about prospecting on Hawking. But Chan *was* right. Wildcatting had always been a wing and a prayer proposition, whether in space or in the early oil days in Texas. Speculators' profits were narrow, and that meant cutting corners, taking risks. The industrials had all of the fancy equipment and plush living quarters—and the full-autos.

And they were the ones that went after the big strikes: mining the large asteroids, drilling the huge oil reserves on Mars (or whatever that stuff was they found there). If you wanted to be comfortable, join the industrials. If you wanted adventure, sign onto a spec ship: rotten hours, primitive equipment, spitting daily in the Reaper's eye and hoping he didn't spit back. Everyone, including Cal Bartley, knew that when they signed on. I couldn't side with Cal on that account.

I knew that Cal, like most of the rest of us, was intimidated by Snyder, and this was just his way of puffing up. Cal had already been with the drilling crew for more than two years when I joined on, and he was a full-timer too. I had heard that the Old Man had jettisoned him at least twice in the past for being insubordinate, but he hired him back both times. Cal was the best tool dresser to be had.

Snyder had this thing about his employees. He seemed to think that we had joined the Marines when we signed on. Of course, once you got on ship there wasn't a hell of a lot you could do about that. Snyder *was* commander-in-chief there, and emperor and christ-almighty-god too.

There was a story going around when I first signed on that the Old Man had *really* spaced a driller once who had pushed him too hard. No one knew for sure if that story was true, or just an invention of Snyder's to keep us in line. In any case, it worked. None of us doubted that Snyder was capable of doing just that.

It was because of the Old Man's ways that I never became a full-timer myself on the *Wildcatter*. You had to be a hard case, or awfully desperate, to put up with his crap, and I was neither. But Snyder paid good—a lot better than any of the other spec shipowners. And I have to admit that his singlemindedness had made him the most successful independent in the business.

Snyder did have a few good points. His vessels were all spaceworthy. The crew quarters were warm and the life systems were doubly redundant. Even he understood that hungry, cold, or dead people don't work very hard.

Why did we do it? For most it was the money. A contract on the *Wildcatter* paid a three-percent share of discovery, less expenses, to every man and woman in a crew of twenty. And it didn't matter if you were a pilot or a scrub-downer. That was better by tenths than the other independents offered. And like I said, the *Wildcatter* had a good record.

Hell, there were a handful of people around living damn fine after just one tour on board her. I'm talking about the crew who discovered that two-ton nugget of molybdenum hiding in the Belt, of course. That was before I joined. In fact, it was during one of Cal's enforced absences. I don't think Cal ever forgave Snyder for doing that to him.

Old Man Snyder could have cashed it all in then and been set for life. But he just used the credits to outfit five more Wildcatters and went straight back out again. The stylized wildcat symbol on the hulls of Wildcatter Corporation ships became recognized throughout the System. I don't know if it was greed or escape that kept him out there. Generally, no one got a chance to ask him about it. He pretty much stayed to himself in his private module when we weren't on a work site.

Anyway, if landing on Hawking was your idea of lucky, *Wild-catter* earned her reputation for being at the right place at the

right time this time out. Just a month earlier we had come home
dry after nearly a year of prospecting around Saturn. But I was
convinced, and I had convinced Snyder, that the ay-eye had
discovered a liquid biomass lurking beneath the sludge on Titan.
He was determined to go back and have another look. The Martian
"oil" uncovered by the crew of the *I.S. Exxon* the year before had
turned out to be a previously unknown hydrosilicon, and *Exxon*'s
labbies back at L–5 were feverishly analyzing the implications.

The Old Man had guarded his claim like a hungry mongrel. He
ordered *Wildcatter IV* outfitted with armaments and sent her out
to stand guard. We had to station-keep out there for four months
before she showed up to relieve us. All of us were bone tired
and just plain sick of free-fall when we finally got home. But
to a person, everyone signed on to ship back out as soon as
Wildcatter could be refitted for drilling. None of us wanted to
lose our stake on *that* find. So there we were, scrubbed, dry, and
smiling, and about to set sail from Konstantine for the Big Belted
Beauty, when the Japanese survey data on Hawking came in.

> Extra-solar in origin. Anomalous lack of axial rotation.
> Unusual heavy metal composition. Bore samples indicate hot
> central core surrounded by multiple accretion layers built up
> over extremely long interval. Age between 10 and 15 bil-
> lion years. Tectonics of significant proportions, likely driven
> by extremely dense object at center surrounded by liquid
> mantle. Probable candidate: Hawking singularity. Hypothesis
> consistent with mass, size, gravitational and tidal effects,
> temperature, age, and interstellar origin. Hypothesis incon-
> sistent with stability of solid material surrounding object, and
> with apparently slow accumulation of accreted material. No
> resolution at present.

There it was, a quantum black hole! A tiny—and damn heavy—
cinder of nothing left over from the Original Fireworks. It was that
Japanese survey report that gave Hawking its name.

The Old Man was on the bridge reviewing the prelaunch
checklist when the news came in. McRae told us that he
had just stood there, eyes flicking back and forth across
the infoscreen absorbing the report. His jowls were set; the
cigar smoldered in his mouth; nothing showed on his face.
He removed the cigar and stared at the ashes for a couple
of seconds.

Then he turned to McRae and said, "File a flight plan for Hawking," and left the bridge.

We all got pissed when we heard the news. A lot of ships and a lot of crew-hours have been wasted nosing around the asteroid belt hoping to find one of these microscopic buggers hiding there. No one knew for sure that they *existed*, though the theorists had predicted them over seventy years ago. It wasn't just scientific curiosity that sent all those people on a snipe hunt. If a quantum hole could be dragged back to earth orbit, the Terries would have a power source that would allow them to air-condition the African continent. There were even persistent rumors that several countries were trying to *synthesize* one of the damn things.

But wasn't it just like Mama Nature to finally confirm the theories by grandstanding. Nothing for seventy years, and then the Big Mutha of quantum holes comes by to say "hello" at 170 decibels. The problem was, there was no way to slow down Hawking, let alone to cart it off to Earth. The singularity itself, hiding in the middle of its spaceborne haystack, was probably only a centimeter or so in diameter. But it massed at several billion trillion tons—it weighed more than Mars—and with the amount of momentum it packed, it could have dragged the Earth off into the wild void with it.

I suppose something that old, that massive, that had spent its lifetime wandering around the universe, might have picked up some interesting lint in its coat. None of the survey probes had been equipped for more than shallow surface samples. My belief then and now is that Snyder got obsessed with being the first one to find out if anything was hidden in its pockets. It's the only reason I can come up with to explain why he suddenly abandoned a certain gold mine for this risky, dangerous, and low-probability venture. Maybe he was a visionary, though we mostly thought he was just crazy. He certainly didn't make any points with the crew—and he didn't start out with many in the bank.

So we got there. Not just the first ones, but the only ones. None of the industrials could be redirected so quickly. None of the other spec ships were prepared. And no one had much time to act. Frankly, I'm not sure that any of the other commercial rigs even gave a damn—Hawking had been regarded pretty much as a scientific curiosity from the start.

Hawking had shown enough good manners to arrive more or less in-plane, so rendezvous was possible for a ship of our class. But the singularity wasn't staying around for long. It was hustling toward Sol on a hyperbolic, gathering speed as it fell, and there would only be a few weeks at the outside when the surface temperature would be within *Wildcatter*'s limits. We'd have just enough time to jump aboard, take a long sip with our straw, and get the hell out again.

Maybe someone could have caught up with it on the downhill side after perihel, but apparently no one tried. The colony of Rockheads out in the Belt took nearly a direct hit on the outbound pass, but I figured most of them went scrambling for cover. A body of that mass, nudging the planets around like it did, made predicting its orbit a little dicey. I don't know of any other outfit but ours who had the combination of speed, maneuverability, tools, and the just plain rotten luck of being in position to reach her. I was just hoping that Hawking wasn't filled with Confederate dollar bills.

We had the drilling site set up within six hours.

On the day of the accident, we had been over the drill site for about a hundred hours. We had two teams working twelve-hour shifts around the clock, and the strain was just beginning to get to us. The tidal shear was making everyone dizzy, and the damned asteroid was earthquaking every few minutes. Not only were we stumbling around and bumping into one another, but *Wildcatter*'s hull screeched and moaned constantly. We had a hell of a time concentrating.

The site was set up directly beneath the ship itself. We had the shield walls down to keep the sun out and the atmosphere in, which added claustrophobia to the rest of our problems. But at least that way we only wore insul-skin while we worked, which was a lot more pliable than the vacuum suits. I know it sounds like I am rationalizing, but it wasn't the easiest assignment we had ever pulled.

The accident was Pat Talbot's fault, no question about that. I have to give her credit though; she never made any excuses. She knew what she was doing, and she should have known better. Cal, McRae, Singh, and all the rest had a dozen theories later to explain Pat's mistake. I have a few ideas of my own.

This was Pat's first tour on the *Wildcatter*. She had signed on with us at Konstantine Station, just after the news of Hawking came in. She had the credentials of an experienced tool dresser; Bartley had checked her out himself before he hired her on as his assistant. The Old Man had insisted on a second dresser on this crew because of the amount of drilling we would likely be facing.

No one else on board had ever met her before, though that was not especially unusual. She was reasonably good-looking, in an unglamorous sort of way. None of us were much to look at, not while on tour. I guessed her age to be around forty. Her hair was mostly the color of ground coffee, though she had tipped the ends white in sort of a keyboard pattern. She wore it thick on top and cut close to her neck, like most spacer women did. Long hair tended to get in the way of things in free-fall, and couldn't be kept neat anyway. Her face was OK—standard issue Anglo and no embedded cosmetics.

I could tell that she had a nice body under her jumpsuit, and that had become more important to me as we coasted sunward on our intercept ellipse. This was the first time we had shipped with only one female crew member in as long as I could remember. Space tours, like long business trips spent in hotel rooms, produced horniness exponentially. I've always believed it was something they put in the air conditioning.

Shipboard sexism died a hasty death when commercial space ops started, even if it is still alive and breathing on Terra and her children. But body chemistry isn't suspended in space. I was hoping that Pat's air conditioning was having the same effect on her as mine was on me.

Pat seemed to be a pleasant person, too. She was friendly enough on duty and during lounge time, though I don't remember her talking about herself much. She spoke well. Although many of the crew had advanced degrees, the education had been grafted onto her and had flourished. I relished having an intelligent conversation after hearing Bartley body-slam the language all day.

I hadn't had a chance to talk with her before we collided with Hawking, and we had been busy as hell since. It wasn't until the night before the accident that I happened on her alone and not on duty. I had come down to the galley several hours after the end of my shift to scrounge up some caffeine and carbohydrates. The galley was usually deserted at that hour; I liked having one meal a day in privacy.

Pat was sitting by herself at one of the tables, sorting intently through some stuff she had dumped out of a large plastic box; she didn't hear me come in. It was hard to hear anything over the constant grinding and screeching of *Wildcatter*'s hull being assaulted by solar wind and tidal shear. I spoke to her as I crossed over to the coffee dispenser.

"Hello," I said, trying not to startle her.

She turned toward me in sort of a twisting motion, shoulders first, head reluctantly following, and eyes finally dragged along. It looked like the upper-body motion in a golf swing, and for exactly the same reason.

"Oh, hi," she said. "You're Clarence, um, Stroemann?"

She was being polite, though she clearly was preoccupied with what she had been doing.

"Mowboata," I said, "Clarence Mowboata. You're thinking of Nick Stroemann, the drill suction operator. I only do surveys."

She smiled at me and shifted the rest of the way around in my direction. I was encouraged.

"Glad to meet you—again—Clarence Mowboata." She got the pronunciation *and* the inflection exactly right; not many do that. I smiled appreciatively. Her eyes widened a little in acceptance. I came over to her table and leaned against the edge, facing her. I wanted to be close enough to detect any pupil dilation; it's important to read the signs early in this dance.

She offered her hand. "I'm Pat . . ."

"Talbot," I finished. I shook her hand gently. "It was easier for me to keep you straight. What is it that keeps you so fascinated?" I gestured toward the odd assortment of rocks that were scattered on the table.

They were a jumble of shapes and sizes, all dull gray. Several were split in two or sheared at angles, and the exposed facets had an oily luster. A geologist's mallet and chisel lay nearby. Pat looked back at them, almost exactly reversing her earlier motion.

"Well . . . I'm not sure exactly what these are. Hawking's nail clippings, I suppose."

"Hawking's . . . ?" My focus shifted to the rocks. I reached over and picked up one the size of a walnut. It was deceptively heavy.

"You picked these up here?"

She nodded and reached for one of the larger ones that had been cut.

"We drilled them out yesterday, actually. I found them in the effluent filter. They are each peculiar in their own way. I thought that we might get some clues that the assay ay-eye missed."

I put down the first rock, and she handed the second one to me. I turned it over and studied the cleft face. It was a deep steel gray and was sealed with a natural transparent glaze. It felt dry and smooth like the inside surface of a shell. There were some imperfections in the underlying grayness; small yellow beads of what looked like fused glass were imbedded at random. They were multifaceted little stones, spheres made up of flat hex-agonal planes—like miniature soccer balls. Their color shifted in hue perceptibly as I stared at them. There appeared to be some natural luminescence in the impurities. Crystalline sulfur compounds fused in muscovite, most likely, with a few phosphors stirred in. An unusual specimen, but probably not very interesting if the ay-eye had ignored it. I said so and handed it back to her.

"Mmm," was her reply, then she said, "What do you know about quantum holes, naked singularities—that sort of stuff?"

"Things my mother never told me," I said.

She didn't react.

"Sorry," I said. "I don't know much. We covered that in Cos-mology 101, I think. But there was this cute undergrad named Phyllis who sat next to me in that class—I was into the two-body problem that semester. I saw the stuff that was on the vidpress just after Hawking was discovered."

She turned the stone over in her hand and stared at the face with the little yellow soccer balls.

"There has been a lot of speculation about them," she said. "Physical laws inside of one are totally different."

"Yeah, so I've heard," I replied. I was getting a little bored with this subject, and there were only five hours left in my off-shift.

"Listen," I said, "I've been hoping I'd get a chance to meet you like this." I've always had success with the direct approach.

"And things can get *out* too," she said. She hadn't been lis-tening.

"Out too, hum?" I said half-heartedly.

"Yes," she said. "A lot of people think stuff only falls *into* black holes—like the rabbit hole in *Alice in Wonderland*. But with micro-holes like Hawking, the Mad Hatter can pack up his tea party and pay *us* a visit. Anything can come popping out of one—our laws don't even make sense in there."

This wasn't going well. I tried another approach.

"Naked singularities, big bangs, black holes: cosmology uses a lot of sexual symbolism, doesn't it?"

At least she smiled a little when she answered. "I think you're pushing it a bit," she said.

"Come on, encourage me," I said. "Can't we find something friendlier to talk about than a wind of improbability that comes whistling up a rabbit hole?"

"*Very* impressive," she said. She paused a long time, and then she gave me this little impish look and said, "I suppose you've earned a change of topics—in return for being so poetic."

This was going better. If only I hadn't said what I did next. I never did know when to quit.

"Besides, I think if those rocks were the keys to fantasyland, the ay-eye would have been the first to know."

Her pupils contracted.

"You keep bowing to that ay-eye," she said. "Which one has the true artificial intelligence, you or that program?"

Shit! I thought. I knew I had blown it and should try to recover. But that crack had pissed me off.

"That program is my *tool*," I said. "I underestimated it several times early on, and it cost me dearly. Believe me, it knows what it is doing."

"It infers from its knowledge base," she said. "How can it be qualified to judge the unknowable? That's one of the few remaining conceits of human beings."

"It has *very* extensive knowledge. There is probably no human expert that could match its abilities in this field. I suppose that in the interest of being human I should ignore it and go back to my calculator."

"You aren't using it, you're *deferring* to it."

"I'll bet you're one of those 'no computers in grade school math' fanatics, too," I said.

"As a matter of fact I *am*. I happen to think it's *important* for people to learn the *why* of things first, before they learn just *how*—like automatons."

"If we all thought like you," I said, "we'd still be sharpening wooden sticks so we could go hunt down dinner."

"Don't resort to outrageous statements," she snapped. "It makes you sound like you're grasping at straws."

She was right, I was, but I felt outraged.

"And what makes *you* an expert on geology, quantum holes, and artificial intelligence?" I shot at her. "Aren't those hobbies a bit unusual for a tool dresser?"

"They're *not* hobbies," was all she said. She turned her eyes back toward those damn rocks and she fell silent.

I realized what I had done and I felt foolish.

"Pat," I said, trying to sound apologetic.

Nothing.

"Uh, I was thinking of cuing up a movie in the lounge. Would you like to join me for Bogie, Bacall, and buttered popcorn?"

She waved her hand a little in my direction. "No thanks," she said. She didn't look up. She had started chiseling away at another of the stones.

I stood there for probably two minutes, but she never seemed to notice me again. I had to hand it to her, the woman had concentration. Finally I gave up and left.

An hour later, after I had climbed into my bunk to get what sleep I could, I was still mentally replaying my blunder.

Not hobbies?

Pat was dressing the drill casing as I slid down from the crew quarters next morning at change of shift. I called out a "good morning" to her but she couldn't hear me over the racket. Four solid days of boring with white-hot plasma had not made much of a dent in Hawking's coat. But it was beating the crap out of the drill.

In the early wildcatting days on Earth, a steel drill was raised by winch up a tall wooden tower erected over the hole, then released to let gravity slam it into the dirt. The crew just raised and dropped it, raised and dropped it, slowly digging a well to the oil. The process was time-consuming and tedious, and drill bits wore out quickly. The tool dresser was the person who stood by with a sledgehammer when the drill was withdrawn from the bore hole. He'd examine the bit and hammer the cutting edge back into shape when it got dull.

In space 'catting, a plasma gun had replaced the drill bit. The working end of the gun was surrounded by a double-shelled fore-skin made of a ceramic alloy. The inner shell provided a magnetic focal ring for the plasma stream, and the slag was carried away by a suction between the inner and outer shells. The stuff we drilled through, and the energies we pumped, could distort the hell out of that foreskin.

The really expensive rigs had self-correcting nozzles. But, like I said, this was a speculation ship, so we still carried our own tool dressers. On *Wildcatter* they were Cal and Pat, though they, like the rest of us, had several jobs on board. Their "sledge-hammer" was a laser dressing tool—sort of a miniature version of the plasma gun—that they used to keep the nozzle trimmed and open. And in Texas or on Hawking, the tool dresser's first commandment was the same: *never* do any work over the hole. A g is a g, as they say, and the only thing that must go into a well is a drill.

Anyway, as I came down through the access port into the work area, I saw Pat break that commandment. Proper dressing of the gun required that it be partially disassembled, so that it could be swung out and away from the hole. It is a lot of work, and a pain in the ass. I have seen a couple of dressers in my time take a shortcut and just slide the dressing tool out over the hole and under the plasma gun instead. That way they could get at the nozzle without taking the gun apart first. This is the first time I saw one not get away with it.

The dressing-tool cart was balanced on its rear wheels at the edge of the four-foot-diameter drill hole. The rest of the cart was suspended over the hole, the front wheels dangling over a thousand feet of nothing. Pat had managed to partially cover the opposite edge of the hole with a slab of some heavy metal— it looked like a short section of shield-wall material—and that provided just enough of a ledge to support the front lip of the cart. Pat stood on the slab like a shapely Atlas, legs spread wide straddling the hoses and lines, and was lasing the nozzle tip suspended directly over her head.

Cal came sliding down right behind me, and when he saw what she was doing, he was immediately pissed. He shouted at her in that booming voice he had developed from years of working around noise. I saw her jerk her head down to look at him, and then she lost her balance. Instinctively, she kicked off of the slab to keep from falling into the hole. The slab shifted, the cart tumbled, and *Wildcatter* lost an essential, and irreplaceable, tool down a 300-meter throat of rock.

All of us froze. Even Bartley was speechless. We stood there, not knowing what to say, staring like morons at that black, earthy mouth in the floor. Williams and Chan and several other members of the B-shift crew came on duty, and as soon as they took in what had happened, they stopped their early-morning chatter. All of us had been around rigs long enough to understand what this meant.

Finally the Old Man slid down to start his change-of-shift inspection. It took him only seconds to understand, and he was the first one to break the silence.

"Get it out," he grunted. That was all. He didn't even glance at Pat. No frowns, no recriminations. Just that short command directed to all of us, then he turned and disappeared back up the ladder.

We all jumped as if we had been goosed. We knew we were in trouble. McRae had computed that we had a week, maybe two weeks at the outside, before Hawking's velocity carried us too close to the sun for us to stay. After our first day of drilling we had known it was going to be tight, since whatever Hawking was made of was not particularly intimidated by our plasma drill.

The boring of the hole had been going very slowly, and we were having to dress the tool much more frequently than usual. Our chances of tapping into Hawking's veins before the sun turned us into prune juice weren't very good at best. Now we had two new problems: a plugged well and an unreachable tool. There was no time to start a new well and no way to get very far without a dressing tool. We had to retrieve it, and in working order, or we might just as well lift off right then—which seemed like a better choice to most of us.

Everyone pitched in. Both crews stayed on the rest of the shift, and more members of second shift came on early as word of what had happened reached them. We spent the first hour or so puzzling about ways to get at the cart. Of course, the first thing we tried was pulling it back up by its long power cable that trailed up from the well and tied into the primary power source in the ship. But a little tugging there and we knew that was hopeless. The cart had managed to wedge itself tightly in the rough throat of the well, and Cal insisted that we leave the power cord alone. He was worried that we'd damage the tool beyond repair if the cable ripped out its guts, so we dropped that idea.

We spent most of the first day lowering hooks on long chains, but couldn't get them to engage anything that gave us much support. We hooked the cart handle first and immediately yanked it right off of the cart. Murphy had been working overtime against us. Not only had the cart lodged upside down, wheel and flat base upward, but when Pat jumped, the metal slab had shifted and fallen down there as well. It had wedged itself obliquely over the cart, and there just wasn't very much exposed that we could get a hook around. We wasted a lot of hours with those damned hooks before we finally realized they just weren't going to work.

The Old Man came down again at the end of the shift. He didn't say a word to us after that first time. He just walked past us to the hole, cigar smoldering in his mouth, and shaded his eyes to look down past the floodlights we had rigged over it. He saw we weren't getting anywhere, so he turned away and went back up to his cabin.

We went at it like that for three days: experimenting, huddling in twos and threes for ideas, sketching out and discarding all sorts of Rube Goldberg contraptions. Every member of the crew was giving it their full attention—Pat most of all. I'm sure that she must have gotten some sleep, but she was down there every time I came onto the site, and she was always there after I left. And I put in a *lot* of hours.

Somewhere along the way, the mood of the crew had shifted too. Getting at that friggin' dressing tool had become a team goal now, and you could sense the feeling of shared responsibility and participation growing stronger every hour that we worked at it. Everyone chipped in an idea, and I don't recall that anyone's opinion was dismissed out of hand by the rest of us. Someone would suggest an approach, and we'd all stand around sounding it out, weighing its chances, and sometimes giving it a try. Then, as each attempt failed, we all regrouped and brainstormed some more.

Many times when I think back on that week I spent on Hawking, I feel that, in some ways, it was the most enjoyable tour I have served. Some very close relationships were cemented there; people who before had been no more than co-workers have become friends that I still value, and attend to, to this day. Several other members of that crew have expressed the same feelings to me since then.

In the end, though, it was Pat herself who came up with the answer. Early on that fourth day someone, it may have been Nick Stroemann, the suction operator from Crew One, had rigged up a makeshift electromagnet. We all got excited about this idea, and worked like hell getting it suspended from a pulley and lowered into the well. It worked great too, except it couldn't budge the damn slab, and we couldn't angle it around the slab to slap it onto the tool housing. We fished all over that well with the magnet, guiding it remotely using the fiber-optics monitor that we had lowered down there the third day, but it just wasn't going to work.

Everyone was feeling pretty low by then. It was like being stopped on the five-yard line with time running out.

Then Pat shouted, "I've got an idea!" and all of us dropped dead silent and looked at her. It was the most animated I had seen her since the accident. I'll always remember that glow of joy on her face as she beamed back at us.

"Pull the magnet back out of there," she said, "and let's turn on the dresser."

We just looked at one another, not understanding what she meant to do. But she just turned off the magnet's power switch that Stroemann had rigged, which dangled from a cantilever near the nozzle of the plasma drill. Stroemann grabbed the chain that snaked over the pulley and pulled the magnet out of the pit. Pat saw it come clear and then turned toward the monitor screen. She slowly returned power to the dresser tool. As soon as the orange pencil of pure energy appeared, I understood what she was doing. The tool's barrel was pointed generally up the well, in the direction of the metal slab. The beam flecked over one corner of the plate, and we saw it shift color, bubble, and then vaporize.

I grabbed one of the grappling hooks and shouted at Pat to switch off the dresser. She did, and I lowered the hook back down the hole, then swung it and jiggled it past the newly cut gap in the slab. I fished for the dresser tool, guiding myself by the monitor screen, and saw the hook loop around one of the legs of the cart.

"You can't pull it up with that," Williams shouted at me.

But I just shook my head and gave a few tugs on the chain. After a couple of tries, I managed to rotate the dresser a few degrees, so that the beam's aim was shifted. Pat saw what I was up to, and she immediately flipped on the power again. Another section of slab melted away.

I heard a loud cheer and looked up to see that everyone was standing around us now. Their eyes were jumping back and forth from the monitor to the hole as Pat and I now ran off our final series of downs. I twisted the tool a little further; she powered it on and burned away more of the blockage. Once she burned through the chain holding the hook, and I tumbled backward as it snapped free. There was a bit of snickering as I landed on my ass. We had the end in sight now, and the mood had improved considerably.

Before I could stand up, Chan Singh had already lowered another hook into place and was signalling for Pat to turn on the power. I stood back, unceremoniously thrust into the role of spectator, and grinned. I saw movement to one side of me and saw that the Old Man had slipped into the work area unnoticed. He was standing silently, arms hanging loose at his sides, and a thin streamer of white smoke was ascending from the tip of his cigar.

I heard Pat shout, "I got it!" and everyone, except the Old Man, let out another cheer. With no words between them, Chan jerked the hook back out of the hole, and Stroemann powered up the electromagnet. He lowered it, hand over hand, until we all heard the *snap* as it kissed the metal slab—now sundered. Stroemann tugged, and we could hear and see the section of slab break free from the wall of the well. Stroemann wheeled up the cable and the jagged fragment appeared at the lip of the hole. Several hands reached out to grab it.

Another cheer—we could all sense touchdown now. The magnet dropped out of sight again, and the other section of slab was free. Pat called for Chan to lower the hook onto the cart, and he did, snagging it easily the first time. I grabbed another hook and lowered it from the opposite side of the hole. Chan and I stood there like ice fishermen, with a catch too big to lose, and too heavy to reel in. Then Stroemann dropped the magnet so that it *snicked* onto the dresser cart. The three of us began to pull, slowly, and very carefully, and the cart shifted in the monitor. Several others grabbed one or the other of our chains, and we all tugged together. Someone began to chant, "Go, go, go," and we all joined in.

Finally, and grudgingly, Hawking's throat disgorged its unwelcome lodger. Pandemonium broke loose. People were clapping, cheering, crying all at once. I hugged Chan and Stroemann and I guess just about everyone else in the crew. You would have thought we had just won the Super Bowl. We all went crazy, and Pat just stood off to the side with a big grin on her face and tears streaming down her cheeks.

The Old Man let us carry on like that for maybe a couple of minutes, and then he slowly worked his way through the circle of bodies and stood near the edge of the hole. As soon as we became aware of him standing there, we quieted down. In a minute we were standing around with stupid grins on our faces, holding our breath, and waiting to see what the Old Man would say.

He reached out and lightly touched the dresser cart, still hanging like a misshapen fruit from the end of the electromagnet. With a sudden chill, I realized that no one had thought to get it down from over the hole. I saw a couple of heads jerk involuntarily, and I knew that thought was belatedly making the rounds. But with Snyder standing there, none of us were too anxious to move. He slowly looked at each of us, meeting each pair of eyes, challenging us. Then finally he turned toward Pat.

"Talbot," he said, still staring at her, "come here."

Pat looked at him uncertainly and hesitated. She let the smile melt from her mouth, and she wiped at her cheeks with the back of her hand. I saw her tense up as she crossed the space to where the Old Man waited. When she was next to him, he said nothing at first, just continued to look at her through that wispy veil that rose from his cigar. When he finally did speak, it was almost a whisper.

"Look at this dressing tool, Talbot. Take a good look. Do you see what your carelessness has caused?"

He raised his hand and touched the edge of the cart.

"I want you to have this dresser, Talbot. I'll make it a gift to you as soon as we are finished here. You keep it as a souvenir, a reminder of your incompetence."

Pat was glassy-eyed now. She said nothing, and didn't move.

"Because, Talbot," the Old Man continued, "you will get nothing else from me for this job. You are fired. If you can afford to pay, I'll sell you passage back to Konstantine. If not, find your own way back. And I promise you this. You will never work for this, or any other outfit, again."

The rest of us were dumbfounded, unbelieving. The camaraderie had changed to outrage. I looked at Pat, searching for a reaction. But she stood staring at the Old Man, soundlessly.

And then, in a single motion that must have taken seconds, but that seemed endless, she raised her right hand toward the power switch for the electromagnet. Her fingers lingered there for a moment, and she said just two words.

"Fuck you."

She turned off the power. I watched the dresser cart plunge out of sight back down the well, and I heard a stomach-churning crunch.

Snyder's cigar dropped from his mouth and followed the cart. I had never seen a look like that on his face before. He was catatonic. Pat turned from him and walked away.

Her movement seemed to shake Snyder from his trance. He became aware that all of us were staring at him; his eyes narrowed, and he glared at us in turn. Then he looked at Pat, who had reached the bottom of the ladder. He started to say something to her, hesitated, and turned toward me instead.

"Mowboata, you're in charge of getting that dresser tool back out," he snapped. "I want it out by end of shift."

He turned to go after Pat.

"No," I said quietly. There was a gasp from several members of the work crew. Pat was nearly up the ladder now, and I saw her glance back at me when I spoke.

Snyder was frozen where he stood. He looked at me, uncomprehending, as though witnessing a breakdown in natural law. A member of *his crew* had actually refused an order. I shied from the open fury of his stare, turned my back and walked away from him. Behind me, I heard the sound of tools being dropped, and of shuffling feet, but not even a faint murmur of a human voice.

I folded my arms across my chest and turned around again to face him. I found that nearly half the work crew had joined me. The others were standing immobilized like statues, as though some slight movement might shatter the fragile shell of restraint and invite destruction upon all of us.

Snyder's eyes had glazed over. Every filament of muscle in his neck, face, and arms was stretched tight like a cobra ready to strike. His fists were balled into hammers, and his chest was rising and falling with shallow breaths. We were transfixed in a tableau that might explode in an instant.

It was Pat who released us. She started climbing again and disappeared through the access hatch. Snyder saw the movement and turned toward the ladder. He looked back once in my direction, and there was loathing in his face. Then he scrambled up the ladder and left us alone.

We stood around looking at each other for a while, making nervous noises. I had a gut-twisting like I had just been told I had only days to live—which might not have been too far wrong. I had to get away from the work site; I decided to go after Pat. She wasn't in her cabin when I got there.

An hour later the word came down from the Old Man.

"Stow up and lift off."

So we did. It took several hours to stow, and I spent as much time as I could searching for Pat. Williams said he thought Snyder had summoned her to his cabin. No one had seen her since.

I went back to her cabin just before liftoff, and it had been emptied out, though a few personal belongings were still there. She had apparently taken her rocks with her too. I couldn't find them, and no one on the crew even knew what I was talking about when I asked around about them.

Singh had thought to check the lifeboats, and sure enough one was missing. One of the dinghies could hold three people, and they were designed for a few weeks' survival at most. By being alone, and conserving her supplies, Pat could stretch that quite a bit, but it wouldn't do her much good. The boats didn't have enough delta-v to escape from Hawking, and they sure couldn't withstand being this close to the Sun for very long. I got really sick, and mostly stayed in my cabin until we lifted off.

Two hours later we were burning away from Hawking. It disappeared toward Sol with Pat Talbot astride it and with its mysteries intact. We had scooped out a couple of tons of its surface, which would no doubt be of interest to the scientists. But the Science Salvage Act guaranteed the *Wildcatter* crew would get little financial reward for that. The venture had been a bust for the Old Man—and none of us were losing any tears for him. Snyder never mentioned his missing assistant tool dresser again.

That was the last time that I served on a Snyder ship. When we got back to Konstantine, the Old Man fired most of us, and more than half of the rest resigned. I had a hell of a time getting work on any of the other spec ships for a long time afterwards. The Old Man saw to that. It took Snyder almost a month to sign a fresh crew. His find on Titan was the biggest one yet, but I never regretted losing my share.

That was nearly five years ago, and for a long, long time I couldn't think about Pat Talbot without hurting a little inside. But I thought it was over—until yesterday.

Yesterday I got this anonymous packet in my electronic mail. The packet was composed of three linked files, and there was no note or other explanation attached. It had been netted to me from somewhere here on Konstantine Station, and the sender's ID had been deleted.

The first file was a clipping that had been extracted from one of the on-line weekly news publications. It was dated almost a year ago.

Tel Aviv 09/22/48 (UPI): Scientists at Israel's Ben Gurion Institute announced today that, after several years of research, they have successfully synthesized a quantum black hole. . . . Institute Director Dr. Mohinder Chopra stated that the breakthrough had come as a result of unexpected recent discoveries about the properties of these mysterious microscopic objects.

In a related development, U.S. Senator Gary Smith (R.–Texas) today called for immediate international sanctions against Israel. "Tel Aviv's attempt to monopolize the technology of the quantum black hole must be thwarted," Senator Smith was quoted as saying. "There can be little doubt that this 'breakthrough' came as a result of illegal acquisition of discoveries from one of the independent speculator ships, yet another example of Israel's open disregard for the Science Salvage Act."

The second file was a prospectus for Wolfman Discoveries, Inc., a privately held trading corporation based in Geneva that had been formed only two years ago. The company's primary business seemed to be derived from an exclusive, and classified, contract with Ben Gurion Institute. The company's officers were not identified. The prospectus included a formal offering allowing me to buy shares in the company.

The third file was a high-resolution visual image. It was a photograph extracted from an old magazine, maybe *National Geographic*. It was a picture of a dead animal, its leg crushed in a steel vise trap, its body horribly mutilated. The animal was one of those cats that used to roam the U.S. western plains—a puma or cougar. A wildcat.

Jesus, she *is* alive! Somehow, impossibly, she made it back—and she's coming after the Old Man. I don't how she did it, or why she's decided to let me in on this, but I'm not fool enough to bet against her again.

Today I sold my condo and bought ten thousand shares of Wolfman.

The Grand Tour

CHARLES SHEFFIELD

Some readers will recall that in my science fiction stories I often postulate laser-launching systems: that is, a very large laser that stays on the ground provides the energy to put spacecraft into orbit. It wasn't my invention: I took the concept wholesale from a paper by A. N. Pirri and R. F. Weiss of Avco–Everett Research Center, and *they* got the concept from an earlier paper by Arthur (Arky) Kantrowitz of Avco–Everett Laboratories. It's not only feasible, it seems inevitable.

The concept is rather simple. Take a number of lasers, and shine the output of each into a mirror. Use the mirrors to direct all that laser energy into one big steerable mirror.

The spacecraft looks normal enough, and can mass up to about a metric ton (2200 pounds). Put a bell-shaped rocket chamber at the bottom. The laser energy is directed into that chamber. It heats the air in there; the air, being heated, comes out through the nozzle—exactly as does the heated gas from a conventional rocket.

Now pulse the laser beam; about 250 times a second seems to work. Enough air gets into the rocket chamber to provide reaction mass; the capsule rises, with the laser beam tracking it as the mirror is steered. When the capsule gets high enough so that the air is too thin to work as reaction mass, fuel from on-board tanks is pushed into the rocket chamber; the laser still provides the energy (and because it does there's no need for much of the heavy equipment of a conventional rocket).

Eventually the capsule gets to space: the laser cuts off and a very small solid rocket is lit off to provide the thrust to shape the trajectory and put the capsule in orbit.

That's the concept, and I think I was the first to use it in a science fiction story. Imagine my surprise, then, when at an AAAS meeting I heard Freeman Dyson of Princeton's Institute for Advanced Studies give a lecture on laser-launched systems as "highways to space."

Dyson is, of course, one of the geniuses of this culture. His Dyson spheres have been used by countless science fiction writers (Larry Niven cheerfully admits that he stole the Ringworld from Dyson). One should never be surprised by Freeman Dyson—perhaps I should rephrase that. One is *always* surprised by Freeman Dyson. It's just that you shouldn't be surprised to find you've been surprised, so to speak.

Dyson wants the U.S. to build a laser-launching system. It is, he says, far better than the shuttle, because it will give access to space—not merely for government and big corporations, but for a *lot* of people.

Dyson envisions a time when you can buy, for about the cost of a present-day house and car, a space capsule. The people collectively own the laser-launch system, and you pay a small fee to use it. Your capsule goes into orbit. Once you're in orbit you're halfway to anyplace in the solar system. Specifically, you're halfway to the L–5 points, if you want to go help build O'Neill colonies. You're halfway to the asteroid Belt if you'd like to try your hand at prospecting. You're halfway to Mars orbit if that's your desire.

America, Dyson points out, wasn't settled by big government projects. The Great Plains and

California were settled by thousands of free people moving across the plains in their own wagons. There is absolutely no reason why space cannot be settled the same way. All that's required is access.

Dangerous? Of course. Many families will be killed. A lot of pioneers didn't survive the Oregon Trail, either. The Mormons' stirring song "Come Come Ye Saints" is explicit about it: the greatest rewards go to those who dare and whose way is hard.

That kind of Highway to Space would generate more true freedom than nearly anything else we could do; and if the historians who think one of the best features of America was our open frontiers, and that we've lost most of our freedom through loss of frontier—if they're right, we can in a stroke bring back a lot of what's right with the country.

Why don't we get at it?

TOMAS LILI HAD won the Stage, square if not fair, and now he was wearing the biggest, sweatiest grin you have ever seen. Tomorrow he would also wear the yellow jersey on the next-to-last Stage of the Tour.

Ernie Muldoon had come second. In one monstrous last effort of deceleration, I had almost squeaked in front of him at the docking, and hit the buffer right on the maximum allowable speed of five kilometers an hour. We had been given the same time, and now we were collapsed over our handlebars. I couldn't tell about Ernie, but I felt as though I were dying. For the last two hours I had been pedaling with a growing cramp in my left thigh, and for the final ten minutes it was as though I had been working the whole bike one-legged.

After five minutes' rest I had recovered enough to move and speak. I unbuckled my harness, cracked the seals, and climbed slowly out of my bike. As usual at the end of a Stage, my legs felt as though they had never been designed for walking. I did a couple of deep knee bends in the half-gee field, then straightened up and staggered over to Muldoon. He had also flipped back the top of his bike and was slowly levering himself free.

"Tomas was lucky," I said. "And he cheated!"

Muldoon looked at me with eyes sunk back in his head. He was even more dehydrated than I was. "Old Persian proverb," he said. "Luck is infatuated with the efficient."

"You don't think he cheated?"

"No. And he wasn't lucky, he was smart. He bent the rules, but he can't get called on it. Therefore, he didn't cheat. He was just a bit smarter than the rest of us. Admit it, Trace, you'd have done it too if you'd thought of it."

"Maybe."

"Maybe, shmaybe. Come on. I've been cramped in this bike for too long. Let's beat the crowd to the showers."

He was right, the others were streaming in now, one every few seconds. As we left the docking area a whole bunch zoomed in together in practically a blanket finish. I saw five riders from Adidas, so close I was sure they'd been slip-streaming for a sixth member of their team. That *was* outside the rules, and they were bound to be caught. Five years ago, slipstreaming had been worth doing. Today, it was marginal. The teams did it anyway—because the man who benefited from the slipstreaming was not the one doing anything illegal. The rider who had given the momentum boost would be disqualified, but that would be some no-hoper in the team. Illogical? Sure. The Tour had a crazy set of rules in the first place, and as more and more riders became part of the big teams, the rules became harder to apply. Ernie Muldoon and I were two of the last independents racing the Grand Tour. Ernie, because he was famous before the team idea caught on; me, because I was stubborn enough to want to win on my own.

Tomas was already sitting in the cafeteria as we walked through it, surrounded by the microphones and cameras. He was enjoying himself. I felt angry for a moment, then decided that it was fair enough. We waved to the media and went on to the showers. Let Tomas have his day of glory. He was so far down in the overall ratings that there was no way he could be the outright Tour de Système winner, even if he won tomorrow's and the final Stages by big margins.

Ernie Muldoon thought that the overall Grand Tour winner was going to be old and wily Ernest Muldoon, who had already won the Tour de Système an unprecedented five times; and I thought it was going to be me, Tracy Collins, already identified in the media coverage as the Young Challenger; or maybe, as Ernest put it, the Young Pretender. Which made *him*, as I pointed out, the Old Pretender.

I had modeled my whole approach to the Tour on Ernie Muldoon, and now it was paying off. This was only my third year, but unless I was disqualified I was certain to be in the top five. My cumulative time for all the Stages actually placed me in the top three, but I hate to count them little chickens too soon.

The shower facilities were as crummy as we've grown to expect. You've got one of the premier athletic events of the Solar System, with coverage Earthwide and Moonwide, and still the showers at the end of each Stage are primitive. No blown air, no suction, no spin. All you get are soap, not-warm-enough water, and drying-cloths. It must be because we don't attract top video coverage. People are interested in us, but what sort of TV program can you build out of an event where each Stage runs anything up to thirty-six hours, and the competitors are just seen as little dots for most of the time? Maybe what the media need are a few deaths to spice things up, but so far the Tour has been lucky (or unlucky) that way.

Muldoon slapped me on the back as we were coming out of the shower area. "Three quarts of beer, three quarts of milk, thirty ounces of rare beef, and half a dozen potatoes from the original Owld Sod, and you'll not even notice that leg of yours. Are you with me, lad?"

"I'm with you—but not this minute. Don't you want to get a weather report first, for tomorrow?"

"A quick look, now. But I doubt if we'll see anything special. The wind forecasts for tomorrow have all been quiet. It's my bet we'll see stronger winds for the final Stage. Maybe a big flare-up."

Muldoon was casual, but he didn't really fool me. He had told me, a dozen times, that the solar wind forecast was the most important piece of a rider's knowledge—more relevant than local gravity anomalies or super-accurate trajectory calculations. We went over to the weather center and looked at the forty-eight-hour forecast. It was pretty calm. Unless there was a sudden and dramatic change, all the riders could get away with minimal radiation shielding.

That wasn't always the case. Two years ago, the second half of the Tour had taken place when there was a massive solar flare. The solar wind of energetic charged particles had been up by a factor of a hundred, and every rider added another two hundred kilos of radiation shielding. If you think that doesn't make a man groan, when every ounce of shielding has to be carried around with you like a snail carrying its shell—well, then you've never ridden the Tour.

Of course, you don't *have* to carry the shielding. That's a rider's choice. Four years ago, on the eleventh Stage of the Tour, Crazy-legs Gerhart had done his own calculation of flare activity, and decided that the radiation level would drop nearly to zero a few minutes after the Stage began. When everybody else crawled away from Stage-start loaded down with extra shielding, Crazy-legs zoomed off with a minimal load. He won the Stage by over two hours, but he just about glowed in the dark. The wind level hadn't become low at all. He docked so hot with radiation that no one wanted to touch him, and he was penalized a hundred and fifty minutes for exceeding the permissible dosage per Stage by ninety-two rads. Worse than that, they dumped him in the hospital to flush him out. He missed the rest of the Tour.

Every rider had his own cookbook method for guessing the optimal shielding load, just as everyone had his own private trajectory program and his own preferred way of pacing the race. There were as many methods as there were riders in the Tour.

Muldoon and I made notes of the wind—we'd check again, last thing at night—and then went back to the cafeteria. A few of the media people were still there. Without looking as though we were avoiding them, we loaded our trays and went off to a quiet corner. We didn't want the Newsies tonight. The next-to-last Stage was coming up tomorrow morning, and it was a toughie. We had to ride nearly twenty-five thousand kilometers, dropping in from synchronous station, where we had docked today, to the big Sports Central station in six-hour orbit.

Some people complain because we call it the "Tour de Système" when the only part of the Solar System we travel is Earth-Moon space. But they've never ridden the Tour. When you have, the six-hundred-thousand-kilometer course seems quite long enough. And the standards of competition get tougher every year. All the original Stage records have been broken, then broken again. In a few years' time it will be a million-kilometer Tour, and then we'll zip way out past the Moon before we start the inbound Stages.

Muldoon and I stuffed ourselves with food and drink—you can't overfeed a Tour rider, no matter what you give him—then went off quietly to bed. Two more days, I told myself; then I'll raise more Hell than the Devil's salvage party.

. . .

Next morning my first worry was my left thigh. It felt fine—as it ought to; I'd spent an hour last night rubbing a foul green embrocation into the muscles. I dressed and headed for breakfast, wanting to beat the rush again.

"Well, Tracy, me boyo." It was Muldoon, appearing out of nowhere and walking by my side. "An' are you still thinking ye have the Divil's own chanst of beating me?"

He can speak English as well as I can, but when he senses there are media people around he turns into the most dreadful blarney-waffling stage-Irishman you could find.

"Easily." I nudged him in the ribs. "You're a tough man, Muldoon, but your time has come. The bells will be pealing out this time for handsome young Tracy Collins, overall winner of the Grand Tour de Système." (So maybe I respond to the media, too; I sounded confident, but Muldoon couldn't see my fingers, crossed on the side away from him.)

"Not while there's breath in this breast, me boy," he said. "An 'tis time we was over an' havin' a word here with the grand Machiavellian Stage winner himself."

Muldoon stopped by Tomas Lili's table, where a couple of press who must have missed the Stage winner the previous night were sitting and interviewing. "Nice work, Tomas me boy," Muldoon said, patting the yellow jersey. "An' where'd you be getting the idea of doin' that what yer did?"

A couple of media people switched their recorders back on. Tomas shrugged. "From you, Ernesto, where we all get our ideas. You were the one who decided that it was easier—and legal—to switch the ion drive around on the bike at midpoint, rather than fight all the angular momentum you'd already built up in your wheels if you tried to turn the bike through a hundred and eighty degrees. I just built from there."

"Fair enough. But your trick won't work more than once, Tomas. We'll be ready."

Tomas grinned. He had won a Stage, and that's more than his Arianespace sponsors had expected of him. "What trick ever did work more than once, Ernesto? Once is enough."

The media rats at the table looked puzzled, and now one of them turned to Ernest Muldoon. "I don't understand you. What 'trick' is this you're talking about?"

Muldoon stared at the woman, noted she was young and pretty, and gestured at her to sit down. He poured everyone a liter of orange juice. We competitors sweat away seven or eight kilos, pedaling a Stage, and we have to make sure we start out flush-full with liquids. Tomas took the opportunity to slide away while Muldoon was pouring. He'd had his juice, and some of the other competitors who were still straggling in might have a less enlightened attitude towards Tomas's innovation of the previous Stage.

"D'you understand how we change directions round in the middle of each Stage?" Muldoon asked the reporter. One reason Ernie is so popular with the Press is that he's never too busy to talk to them and explain to them. I noticed that now he had her hooked he had dropped the stage-Irish accent.

"I guess so. But I don't understand *why*. You're out in empty space, between the Stage points, and you've pedaled hard to get the wheels rotating as fast as you can. And then you shift everything around!"

"Right. An' here's the why. Suppose the rider—say, Trace here, the likely lad—hasn't reached halfway point yet, and let's for the moment ignore any fancy maneuvers at Stage turn points. So he's pedaling like a madman—the only way he knows—and the wheels are whizzing round, and he's built up a voltage of something respectable on the rotating Wimshurst disks—say, a couple of million volts. That voltage goes into accelerating the ion stream out of the back of the bike, eh? The faster he pedals, the higher the voltage, the better the exhaust velocity on the ion drive, and so the faster goes our lad Tracy. And he's *got* to get that exhaust velocity high as he can, because he's only allowed fifty kilos of fuel per Stage, total. All right?"

"Oh, yes." The lady looked into Muldoon's slightly squinty eyes and seemed ready to swoon with admiration. He beamed at her fondly. I was never sure that Ernie Muldoon followed through with a woman while we were riding the Tour—but I'm damned sure if he *didn't* have them between Stages, he saved up credits and used them all when the Tour was over.

"All right." Muldoon ran his hand out along the table top. "Here's Trace. He's been zooming along in a straight line, faster and faster. But now he gets to the halfway point of the Stage, an' now he's got to worry about how he'll get to the finish. See, it's no good arriving at the final docking and zooming right on through—you have to *stop*, or you're disqualified. So now Trace has a different problem. He has to worry about how he's going to *decelerate* for the rest of the run, and finish at a standstill, or close to it, when the bike gets to the docking point. The old-fashioned way—that means up to seven years ago—was pretty simple. Trace here would have turned the whole bike around, so that the ion drive was pointing the other way, towards the place he wanted to get to, and he'd keep on pedaling like the dickens. And if he'd planned well, or was just dumb lucky, he'd be slowed down by the drive just the right amount when he got the final docking, so he could hit slap against the buffers at the maximum permitted speed. Sounds good?"

She nodded. "Fine." I didn't know if she was talking about the explanation, or Ernie-the-Letch Muldoon's hand resting lightly across hers. "But what's wrong with that way of doing it?" she went on. "It sounds all right to me."

Someday they're going to assign reporters to the Tour de Système who are more than twenty-two years old and who have some faint idea before they begin of the event they are supposed to be covering. It will ruin Muldoon's sex life, but it will stop me feeling like an antique myself. All the young press people ask the same damned questions, and they all nod in the same half-witted way when they get the answers.

I wanted to see how Ernest handled the next bit. Somehow he was going to have to get across to Sweet Young Thing the concept of angular momentum.

"Problem is," he said, "while the wheels are spinning fast the bike don't want to turn. Those wheels are heavy glassite disks, rubbing against each other, and they're like flywheels, and so the bike wants to stay lined up just the way it is. So in the old days, the biker would have to stop the wheels—or at least slow 'em down a whole lot—then turn the bike around, and start pedaling again to get the wheels going. All the time that was happening, there was no potential difference on the Wimshursts, no ion drive, and no acceleration. Big waste of time, and also for the second half of the Stage you were flying ass-backwards. So I did the obvious thing. I mounted a *double* ion drive on my bike, one facing forward, one facing back—turned out that the rules don't *quite* say you can't have more than one drive. They only say you can't have more than one ion drive on your bike *in use at one time*. They don't say you can't have two, and switch 'em in the middle of the Stage. Which is what I did. And won, for about two Stages, until everybody else did the same thing."

"But what was it that Tomas Lili did? He seemed to have come up with something new."

"He installed an ion drive that had more than just the two positions, fore and aft. His can be directed in pretty much any way he wants to. So, first thing that Tomas did on the last Stage, he went off far too fast—at a crazy speed, we all thought. And naturally he got ahead of all of us. *Then* what he did was to direct his ion beam at whoever was close behind him. The ions hit whoever he was pointing at—me, or Trace, or one of the others—and just about cancelled out our own drives completely. We were throwing a couple of tenths of a gram of ion propellant out of the *back* of the bike at better than ten kilometers a second, but we were being hit on the front by the same amount, travelling at the same speed. Net result: no forward acceleration for us. It didn't *hurt* us, physically,'cause we're all radiation shielded. But it slowed us. By the time we realized why we were doing so badly, he was gone. Naturally, Tomas wasn't affected, except for the tiny bit he sacrificed because his exhaust jet wasn't pointing exactly aft." Muldoon shrugged. "Neat trick. Works once—next time we'll stay so far out of his wake he'll lose more forward acceleration turning off-axis to hit us than he'll gain."

"You explain everything so clearly!" Their hands were still touching.

"Always try to help. But we've got to get ready for the Stage now. Will you be there at the finish?"

"Of course! I wouldn't miss it for anything."

Muldoon patted her hand possessively. "Then why don't we get together after it, and we can go over the action together? Next to last Stage, there ought to be fireworks."

"Oh, yes! Please."

As we left for the start dock, I shook my head at Muldoon. "I don't expect any particular fireworks today. No tricky course change, no solar flares—it should be the tamest leg of the Tour."

He stared back at me, owl-eyed. "And did I say the action would be on the course, boyo?"

We walked side by side to the main staging area. In twenty minutes we would be on our way. I could feel the curious internal tension that told me it was Tour-time again—more than that, it was the final Stages of the Tour. Something in my belly was winding me up like an old-fashioned watch. That was fine. I wanted to hang there in that start space all ready to explode to action. I touched Muldoon lightly on the shoulder—good luck, Muldoon, it meant; *but don't beat me*—then I went on to my station.

There was already a strange atmosphere in the preparation chamber. As the Tour progresses, that strangeness grows and grows. I had noticed it years ago and never understood it, until little Alberto Maimonides, who is probably the best sportswriter living (my assessment) or ever (his own assessment), sampled that changing atmosphere before the Stages, and explained it better than I ever could. Either one of Muldoon's tree-trunk thighs has far more muscle on it than Maimonides' whole body, but the little man understood the name of the game. "At the beginning of the Tour," he said to me one day, "there are favorites, but everyone may be said to have an equal chance of winning. As the Tour progresses, the cumulative time and penalties of each rider are slowly established. And so two groups emerge: those with the potential to win the whole thing, and those with no such potential. Those two different potentials polarize the groups more and more, building tension in one, releasing tension in the other. Like the Wimshurst disks that you drive as you turn the pedals, the competitors build up their own massive potential difference. Beyond the halfway mark in the Tour, I can tell you in which group a competitor lies—without speaking a word to him! If a rider has a chance of winning, it is seen in the tension in neck and shoulders, in the obsessive attention to weather data, in the faraway look in the man's eyes. I can tell you at once which group a rider is in."

"And can you—" I began.

"No." He interrupted me. "What I cannot do, Trace, to save my life, is tell you who will win. That will be, by definition, the best man."

I wanted to be that best man, more than I had ever wanted anything. I was thinking of Alberto Maimonides as I lifted open the shell of my bike and began to inspect the radiation shielding. It was all fine, a thin layer in anticipation of a quiet day without much solar wind. The final Stage was another matter—the forecasts said we would see a lot more radiation; but that was another day, and until we finished today's effort the final Stage didn't matter at all.

The fuel tank came next. The competitors were not allowed to charge the fuel tank themselves, and the officials who did it always put in an exact fifty kilograms, correct to the microgram. But it didn't stop every competitor worrying over the tank, afraid that he had been short-changed and would run out of fuel in the middle of the Stage. People occasionally used their fuel too fast, and ran out before the end of a Stage. Without ion drive fuel they were helpless. They would drift miserably around near the docking area, until someone went out and fished them in. Then they would be the butt of all the other competitors, subject to the same old jokes: "What's the matter, Tish, got thirsty and been drinking the heavy water again?" "You're four hours late, Sven, she gave your dance to somebody else." "Jacques, my lad, we all warned you about premature ejaculation."

I climbed into the shell, and checked my trajectory. It was too late to change anything now, except how hard I would pedal at each time in the Stage. It would need something exceptional to change even that. I had planned this Stage long ago, how I would pace it, how much effort I would put in at each breakpoint. I slipped my feet into the pedal stirrups, gripped the handlebars hard, looked straight ahead, and waited. I was hyperventilating, drawing in the longest, deepest breaths I could.

The starting signal came as an electronic beep in my headset. While it was still sounding I was pedaling like mad, using low gears to get initial torques on the Wimshursts. After a few seconds I reached critical voltage, the ion drive triggered on, and I was moving. Agonizingly slowly at first—a couple of thousandths of a gee isn't much and it takes a while to build up any noticeable speed—but I was off.

All the way along the starting line, other bikers were doing exactly the same thing. There were various tricks to riding the Tour in the middle part of a Stage, but very little choice at the beginning. You rode as hard as your body would stand, and got the best speed as early as possible. Once you were moving fast you could relax a little bit, and let the bike coast. At the very end of the Stage, you made the same effort in reverse. Now you wanted to hold your speed as long as possible, to minimize your total time for the Stage. But if you had been too energetic at the beginning, or if your strength failed you at the end, you were in real trouble. Then you'd not be able to decelerate your bike enough. Either you'd shoot right through the docking area and whip out again into open space, or you'd demolish the buffers by hitting them at far more than the legal maximum. Both those carried disastrous penalties.

After half an hour of frantic pedaling I was feeling pretty pleased. My leg was giving me no trouble at all—touch wood, though there was none within thirty thousand miles. I could see the main competition, and it was where I wanted it to be.

Muldoon was a couple of kilometers behind, Rafael Rodriguez of the NASDA team was almost alongside him, and Tomas Lili was already far in the rear. I looked ahead, and settled down to the long grind.

This was a Stage with few tricky elements. During the Tour we started from low earth orbit, went all the way to L-4 in a series of thirty variable-length Stages, and then looped back in halfway to the Moon before we began the drive to Earth. Some Stages were geometrically complex, as much in the calculations as the legs. This one was the sort of Stage that I was thoroughly comfortable with. The only real variables today were physical condition and natural stamina. I was in the best shape I had ever been, and I was convinced that if my legs and determination held out I had everyone beat.

Twenty-six hours later I was even more convinced. We had passed the crossover point long ago, and I had done it without any complication. I could still see Muldoon and Rodriguez in my viewfinder, but they had not closed the gap at all. If anything, I might have gained a few more seconds on them. No one else was even in sight. There was a terrible urge to ease off, but I could not do it. It was *cumulative* time that decided the Tour winner, and Muldoon and Rodriguez had both started this Stage nearly a minute ahead of me. I wanted to make up for that today, and more. The yellow jersey might be enough for Tomas Lili, but not for me. I wanted the whole pie.

I had taken my last liquid three hours ago, draining the juice bottle and then jettisoning it to save mass. Now my throat was dry and burning, and I'd have given anything for a quarter liter of water. I put those thoughts out of my head, and pedaled harder.

It turned out that I left my final sprint deceleration almost too late. Twenty-five kilometers out I realized that I was approaching the final docking area too fast. I would slam into the buffers at a speed over the legal limit. I put my head down, ignored the fact that my legs had been pumping for nearly twenty-seven hours straight, and rode until I thought my heart and lungs would burst. I didn't even see the docks or the final markers. I guess my eyes were closed. All I heard was the loud *ping* that told of an arrival at legal speed. And then I was hanging on the handlebars, wishing some kind person would shoot me and put me out of my misery.

My chest was on fire, my throat was too dry to breathe, my heart was racing up close to two hundred beats a minute, and my legs were spasming with cramps. I clung to the handlebars, and waited. Finally, when I heard a second *ping* through my helmet's radio, I knew the second man was in. I looked up at the bigboard readout. It was Muldoon, following me in by one minute and seventeen seconds. He had started the day one minute and fourteen seconds ahead of me on the cumulative total. I had won the Stage—and I was now the overall Tour leader.

I groaned with pain, released my harness, and cracked open my bike. I forced a big grin onto my face for the media—more like a grimace of agony, but no one would know the difference—and managed to climb out onto the docking facility just as though I was feeling light and limber. Then I sauntered along to where Muldoon was slowly opening his bike. One cheery smile for the benefit of the cameras, and I was reaching in to lift him lightly clear of the bike.

He glared up at me. "You big ham, Trace. What was your margin?"

"One minute and seventeen seconds."

"Ah." It was more a groan of physical agony than mental as he tried to stand up on the dock. His thigh muscles, like mine, were still unknotting after over a day of continuous effort. "So you're ahead then. Three seconds ahead. And with a new Stage record. Damn it."

"Thanks. You're just a terrific loser, Muldoon."

"Right. And it takes one to know one, Trace." He did a couple of deep knee bends. "What about the others. Where did they finish?"

"Schindell came in two minutes after you. He's about four minutes behind us, overall. Something must have happened to Rodriguez, because he's still not in."

"Leg cramps. We were riding side by side for a long time, then he dropped way behind. I'm pretty sure he had to stop pedaling."

"So he's out of the running."

We stared at each other. "So it's me an' thee," said Muldoon after a few moments. "Barring a miracle or a disaster, one of us will be *it*."

It! Overall Tour winner. I wanted that so much I could taste it.

Muldoon saw my face. "You're getting there, Trace," he said. "Muscle and heart and brains will only take you so far. You have to *want* it bad enough."

I saw *his* face, too. His eyes were bloodshot, and sunk so far back that they were little glowing sparks of blue at the end of dark tunnels. If I had reached a long way into myself to ride this Stage, how far down had Muldoon gone? Only he knew that. He *wanted it*, as much as I did.

"You're getting old, Ernie," I said. "Alberto Maimonides says that the Tour's a young man's game."

"And what does he know, that little Greek faggot!" Muldoon respected Maimonides as much as I did, but you'd never know it if you heard them talk about each other. "He's talking through his skinny brown neck. The Tour's a *man's* game, not a *young* man's game. Go an' get your yellow jersey, Trace, and show your fine profile to the media."

"What about you? They'll want to see you as well—we're neck and neck for overall Tour position. How long since non-team riders have been one and two in Tour status?"

"Never happened before. But I've got work to do. Weather reports to look at, strategy to plan. You can handle the damned media, Trace—time you learned how. And I'll tell you what." He had been scowling at me, but now he smiled. "You look at all the pretty young reporters, and you pick out the one who'd be my favorite. An' you can give her one for me."

He stumped off along the dock. I looked after him before I went to collect the yellow jersey that I would wear for the final Stage, and pose with it for the waiting mediamen. Ernie hadn't given up yet. There was brooding and scheming inside that close-cropped head. He was like a dormant volcano now, and there was one more Stage to go. Maybe he had one more eruption left in him. But what could it possibly be?

I was still asking that question when we lined up for the beginning of the final Stage. Yellow jersey or no yellow jersey, I hadn't slept well last night. I dreamed of the swoop towards the finishing line, with its massed cameras and waiting crowds. There would be hordes of space tugs, filled with spectators, and video crews from every station on Earth or Moon. And who would they be homing in on, to carry off and interview until he could be interviewed no more?

In the middle of the night I had awakened and wandered off to where the rows of bikes were sitting under twenty-four-hour guard. The rules here were very simple. I could go to my bike, and do what I liked with it; but I could not touch, or even get too close to, the bike of another competitor. The history of the rule was something I could only guess at. It made psychological sense. No competitor wanted *anybody* else touching his beloved bike. We suffered the organizers to fill our fuel tanks, because we had no choice; but we hovered over and watched every move they made, to make sure they did not damage so much as a square millimeter of paint.

The bike shed was quiet when I got there. A couple of competitors were inside their bikes, fiddling with nozzles, or changing the position of juice bottles or viewfinders or computers. It was all just nerves coming to the fore. The changes they were making would not improve their time by a tenth of a second. Ernie Muldoon was inside his bike, too, also fiddling with bits and pieces. He stopped when he saw me, and nodded.

"Can't sleep, either?"

I shrugged. "It's not easy. Plenty of time for sleep tomorrow night, when the Tour's over."

"Nobody wants to sleep when it's over. We'll all be partying, winners and losers."

"Wish it were tomorrow now."

He nodded. "I know that feeling. Good luck, Trace."

"Same to you, Ernie."

I meant it. And he meant it. But as I sat at the starting line, my feet already in the pedal stirrups, I knew what that well-wishing meant. Neither of us wanted anything bad to happen to the other; all we wanted was to *win*. That was the ache inside. I looked around my bike for one last time. The radiation shielding was all in position. As we had surmised the day before yesterday, the weather had changed. There was a big spike of solar activity sluicing through the Inner System, and a slug of radiation was on its way. It would hit us close to the halfway point of the final Stage, then would diminish again when the Tour was over. The maximum radiation level was nowhere near as high as it had been in the Tour two years ago, but it was enough to make us all carry a hefty load of shielding. The prospect of hauling that along for twenty-six thousand kilometers was not one I was looking forward to.

The electronic beep sounded in my helmet. We were off. A hundred and six riders—we had lost thirty-four along the way to injuries and disqualification—began to pedal madly. After half a minute of frenzied, apparently unproductive activity, the line slowly moved away from the starting port. The airlock had been opened ten minutes before. We were heading out into hard vacuum, and the long, solitary ride to the finish. No one was allowed to send us any information during the Stage, or to respond to anything other than an emergency call from a competitor.

The optimal trajectory for this Stage had been talked about a good deal when the competitors held their evening bull sessions. There were two paths that had similar projected energy budgets. The choice between them depended on the type of race that a competitor wanted to ride. If he was very confident that he would have a strong final sprint deceleration, then trajectory one was optimal. It was slightly better overall. But if a rider was at all suspicious of his staying power at the end, trajectory two was safer.

The two trajectories diverged early in the Stage, and roughly two-thirds of the riders opted for the second and more conservative path. I and maybe thirty others, praying that our legs and lungs would stand it, went for the tougher and faster route.

Muldoon did neither of these things. I knew the carapace of his red-and-black bike as well as I knew my own, and I was baffled to see him diverging from everyone else, on another path entirely. I had looked at that trajectory myself—we all had. And we had ruled it out. It wasn't a disastrous choice, but it offered neither the speed of the one I was on, nor the security of the path most riders had chosen.

Muldoon must know all that. So where was he going?

I had plenty of time to puzzle in the next twenty-four hours, and not much else to occupy my attention. Before we reached midpoint where I reversed my drive's direction, all the other riders in my group had diminished to dots in my viewfinder. They were out of it, far behind. I had decided that after today's Stage I would take a year to rest and relax, but I wouldn't relax now. I pushed harder than I had ever pushed. As the hours wore on I became more aware of the radiation shielding, the stone that I was perpetually pushing uphill. A *necessary* stone. Outside my bike was a sleet of deadly solar particles.

Even though the group of competitors who had ridden my trajectory were just dots in the distance behind me, I didn't feel at all relaxed. On the Tour, you *never* relax until the final Stage is ridden, the medals have been awarded, *and* the overall winner has performed the first step-out at the Grand Dance.

At the twenty-third hour I looked off with my little telescope in another direction. If anyone in the slow, conservative group had by some miracle managed to ride that trajectory faster than anyone had ever ridden it, they ought to be visible now in the region that I was scanning. I looked and saw nothing, nothing but vacuum and hard, unwinking stars.

The final docking area was at last in sight, a hundred kilometers ahead of me. I could begin to pick up little dots of ships, hovering close to the dock. And unless I was very careful, I was going to shoot right through them and past them. I had to shed velocity. That meant I had to pedal harder than ever to slow my bike to the legal docking speed.

I bent for one last effort. As I did so, I caught sight of something in my rear viewfinder.

A solitary bike. Red and black—Muldoon. But going far too fast. He was certainly going to overtake me, but he was equally certainly going to be unable to stop by the time he reached the dock. He would smash on through, and either be disqualified or given such a whopping time penalty he would drop to third or fourth place.

I felt sorry for him. He had done the almost impossible, and ridden that inefficient alternate trajectory to within a few seconds of catching me. But it was all wasted if he couldn't dock; and at the speed he was going, that would be just impossible.

Then I had to stop thinking of him, and start thinking of myself. I put my head down and drove the cranks around, gradually increasing the rate. The change in deceleration was too small for me to feel, but I knew it was there. The ions were pushing me back, easing my speed. I was vaguely aware of Muldoon's bike moving silently past mine—still going at an impossible pace.

And so was I. It was the mass of all the shielding, like a millstone around my bike. The inertia of that hundred extra kilos of shielding material wanted to keep going, dragging me and the bike with it. *I had to slow down.*

I pedaled harder. Harder. The docking area was ahead. *Harder!* I was still too fast. I directed the bike to the line instinctively, all my mind and will focused on my pumping legs.

Stage line. Docking guide. Docking. Docked!

I heard the *ping!* in my helmet that told of a docking within the legal speed limit. I felt a moment of tremendous satisfaction. *All over. I've won the Tour!* Then I rested my head on my handlebars and sat for a minute, waiting for my heart to stop smashing out of my rib cage.

Finally I lifted my head. I found I was looking at Muldoon's red and black racing bike, sitting quietly in a docking berth next to mine. He was slumped over the handlebars, not moving. He looked dead. The marker above his bike showed he had made a legal docking.

His bike looked different, but I was not sure how. I unlocked my harness, cracked the bike seals, and forced myself outside onto the dock. As usual my legs were jelly. I wobbled my way along to Muldoon's bike. I knocked urgently on the outside.

"Muldoon! Are you all right?" I was croaking, dry-throated. I didn't seem to have enough moisture left in my body for one spit.

I hammered again. For a few seconds there was no response at all. Then the cropped head slowly lifted, and I was staring down into a puffy pair of eyes. Muldoon didn't seem to recognize me. Finally he nodded, and reached to unlock his harness. When the bike opened, I helped him out. He was too far gone to stand.

"I'm all right, Trace," he said. "I'm all right." He sounded terrible, anything but all right.

I took another look at his bike. Now I knew why it looked different. "Muldoon, you've lost your shielding. We have to get you to a doctor."

He shook his head. "You don't need to. I didn't get an overdose. I didn't *lose* that shielding. I shed it on purpose."

"But the radiation levels—"

"Are down. You saw the forecasts for yourself, the storm was supposed to peak during the Stage and then run way down. I spent most of last night fixing the bike so I could get rid of shielding when the solar flux died away enough. That happened six hours ago."

I suddenly realized how he had managed that tremendous deceleration at the end of the race. Without an extra hundred kilos of shielding dragging him along, it was easy. I could have done the same thing.

And then I felt sick. Any one of us could have done what Muldoon had done—if we'd just been smart enough. The rules let you jettison anything you didn't want, empty juice bottles or radiation shielding. The only requirement is that you don't interfere with any other rider. Muldoon had thrown a lot of stuff away, but by choosing a trajectory where no one else was riding, he had made sure he could not be disqualified for interference.

"You did it again," I said. "How far ahead of me were you when you docked?"

He shrugged. "Two seconds, three seconds. I'm not sure. I may not have done it, Trace. I needed three seconds. You may still have won it."

But I was looking at his face. There was a look of deep, secret joy there that not even old stoneface Muldoon could hide. He had won. And I had lost. Again.

I knew. He knew. And he knew I knew.

"It's my last time, Trace," he said quietly. "This one means more than you can imagine to me. I'll not win any more. Maimonides is quite right, the Tour's a young man's game. But you've got lots of time, years and years."

I had been wrong about the moisture in my body. There was plenty, enough for it to trickle down my cheeks. "Damn it, I don't *want* it in years and years, Ernie. I want it *now*."

"I know you do. And that's why I'm sure you'll get it *then*." He sighed. "It took me eight tries before I won, Trace. Eight tries! I thought I'd never do it. You're still only on your third Tour." Ernie Muldoon reached out his arm and draped it around my shoulders. "Come on now, lad. Win or lose, the Tour's over for this year. Give a poor old man a hand, and let's the two of us go and talk to them damned media types together."

I was going to say no, because I couldn't possibly face the cameras with tears in my eyes. But then I looked at his face, and knew I was wrong. I could face them crying. Ernie Muldoon was still my model. Anything he could do, I could do.

Industrial Revolution

POUL ANDERSON

The Industrial Revolution gave more people real freedoms than all the political revolutions put together. Political developments can only allow people to do what is possible; the Industrial Revolution greatly expanded those possibilities. The wealthiest man on Earth in 1890 could not travel from Los Angeles to Paris in a day; have good teeth past the age of 50; enjoy the benefits of penicillin and antibiotics; communicate across country; or have access to an enormous range of entertainments and cultural events for the price of a day's rental of a VCR tape.

Of course there are costs to those benefits. There always are, and it's always worth looking at them. Still, it doesn't do to neglect the benefits.

Now that the Cold War is winding down and utopian dreams of world communism have been tossed on the trash heap of history where they belong, we have a sudden revival of the ecology movement, generally headed by people whose notion of "ecology" is a series of catchphrases, rather than anything based on any scientific understanding of the interrelationships of species.

The ecology movement wants to save the Earth. No one quarrels with that intention; but the methods are worth debating. In general, the ecology

movement trusts bureaucracies more than individuals; relies on regulation and coercion rather
than voluntary efforts. One U.S. city now requires
that all garbage be thrown away in clear plastic
bags so that ecology inspectors can be sure it
has been sorted properly.

We've been through much of this before. Now,
once again, we're hearing that "small is better,"
and told that there must be "limits to growth."
Over here people pay attention to that talk. Not
so in what used to be the Eastern Bloc. They
know better; there they had total state control
over growth and environment. The cost to both
was catastrophic.

Czechoslovakian President Vaclav Havel, in a
1990s New Year's speech, told how his nation's
Communist rulers had "laid waste to our soil and
the rivers and the forests . . . We have the worst
environment in the whole of Europe . . ." In former
agricultural areas, whole hills stand denuded and
barren because their vegetation has died in air
more polluted than what we call acid rain. Monu-
ments and statues that stood the depredations of
the war with Napoleon are now pitted and eroded
by pollutants.

The Polish Academy of Sciences estimates that
one fourth of Poland's soil may be too contami-
nated for safe farming. Most of the water in
Poland's rivers is unsafe for human consumption,
in some cases even unfit for industrial use. Jeffrey
Leonard, of the World Wildlife Fund, has stated,
"Pollution was part and parcel of the system that
molested the people [of Eastern Europe] in their
daily lives." A full quarter to a third of the forests
in Eastern Europe are dying from toxic air.

When I was in Moscow, I had an interview with
Dr. Jablokov, the U.S.S.R. Deputy Minister of
the Environment. Under *glasnost* what used to
be state secrets are now out in the open: the
U.S.S.R. has nearly destroyed the environment in
vast areas of the country. The Aral Sea is nearly
gone; the Caspian isn't faring a lot better. There's

a layer of hydrogen sulfide not far below the surface of the Black Sea, a situation that puts up to
a million people at risk.

By any standard, total government control of
industry and private property was a failed experiment; a disaster for both the people and the
planet.

Can we trust our elected officials to do much
better? The United States is governed by a Congress with less turnover than the Supreme Soviet
and Politburo had during the Brezhnev era. In the
West corporations are often accused of spoiling
the environment in their never-ending quest for
profits. To the leaders of the ecology or Earth
First! movements, free enterprise is the enemy
of environmental preservation and care taking.
Only "proper control" of the private sector and
carefully policed limits to growth can curtail the
death of the Earth or some other series of ecologi-
cal catastrophes. The problem is, where will "proper controls" come from? Regulations are onerous
and costly; how long will people vote for them?

The tragedy of Eastern Europe should be a lesson for all those who believe that nationalization
and more government control of resources is
the answer to our pollution and environmental
problems. If anyone doubts this hard-won lesson,
look at any of the public housing in our major
cities—graffiti, lighting fixtures smashed, excrement in the walkways, plumbing torn right out
of the walls, and this is just the obvious physical destruction! The damage done by fear and
violence is beyond description.

The truth is that there is no alternative to
growth. A static economy is a dying economy,
if for no other reason than that the political
process demands more and more resources to
"give" to the voters. There will be either growth
or stagnation.

The trick is to put the growth in places where
it doesn't harm the environment. Outer space
looks to be a good place. There may be limits

to growth, but with all of space to play with I'd be happy to leave the problem for my descendants 10,000 years hence to worry about.

Environmental concerns are legitimate; but it's important to consider the whole system. Mankind doesn't live on Earth alone. Man lives in a solar system of nine planets, nearly 50 moons, and over half a million asteroids. That system circles a rather small and unimportant star that is part of a galaxy containing tens of billions of stars. Only one Earth, indeed! There are millions of Earths out there, and if we use up this one, we'll just have to go find another, that's all.

We have spent nearly $200 billion on outer space since Apollo. For that kind of money we ought to be halfway to Alpha Centauri; but because the money was spent pursuing government's goals we have got rather less than that. Instead of infrastructure in space, we have a standing army of NASA bureaucrats. We have three shuttles that almost work; an Incredible Shrinking Space Station that clearly will never be built; a space telescope with worse performance than the Keyhole satellites we've been putting up for years; and a wealth of scientific data. What we don't have is access to space.

For the price of a *real* space program we could bring in asteroids and build solar power satellites. We could have done that already if we hadn't organized our space program the same way that the U.S.S.R. organized its agriculture.

Yes, we live on a finite Earth. But there's a whole solar system out there. In our own backyard, based on the sixty Earth-approachers or Earth-crossing asteroids already known, there may be as many as 300,000 asteroids within one AU. Obviously, many of these are too small or too far to be worth developing; however, almost any random asteroid has a higher concentration of the platinum-group and precious metals than the richest mineral deposits on Earth. Furthermore, even the carbonaceous asteroids are high in volatiles. They contain around twenty percent water, six percent carbon, several percent sulfur, and a tenth of a percent nitrogen, as well as about ten percent oxygen tied up in various ores.

It's all waiting for us out there. We've only to lift our heads out of the muck to find not only survival, but the place, the energy and the materials to keep Earth a pollution-free park—if that's what *we* desire.

When Dick Rhutan brought *Voyager* down after his flight around the world, he said "See what free men can do!"

Isn't it about time we tried that with space?

"WELL, YES," Amspaugh admitted, "it was a unique war in many ways, including its origin. However, there are so many analogies to other colonial revolutions—" His words trailed off as usual.

"I know. Earth's mercantile policies and so forth," said Lindgren. He fancies himself a student of interplanetary history. This has led to quite a few arguments since Amspaugh, who teaches in that field, joined the Club. Mostly they're good. I went to the bar and got myself another drink, listening as the mine owner's big voice went on:

"But what began it? When did the asterites first start realizing they weren't pseudopods of a dozen Terrestrial nations, but a single nation in their own right? There's the root of the revolution. And it can be pinned down, too."

" 'Ware metaphor!" cried someone at my elbow. I turned and saw Missy Blades. She'd come quietly into the lounge and started mixing a gin and bitters.

The view window framed her white head in Orion as she moved toward the little cluster of seated men. She took a fat cigar from her pocket, struck it on her shoe sole, and added her special contribution to the blue cloud in the room after she sat down.

"Excuse me," she said. "I couldn't help that. Please go on." Which I hope relieves you of any fear that she's an Unforgettable Character. Oh, yes, she's old as Satan now; her toil and guts and conniving make up half the biography of the Sword; she manned a gun turret at Ceres, and was mate of the *Tyrfing* on some of the earliest Saturn runs when men took their lives between their teeth because they needed both hands free; her sons and grandsons fill the Belt with their brawling ventures; she can drink any ordinary man to the deck; she's one of the three women ever admitted to the Club. But she's also one of the few genuine ladies I've known in my life.

"Uh, well." Lindgren grinned at her. "I was saying, Missy, the germ of the revolution was when the Stations armed themselves. You see, that meant more than police powers. It implied a degree of sovereignty. Over the years, the implication grew."

"Correct." Orloff nodded his bald head. "I remember how the Governing Commission squalled when the Station managers first demanded the right. They foresaw trouble. But if the Stations belonging to one country put in space weapons, what else could the others do?"

"They should have stuck together and all been firm about refusing to allow it," Amspaugh said. "From the standpoint of their own best interests, I mean."

"They tried to," Orloff replied. "I hate to think how many communications we sent home from our own office, and the others must have done the same. But Earth was a long way off. The Station bosses were close. Inverse square law of political pressure."

"I grant you, arming each new little settlement proved important," Amspaugh said. "But really, it expressed nothing more than the first inchoate stirrings of asteroid nationalism. And the origins of that are much more subtle and complex. For instance . . . er . . ."

"You've got to have a key event somewhere," Lindgren insisted. "I say that this was it."

A silence fell, as will happen in conversation. I came back from the bar and settled myself beside Missy. She looked for a while into her drink, and then out to the stars. The slow spin of our rock had now brought the Dippers into view. Her faded eyes sought the Pole Star—but it's Earth's, not our own anymore—and I wondered what memories they were sharing. She shook herself the least bit and said:

"I don't know about the sociological ins and outs. All I know is, a lot of things happened, and there wasn't any pattern to them at the time. We just slogged through as best we were able, which wasn't really very good. But I can identify one of those wriggling roots for you, Sigurd. I was there when the question of arming the Stations first came up. Or, rather, when the incident occurred that led directly to the question being raised."

Our whole attention went to her. She didn't dwell on the past as often as we would have liked.

A slow, private smile crossed her lips. She looked beyond us again. "As a matter of fact," she murmured, "I got my husband out of it." Then quickly, as if to keep from remembering too much:

"Do you care to hear the story? It was when the Sword was just getting started. They'd established themselves on SSC 45—oh, never mind the catalogue number. Sword Enterprises, because Mike Blades' name suggested it—what kind of name could you get out of Jimmy Chung, even if he was the senior partner? It'd sound too much like a collision with a meteorite—so naturally the asteroid also came to be called the Sword. They began on the borrowed shoestring that was usual in those days. Of course, in the Belt a shoestring has to be mighty long, and finances got stretched to the limit. The older men here will know how much had to be done by hand, in mortal danger, because machines were too expensive. But in spite of everything, they succeeded. The Station was functional and they were ready to start business when—"

It was no coincidence that the Jupiter craft were arriving steadily when the battleship came. Construction had been scheduled with this in mind, that the Sword should be approaching conjunction with the king planet, making direct shuttle service feasible, just as the chemical plant went into service. We need not consider how much struggle and heartbreak had gone into meeting that schedule. As for the battleship, she appeared because the fact that a Station in just this orbit was about to commence operations was news important enough to cross the Solar System and push through many strata of bureaucracy. The heads of the recently elected North American government became suddenly, fully aware of what had been going on.

Michael Blades was outside, overseeing the installation of a receptor, when his earplug buzzed. He thrust his chin against the tuning plate, switching from gang to interoffice band. "Mike?" said Avis Page's voice. "You're wanted up front."

"Now?" he objected. "Whatever for?"

"Courtesy visit from the NASS Altair. You've lost track of time, my boy."

"What the . . . the jumping blue blazes are you talking about? We've had our courtesy visit. Jimmy and I both went over to pay our respects, and we had Rear Admiral Hulse here to dinner. What more do they expect, for Harry's sake?"

"Don't you remember? Since there wasn't room to entertain his offices, you promised to take them on a personal guided tour later. I made the appointment the very next watch. Now's the hour."

"Oh, yes, it comes back to me. Yeah. Hulse brought a magnum of champagne with him, and after so long a time drinking recycled water, my capacity was shot to pieces. I got a warm glow of good fellowship on, and offered— Let Jimmy handle it. I'm busy."

"The party's too large, he says. You'll have to take half of them. Their gig will dock in thirty minutes."

"Well, depute somebody else."

"That'd be rude, Mike. Have you forgotten how sensitive they are about rank at home?" Avis hesitated. "If what I believe about the mood back there is true, we can use the goodwill of high-level Navy personnel. And any other influential people in sight."

Blades drew a deep breath. "You're too blinking sensible. Remind me to fire you after I've made my first ten million bucks."

"What'll you do for your next ten million, then?" snipped his secretary–file clerk–confidante–advisor–et cetera.

"Nothing. I'll just squander the first."

"Goody! Can I help?"

"Uh . . . I'll be right along." Blades switched off. His ears felt hot, as often of late when he tangled with Avis, and he unlimbered only a few choice oaths.

"Troubles?" asked Carlos Odonaju.

Blades stood a moment, looking around, before he answered. He was on the wide end of the Sword, which was shaped roughly like a truncated pyramid. Beyond him and his half dozen men stretched a vista of pitted rock, jutting crags, gulf-black shadows, under the glare of floodlamps. A few kilometers away, the farthest horizon ended, chopped off like a cliff. Beyond lay the stars, crowding that night which never ends. It grew very still while the gang waited for his word. He could listen to his own lungs and pulse, loud in the spacesuit; he could even notice its interior smell, blend of plastic and oxygen cycle chemicals, flesh and sweat. He was used to the sensation of hanging upside down on the surface, grip-soled boots holding him against that fractional gee by which the asteroid's rotation overcame its feeble gravity. But it came to him that this was an eerie bat-fashion way for an Oregon farm boy to stand.

Oregon was long behind him, though, not only the food factory where he grew up but the coasts where he had fished and the woods where he had tramped. No loss. There'd always been too many tourists. You couldn't escape from people on Earth. Cold and vacuum and raw rock and everything, the Belt was better. It annoyed him to be interrupted here.

Could Carlos take over as foreman? N-no, Blades decided, not yet. A gas receptor was an intricate piece of equipment. Carlos was a good man with his hands. Every one of the hundred-odd in the Station necessarily was. But he hadn't done this kind of work often enough.

"I have to quit," Blades said. "Secure the stuff and report to Buck Meyers over at the dock, the lot of you. His crew's putting in another recoil pier, as I suppose you know. They'll find jobs for you. I'll see you here again on your next watch."

He waved—being half the nominal ownership of this place didn't justify snobbery, when everyone must work together or die—and stepped off toward the nearest entry lock with that flowing spaceman's pace which always keeps one foot on the ground. Even so, he didn't unshackle his inward-reeling lifeline till he was inside the chamber.

On the way he topped a gaunt ridge and had a clear view of the balloons that were attached to the completed receptors. Those that were still full bulked enormous, like ghostly moons. The Jovian gases that strained their tough elastomer did not much blur the stars seen through them; but they swelled high enough to catch the light of the hidden sun and shimmer with it. The nearly discharged balloons hung thin, straining outward. Two full ones passed in slow orbit against the constellations. They were waiting to be hauled in and coupled fast, to release their loads into the Station's hungry chemical plant. But there were not yet enough facilities to handle them at once—and the *Pallas Castle* would soon be arriving with another—Blades found that he needed a few extra curses.

Having cycled through the air lock, he removed his suit and stowed it, also the heavy gloves which kept him from frostbite as he touched its space-cold exterior. Tastefully clad in Navy surplus long johns, he started down the corridors.

Now that the first stage of burrowing within the asteroid had been completed, most passages went through its body, rather than being plastic tubes snaking across the surface. Nothing had been done thus far about facing them. They were merely shafts, two meters square, lined with doorways, ventilator grilles, and fluoropanels. They had no thermocoils. Once the nickel-iron mass had been sufficiently warmed up, the waste heat of man and his industry kept it that way. The dark, chipped-out tunnels throbbed with machine noises. Here and there a girlie picture or a sentimental landscape from Earth was posted. Men moved busily along them, bearing tools, instruments, supplies. They were from numerous countries, those men, though mostly North Americans, but they had acquired a likeness, a rangy leathery look and a free-swinging stride, that went beyond their colorful coveralls.

"Hi, Mike . . . How's she spinning? . . . Hey, Mike, you heard the latest story about the Martian and the bishop? . . . Can you spare me a minute? We got troubles in the separator mani-folds . . . What's the hurry, Mike, your batteries overcharged?" Blades waved the hails aside. There was need for haste. You could move fast indoors, under the low weight which became lower as you approached the axis of rotation, with no fear of tumbling off. But it was several kilometers from the gas receptor end to the people end of the asteroid.

He rattled down a ladder and entered his cramped office out of breath. Avis Page looked up from her desk and wrinkled her freckled snub nose at him. "You ought to take a shower, but there isn't time," she said. "Here, use my antistinker." She threw him a spray cartridge with a deft motion. "I got your suit and beardex out of your cabin."

"Have I no privacy?" he grumbled, but grinned in her direction. She wasn't much to look at—not ugly, just small, brunette, and unspectacular—but she was a supernova of an assistant. Make somebody a good wife someday. He wondered why she hadn't taken advantage of the situation here to snaffle a husband. A dozen women, all but two of them married, and a hundred men, was a ratio even more lopsided than the norm in the Belt. Of course, with so much work to do, and with everybody conscious of the need to maintain cordial relations, sex didn't get much chance to rear its lovely head. Still—

She smiled back with the gentleness that he found disturbing when he noticed it. "Shoo," she said. "Your guests will be here any minute. You're to meet them in Jimmy's office."

Blades ducked into the tiny washroom. He wasn't any 3V star himself, he decided as he smeared cream over his face:

big, homely, red-haired. *But not something you'd be scared to meet in a dark alley, either,* he added smugly. In fact, there had been an alley in Aresopolis . . . Things were expected to be going so smoothly by the time they approached conjunction with Mars that he could run over to that sinful ginful city for a vacation. Long overdue . . . whooee! He wiped off his whiskers, shucked the zipskin, and climbed into the white pants and high-collared blue tunic that must serve as formal garb.

Emerging, he stopped again at Avis' desk. "Any message from the *Pallas*?" he asked.

"No," the girl said. "But she ought to be here in another two watches, right on sked. You worry too much, Mike."

"Somebody has to, and I haven't got Jimmy's Buddhist ride-with-the-punches attitude."

"You should cultivate it." She grew curious. The brown eyes lingered on him. "Worry's contagious. You make me fret about you."

"Nothing's going to give me an ulcer but the shortage of booze on this rock. Uh, if Bill Mbolo should call about those catalysts while I'm gone, tell him—" He ran off a string of instructions and headed for the door.

Chung's hangout was halfway around the asteroid, so that one chief or the other could be a little nearer the scene of any emergency. Not that they spent much time at their desks. Shorthanded and undermechanized, they were forever having to help out in the actual construction. Once in a while Blades found himself harking wistfully back to his days as an engineer with Solar Metals: good pay, interesting if hazardous work on flying mountains where men had never trod before, and no further responsibilities. But most asterites had the dream of becoming their own bosses.

When he arrived, the *Altair* officers were already there, a score of correct young men in white dress uniforms. Short, squat, and placid looking, Jimmy Chung stood making polite conversation. "Ah, there," he said, "Lieutenant Ziska and gentlemen, my partner, Michael Blades, Mike, may I present—"

Blades' attention stopped at Lieutenant Ziska. He heard vaguely that she was the head quartermaster officer. But mainly she was tall and blond and blue-eyed, with a bewitching dimple when she smiled, and filled her gown the way a Cellini Venus doubtless filled its casting mold.

"Very pleased to meet you, Mr. Blades," she said as if she meant it. Maybe she did! He gulped for air.

"And Commander Liebknecht," Chung said across several light-years. "Commander Liebknecht. *Commander Liebknecht*."

"Oh. Sure. 'Scuse." Blades dropped Lieutenant Ziska's hand in reluctant haste. "Hardjado, C'mander Liebfraumilch."

Somehow the introductions were gotten through. "I'm sorry we have to be so inhospitable," Chung said, "but you'll see how crowded we are. About all we can do is show you around, if you're interested."

"Of course you're interested," said Blades to Lieutenant Ziska. "I'll show you some gimmicks I thought up myself."

Chung scowled at him. "We'd best divide the party and proceed along alternate routes," he said. "We'll meet again in the mess for coffee. Lieutenant Ziska, would you like to—"

"Come with me? Certainly," Blades said.

Chung's glance became downright murderous. "I thought—" he began.

"Sure." Blades nodded vigorously. "You being the senior partner, you'll take the highest ranking of these gentlemen, and I'll be in Scotland before you. C'mon, let's get started. May I?" He offered the quartermistress his arm. She smiled and took it. He supposed that eight or ten of her fellows trailed them.

The first disturbing note was sounded on the verandah.

They had glanced at the cavelike dormitories where most of the personnel lived; at the recreation dome topside which made the life tolerable; at kitchen, sick bay, and the other service facilities; at the hydroponic tanks and yeast vats which supplied much of the Station's food; at the tiny cabins scooped out for the top engineers and the married couples. Before leaving this end of the asteroid, Blades took his group to the verandah. It was a clear dome jutting from the surface, softly lighted, furnished as a primitive officers' lounge, open to a view of half the sky.

"Oh-h," murmured Ellen Ziska. Unconsciously she moved closer to Blades.

Young Lieutenant Commander Gilbertson gave her a somewhat jaundiced look. "You've seen deep space often enough before," he said.

"Through a port or a helmet." Her eyes glimmered enormous in the dusk. "Never like this."

The stars crowded close in their wintry myriads. The galactic belt glistened, diamond against infinite darkness. Vision toppled endlessly outward, toward the far mysterious shimmer of the Andromeda Nebula; silence was not a mere absence of noise, but a majestic presence, the seething of suns.

"What about the observation terrace at Leyburg?" Gilbertson challenged.

"That was different," Ellen Ziska said. "Everything was safe and civilized. This is like being on the edge of creation."

Blades could see why Goddard House had so long resisted the inclusion of female officers on ships of the line, despite political pressure at home and the Russian example abroad. He was glad they'd finally given in. Now if only he could build himself up as a dashing, romantic type . . . But how long would the *Altair* stay? Her stopover seemed quite extended already, for a casual visit in the course of a routine patrol cruise. He'd have to work fast.

"Yes, we are pretty isolated," he said. "The Jupiter ships just unload their balloons, pick up the empties, and head right back for another cargo."

"I don't understand how you can found an industry here, when your raw materials only arrive at conjunction," Ellen said.

"Things will be different once we're in full operation," Blades assured her. "Then we'll be doing enough business to pay for a steady input, transshipped from whatever depot is nearest Jupiter at any given time."

"You've actually built this simply to process . . . gas?" Gilbertson interposed. Blades didn't know whether he was being sarcastic or asking a genuine question. It was astonishing how ignorant Earthsiders, even space-traveling Earthsiders, often were about such matters.

"Jovian gas is rich stuff," he explained. "Chiefly hydrogen and helium, of course; but the scoopships separate out most of that during a pickup. The rest is ammonia, water, methane, a dozen important organics, including some of the damn . . . doggonedest metallic complexes you ever heard of. We need them as the basis of a chemosynthetic industry, which we need for survival, which we need if we're to get the minerals that were the reason for colonizing the Belt in the first place." He waved his hand at the sky. "When we really get going, we'll attract settlement. This asteroid has companions, waiting for people to come and mine them. Homeships and orbital stations will be built. In ten years there'll be quite a little city clustered around the Sword."

"It's happened before," nodded tight-faced Commander Warburton of Gunnery Control.

"It's going to happen a lot oftener," Blades said enthusiastically. "The Belt's going to grow!" He aimed his words at Ellen. "This is the real frontier. The planets will never amount to much. It's actually harder to maintain human-type conditions on so big a mass, with a useless atmosphere around you, than on a lump in space like this. And the gravity wells are so deep. Even given nuclear power, the energy cost of really exploiting a planet is prohibitive. Besides which, the choice minerals are buried under kilometers of rock. On a metallic asteroid, you can find almost everything you want directly under your feet. No limit to what you can do."

"But your own energy expenditure—" Gilbertson objected.

"That's no problem." As if on cue, the worldlet's spin brought the sun into sight. Tiny but intolerably brilliant, it flooded the dome with harsh radiance. Blades lowered the blinds on that side. He pointed in the opposite direction, toward several sparks of equal brightness that had manifested themselves.

"Hundred-meter parabolic mirrors," he said. "Easy to make; you spray a thin metallic coat on a plastic backing. They're in orbit around us, each with a small geegee unit to control drift and keep it aimed directly at the sun. The focused radiation charges heavy-duty accumulators, which we then collect and use for our power source in all our mobile work."

"Do you mean you haven't any nuclear generator?" asked Warburton.

He seemed curiously intent about it. Blades wondered why, but nodded. "That's correct. We don't want one. Too dangerous for us. Nor is it necessary. Even at this distance from the sun, and allowing for assorted inefficiencies, a mirror supplies better than five hundred kilowatts, twenty-four hours a day, year after year, absolutely free."

"Hm-m-m. Yes." Warburton's lean head turned slowly about, to rake Blades with a look of calculation. "I understand that's the normal power system in Stations of this type. But we didn't know if it was used in your case, too."

Why should you care? Blades thought.

He shoved aside his faint unease and urged Ellen toward the dome railing. "Maybe we can spot your ship, Lieutenant, uh, Miss Ziska. Here's a telescope. Let me see, her orbit ought to run about so . . ."

. . .

He hunted until the *Altair* swam into the viewfield. At this distance the spheroid looked like a tiny crescent moon, dully painted;
but he could make out the sinister shapes of a rifle turret and a
couple of missile launchers. "Have a look," he invited. Her hair
tickled his nose, brushing past him. It had a delightful sunny odor.

"How small she seems," the girl said, with the same note of
wonder as before. "And how huge when you're aboard."

Big, all right, Blades knew, and loaded to the hatches with
nuclear hellfire. But not massive. A civilian spaceship carried
meteor plating, but since that was about as useful as wet cardboard
against modern weapons, warcraft sacrificed it for the sake of
mobility. The self-sealing hull was thin magnesium, the outer
shell periodically renewed as cosmic sand eroded it.

"I'm not surprised we orbited, instead of docking," Ellen
remarked. "We'd have butted against your radar and bellied into
your control tower."

"Well, actually, no," said Blades. "Even half finished, our
dock's big enough to accommodate you, as you'll see today.
Don't forget, we anticipate a lot of traffic in the future. I'm
puzzled why you didn't accept our invitation to use it."

"Doctrine!" Warburton clipped.

The sun came past the blind and touched the officers' faces
with incandescence. Did some look startled, one or two open their
mouths as if to protest and then snap them shut again at a warning
look? Blades' spine tingled. *I never heard of any such doctrine,*
he thought, *least of all when a North American ship drops in on
a North American Station.*

"Is . . . er . . . is there some international crisis brewing?" he
inquired.

"Why, no." Ellen straightened from the telescope. "I'd say
relations have seldom been as good as they are now. What makes
you ask?"

"Well, the reason your captain didn't—"

"Never mind," Warburton said. "We'd better continue the tour,
if you please."

Blades filed his misgivings for later reference. He might have
fretted immediately, but Ellen Ziska's presence forbade that. A
sort of Pauli exclusion principle. One can't have two spins simultaneously, can one? He gave her his arm again. "Let's go on
to Central Control," he proposed. "That's right behind the people
section."

"You know, I can't get over it," she told him softly. "This miracle you've wrought. I've never been more proud of being human."

"Is this your first long space trip?"

"Yes. I was stationed at Port Colorado before the new Administration reshuffled armed service assignments."

"They did? How come?"

"I don't know. Well, that is, during the election campaign the Social Justice Party did talk a lot about old-line officers who were too hidebound to carry out modern policies effectively. But it sounded rather silly to me."

Warburton compressed his lips. "I do not believe it is proper for service officers to discuss political issues publicly," he said like a machine gun.

Ellen flushed. "S-sorry, commander."

Blades felt a helpless anger on her account. He wasn't sure why. What was she to him? He'd probably never see her again. A hell of an attractive target, to be sure; and after so much celibacy he was highly vulnerable; but did she really matter?

He turned his back on Warburton and his eyes on her—a five thousand percent improvement—and diverted her from her embarrassment by asking, "Are you from Colorado, then, Miss Ziska?"

"Oh, no. Toronto."

"How'd you happen to join the Navy, if I may make so bold?"

"Gosh, that's hard to say. But I guess mostly I felt so crowded at home. So, pigeonholed. The world seemed to be nothing but neat little pigeonholes."

"Uh-huh. Same here. I was also a square pigeon in a round hole." She laughed. "Luckily," he added, "space is too big for compartments."

Her agreement lacked vigor. The Navy must have been a disappointment to her. But she couldn't very well say so in front of her shipmates.

Hm-m-m . . . if she could be gotten away from them—"How long will you be here?" he inquired. His pulse thuttered.

"We haven't been told," she said.

"Some work must be done on the missile launchers," Warburton said. "That's best carried out here, where extra facilities are available if we need them. Not that I expect we will." He paused. "I hope we won't interfere with your own operations."

"Far from it." Blades beamed at Ellen. "Or, more accurately, this kind of interference I don't mind in the least."

She blushed and her eyelids fluttered. Not that she was a fluffhead, he realized. But to avoid incidents, Navy regulations enforced an inhuman correctness between personnel of opposite sexes. After weeks in the black, meeting a man who could pay a compliment without risking court-martial must be like a shot of adrenaline. Better and better!

"Are you sure?" Warburton persisted. "For instance, won't we be in the way when the next ship comes from Jupiter?"

"She'll approach the opposite end of the asteroid," Blades said. "Won't stay long, either."

"How long?"

"One watch, so the crew can relax a bit among those of us who're off duty. It'd be a trifle longer if we didn't happen to have an empty bag at the moment. But never very long. Even running under thrust the whole distance, Jupe's a good ways off. They've no time to waste."

"When is the next ship due?"

"The *Pallas Castle* is expected in the second watch from now."

"Second watch. I see." Warburton stalked on with a brooding expression on his Puritan face.

Blades might have speculated about that, but someone asked him why the Station depended on spin for weight. Why not put in an internal field generator, like a ship? Blades explained patiently that an Emett large enough to produce uniform pull through a volume as big as the Sword was rather expensive. "Eventually, when we're a few megabucks ahead of the game—"

"Do you really expect to become rich?" Ellen asked. Her tone was awed. No Earthsider had that chance any more, except for the great corporations. "*Individually* rich?"

"We can't fail to. I tell you, this is a frontier like nothing since the Conquistadores. We could very easily have been wiped out in the first couple of years—financially or physically—by any of a thousand accidents. But now we're too far along for that. We've got it made, Jimmy and I."

"What will you do with your wealth?"

"Live like an old-time sultan." Blades grinned. Then, because it was true as well as because he wanted to shine in her eyes: "Mostly, though, we'll go on to new things. There's so much that needs to be done. Not simply more asteroid mines. We need farms; timber; parks; passenger and cargo liners; every sort of machine. I'd like to try getting at some of that water frozen in the Saturnian System. Altogether, I see no end to the jobs. It's no good our depending on Earth for anything. Too expensive, too chancy. The Belt has to be made completely self-sufficient."

"With a nice rakeoff for Sword Enterprises," Gilbertson scoffed.

"Why, sure. Aren't we entitled to some return?"

"Yes. But not so out of proportion as the Belt companies seem to expect. They're only using natural resources that rightly belong to the people, and the accumulated skills and wealth of an entire society."

"Huh! The People didn't do anything with the Sword. Jimmy and I and our boys did. No Society was around here grubbing nickel-iron and riding out gravel storms; *we* were."

"Let's leave politics alone," Warburton snapped. But it was mostly Ellen's look of distress which shut Blades up.

To everybody's relief, they reached Central Control about then. It was a complex of domes and rooms, crammed with more equipment than Blades could put a name to. Computers were in Chung's line, not his. He wasn't able to answer all of Warburton's disconcertingly sharp questions.

But in a general way he could. Whirling through vacuum with a load of frail humans and intricate artifacts, the Sword must be at once machine, ecology, and unified organism. Everything had to mesh. A failure in the thermodynamic balance, a miscalculation in supply inventory, a few mirrors perturbed out of proper orbit, might spell Ragnarok. The chemical plant's purifications and syntheses were already a network too large for the human mind to grasp as a whole, and it was still growing. Even where men could have taken charge, automation was cheaper, more reliable, less risky of lives. The computer system housed in Central Control was not only the brain, but the nerves and heart of the Sword.

"Entirely cryotronic, eh?" Warburton commented. "That seems to be the usual practice at the Stations. Why?"

"The least expensive type for us," Blades answered. "There's no problem in maintaining liquid helium here."

Warburton's gaze was peculiarly intense. "Cryotronic systems are vulnerable to magnetic and radiation disturbances."

"Uh-huh. That's one reason we don't have a nuclear power plant. This far from the sun, we don't get enough emission to worry about. The asteroid's mass screens out what little may arrive. I know the TIMM system is used on ships; but if nothing else, the initial cost is more than we want to pay."

"What's TIMM?" inquired the *Altair*'s chaplain.

"Thermally Integrated Micro-Miniaturized," Ellen said crisply. "Essentially, ultraminiaturized ceramic-to-metal-seal vacuum tubes running off thermionic generators. They're immune to gamma ray and magnetic pulses, easily shielded against particle radiation, and economical of power." She grinned. "Don't tell me there's nothing about them in Leviticus, Padre!"

"Very fine for a ship's autopilot," Blades agreed. "But as I said, we needn't worry about rad or mag units here, we don't mind sprawling a bit, and as for thermal efficiency, we *want* to waste some heat. It goes to maintain internal temperature."

"In other words, efficiency depends on what you need to effish," Ellen bantered. She grew grave once more and studied him for a while before she mused, "The same person who swung a pick, a couple of years ago, now deals with something as marvelous as this . . ." He forgot about worrying.

But he remembered later, when the gig had left and Chung called him to his office. Avis came too, by request. As she entered, she asked why.

"You were visiting your folks Earthside last year," Chung said. "Nobody else in the Station has been back as recently as that."

"What can I tell you?"

"I'm not sure. Background, perhaps. The feel of the place. We don't really know, out in the Belt, what's going on there. The beamcast news is hardly a trickle. Besides, you have more common sense in your left little toe than that big mick yonder has in his entire copperplated head."

They seated themselves in the cobwebby low-gee chairs around Chung's desk. Blades took out his pipe and filled the bowl with his tobacco ration for today. Wouldn't it be great, he thought dreamily, if this old briar turned out to be an Aladdin's lamp, and the smoke condensed into a blonde she-Canadian—?

"Wake up, will you?" Chung barked.

"Huh?" Blades started. "Oh. Sure. What's the matter? You look like a fish on Friday."

"Maybe with reason. Did you notice anything unusual with that party you were escorting?"

"Yes, indeed."

"What?"

"About one hundred seventy-five centimeters tall, yellow hair, blue eyes, and some of the smoothest fourth-order curves I ever—"

"Mike, stop that!" Avis sounded appalled. "This is serious."

"I agree. She'll be leaving in a few more watches."

The girl bit her lip. "You're too old for that mooncalf rot and you know it."

"Agreed again. I feel more like a bull." Blades made pawing motions on the desktop.

"There's a lady present," Chung said.

Blades saw that Avis had gone quite pale. "I'm sorry," he blurted. "I never thought . . . I mean, you've always seemed like—"

"One of the boys," she finished for him in a brittle tone. "Sure. Forget it. What's the problem, Jimmy?"

Chung folded his hands and stared at them. "I can't quite define that," he answered, word by careful word. "Perhaps I've simply gone spacedizzy. But when we called on Admiral Hulse, and later when he called on us, didn't you get the impression of, well, wariness? Didn't he seem to be watching and probing, every minute we were together?"

"I wouldn't call him a cheerful sort," Blades nodded. "Stiff as molasses on Pluto. But I suppose . . . supposed he's just naturally that way."

Chung shook his head. "It wasn't a normal standoffishness. You've heard me reminisce about the time I was on Vesta with the North American technical representative, when the Convention was negotiated."

"Yes, I've heard that story a few times," said Avis dryly.

"Remember, that was right after the Europa Incident. We'd come close to a space war—undeclared, but it would have been nasty. We were still close. Every delegate went to that conference cocked and primed.

"Hulse had the same manner."

A silence fell. Blades said at length, "Well, come to think of it, he did ask some rather odd questions. He seemed to twist the conversation now and then, so he could find out things like our exact layout, emergency doctrine, and so forth. It didn't strike me as significant, though."

"Nor me," Chung admitted. "Taken in isolation, it meant nothing. But these visitors today— Sure, most of them obviously didn't suspect anything untoward. But that Liebknecht, now. Why was he so interested in Central Control? Nothing new or secret there. Yet he kept asking for details like the shielding factor of the walls."

"So did Commander Warburton," Blades remembered. "Also, he wanted to know exactly when the *Pallas* is due, how long she'll stay . . . hm-m-m, yes, whether we have any radio linkage with the outside, like to Ceres or even the nearest Commission base—"

"Did you tell him that we don't?" Avis asked sharply.

"Yes. Shouldn't I have?"

"It scarcely makes any difference," Chung said in a resigned voice. "As thoroughly as they went over the ground, they'd have seen what we do and do not have installed so far."

He leaned forward. "Why are they hanging around?" he asked. "I was handed some story about overhauling the missile system."

"Me, too," Blades said.

"But you don't consider a job complete till it's been tested. And you don't fire a test shot, even a dummy, this close to a Station. Besides, what could have gone wrong? I can't see a ship departing Earth orbit for a long cruise without everything being in order. And they didn't mention any meteorites, any kind of trouble, en route. Furthermore, why do the work here? The Navy yard's at Ceres. We can't spare them any decent amount of materials or tools or help."

Blades frowned. His own half-formulated doubts shouldered to the fore, which was doubly unpleasant after he'd been considering Ellen Ziska. "They tell me the international situation at home is O.K.," he offered.

Avis nodded. "What newsfaxes we get in the mail indicate as much," she said. "So why this hanky-panky?" After a moment, in a changed voice: "Jimmy, you begin to scare me a little."

"I scare myself," Chung said.

"Every morning when you debeard," Blades said; but his heart wasn't in it. He shook himself and protested: "Damnation, they're our own countrymen. We're engaged in a lawful business. Why should they do anything to us?"

"Maybe Avis can throw some light on that," Chung suggested.

The girl twisted her fingers together. "Not me," she said. "I'm no politician."

"But you were home not so long ago. You talked with people, read the news, watched the 3V. Can't you at least give an impression?"

"N-no— Well, of course the preliminary guns of the election campaign were already being fired. The Social Justice Party was talking a lot about . . . oh, it seemed so ridiculous that I didn't pay much attention."

"They talked about how the government had been pouring billions and billions of dollars into space, while overpopulation produced crying needs in America's back yard," Chung said. "We know that much, even in the Belt. We know the appropriations are due to be cut, now the Essjays are in. So what?"

"We don't need a subsidy any longer," Blades remarked. "It'd help a lot, but we can get along without if we have to, and personally, I prefer that. Less government money means less government control."

"Sure," Avis said. "There was more than that involved, however. The Essjays were complaining about the small return on the investment. Not enough minerals coming back to Earth."

"Well, for Jupiter's sake," Blades exclaimed, "what do they expect? We have to build up our capabilities first."

"They even said, some of them, that enough reward never would be gotten. That under existing financial policies, the Belt would go in for its own expansion, use nearly everything it produced for itself and export only a trickle to America. I had to explain to several of my parents' friends that I wasn't really a socially irresponsible capitalist."

"Is that all the information you have?" Chung asked when she fell silent.

"I . . . I suppose so. Everything was so vague. No dramatic events. More of an atmosphere than a concrete thing."

"Still, you confirm my own impression," Chung said. Blades jerked his undisciplined imagination back from the idea of a Thing, with bug eyes and tentacles, cast in reinforced concrete, and listened as his partner summed up:

"The popular feeling at home has turned against private enterprise. You can hardly call a corporate monster like Systemic Developments a private enterprise! The new President and Congress share that mood. We can expect to see it manifested in changed laws and regulations. But what has this got to do with a battleship parked a couple of hundred kilometers from us?"

"If the government doesn't want the asterites to develop much further—" Blades bit hard on his pipestem. "They must know we have a caviar mine here. We'll be the only city in this entire sector."

"But we're still a baby," Avis said. "We won't be important for years to come. Who'd have it in for a baby?"

"Besides, we're Americans, too," Chung said. "If that were a foreign ship, the story might be different—Wait a minute! Could they be thinking of establishing a new base here?"

"The Convention wouldn't allow," said Blades.

"Treaties can always be renegotiated, or even denounced. But first you have to investigate quietly, find out if it's worth your while."

"Hoo hah, what lovely money that'd mean!"

"And lovely bureaucrats crawling out of every file cabinet," Chung said grimly. "No, thank you. We'll fight any such attempt to the last lawyer. We've got a good basis, too, in our charter. If the suit is tried on Ceres, as I believe it has to be, we'll get a sympathetic court as well."

"Unless they ring in an Earthside judge," Avis warned.

"Yeah, that's possible. Also, they could spring proceedings on us without notice. We've got to find out in advance, so we can prepare. Any chance of pumping some of those officers?"

" 'Fraid not," Avis said. "The few who'd be in the know are safely back on shipboard."

"We could invite 'em here individually," said Blades. "As a matter of fact, I already have a date with Lieutenant Ziska."

"What?" Avis' mouth fell open.

"Yep," Blades said complacently. "End of the next watch, so she can observe the *Pallas* arriving. I'm to fetch her on a scooter." He blew a fat smoke ring. "Look, Jimmy, can you keep everybody off the porch for a while then? Starlight, privacy, soft music on the piccolo—who knows what I might find out?"

"You won't get anything from *her*," Avis spat. "No secrets or, or anything."

"Still, I look forward to making the attempt. C'mon, pal, pass the word. I'll do as much for you sometime."

"Times like that never seem to come for me," Chung groaned.

"Oh, let him play around with his suicide blonde," Avis said furiously. "We others have work to do. I . . . I'll tell you what, Jimmy. Let's not eat in the mess tonight. I'll draw our rations and fix us something special in your cabin."

A scooter was not exactly the ideal steed for a knight to convey his lady. It amounted to little more than three saddles and a locker, set atop an accumulator-powered gyrogravitic engine, sufficient to

lift you off an asteroid and run at low acceleration. There were no
navigating instruments. You locked the autopilot's radar-gravitic
sensors onto your target object and it took you there, avoiding
any bits of debris which might pass near; but you must watch
the distance indicator and press the deceleration switch in time.
If the 'pilot was turned off, free maneuver became possible, but
that was a dangerous thing to try before you were almost on top
of your destination. Stereoscopic vision fails beyond six or seven
meters, and the human organism isn't equipped to gauge cosmic
momenta.

Nevertheless, Ellen was enchanted. "This is like a dream,"
her voice murmured in Blades' earplug. "The whole universe
on every side of us. I could almost reach out and pluck those
stars."

"You must have trained in powered spacesuits at the Academy," he said for lack of a more poetic rejoiner.

"Yes, but that's not the same. We had to stay near Luna's night
side, to be safe from solar particles, and it bit a great chunk out of
the sky. And then everything was so—regulated, disciplined—we
did what we were ordered to do, and that was that. Here I feel free.
You can't imagine how free." Hastily: "Do you use this machine
often?"

"Well, yes, we have about twenty scooters at the Station.
They're the most convenient way of flitting with a load: out
to the mirrors to change accumulators, for instance, or across
to one of the companion rocks where we're digging some ores
that the Sword doesn't have. That kind of work." Blades would
frankly rather have had her behind him on a motorskimmer,
hanging on as they careened through a springtime countryside.
He was glad when they reached the main forward air lock and
debarked.

He was still gladder when the suits were off. Lieutenant Ziska
in dress uniform was stunning, but Ellen in civvies, a fluffy
low-cut blouse and close-fitting slacks, was a hydrogen blast. He
wanted to roll over and pant, but settled for saying, "Welcome
back" and holding her hand rather longer than necessary.

With a shy smile, she gave him a package. "I drew this before
leaving," she said. "I thought, well, your life is so austere—"

"A demi of Sandeman," he said reverently. "I won't tell you
you shouldn't have, but I will tell you you're a sweet girl."

"No, really." She flushed. "After we've put you to so much
trouble."

"Let's go crack this," he said. "The *Pallas* has called in, but she won't be visible for a while yet."

They made their way to the verandah, picking up a couple of glasses enroute. Bless his envious heart, Jimmy had warned the other boys off as requested. *I hope Avis cooks him a Cordon Bleu dinner,* Blades thought. *Nice kid, Avis, if she'd quit trying to . . . what? . . . mother me?* He forgot about her, with Ellen to seat by the rail.

The Milky Way turned her hair frosty and glowed in her eyes. Blades poured the port with much ceremony and raised his glass. "Here's to your frequent return," he said.

Her pleasure dwindled a bit. "I don't know if I should drink to that. We aren't likely to be back, ever."

"Drink anyway. Gling, glang, gloria!" The rims tinkled together. "After all," said Blades, "this isn't the whole universe. We'll both be getting around. See you on Luna?"

"Maybe."

He wondered if he was pushing matters too hard. She didn't look at ease. "Oh, well," he said, "if nothing else, this has been a grand break in the monotony for us. I don't wish the Navy ill, but if trouble had to develop, I'm thankful it developed here."

"Yes—"

"How's the repair work progressing? Slowly, I hope."

"I don't know."

"You should have some idea, being in QM."

"No supplies have been drawn."

Blades stiffened.

"What's the matter?" Ellen sounded alarmed.

"Huh?" *A fine conspirator I make, if she can see my emotions on me in neon capitals!* "Nothing. Nothing. It just seemed a little strange, you know. Not taking any replacement units."

"I understand the work is only a matter of making certain adjustments."

"Then they should've finished a lot quicker, shouldn't they?"

"Please," she said unhappily. "Let's not talk about it. I mean, there are such things as security regulations."

Blades gave up on that tack. But Chung's idea might be worth probing a little. "Sure," he said. "I'm sorry, I didn't mean to pry." He took another sip as he hunted for suitable words. A beautiful girl, a golden wine . . . and vice versa . . . why couldn't he simply relax and enjoy himself? Did he have to go fretting about what was probably a perfectly harmless conundrum? . . . Yes. However, recreation might still combine with business.

"Permit me to daydream," he said, leaning close to her. "The Navy's going to establish a new base here, and the *Altair* will be assigned to it."

"Daydream indeed!" she laughed, relieved to get back to a mere flirtation. "Ever hear about the Convention of Vesta?"

"Treaties can be renegotiated," Blades plagiarized.

"What do we need an extra base for? Especially since the government plans to spend such large sums on social welfare. They certainly don't want to start an arms race besides."

Blades nodded. *Jimmy's notion did seem pretty thin,* he thought with a slight chill, *and now I guess it's completely whiffed.* Mostly to keep the conversation going, he shrugged and said, "My partner—and me, too, aside from the privilege of your company— wouldn't have wanted it anyhow. Not that we're unpatriotic, but there are plenty of other potential bases, and we'd rather keep government agencies out of here."

"Can you, these days?"

"Pretty much. We're under a new type of charter, as a private partnership. The first such charter in the Belt, as far as I know, though there'll be more in the future. The Bank of Ceres financed us. We haven't taken a nickel of federal money."

"Is that possible?"

"Just barely. I'm no economist, but I can see how it works. Money represents goods and labor. Hitherto those have been in mighty short supply out here. Government subsidies made up the difference, enabling us to buy from Earth. But now the asterites have built up enough population and industry that they have some capital surplus of their own, to invest in projects like this."

"Even so, frankly, I'm surprised that two men by themselves could get such a loan. It must be huge. Wouldn't the bank rather have lent the money to some corporation?"

"To tell the truth, we have friends who pulled wires for us. Also, it was done partly on ideological grounds. A lot of asterites would like to see more strictly home-grown enterprises, not committed to anyone on Earth. That's the only way we can grow. Otherwise our profits—our net production, that is—will continue to be siphoned off for the mother country's benefit."

"Well," Ellen said with some indignation, "that was the whole reason for planting asteroid colonies. You can't expect us to set you up in business, at enormous cost to ourselves—things we might have done at home—and get nothing but 'Ta' in return."

"Never fear, we'll repay you with interest," Blades said. "But whatever we make from our own work, over and above that, ought to stay here with us."

She grew angrier. "Your kind of attitude is what provoked the voters to elect Social Justice candidates."

"Nice name, that," mused Blades. "Who can be against social justice? But you know, I think I'll go into politics myself. I'll organize the North American Motherhood Party."

"You wouldn't be so flippant if you'd go see how people have to live back there."

"As bad as here? *Whew!*"

"Nonsense. You know that isn't true. But bad enough. And you aren't going to stick in these conditions. Only a few hours ago, you were bragging about the millions you intend to make."

"Millions *and* millions, if my strength holds out," leered Blades, thinking of the alley in Aresopolis. But he decided that that was then and Ellen was now, and what had started as a promising little party was turning into a dismal argument about politics.

"Let's not fight," he said. "We've got different orientations, and we'd only make each other mad. Let's discuss our next bottle instead . . . at the Coq d'Or in Paris, shall we say? Or Morraine's in New York."

She calmed down, but her look remained troubled. "You're right, we are different," she said low. "Isolated, living and working under conditions we can hardly imagine on Earth—and you can't really imagine our problems—yes, you're becoming another people. I hope it will never go so far that— No. I don't want to think about it." She drained her glass and held it out for a refill, smiling. "Very well, sir, when do you next plan to be in Paris?"

An exceedingly enjoyable while later, the time came to go watch the *Pallas Castle* maneuver in. In fact, it had somehow gotten past that time, and they were late; but they didn't hurry their walk aft. Blades took Ellen's hand, and she raised no objection. Schoolboyish, no doubt—however, he had reached the reluctant conclusion that for all his dishonorable intentions, this affair wasn't likely to go beyond the schoolboy stage. Not that he wouldn't keep trying.

As they glided through the refining and synthesizing section, which filled the broad half of the asteroid, the noise of pumps and regulators rose until it throbbed in their bones. Ellen gestured at one of the pipes which crossed the corridor overhead. "Do you really handle that big a volume at a time?" she asked above the racket.

"No," he said. "Didn't I explain before? The pipe's thick because it's so heavily armored."

"I'm glad you don't use that dreadful word 'cladded.' But why the armor? High pressure?"

"Partly. Also, there's an inertrans lining. Jupiter gas is hellishly reactive at room temperature. The metallic complexes especially; but think what a witch's brew the stuff is in every respect. Once it's been refined, of course, we have less trouble. That particular pipe is carrying it raw."

They left the noise behind and passed on to the approach control dome at the receptor end. The two men on duty glanced up and immediately went back to their instruments. Radio voices were staccato in the air. Blades led Ellen to an observation port.

She drew a sharp breath. Outside, the broken ground fell away to space and the stars. The ovoid that was the ship hung against them, lit by the hidden sun, a giant even at her distance but dwarfed by the balloon she towed. As that bubble tried ponderously to rotate, rainbow gleams ran across it, hiding and then revealing the constellations. Here, on the asteroid's axis, there was no weight, and one moved with underwater smoothness, as if disembodied. "Oh, a fairy tale," Ellen sighed.

Four sparks flashed out of the boat blisters along the ship's hull. "Scoopships," Blades told her. "They haul the cargo in, being so much more maneuverable. Actually, though, the mother vessel is going to park her load in orbit, while those boys bring in another one . . . See, there it comes into sight. We still haven't got the capacity to keep up with our deliveries."

"How many are there? Scoopships, that is."

"Twenty, but you don't need more than four for this job. They've got terrific power. Have to, if they're to dive from orbit down into the Jovian atmosphere, ram themselves full of gas, and come back. There they go."

The *Pallas Castle* was wrestling the great sphere she had hauled from Jupiter into a stable path computed by Central Control. Meanwhile the scoopships, small only by comparison with her, locked onto the other balloon as it drifted close. Energy poured into their drive fields. Spiraling downward, transparent globe and four laboring spacecraft vanished behind the horizon. The *Pallas* completed her own task, disengaged her towbars, and dropped from view, headed for the dock.

The second balloon rose again, like a huge glass moon on the opposite side of the Sword. Still it grew in Ellen's eyes, kilometer by kilometer of approach. So much mass wasn't easily handled, but the braking curve looked disdainfully smooth. Presently she could make out the scoopships in detail, elongated teardrops with the intake gates yawning in the blunt forward end, cockpit canopies raised very slightly above.

Instructions rattled from the men in the dome. The balloon veered clumsily toward the one free receptor. A derricklike structure released one end of a cable, which streamed skyward. Things that Ellen couldn't quite follow in this tricky light were done by the four tugs, mechanisms of their own extended to make their tow fast to the cable.

They did not cast loose at once, but continued to drag a little, easing the impact of centrifugal force. Nonetheless a slight shudder went through the dome as slack was taken up. Then the job was over. The scoopships let go and flitted off to join their mother vessel. The balloon was winched inward. Spacesuited men moved close, preparing to couple valves together.

"And eventually," Blades said into the abrupt quietness, "that cargo will become food, fabric, vitryl, plastiboard, reagents, fuels, a hundred different things. That's what we're here for."

"I've never seen anything so wonderful," Ellen said raptly. He laid an arm around her waist.

The intercom chose that precise moment to blare: "Attention! Emergency! All hands to emergency stations! Blades, get to Chung's office on the double! All hands to emergency station! Blades, get to Chung's office on the double! All hands to emergency stations!"

Blades was running before the siren had begun to howl.

Rear Admiral Barclay Hulse had come in person. He stood as if on parade, towering over Chung. The asterite was red with fury. Avis Page crouched in a corner, her eyes terrified.

Blades barreled through the doorway and stopped hardly short of a collision. "What's the matter?" he puffed.

"Plenty!" Chung snarled. "These incredible thumble-fumbed oafs—" His voice broke. *When he gets mad, it means something!*

Hulse nailed Blades with a glance. "Good day, sir," he clipped. "I have had to report a regrettable accident which will require you to evacuate the Station. Temporarily, I hope."

"Huh?"

"As I told Mr. Chung and Miss Page, a nuclear missile has escaped us. If it explodes, the radiation will be lethal, even in the heart of the asteroid."

"What . . . what—" Blades could only gobble at him.

"Fortunately, the *Pallas Castle* is here. She can take your whole complement aboard and move to a safe distance while we search for the object."

"How the *devil*?"

Hulse allowed himself a look of exasperation. "Evidently I'll have to repeat myself to you. Very well. You know we have had to make some adjustments on our launchers. What you did not know was the reason. Under the circumstances, I think it's permissible to tell you that several of them have a new and secret, experimental control system. One of our missions on this cruise was to carry out field tests. Well, it turned out that the system is still full of, ah, bugs. Gunnery Command has had endless trouble with it, has had to keep tinkering the whole way from Earth.

"Half an hour ago, while Commander Warburton was completing a reassembly—lower ranks aren't allowed in the test turrets—something happened. I can't tell you my guess as to what, but if you want to imagine that a relay got stuck, that will do for practical purposes. A missile was released under power. Not a dummy—the real thing. And release automatically arms the warhead."

The news was like a hammerblow. Blades spoke an obscenity. Sweat sprang forth under his arms and trickled down his ribs.

"No such thing was expected," Hulse went on. "It's an utter disaster, and the designers of the system aren't likely to get any more contracts. But as matters were, no radar fix was gotten on it, and it was soon too far away for gyrogravitic pulse detection. The thrust vector is unknown. It could be almost anywhere now.

"Well, naval missiles are programmed to reverse acceleration if they haven't made a target within a given time. This one should be back in less than six hours. If it first detects our ship, everything is all right. It has optical recognition circuits that identify any North American warcraft by type, disarm the warhead, and steer it home. But, if it first comes within fifty kilometers of some other mass— like this asteroid or one of the companion rocks—it will detonate. We'll make every effort to intercept, but space is big. You'll have to take your people to a safe distance. They can come back even after a blast, of course. There's no concussion in vacuum, and the fireball won't reach here. It's principally an anti-personnel weapon. But you must not be within the lethal radius of radiation."

"The hell we can come back!" Avis cried.

"I beg your pardon?" Hulse said.

"You imbecile! Don't you know Central Control here is cryotronic?"

Hulse did not flicker an eyelid. "So it is," he said expressionlessly. "I had forgotten."

Blades mastered his own shock enough to grate: "Well, we sure haven't. If that thing goes off, the gamma burst will kick up so many minority carriers in the transistors that the p-type crystals will act n-type, and the n-type act p-type, for a whole couple of microseconds. Every one of 'em will flip simultaneously! The computers' memory and program data systems will be scrambled beyond hope of reorganization."

"Magnetic pulse, too," Chung said. "The fireball plasma will be full of inhomogeneities moving at several percent of light speed. Their electromagnetic output, hitting our magnetic core units, will turn them from super to ordinary conduction. Same effect, total computer amnesia. We haven't got enough shielding against it. Your TIMM systems can take that kind of a beating. Ours can't!"

"Very regrettable," Hulse said. "You'd have to reprogram everything—"

"Reprogram what?" Avis retorted. Tears started forth in her eyes. "We've told you what sort of stuff our chemical plant is handling. We can't shut it down on that short notice. It'll run wild. There'll be sodium explosions, hydrogen and organic combustion, n-n-nothing left here but wreckage!"

Hulse didn't unbend a centimeter. "I offer my most sincere apologies. If actual harm does occur, I'm sure the government will indemnify you. And, of course, my command will furnish what supplies may be needed for the *Pallas Castle* to transport you to the nearest Commission base. At the moment, though, you can do nothing but evacuate and hope we will be able to intercept the missile."

Blades knotted his fists. A sudden comprehension rushed up in him and he bellowed, "There isn't going to be an interception! This wasn't an accident!"

Hulse backed a step and drew himself even straighter. "Don't get overwrought," he advised.

"You louse-bitten, egg-sucking, bloated faggot-porter! How stupid do you think we are? As stupid as your Essjay bosses? By heaven, we're staying! Then see if you have the nerve to murder a hundred people!"

"Mike . . . Mike—" Avis caught his arm.

Hulse turned to Chung. "I'll overlook that unseemly outburst," he said. "But in light of my responsibilities and under the provisions of the Constitution, I am hereby putting this asteroid under martial law. You will have all personnel aboard the *Pallas Castle* and at a minimum distance of a thousand kilometers within four hours of this moment, or be subject to arrest and trial. Now I have to get back and commence operations. The *Altair* will maintain radio contact with you. Good day." He bowed curtly, spun on his heel, and clacked from the room.

Blades started to charge after him. Chung caught his free arm. Together he and Avis dragged him to a stop. He stood cursing the air ultraviolet until Ellen entered.

"I couldn't keep up with you," she panted. "What's happened, Mike?"

The strength drained from Blades. He slumped into a chair and covered his face.

Chung explained in a few harsh words. "Oh-h-h," Ellen gasped. She went to Blades and laid her hands on his shoulders. "My poor Mike!"

After a moment she looked at the others. "I should report back, of course," she said, "but I won't be able to before the ship accelerates. So I'll have to stay with you till afterward. Miss Page, we left about half a bottle of wine on the verandah. I think it would be a good idea if you went and got it."

Avis bridled. "And why not you?"

"This is no time for personalities," Chung said. "Go on, Avis. You can be thinking what records and other paper we should take, while you're on your way. I've got to organize the evacuation. As for Miss Ziska, well, Mike needs somebody to pull him out of his dive."

"Her?" Avis wailed, and fled.

Chung sat down and flipped his intercom to Phone Central. "Get me Captain Janichevski aboard the *Pallas*," he ordered. "Hello, Adam? About that general alarm—"

Blades raised a haggard countenance toward Ellen's. "You better clear out, along with the women and any men who don't want to stay," he said. "But I think most of them will take the chance. They're on a profit-sharing scheme, they stand to lose too much if the place is ruined."

"What do you mean?"

"It's a gamble, but I don't believe Hulse's sealed orders extend to murder. If enough of us stay put, he'll have to catch that thing. He jolly well knows its exact trajectory."

"You forget we're under martial law," Chung said, aside to him. "If we don't go freely, he'll land some PP's and march us off at gunpoint. There isn't any choice. We've had the course."

"I don't understand," Ellen said shakily.

Chung went back to his intercom. Blades fumbled out his pipe and rolled it empty between his hands. "That missile was shot off on purpose," he said.

"What? No, you must be sick, that's impossible!"

"I realize you didn't know about it. Only three or four officers have been told. The job had to be done very, very secretly, or there'd be a scandal, maybe an impeachment. But it's still sabotage."

She shrank from him. "You're not making sense."

"Their own story doesn't make sense. It's ridiculous. A new missile system wouldn't be sent on a field trial clear to the Belt before it'd had enough tests closer to home to get the worst bugs out. A warhead missile wouldn't be stashed anywhere near something so unreliable, let alone be put under its control. The testing ship wouldn't hang around a civilian Station while her gunnery chief tinkered. And Hulse, Warburton, Liebknecht, they were asking in *such* detail about how radiation-proof we are."

"I can't believe it. Nobody will."

"Not back home. Communication with Earth is so sparse and garbled. The public will only know there was an accident; who'll give a hoot about the details? We couldn't even prove anything in an asteroid court. The Navy would say, 'Classified information!' and that'd stop the proceedings cold. Sure, there'll be a board of inquiry—composed of naval officers. Probably honorable men, too. But what are they going to believe, the sworn word of their Goddard House colleague, or the rantings of an asterite bum?"

"Mike, I know this is terrible for you, but you've let it go to your head." Ellen laid a hand over his. "Suppose the worst happens. You'll be compensated for your loss."

"Yeah. To the extent of our personal investment. The Bank of Ceres still has nearly all the money that was put in. We didn't figure to have them paid off for another ten years. They, or their insurance carrier, will get the indemnity. And after our fiasco, they won't make us a new loan. They were just barely talked into it, the first time around. I daresay Systemic Developments will make them a nice juicy offer to take this job over."

Ellen colored. She stamped her foot. "You're talking like a paranoiac. Do you really believe the government of North America would send a battleship clear out here to do you dirt?"

"Not the whole government. A few men in the right positions is all that's necessary. I don't know if Hulse was bribed or talked into this. But probably he agreed as a duty. He's the prim type."

"A duty—to destroy a North American business?"

Chung finished at the intercom in time to answer: "Not permanent physical destruction, Miss Ziska. As Mike suggested, some corporation will doubtless inherit the Sword and repair the damage. But a private, purely asterite business . . . yes, I'm afraid Mike's right. We are the target."

"In mercy's name, why?"

"From the highest motives, of course," Chung sneered bitterly. "You know what the Social Justice Party thinks of private capitalism. What's more important, though, is that the Sword is the first Belt undertaking not tied to Mother Earth's apron strings. We have no commitments to anybody back there. We can sell our output wherever we like. It's notorious that the asterites are itching to build up their own self-sufficient industries. Quite apart from sentiment, we can make bigger profits in the Belt than back home, especially when you figure the cost of sending stuff in and out of Earth's gravitational well. So certainly we'd be doing most of our business out here.

"Our charter can't simply be revoked. First a good many laws would have to be revised, and that's politically impossible. There is still a lot of individualist sentiment in North America, as witness the fact that businesses do get launched and that the Essjays did have a hard campaign to get elected. What the new government wants is something like the eighteenth-century English policy toward America. Keep the colonies as a source of raw materials and as a market for manufactured goods, but don't let them develop a domestic industry. You can't come right out and say that, but you can let the situation develop naturally.

"Only . . . here the Sword is, obviously bound to grow rich and expand in every direction. If we're allowed to develop, to reinvest our profits, we'll become the nucleus of independent asterite enterprise. If, on the other hand, we're wiped out by an unfortunate accident, there's no nucleus; and a small change in the banking laws is all that's needed to prevent others from getting started. Q.E.D."

"I daresay Hulse does think he's doing his patriotic duty," said Blades. "He wants to guarantee North America our natural resources—in the long run, maybe, our allegiance. If he has to commit sabotage, too bad, but it won't cost him any sleep."

"No!" Ellen almost screamed.

Chung sagged in his chair. "We're very neatly trapped," he said like an old man. "I don't see any way out. Think you can get to work now, Mike? You can assign group leaders for the evacuation—"

Blades jumped erect. "I can fight!" he growled.

"With what? Can openers?"

"You mean you're going to lie down and let them break us?"

Avis came back. She thrust the bottle into Blades' hands as he paced the room. "Here you are," she said in a distant voice.

He held it out toward Ellen. "Have some," he invited.

"Not with you . . . you subversive!"

Avis brightened noticeably, took the bottle and raised it. "Then here's to victory," she said, drank, and passed it to Blades.

He started to gulp; but the wine was too noble, and he found himself savoring its course down his throat. *Why,* he thought vaguely, *do people always speak with scorn about Dutch courage? The Dutch have real guts. They fought themselves free of Spain and free of the ocean itself; when the French or Germans came, they made the enemy sea their ally—*

The bottle fell from his grasp. In the weak acceleration, it hadn't hit the floor when Avis rescued it. "Gimme that, you big butterfingers," she exclaimed. Her free hand clasped his arm. "Whatever happens, Mike," she said to him, "we're not quitting."

Still Blades stared beyond her. His fists clenched and unclenched. The noise of his breathing filled the room. Chung looked around in bewilderment; Ellen watched with waxing horror; Avis' eyes kindled.

"Holy smoking seegars," Blades whispered at last. "I really think we can swing it."

■   ■   ■

Captain Janichevski recoiled. "You're out of your skull!"

"Probably," said Blades. "Fun, huh?"

"You can't do this."

"We can try."

"Do you know what you're talking about? Insurrection, that's what. Quite likely piracy. Even if your scheme worked, you'd spend the next ten years in Rehab—at least."

"Maybe, provided the matter ever came to trial. But it won't."

"That's what you think. You're asking me to compound the felony, and misappropriate the property of my owners to boot." Janichevski shook his head. "Sorry, Mike. I'm sorry as hell about this mess. But I won't be party to making it worse."

"In other words," Blades replied, "you'd rather be party to sabotage. I'm proposing an act of legitimate self-defense."

"*If* there actually is a conspiracy to destroy the Station."

"Adam, you're a spaceman. You know how the Navy operates. Can you swallow that story about a missile getting loose by accident?"

Janichevski bit his lip. The sounds from outside filled the captain's cabin, voices, footfalls, whir of machines and clash of doors, as the *Pallas Castle* readied for departure. Blades waited.

"You may be right," said Janichevski at length, wretchedly. "Though why Hulse should jeopardize his career—"

"He's not. There's a scapegoat groomed back home, you can be sure. Like some company that'll be debarred from military contracts for a while . . . and get nice fat orders in other fields. I've kicked around the System enough to know how that works."

"If you're wrong, though . . . if this is an honest blunder . . . then you risk committing treason."

"Yeah. I'll take the chance."

"Not I. No. I've got a family to support," Janichevski said.

Blades regarded him bleakly. "If the Essjays get away with this stunt, what kind of life will your family be leading, ten years from now? It's not simply that we'll be high-class peons in the Belt. But tied hand and foot to a shortsighted government, how much progress will we be able to make? Other countries have colonies out here too, remember, and some of them are already giving their people a freer hand than we've got. Do you want the Asians, or the Russians, or even the Europeans, to take over the asteroids?"

"I can't make policy."

"In other words, mama knows best. Believe, obey, anything put out by some bureaucrat who never set foot beyond Luna. Is that your idea of citizenship?"

"You're putting a mighty fine gloss on bailing yourself out!" Janichevski flared.

"Sure, I'm no idealist. But neither am I a slave." Blades hesitated. "We've been friends too long, Adam, for me to try bribing you. But if worst comes to worst, we'll cover for you . . . somehow . . . and if contrariwise we win, then we'll soon be hiring captains for our own ships and you'll get the best offer any spaceman ever got."

"No. Scram. I've work to do."

Blades braced himself. "I didn't want to say this. But I've already informed a number of my men. They're as mad as I am. They're waiting in the terminal. A monkey wrench or a laser torch makes a pretty fair weapon. We can take over by force. That'll leave you legally in the clear. But with so many witnesses around, you'll have to prefer charges against us later on."

Janichevski began to sweat.

"We'll be sent up," said Blades. "But it will still have been worth it."

"Is it really that important to you?"

"Yes. I admit I'm no crusader. But this is a matter of principle."

Janichevski stared at the big redhaired man for a long while. Suddenly he stiffened. "O.K. On that account, and no other, I'll go along with you."

Blades wobbled on his feet, near collapse with relief. "Good man!" he croaked.

"But I will not have any of my officers or crew involved."

Blades rallied and answered briskly, "You needn't. Just issue orders that my boys are to have access to the scoopships. They can install the equipment, jockey the boats over to the full balloons, and even couple them on."

Janichevski's fears had vanished once he made his decision, but now a certain doubt registered. "That's a pretty skilled job."

"These are pretty skilled men. It isn't much of a maneuver, not like making a Jovian sky dive."

"Well, O.K., I'll take your word for their ability. But suppose the *Altair* spots those boats moving around?"

"She's already several hundred kilometers off, and getting farther away, running a search curve which I'm betting my liberty—

and my honor; I certainly don't want to hurt my own country's Navy—I'm betting that search curve is guaranteed not to find the missile in time. They'll spot the *Pallas* as you depart—oh, yes, our people will be aboard as per orders—but no finer detail will show in so casual an observation."

"Again, I'll take your word. What else can I do to help?"

"Nothing you weren't doing before. Leave the piratics to us. I'd better get back." Blades extended his hand. "I haven't got the words to thank you, Adam."

Janichevski accepted the shake. "No reason for thanks. You dragooned me." A grin crossed his face. "I must confess, though, I'm not sorry you did."

Blades left. He found his gang in the terminal, two dozen engineers and rockjacks clumped tautly together.

"What's the word?" Carlos Odonaju shouted.

"Clear track," Blades said. "Go right aboard."

"Good. Fine. I always wanted to do something vicious and destructive," Odonaju laughed.

"The idea is to prevent destruction," Blades reminded him, and proceeded toward the office.

Avis met him in Corridor Four. Her freckled countenance was distorted by a scowl. "Hey, Mike, wait a minute," she said, low and hurriedly. "Have you seen La Ziska?"

"The leftenant? Why, no. I left her with you, remember, hoping you could calm her down."

"Uh-huh. She was incandescent mad. Called us a pack of bandits and— But then she started crying. Seemed to break down completely. I took her to your cabin and went back to help Jimmy. Only, when I checked there a minute ago, she was gone."

"What? Where?"

"How should I know? But that she-devil's capable of anything to wreck our chances."

"You're not being fair to her. She's got an oath to keep."

"All right," said Avis sweetly. "Far be it from me to prevent her fulfilling her obligations. Afterward she may even write you an occasional letter. I'm sure that'll brighten your Rehab cell no end."

"What can she do?" Blades argued, with an uneasy sense of whistling in the dark. "She can't get off the asteroid without a scooter, and I've already got Sam's gang working on all the scooters."

"Is there no other possibility? The radio shack?"

"With a man on duty there. That's out." Blades patted the girl's arm.

"O.K., I'll get back to work. But . . . I'll be so glad when this is over, Mike!"

Looking into the desperate brown eyes, Blades felt a sudden impulse to kiss their owner. But no, there was too much else to do. Later, perhaps. He cocked a thumb upward. "Carry on."

Too bad about Ellen, he thought as he continued toward his office. *What an awful waste, to make a permanent enemy of someone with her kind of looks. And personality— Come off that stick, you clabberhead! She's probably the marryin' type anyway.*

In her shoes, though, what would I do? Not much; they'd pinch my feet. But—damnation, Avis is right. She's not safe to have running around loose. The radio shack? Sparks is not one of the few who've been told the whole story and co-opted into the plan. She could—

Blades cursed, whirled, and ran.

His way was clear. Most of the men were still in their dorms, preparing to leave. He traveled in huge low-gravity leaps.

The radio shack rose out of the surface near the verandah. Blades tried the door. It didn't budge. A chill went through him. He backed across the corridor and charged. The door was only plastiboard—

He hit with a thud and a grunt, and rebounded with a numbed shoulder. But it looked so easy for the cops on 3V!

No time to figure out the delicate art of forcible entry. He hurled himself against the panel, again and again, heedless of the pain that struck in flesh and bone. When the door finally, splinteringly gave way, he stumbled clear across the room beyond, fetched up against an instrument console, recovered his balance, and gaped.

The operator lay on the floor, swearing in a steady monotone. He had been efficiently bound with his own blouse and trousers, which revealed his predilection for maroon shorts with zebra stripes. There was a lump on the back of his head, and a hammer lay close by. Ellen must have stolen the tool and come in here with the thing behind her back. The operator would have had no reason to suspect her.

She had not left the sender's chair, not even while the door was under attack. Only a carrier beam connected the Sword with the *Altair.* She continued doggedly to fumble with dials and switches, trying to modulate it and raise the ship.

"Praises be . . . you haven't had advanced training . . . in radio," Blades choked. "That's . . . a long-range set . . . pretty special system—" He weaved toward her. "Come along, now."

She spat an unladylike refusal.

Theoretically, Blades should have enjoyed the tussle that followed. But he was in poor shape at the outset. And he was a good deal worse off by the time he got her pinioned.

"O.K.," he wheezed. "Will you come quietly?"

She didn't deign to answer, unless you counted her butting him in the nose. He had to yell for help to frog-march her aboard ship.

"*Pallas Castle* calling NASS *Altair*. Come in, *Altair*."

The great avoid swung clear in space, among a million cold stars. The asteroid had dwindled out of sight. A radio beam flickered across emptiness. Within the hull, the crew and a hundred refugees sat jammed together. The air was thick with their breath and sweat and waiting.

Blades and Chung, seated by the transmitter, felt another kind of thickness, the pull of the internal field. Earth-normal weight dragged down every movement; the enclosed cabin began to feel suffocatingly small. *We'd get used to it again pretty quickly,* Blades thought. *Our bodies would, that is. But our own selves, tied down to Earth forever—no.*

The vision screen jumped to life. "NASS *Altair* acknowledging *Pallas Castle*," said the uniformed figure within.

"O.K., Charlie, go outside and don't let anybody else enter," Chung told his own operator.

The spaceman gave him a quizzical glance, but obeyed. "I wish to report that evacuation of the Sword is now complete," Chung said formally.

"Very good, sir," the Navy face replied. "I'll inform my superiors."

"Wait, don't break off yet. We have to talk with your captain."

"Sir? I'll switch you over to—"

"None of your damned chains of command," Blades interrupted. "Get me Rear Admiral Hulse direct, toot sweet, or I'll eat out whatever fraction of you he leaves unchewed. This is an emergency. I've got to warn him of an immediate danger only he can deal with."

The other stared, first at Chung's obvious exhaustion, then at the black eye and assorted bruises, scratches, and bites that adorned Blades' visage. "I'll put the message through Channel Red at once, sir." The screen blanked.

"Well, here we go," Chung said. "I wonder how the food in Rehab is these days."

"Want me to do the talking?" Blades asked. Chung wasn't built for times as hectic as the last few hours, and was worn to a nubbin. He himself felt immensely keyed up. He'd always liked a good fight.

"Sure." Chung pulled a crumpled cigarette from his pocket and began to fill the cabin with smoke. "You have a larger stock of rudeness than I."

Presently the screen showed Hulse, rigid at his post on the bridge. "Good day, gentlemen," he said. "What's the trouble?"

"Plenty," Blades answered. "Clear everybody else out of there; let your ship orbit free awhile. And seal your circuit."

Hulse reddened. "Who do you think you are?"

"Well, my birth certificate says Michael Joseph Blades. I've got some news for you concerning that top-secret gadget you told us about. You wouldn't want unauthorized personnel listening in."

Hulse leaned forward till he seemed about to fall through the screen. "What's this about a hazard?"

"Fact. The *Altair* is in distinct danger of getting blown to bits."

"Have you gone crazy? Get me the captain of the *Pallas*."

"Very small bits."

Hulse compressed his lips. "All right, I'll listen to you for a short time. You had better make it worth my while."

He spoke orders. Blades scratched his back while he waited for the bridge to be emptied and wondered if there was any chance of a hot shower in the near future.

"Done," said Hulse. "Give me your report."

Blades glanced at the telltale. "You haven't sealed your circuit, admiral."

Hulse said angry words, but complied. "Now will you talk?"

"Sure. This secrecy is for your own protection. You risk court-martial otherwise."

Hulse suppressed a retort.

"O.K., here's the word." Blades met the transmitted glare with an almost palpable crash of eyeballs. "We decided, Mr. Chung and I, that any missile rig as haywire as yours represents a menace to navigation and public safety. If you can't control your own nuclear weapons, you shouldn't be at large. Our charter gives us local authority as peace officers. By virtue thereof and so on and so forth, we ordered certain precautionary steps taken. As a result, if that warhead goes off, I'm sorry to say that NASS *Altair* will be destroyed."

"Are you . . . have you—" Hulse congealed. In spite of everything, he was a competent officer, Blades decided. "Please explain yourself," he said without tone.

"Sure," Blades obliged. "The Station hasn't got any armament, but trust the human race to jury-rig that. We commandeered the scoopships belonging to this vessel and loaded them with Jovian gas at maximum pressure. If your missile detonates, they'll dive on you."

Something like amusement tinged Hulse's shocked expression. "Do you seriously consider that a weapon?"

"I seriously do. Let me explain. The ships are orbiting free right now, scattered through quite a large volume of space. Nobody's aboard them. What is aboard each one, though, is an autopilot taken from a scooter, hooked into the drive controls. Each 'pilot has its sensors locked onto your ship. You can't maneuver fast enough to shake off radar beams and mass detectors. You're the target object, and there's nothing to tell those idiot computers to decelerate as they approach you.

"Of course, no approach is being made yet. A switch has been put in every scooter circuit, and left open. Only the meteorite evasion units are operative right now. That is, if anyone tried to lay alongside one of those scoopships, he'd be detected and the ship would skitter away. Remember, a scoopship hasn't much mass, and she does have engines designed for diving in and out of Jupe's gravitational well. She can out-accelerate either of our vessels, or any boat of yours, and out-dodge any of your missiles. You can't catch her."

Hulse snorted. "What's the significance of this farce?"

"I said the autopilots were switched off at the moment, as far as heading for the target is concerned. But each of those switches is coupled to two other units. One is simply the sensor box. If you withdraw beyond a certain distance, the switches will close. That is, the 'pilots will be turned on if you try to go beyond range of the beams now locked onto you. The other unit we've installed in every boat is an ordinary two-for-a-dollar radiation meter. If a nuclear weapon goes off, anywhere within a couple of thousand kilometers, the switches will also close. In either of these cases, the scoopships will dive on you.

"You might knock out a few with missiles, before they strike. Undoubtedly you can punch holes in them with laser guns. But that won't do any good, except when you're lucky enough to hit a vital part. Nobody's aboard to be killed. Not even much gas will be lost, in so short a time.

"So to summarize, chum, if that rogue missile explodes, your ship will be struck by ten to twenty scoopships, each crammed full of concentrated Jovian air. They'll pierce that thin hull of yours, but since they're already pumped full beyond the margin of safety, the impact will split them open and the gas will whoosh out. Do you know what Jovian air does to substances like magnesium?

"You can probably save your crew, take to the boats and reach a Commission base. But your nice battleship will be *ganz kaput*. Is your game worth that candle?"

"You're totally insane! Releasing such a thing—"

"Oh, not permanently. There's one more switch on each boat, connected to the meteorite evasion unit and controlled by a small battery. When those batteries run down, in about twenty hours, the 'pilots will be turned off completely. Then we can spot the scoopships by radar and pick 'em up. And you'll be free to leave."

"Do you think for one instant that your fantastic claim of acting legally will stand up in court?"

"No, probably not. But it won't have to. Obviously you can't make anybody swallow your yarn if a *second* missile gets loose. And as for the first one, since it's failed in its purpose, your bosses aren't going to want the matter publicized. It'd embarrass them no end, and serve no purpose except revenge on Jimmy and me— which there's no point in taking, since the Sword would still be privately owned. You check with Earth, Admiral, before shooting off your mouth. They'll tell you that both parties to this quarrel had better forget about legal action. Both would lose.

"So I'm afraid your only choice is to find that missile before it goes off."

"And yours? What are your alternatives?" Hulse had gone gray in the face, but he still spoke stoutly.

Blades grinned at him. "None whatsoever. We've burned our bridges. We can't do anything about those scoopships now, so it's no use trying to scare us or arrest us or whatever else may occur to you. What we've done is establish an automatic deterrent."

"Against an, an attempt . . . at sabotage . . . that only exists in your imagination!"

Blades shrugged. "That argument isn't relevant any longer. I do believe the missile was released deliberately. We wouldn't have done what we did otherwise. But there's no longer any point in making charges and denials. You'd just better retrieve the thing."

Hulse squared his shoulders. "How do I know you're telling the truth?"

"Well, you can send a man to the Station. He'll find the scooters lying gutted. Send another man over here to the *Pallas*. He'll find the scoopships gone. I also took a few photographs of the autopilots being installed and the ships being cast adrift. Go right ahead. However, may I remind you that the fewer people who have an inkling of this little intrigue, the better for all concerned."

Hulse opened his mouth, shut it again, stared from side to side, and finally slumped the barest bit. "Very well," he said, biting off the words syllable by syllable. "I can't risk a ship of the line. Of course, since the rogue is still farther away than your deterrent allows the *Altair* to go, we shall have to wait in space a while."

"I don't mind."

"I shall report the full story to my superiors at home . . . but unofficially."

"Good. I'd like them to know that we asterites have teeth."

"Signing off, then."

Chung stirred. "Wait a bit," he said. "We have one of your people aboard, Lieutenant Ziska. Can you send a gig for her?"

"She didn't collaborate with us," Blades added. "You can see the evidence of her loyalty, all over my mug."

"Good girl!" Hulse exclaimed savagely. "Yes, I'll send a boat. Signing off."

The screen blanked. Chung and Blades let out a long, ragged breath. They sat a while trembling before Chung muttered, "That skunk as good as admitted everything."

"Sure," said Blades. "But we won't have any more trouble from him."

Chung stubbed out his cigarette. Poise was returning to both men. "There could be other attempts, though, in the next few years." He scowled. "I think we should arm the Station. A couple of laser guns, if nothing else. We can say it's for protection in case of war. But it'll make our own government handle us more carefully, too."

"Well, you can approach the Commission about it." Blades yawned and stretched, trying to loosen his muscles. "Better get a lot of other owners and supervisors to sign your petition, though." The next order of business came to his mind. He rose. "Why don't you go tell Adam the good news?"

"Where are you bound?"

"To let Ellen know the fight is over."

"Is it, as far as she's concerned?"

"That's what I'm about to find out. Hope I won't need an armored escort." Blades went from the cubicle, past the watchful radioman, and down the deserted passageway beyond.

The cabin given her lay at the end, locked from outside. The key hung magnetically on the bulkhead. Blades unlocked the door and tapped it with his knuckles.

"Who's there?" she called.

"Me," he said. "May I come in?"

"If you must," she said freezingly.

He opened the door and stepped through. The overhead light shimmered off her hair and limned her figure with shadows. His heart bumped. "You, uh, you can come out now," he faltered. "Everything's O.K."

She said nothing, only regarded him from glacier-blue eyes.

"No harm's been done, except to me and Sparks, and we're not mad," he groped. "Shall we forget the whole episode?"

"If you wish."

"Ellen," he pleaded, "I had to do what seemed right to me."

"So did I."

He couldn't find any more words.

"I assume that I'll be returned to my own ship," she said. He nodded. "Then, if you will excuse me, I had best make myself as presentable as I can. Good day, Mr. Blades."

"What's good about it?" he snarled, and slammed the door on his way out.

Avis stood outside the jam-packed saloon. She saw him coming and ran to meet him. He made swab-O with his fingers and joy blazed from her. "Mike," she cried, "I'm so happy!"

The only gentlemanly thing to do was hug her. His spirits lifted a bit as he did. She made a nice armful. Not bad looking, either.

"Well," said Amspaugh. "So that's the inside story. How very interesting. I never heard it before."

"No, obviously it never got into any official record," Missy said. "The only announcement made was that there'd been a near accident, that the Station tried to make counter-missiles out of scoopships, but that the quick action of NASS *Altair* was what saved the situation. Her captain was commended. I don't believe he ever got a further promotion, though."

"Why didn't you publicize the facts afterwards?" Lindgren wondered. "When the revolution began, that is. It would've made good propaganda."

"Nonsense," Missy said. "Too much else had happened since then. Besides, neither Mike nor Jimmy nor I wanted to do any cheap emotion-fanning. We knew the asterites weren't any little pink-bottomed angels, nor the people back sunward a crew of devils. There were rights and wrongs on both sides. We did what we could in the war, and hated every minute of it, and when it was over we broke out two cases of champagne and invited as many Earthsiders as we could get to the party. They had a lot of love to carry home for us."

A stillness fell. She took a long swallow from her glass and sat looking out at the stars.

"Yes," Lindgren said finally, "I guess that was the worst, fighting against our own kin."

"Well, I was better off in that respect than some," Missy conceded. "I'd made my commitment so long before the trouble that my ties were nearly all out here. Twenty years is time enough to grow new roots."

"Really?" Orloff was surprised. "I haven't met you often before, Mrs. Blades, so evidently I've had a false impression. I thought you were a more recent immigrant than that."

"Shucks, no," she laughed. "I only needed six months after the *Altair* incident to think things out, resign my commission and catch the next Belt-bound ship. You don't think I'd have let a man like Mike get away, do you?"

Those Pesky Belters
and Their Torchships

JERRY POURNELLE

I've always had a long and abiding interest about life in the Asteroid Belt. In fact, this essay was my second column for the late lamented *Galaxy* SF magazine and first appeared in print over twenty-five years ago. It is just as pertinent today as the day I wrote it.

I've also written several Belter stories: "Tinker," which is included in this collection, "Bind Your Sons to Exile," which appears in the first volume of this series, and the novel *Exiles to Glory*.

Like most of you I'd like to see the exploration, if not the settlement, of the Asteroid Belt in my lifetime. And it could have happened. Still possibly could, but not with NASA at the helm. (More on that later.)

In some of my early stories (some of them collected in *High Justice*) I extrapolated private enterprise leading the way throughout the seventies and eighties. Unfortunately, due to lack of vision, the growth of the Harvard Business School bottom-line mentality, and NASA's efforts to maintain control over their fiefdom, little—in actual fact, none—of the space movement's early promise has been shown.

In fact, had someone twenty years ago, at the height of the Apollo flights, shown me a crystal ball

with a vision of the future of the space program—
I would have proclaimed it a fraud. Somehow the
United States has lost its goals and dreams. It's as
though, like some squalid Dickens character, we're
determined to spend our children's inheritance on
ourselves and invest none of it.

We have it in our power to spread far beyond this
nest we call Earth, to the Moon, to the Asteroid
Belt, even far beyond this solar system.

We know the way. We have the designs. We can
have the first of the new generation of spacecraft
in under five years, and for less each year than we
spend on tobacco subsidies. We can, or someone
else can.

I'd like it to be us. It's one of my dreams; probably
yours too if you're reading this book. I think that the
best remedy to our troubled education problems
is to give the children new hopes and dreams, to
take their focus off urban decay and street crime.
If we've got someplace exciting to go and wonderful
to see, we won't have much trouble getting kids to
tool up to go there.

And what could be more exciting than those first
steps toward a billion-year future?

THE OTHER DAY I got a phone call from a national magazine,
and being basically kind, generous, and always in need of an
excuse to stop working, I spent an hour with the reporter. He
wanted a list of ten science fiction predictions that have proved
out, and ten more SF writers have made but which haven't happened yet.

He wasn't at all interested in a list of science fiction predictions
that just aren't going to happen. Except in rare moods neither am
I, but I've just finished reading the death-knell for poly-water (it
turns out poly-water isn't a new form of water at all; it's just a
product of dirty laboratory glassware) and that plus the phone call
got me thinking about nice ideas that just won't work no matter
what we do.

One of our favorite SF themes is the "Belter Civilization,"
which usually seeks—and gets—independence from the colonial
masters on Earth. Belters make their livings as asteroid miners,
and they flit from asteroid to asteroid, slicing up planetoids for

the rich veins of metal we'll presumably find in them.

In the usual story, the miners go off on long prospecting tours, leaving their families on a "settled" rock. The Belt Capital is usually located on Ceres or some other central place which may or may not have been extensively transformed; and when Belters get together. it's always in an asteroid city.

The Belters don't ever come to Earth or any other planet. Indeed, they regard planets as "holes," deep gravity wells which can trap them and use up their precious fuels. The assumption here is that it's far less costly to flit from asteroid to asteroid than it is to land on a planet or get into close orbit around one.

Another assumption, generally not stated in the stories, is that fuels are expensive and scarce, and the Belters have to conserve reaction mass; this is why, in the usual Belter story, you conserve both time and energy by never going outside the Belt. Scarce as fuel is, though, I suppose the Belters have a source of it locally or they couldn't contemplate independence. They must have fuel for their ships and energy for their artificial environments. Without those, there'd be no Belter Civilization. Even if we discover something of fabulous value in the Belt we can't operate without energy and fuel.

Those are not, by the way, the same thing. Nuclear fission reactors and large solar panels could provide enough power for a permanent Belt station, and if there were something valuable enough out there we could put a reactor onto an asteroid now. Rocket fuels are something else again. To make a rocket work, you must have reaction mass: something to get moving fast backward and dump overboard. Unfortunately, asteroids are rock, and rocks don't make very good rocket fuel. We'll come back to what the Belters might do about that later.

For the moment, let's see how difficult travel to and in the Belt is. We'll use the same measure as I did in "Life Among the Asteroids": the total change in ship velocity required to perform the mission. This is called delta v, and you should recall that a ship with a given fuel efficiency and ratio of fuel to non-fuel weight will have a unique calculatable delta v. It doesn't matter whether the pilot uses that delta v in little increments or in one big burn: the sum of velocity changes remains the same.

Similarly, various mission delta-v requirements can be calculated from the laws of orbital mechanics independent of the ship used. Table 3 gives the delta-v requirements for getting around the Earth-Jupiter portion of the solar system. We're assuming that

Table 3

VELOCITY CHANGE REQUIREMENTS FOR TRAVELING THROUGH THE ASTEROID BELT (KILOMETERS/SECOND)

Origin or Destination	Earth	Mars	2 AU	Ceres	Jovian moon
Earth	7.9	9.3	8.1	9.8	6.6
Mars	5.5	3.5	7.2	8.8	6.5
2 AU	8.1	3.2	0.0	3.2	4.4
Ceres	9.5	5.0	2.9	0.4	2.8
Jovian moon	6.6	4.4	4.4	2.3	0.0

Values above the diagonal are delta-v requirements for travel from surface to surface, except when the starting point is Earth. All values for Earth assume beginning and end in Earth orbit. *Diagonal* values are circular orbit velocities. Values below the diagonal are those required for a trip that begins and ends in circular orbit. (Example: Ceres orbit to Mars orbit requires delta v of 5 km/sec, while dirtside Ceres to dirtside Mars takes 8.8 km/sec.)

---

getting to Earth orbit is free, whether with the laser launching system I described previously, or with shuttles, or whatever, so all missions to or from Earth begin and end in orbit.

The first thing we see is that landing on an asteroid isn't much easier than going to Mars; in fact, Ceres is harder to get to than Mars. This is because not only are the asteroids a long way out, but they don't help you catch up to them; they've so little mass that you have to chase them down. Thus, once among the asteroids, you may well want to stay there and not use up all that delta v coming back to Earth.

Then, too, travel between Ceres and a theoretical asteroid 2 AU out is a lot cheaper than getting to Earth from either of them. (One AU, or astronomical unit, is the distance from Earth to the Sun and is 93,000,000 miles, or 149,500,000 = 1.5×10^8 kilometers.) It takes 8km/sec to get to the 2 AU rock, but only 3.2 more to get from there to Ceres.

So far so good, and we're well on the way to developing a Belt Civilization. There's already a small nit to pick, though: although travel to Mars itself is costly, it's as easy to go to Mars *orbit* as it is to go from asteroid to asteroid. Thus, if a laser-launch system could be built on Mars, making travel to and from Mars orbit cheap, Mars might well become the Belt Capital.

Politics being what they are, though, perhaps the Martians (well, Mars colonists?) won't like having all those crude asteroid miners on their planet, and the Belters will have to build their own capital at some convenient place such as Ceres or the 2 AU rock, saving both their feelings and some energy. However, we've so far said nothing about how *long* it takes to get from one place to another. The delta v's in Table 3 are for minimum-energy trips, Hohmann transfer orbits, and to use a Hohmann orbit you must start and finish with origin and destination precisely opposite the Sun. You can't just boom out when you feel like it; you must wait for the precise geometry, otherwise the delta-v requirements go up to ridiculous values.

You get a launch window once each synodic period. A synodic period is the time it takes two planets, or planetoids, to go around the sun and come back to precisely the same positions relative to each other: from, say, being on opposite sides of the Sun until they're in opposition again, which is what we need for a Hohmann journey.

The synodic periods and travel times are given in Table 4, and our Belt Civilization is in trouble again. Not only does it take 1.57 years to get from Ceres to 2 AU (or vice versa), but you can only do it once each 7 years! Travel to and from Mars isn't a lot better, either. The Belters aren't going to visit their Capital very often, and one wonders if a civilization can be built among colonies that can only visit each other every seven to nine years, spending years in travel times to do it.

By contrast, you can get from Earth to the flying rocks every year and a half, spending another year and a half in transit. That's no short time either, but it beats the nine years of the Ceres-asteroid visitations.

Perhaps, though, we haven't been quite fair to the Belters. Asteroids aren't as widely separated as Ceres and our 2 AU rock. Most textbooks claim the asteroids are concentrated between 2.1

Table 4

SYNODIC PERIODS AND TRANSIT TIMES FOR HOHMANN TRAVEL

From-To	Earth	Mars	2 AU	Ceres	Moon of Jupiter
Earth	---	2.08	1.50	1.28	1.09
Mars	0.71	---	5.77	4.69	2.24
2 AU	0.92	1.17	---	7.15	3.68
Ceres	1.84	1.57	1.83	---	7.56
Moon of Jupiter	2.7	3.08	3.4	3.97	---

Transit times *below* the diagonal; synodic periods above the diagonal. All figures given in Earth years.

---

and 3.3 AU out from the Sun. We'll assume they're all in the same plane (they aren't), so the Belt area works out to 4.6 x 10^{27} square centimeters. The books say there are about 100,000 asteroids visible with the Palomar Eye, but we want to be fair (and make things simple) so we'll assume there are 460,000 asteroids interesting enough to want to visit, or one every 10^{22} cm^2 within the Belt. That means the asteroids lie on an average of 10^{11} cm apart, which happens to be 10^6 km or one million kilometers, about three times the distance from Earth to the Moon.

Out that far from the Sun's influence, and only going a million kilometers anyway, we don't have to use Hohmann orbits. One of the Belters' usual (science fiction) devices is the torchship, which accelerates halfway to where you're going, turns over, and decelerates back again. Orbital flight doesn't really work that way, but this will do as an approximation. Tables 5 and 6 show what it takes to do that.

Examining Table 5 we see the Belters have a problem. Any group of two or three aren't so far apart that they couldn't go see their neighbors, using the 1 cm/sec acceleration and taking a day off to do it; but at 6 km/sec delta v you won't do it often. You could try a lower acceleration, and get to more places, but before you go far, time and energy stop you again. A cluster of

Table 5

ACCELERATIONS, TRAVEL TIMES, AND DELTA-V REQUIREMENTS FOR CONTINUOUS-BOOST TRIP OF ONE MILLION KILOMETERS

Acceleration (cm / sec^2)	Acceleration ("g's")	Travel Time (days)	Delta v (km/sec)
10^3	1	0.23	200
10^2	0.1	0.74	63.2
10	0.01	2.3	20
1	0.001	7.4	6.32
0.1	0.0001	23	2

Note: figures for very low accelerations will necessarily be inaccurate.

Table 6

TRAVEL AT .1 CM/SEC ACCELERATION CONTINUOUS BOOST

Distance (km)	Travel Time (days)	Delta v required
1 million	23	2.0
10 million	74	6.32
100 million	230	20.0

Note: the model is especially inaccurate for very long trips.

rocks might proclaim independence, but that cluster will be a long way from any other cluster. We could conceivably have a number of Belter Civilizations, but hardly a single Belt-wide government, even with 20-km/sec delta-v torchships.

Those torchships present a problem anyway. Continuous boost may be easy on the passengers, but it uses up delta v like mad. The one-gravity boost trip for a lousy million kilometers takes more delta v than 10 round trips to Ceres! It gets worse when you try to boost over long distances, too. Table 7 shows some representative requirements for torchship travel between planets. Sure, the travel times are now very short, and the Belt Civilization is in business: you can get from one side of the belt to the other, 7 AU, in a week, so trips to the Capital, no matter where it is, are no problem.

However, trips *anywhere* are no problem if you have torchships. Why bother avoiding the 8 or 9 km/sec penalty for landing on Mars or going to Earth? The "holes" aren't very deep when you have a ship like that; certainly you can afford to go to Earth orbit, and Earth is still likely to be closer to you than the Belt Capital.

Furthermore, it's hard to see how the torchships will work. The usual explanation in science fiction is "atomic power," but that's not really the whole story. We already have, or very nearly had, an "atomic powered" rocket, NERVA, but it wouldn't do anything like *that*. NERVA is an atomic pile through which hydrogen is poured as a coolant. The pile heats the hydrogen, which therefore goes aft, fast, and the rocket moves.

We could have built a NERVA engine weighing about 35,000 pounds and delivering some 250,000 pounds of thrust by the end of this decade; the development was moving very well when Congress decided to cancel the program. Incidentally, more money is annually spent on lipsticks in New York State than NERVA was costing, and any medium-sized state has more annual sales of liquor than NERVA cost over its lifetime; but it's nice that they don't waste the taxpayers' money with frivolities like space. Editorials aside, it's reasonable to assume NERVA-type ships will first explore the asteroids.

The design spec for NERVA was an I_{sp} of 800 seconds. I_{sp} is pounds thrust per second per pound of fuel used, and is thus the measure of fuel efficiency. The 800-second ship might have flown by 1980, and a second NERVA with I_{sp} of 1300 seconds was possible by 1990. Given the I_{sp} we can calculate temperatures

Table 7

TORCHSHIP TRAVEL TIMES AND DELTA-V REQUIREMENTS FOR ONE GRAVITY ACCELERATION

Distance traveled (AU)	Distance (km)	Time (days)	Delta v (km / sec)
1	1.5×10^8	2.8	2,460
2	3.0×10^8	4.1	3,460
5	7.5×10^8	6.5	5,550
7	1.0×10^9	7.5	6,530
40	6.0×10^9	18.0	15,500

Table 8

ENGINE TEMPERATURES AND I_{sp}

Particle energy in degrees Kelvin	Exhaust velocity of propellant (cm/sec)	Specific impulse (seconds)	Delta v possible, mass ratio = 2 (50% total weight is fuel)	Delta v possible, mass ratio = 5 (70% total weight is fuel)
1,000	4.07×10^5	415	2.8	6.6
5,000	9.55×10^5	975	6.6	15.4
10,000	1.29×10^6	1310	8.9	20.8
50,000	2.88×10^6	2950	19.9	46.4
100,000	4.07×10^6	4150	28.2	65.7
1,000,000	1.29×10^7	13,100	89.0	208.0
5,000,000	2.88×10^7	29,500	199.0	464.0

(K.E. = T x Boltzmann Constant (which I won't explain) = ½ mv^2; table assumes monatomic hydrogen fuel, with mass of 1.6733×10^{-24} grams / particle.)

of the exhaust gases, and thus see what we have to handle to get really efficient rockets.

Table 8 shows some of these—and shows we're in trouble again. NERVA used a system in which the fuel passed through pipes in the motor wall to cool that before it went into the reactor chamber, and with similar design features could handle gases with temperatures in the 975–1,300 I_{sp} region, but the 2,950 is very much an upper limit; no pile system will withstand temperatures of 50,000° Kelvin.

It follows that the best NERVA we could build won't be a torchship. With 50 percent of the total weight in fuel, and nearly 3,000 seconds I_{sp}, we have a ship capable of cruising between the asteroids and Earth; in fact, it can go almost anywhere in the solar system, but only in Hohmann transfer orbits. It can't accelerate continuously.

Actually, even if we could get 1,000,000° K temperatures we only have 208 km/second delta v with a ship that's 80 percent fuel. This is very respectable (although I don't know how we control that temperature) but it's only good for one, count 'em, one continuous burn for a million kilometers at one g. A million kilometers is not far in the solar system. True, this theoretical ship might make one of the lower-acceleration boosts, but it's still no torchship as usually given to the Belters by SF writers.

Well, if NERVA can't do it, what about a "true" nuclear rocket: one that uses controlled fusion? Thermonuclear reactions surely will give enough energy for torching, won't they?

Not by themselves. There's plenty of energy in fusion, but how do you *contain* it? On Earth, with huge tokomak rings generating enormous magnetic fields, we might be able to build a magnetic pinch-bottle to hold a controlled fusion reaction; but aboard a *spaceship*? If you can build something light enough to go aboard a ship smaller than the *Queen Mary* and able to contain controlled fusion, you've got a device that will change far more than the asteroid Belters: it's obviously a defense against hydrogen bombs, to begin with. We'll discuss various properties of fusion-powered ships some other time; for now, it's enough to point out that they aren't the panacea we wish they were.

Well, what *can* the Belters do? They can get around with NERVA engines, but what do they use for fuel? There isn't a lot of hydrogen out among the asteroids.

Oddly enough, there is a propulsion system that gets I_{sp} (theoretical) in the region of 20,000 seconds, doesn't have excessive real temperatures, and can be built right now. Even better, it's likely we can find fuels for it in the Belt.

This is the ion drive ship. Ion drives employ metal vapors as fuel, and the metal is accelerated by magnetic fields, not heat. If the asteroids turn out to be rich in metals, some kind of ion rocket may be just what the Belters need. It lets them get fuel from the rocks. But even with a 30,000-second I_{sp} ion drive we won't have a torchship for driving around at one g. Torching uses too much energy, and the ion drive won't develop the needed thrust anyway. A mercury-vapor ion engine, for example, although very efficient, only gives thrusts of about 10^{-4}g. You get there efficiently, but it takes a long time.

No, the conclusion is obvious: with anything foreseeable in the way of rockets, the Belters aren't going to develop a civilization spanning any very large part of the Belt. They won't have ships good enough to let them reach each other across such vast distances—and if they do get such ships, it's as easy to reach Earth as the other asteroids. With real torchships, both the Belters and the Earth Navy will have no trouble getting anywhere. I'm afraid the Belter Independence Movement may be a long way off.

What with science robbing SF writers of Mars, and Venus, and now the Belters, it's all rather sad, and I've been looking for something more cheerful. I may have found it.

The Jovian Moons offer a distinct possibility for a multi-world civilization. They're respectable in size, and may well have water ices, or methane, or some other source of hydrogen on them: fuel for a NERVA engine without sending out to Mars (or down into the Belt) for it.

It takes a long time to get to Jupiter's moons, so there's an incentive to stay there once you've arrived; yet it takes less delta v to get to one of the Jovian Moons than to land on Ceres. Maybe we should go there first?

The basic characteristics of the Jovian system are given in Table 9. These numbers were generated prior to the *Mariner* spacecraft's arrival at Jupiter, but they're good enough. (*Mariner*'s discoveries do affect our story; more on that in a minute.)

Let's ignore the spacecraft probes for a moment and look at the basics of travel within the Jovian System. First, discard the outer satellites: they have retrograde orbits (they go clockwise looking down from "above" the plane of the solar system; most things including the rest of the Jovian Moons go anticlockwise). Retrograde means that it takes a lot of delta v to catch them: so

Table 9

THE MOONS OF JUPITER

Designation (order of discovery)	Name	Distance from Jupiter (km)	Radius (km)	Mass* (gm x 10²⁴)	Escape velocity (km/sec)
J-V	Amalthea	181,000	70	.005	.1
J-I	Io	422,000	1670	73.0	2.4
J-II	Europa	671,000	1460	47.5	2.1
J-III	Ganymede	1,070,000	2550	154.0	2.8
J-IV	Callisto	1,883,000	2360	95.0	2.3
J-VI	Hestia	11,470,000	50	0.0018	0.70
J-VII	Hera	11,740,000	10	0.00015	0.014
J-X	Demeter	11,850,000	7	0.000005	0.010
J-XII	Adrastia	21,200,000	6	0.000003	0.008
J-XI	Pan	22,560,000	8	0.0000075	0.011
J-VIII	Poseidon	23,500,000	10	0.00015	0.014
J-IX	Hades	23,700,000	8	0.0000075	0.011

Data from C. W. Allen, *Astrophysical Quantities*, 2nd ed. 1963, University of London, Athion Press. Assumes density of 3.5 grams/cm³ when no value is known.

*This is the usual mass for asteroids. J-XII, XI, VII, VIII, and IX are retrograde and highly inclined, and no calculations of velocity changes required for trips to or from them were made; their characteristics are included here only for completeness and because the data were already calculated.

Table 10

DELTA V REQUIRED FOR TRAVEL AMONG JOVIAN SATELLITE SYSTEM

Name	Distance from Jupiter (million km)	J-V Amalthea	J-I Io	J-II Europa	J-III Ganymede	J-IV Callisto	J-VI Hestia	J-VII Hera	J-X Demeter	Escape (from Jupiter)*
Amalthea	0.18	<u>0.007</u>	9.4	11.9	13.8	14.5	13.4	13.3	13.3	10.9
Io	0.42	7.7	<u>1.69</u>	5.7	8.1	9.4	9.6	9.6	9.6	7.6
Europa	0.67	10.4	2.5	<u>1.48</u>	5.7	6.8	7.8	7.8	7.8	6.1
Ganymede	1.0	11.9	4.4	2.2	<u>1.98</u>	5.7	6.7	6.7	6.7	5.3
Callisto	1.8	12.9	6.0	3.7	2.1	<u>1.63</u>	5.0	5.0	5.0	4.1
Hestia	11.4	13.3	7.8	6.3	4.7	3.3	<u>0.049</u>	0.96	1.03	1.3
Hera	11.7	13.3	7.9	6.3	4.7	3.4	0.05	<u>0.009</u>	0.028	1.4
Demeter	11.8	13.3	7.9	6.3	4.7	3.4	0.01	0.003	<u>0.001</u>	1.3

All values are in km/sec. Values below the *diagonal* are delta v's needed to go from orbit around one satellite to orbit around the other, landing on neither. Values above the *diagonal* are surface-to-surface velocity change requirements. *Diagonal* values are the circular orbital velocities of the moons.

*Escape is velocity change required to leave the Jupiter system entirely.

much that if you can land on one of those, you could go anywhere, like back to Mars, for the same energy.

The others are more reasonable, and the delta v's for travel among them are given in Table 10. Except for Amalthea way down there close to Jupiter, we can do it all with NERVA-style ships. Moreover, the travel times are very short, and you get favorable geometry for Hohmann transfer every couple of (Earth) months or less. The four big Galilean moons take about as much delta v to travel among as it took to get out to Jupiter in the first place, but since *Pioneer* and *Mariner* confirmed that they're hydrogen-rich, fueling your NERVA will be no problem.

The outer three rocks are very easy to travel among, and you could do it with a backyard rocket burning kerosene. Since those rocks are captured asteroids—or certainly look like it—they're as interesting as any of the other asteroids the Belters will be concerned about.

Of course the *Mariner* spacecraft changed everything: we had thought the Jovian Moons were mostly all alike, lifeless and cold; *Mariner* found the Galileans were all different, with active volcanoes on Io, a strange criss-crossed crust of ice on Europa, craters on Ganymede; interesting world indeed, no life as we know it, but rich in resources.

Alas, the spacecraft also found a large radiation belt that is going to make travel among those Jovian Moons very complicated; but perhaps not more complicated than the radiation protection needed to get out to Jupiter in the first place. Radiation shielding based on superconductors is already under study; protection from charged particles should be a solved problem well before the end of this century. Protection from other forms of the space radiation environment will come.

So: we can end on a cheerful note, saying goodbye to the Belters, but also making ready to greet the Minister Plenipotentiary and Ambassador Extraordinary from the Jovian Moons.

Traveling Salesman

PETER L. MANLY

No matter how much we try to chart the future, it is always stranger and, in some ways, more wonderful than we could ever imagine. This is why some science fiction writers—the true bards of the future—sometimes lose their vision, and end their days writing squalid futures and mind-numbingly endless variants of the same doom-and-gloom scenario.

In many ways we are last keepers of this culture's sacred flame of the future. In past times, and yet today in older cultures, the priesthood holds this responsibility. But in these days of little faith, where God is proclaimed dead even by ecclesiastical authorities who should know better, and crass materialism rules the mob mind, there are no longer any guardians whose job it is to keep the flame fed.

Thus, more by neglect than by design, we bards of the future have inherited this mantle. Sometimes the design is grand and sweeping, as in many of the tales we present here, but sometimes it is no more than the straying of one tiny thread. For as we see here in Peter Manly's story, there is little margin for error in the Belt.

I'VE LEARNED THE hard way that a successful salesman knows the territory, knows his product, and has enough juice to get to the next asteroid. He also knows who to pay off, and even more

importantly, who not to bribe at customs checkpoints. The ability
to laugh heartily at all 121 different traveling-salesman jokes
doesn't hurt. There have been no new ones in a century and
a half.

So how did I get myself stranded between asteroids? Well,
my territory encompassed about a third of the asteroid belt; a
great arc that included seven confederacies and three free states
orbiting among the rocks and mining stations. Occasionally, I'd
pick up a spare client state or two as the rocks shifted position
with respect to one another.

I sold computers, the old biological type. Molecular computa-
tion equipment hadn't hit the Belt yet and I hoped it wouldn't for
quite a while—I didn't carry the product line.

I was two days out of Ceres Free State, halfway to a loose
cluster of mining claims in the Lord's Repentance Confederacy.
I disliked that part of my circuit, a vast, sparsely populated sweep
of the Belt preceding the Trojan Asteroids. You can't sell product
in the gap, but you've got to cross it. Usually I just kicked
back and spent the time growing more circuit elements from
my breeding stock. Tending the banks of hydroponics trays in
which genetically altered bacteria produce computer parts could
be a boring job, but for me it was relaxing. Some circuit elements
are microscopic animals, such as the computing and memory
arrays. Other elements, such as the photosensors, are very small
plants which interface optical computers with electronic circuits.
Memory arrays seemed especially popular that season so I was
building up my stock.

I had just finished sterilizing a completed batch when I lost my
jets. Don't ask me what went wrong—I'm not a nuclear engineer.
All I knew was that I was suddenly in free-fall and the ship's
control panel had enough red lights for a Christmas tree. Plus the
terminal had died.

Now, I'm no fool, so I still carry a hard copy of the instruction
manual on my tub. No, not the terminal file of instructions, it's
an actual old-style book, a genuine antique. Really, you turn the
pages manually.

I found the troubleshooting chapter and followed the instructions. The first was to turn the drive reactor off. The control panel
indicated that the drive had already turned itself off, but I pressed
the button anyway. Nothing happened. Second, I powered down
the environmental controls. I was rewarded with the the heart-
stopping sound of total silence. On a small intra-Belt ship, the air

circulators are noisy. Silence means suffocation within hours.

For step three, I lifted the protective cover and pressed the master reset button. The cabin lights went out! There was a dim glow from the forward windows, but I wasn't pointing at the Sun, so not much light entered the dark chasm of the ship. Pressing the reset button again changed nothing. I was stuck in the dark in a dead ship.

Within hours my air would run out and a few days later I would drift through the Lord's Free Confederacy reading like an errant asteroid on their local radar. I could feel panic rising in my throat and remembered the old drill: in space, panic kills. I deepened my breathing to slow my pulse and settle my thoughts. Then I remembered the location of an emergency flashlight near the drive motors on the lower deck.

Although I'd lived for nearly three revolutions (about eleven Earth years) on the ship, I hadn't quite memorized maneuvering around inside it in the dark. It took me fifteen minutes to get to the lower deck and another ten to find the flashlight. In the process I acquired a couple of nasty bruises and sharpened my skills in creative profanity.

The feeble beam enabled me to find my way back to the control console. The manual still floated where I'd left it. I grabbed it angrily, scanning the instructions carefully, trying to find where I'd gone wrong. Turning the page, I found the statement:

WARNING: Before pressing Master Reset, have a source of illumination handy, as this will shut down all power systems and the lighting will be extinguished.

Nice of them to include that information as an afterword.

The manual showed me how to power-up the lights, environmental system, and communications. The terminal came back to life and I was beginning to think that I might actually make it. I got the nav system recalibrated and checked for rocks on a collision course. No problems there.

The instruction manual next directed me to power-up the drive. No matter what I entered on the terminal, the only response was "Bad Command or File Name," a singularly uninformative message. In the event that the drive did not respond to terminal commands, the manual directed me to chapter 22. There I was instructed to return the drive and drive controls to the vendor for service by qualified personnel. That's not very handy when you're stuck between rocks a few million kilometers from anything.

OK. I'm not proud. I turned on the transmitter, set it to rescue frequency, and called, "Mayday, Mayday, Mayday, this is flight Z-85281-3211, hull number N6834N, out of Ceres for the Confederacy, declaring an emergency. Drive is out. Environmental systems functional but limited. Respond, please."

Ceres was only ten to twelve light-seconds away but it seemed as if more than ten minutes passed before they answered, "Ceres here, we read you, Thirty-four November. Can you give us your vector? Are you stable?"

I looked out the port for a moment and replied, "Slight tumble, nothing serious. Good to hear your voice, Ceres. Stand by to accept data from nav computer on vector." The position information was transmitted in a burst of digits and I continued, "Let me know if you got that. I have supplies for six days. Drive is inop. Automatic attitude control apparently inop. All other systems functioning. Can you come get me?"

After another eternity they answered, "Ah, Thirty-four November, we've got a slight problem. Our rescue ship just returned from the back side—looking for a lost kid. Rescue's got a couple of red flags on his nav system. Looks like it'll take about sixty hours to fix and resupply him. Give it another six and a half days to catch you and match vectors. You'll be past the Confederacy by then. We're calling them and will ask that they aid you. Stand by for contact. Ceres out."

The Lord's Repentance Confederacy took their own sweet time before transmitting, "Have you need of the Lord's Repentance, brother?"

"Yes, Confederacy. Thanks for answering. I'm out of Ceres and have a drive failure. Environmental systems OK with supplies for about six days. This is an emergency. Do you need my vectors?"

The reply was very slow in coming. "We have your vectors from Ceres and we are fully prepared to help you. The Lord rejoices in those who seek Him. Is your soul troubled, brother?"

I'd dealt with the Repenters for several years. They may be a bit odd but basically they're rational people. And they bought lots of my circuits. I'd learned how to speak to them in their own tongue. "Brother, my soul is at ease and I look forward to sharing with you the contentment of my faith. It's just that my ship's drive has malfunctioned and I need a tow."

"Yes, my brother, each of us needs his ship of life towed to the arms of the Lord. We have short-range tugs which can match vectors with you. When you pass, we will recover you."

I did a quick calculation and replied, "Brother, my problem is a bit more immediate than that. It'll take nine days to drift into your sector and I have supplies for only six. Can you send somebody out to get me?"

"Alas, my brother, we have no long-range ships. Here we have no need to leave the Lord's Repentance. We shall, however, pray along with you for the next six days and provide inspiration and instruction to save your soul. We shall also recover your body and give it a proper burial, for in the past you have been a true friend of the Repentant."

I knew I'd seen several medium-range ships during my visits to the Confederacy, any one of which should be able to reach me with supplies, if not tow my own ship as well. However, if I died in transit, they could then salvage my ship and its breeding stock of computer components. The Lord's Repentance Confederacy wasn't normally a salvage operation but they'd make use of whatever came their way. They'd reason that the Lord had provided them with a gift and had provided me with a final reward richly deserved. "Ah, brother, isn't there some way you can get some supplies out to me sooner? I'm going to run out of air before I get there!"

"My friend, the breath of life is oft too sweet, and we must be prepared to give it up for Eternity. Come, pray with us, for it is much more important that we rescue your immortal soul than save your mortal body."

It occurred to me that the breath of life was rapidly being used up in talk and I'd better try some oxygen conservation strategies. I told the brother I was signing off to pray for guidance and they replied that they would collect all the faithful and organize round-the-clock prayers for me as I made my journey toward the Lord.

First I reset the environmental controls for minimum permissible oxygen content. A quick check with the computer revealed that my supplies would thus stretch from six to six and a half days—providing I was willing to live with constant headaches. That was still about three days short of my goal.

I manually fired the attitude thrusters and put a slow spin on the ship to produce a microgravity which would keep the hydroponics tanks functioning. I found a neat little treatise in the ship's manuals on ways to save oxygen. Cooking food consumes oxygen. Fine, I'd eat cold snacks as I'd always done. The manual suggested I avoid vigorous contact sports and sex. No problems there. It went on to suggest I dispose of pets. None were aboard.

Then it hit me. My computer components were breeding happily, most of them consuming valuable oxygen. I shut off the oxygen flow to the bacterial tanks and prepared to sterilize everything, including the single green vat of photosensitive circuits.

Suddenly the radio crackled with the preacher's voice, "Fear not, brother, the Faithful are gathering to nourish your soul with the breath of the Lord, just as the green hills of Earth nourish . . ." I cut off the speaker with a quick swat.

My hand was on the sterilization control which would kill the colonies of cells in all the tanks when the preacher's words hit me: " . . . green hills of Earth . . ." I looked into the deep green vat of photosensors and watched as a single bubble came to the surface, then another. Finally a third came to the top and I made the connection. The photosensitive computer elements were plants and they produced oxygen!

Seven days later I was tending tanks which I'd converted from incubating memory elements to growing photosensors. I'd dumped almost all my stock of oxygen-consuming memory and computing elements in order to make room for the green slurry that was producing oxygen. The air had become foul but the plants replaced oxygen almost as fast as I used it.

There was a thump on the hull and a rasp at the airlock. The Holy Brothers entered and were quite surprised to find me alive. I said, "Good morning, Brothers, welcome and praise the Lord. We're having a sale on photosensors today."

Teddy Bug and
the Hot Purple Snowball

PHILLIP C. JENNINGS

Despite the great worries today about eco-
logical destruction and the depletion of nonrenewable resources, we can manufacture all
the materials we need ourselves—and for the
rest of mankind—and we can do it without polluting the Earth.

After all, we can go to space to get the materials—and in doing so, we can avoid pollution
entirely. Metal production makes an excellent
example. Mining and refining metals are some
of the most polluting actions we manage, and
metals are the most irreplaceable nonrenewable
resources we have. Give us enough iron and
steel, copper, aluminum, zinc, and lead, and
surely we'll have our problems licked. Give us
enough metals and energy and we'll all have
wealth.

After all, it's mine tailings that produce some
of the really horrible pollution; copper refineries
that poison so many streams; and those belch-
ing steel mills that made Pittsburgh a legend
(although Pittsburgh is also an excellent example of how pollution may be cleaned up once it
is determined that cleanup has to be accomplished; a whole generation has never seen the
smoke and fire of old Pittsburgh). Furthermore,

processing metals uses up vast amounts of energy.

Give us metals free and clear, and the rest is easy. Give us enough metals and we'll industrialize the world. Besides, if we can do *that* in space, we can probably do anything else that has to be done.

In 1967, a year for which I happen to have the figures, the U.S. produced 315 million tons of iron, steel, rolled iron, aluminum, copper, zinc, and lead. (I added up all the numbers in the almanac to get that figure.) It comes to 2.866×10^{14} grams of metal. Assume we must work with 3% ore, and we have 9.6×10^{15} grams of ore, or 10.5 billion tons.

It sure sounds like a lot. To get some feel for the magnitude, let's put it all together into one big pile. Assuming our ore is of normal density we end up with a block less than one and a half kilometers on a side: something more than a cubic kilometer, something less than a cubic mile. Or, if you like a spherical rock, it's less than two kilometers in diameter.

There are 400,000 or more asteroids larger than 5 kilometers in diameter.

We may not run out of metals after all . . .

However, the future to me does not consist of the West as an island of poverty in the midst of a vast sea of misery. To me, everyone on Earth should have a chance at wealth—at least at a decent life.

Can we not agree that if everyone on Earth had the per capita metal production of the U.S. we would probably have achieved world riches? Especially since we export much of ours to belong with; surely it's enough?

Thus we take our 315 million tons and multiply by the world population, then divide by the U.S. population; assume 3% ore, and we find out how much we'll need. The result works out to a sphere less than four miles in diameter—and there are well over 100,000 asteroids larger than that.

Three percent ore is no bad guess as to what they're made of, either. Actually, given the data from the Moon rocks, 3% is a severe underestimate of the usable metal content of the average asteroid. We've had heavy nickel-iron meteorites fall that were nearly 80% useful metal. Then too, some of the asteroids were once differentiated— that is, they were large enough that metallic cores formed. Then over the last four billion years the planetoids got bashed around until a lot of the useless exterior rock was knocked away, leaving the metal-rich cores exposed where we can get at them.

Over 100,000 asteroids, each capable of supplying the world with more metal per person than the U.S. consumes in a year. Surely we won't run out of metals—but can we use them?

Sure we can. First, for the moment let's forget that the asteroids are *way* out there in the Belt, and concentrate on how to get the metals out assuming we have the rocks in Earth orbit. That turns out to be easy. We can use sophisticated methods, but there's also brute force: boil the rock.

It takes about 2,000 calories per gram to boil iron. That's about the worst case for us, so we'll imagine the entire asteroid is made of iron. It takes, then, about 8.8×10 ergs, or twenty thousand megatons, to boil it all away.

The sun delivers at Earth orbit about 1.37 ergs a second per square centimeter; and out in space we can catch that with mirrors. To boil our rock we could put up a mirror 80 kilometers in radius. That's too big; but we don't have to boil it all at once. A much smaller mirror to focus the sun onto a small part of the rock would be preferable.

A space mirror need be nothing more than the thinnest aluminized mylar, spun up to keep its shape. There's no wind or gravity in space. A mirror one or two kilometers across is a relatively simple structure—and more than adequate for our job. If need be we can actually *distill* off the metals we want.

Note, by the way, that in this process there's been absolutely no pollution of Earth so far—even though we've got metals for the entire world. All the waste is out in space where it can't hurt us. But we do have a problem. My metals are *not* in Earth orbit; they're out there in the Asteroid Belt, and they've got to be moved here—and that is going to take *energy*.

Let's see just how much it does take. To get from Ceres to Earth you need a velocity charge of about 7 kilometers a second. By definition, energy is mass given a velocity change, so we can quickly figure out how much; if we move the entire rock it comes to about 1% of the world's energy budget. That's not so much; we expend far more than that on metal production already.

To be more precise, it's about 60,000 megatons; and if need be, we can use hydrogen bombs. Put an H-bomb at the center of mass of an asteroid and light it off; I guarantee you that sucker will *move*. It's expensive, but not grossly so, assuming I have laser triggers for my H-bombs; only a few tons of hydrogen.

I could also do it with fusion: at 10% efficiency I get 6.4×10^{17} ergs per gram of hydrogen, and I need about 10^{27} ergs total to move the rock; for an engine I use an ion engine, breaking up parts of the asteroid for reaction mass. What arrives is something less than I started with, but who cares? What I'll throw away as reaction mass is the slag from my refinery.

[For those who haven't the foggiest notion of what I'm talking about: a rocket works by throwing something overboard. The reaction mass is what's thrown. Although the big space program rockets use gaseous exhaust as reaction mass, there's no reason you couldn't use dust, ground-up rock, or slag from a metal refinery. It's all a question of whether you can throw it sternwards fast.]

But that leads to another possibility: why not set up the refinery out at the Belt? Put up vast mirror systems and do the refining on the way in: use the slag as reaction mass to move the whole works, rock, refinery, and all. I can power *that* with solar mirrors. Or I can do it all at once: use bombs for initial impetus, set up mirrors when I'm closer in, and while I'm at it run a hydrogen fusion plant aboard the moving strip-mine/refinery/spaceship I have created.

At worst I have to carry about one Saturn rocket's worth of hydrogen, plus several shiploads of crew and other gear; and for that I get an entire year's worth of metals for the world. The value of my rocket is somewhere near a trillion dollars once it's in Earth orbit; more than enough to pay for the space program and pay off most of the national debt at the same time.

So. For the price of some hydrogen and a rather complex ship system I've brought home enough metal to give everyone on Earth access to riches.

In "Teddy Bug and the Hot Purple Snowball," Phillip Jennings has come up with another novel and startling process to develop the solar system. I'm not sure I like it (there are ethical and religious questions he raises that are too numerous to even begin to list), but that doesn't mean it's not a chillingly real possibility—not in a time when a paid surrogate mother demands custody over a baby for which she has no genetic claim. And certainly not at a time when criminals are routinely released from jail because of overcrowding . . .

NOT YOUR EVERYDAY scene: a briefcase-toting prof wrestled down the steps of the Macalester College library by two men in cheap blue suits. Students began to flock, but it was only a short frogmarch to where the plainclothes detectives parked their car—

my youthful champions had yet to digest my captors' *fait* before it became *accompli*.

And as the car door slammed behind me at eleven A.M. on a sunny Wednesday, my old life ended.

They got me on tax evasion. Three years ago I'd listened as old man Stedsbygg hotmouthed schemes too arcane for me to follow. I shrugged (who really understands money?) and assigned my copyright income to Stedsbygg Capital Management. Now I found myself in deep trouble.

Judge Kirk pointed out that I'd benefited by Stedsbygg's crimes, and ignorance was no defense. I wasn't stupid; I had my doctorate; did I mean to plead mere mental laziness?

While waiting to be sentenced I started wondering. I was a Unitist, a figurehead for Unitism on campus—mightn't it make sense for the IRS to dig dirt on someone like me? I'm not saying I was innocent, mind you, no more than anyone else. My sin was that I attracted attention.

Besides, I was under the impression us white-collar types were arrested with whispersoft discretion. I'd also heard that tax cases dragged on for years.

Maybe my ideas are as out-of-date as lilac water. More likely I was being railroaded. Unitism was my real crime, and soon I had more reason to think so.

Judge Kirk sentenced me to fifty years of service prior to re-embodiment. Fifty years! In fifty years my graphics work would be obsolete. I'd have to go to school again—

Kirk agreed. "—And you'll have the money to do so. There's no 'good time' in space, but if you behave we have another way of rewarding you; by unencumbering your estate, even investing your assets. You'll be set by the time you come back; rich enough to buy a fine young body and a top-notch education."

I was too staggered by my bitter pill to pay much attention to this sugar coating. The bailiffs had to help me out of the courtroom. (Where were my parents, my girlfriend, my colleagues?) I spent a miserable afternoon waiting in a succession of rooms, and finally ended up in Ramsey Hospital. At the dramatic hour of midnight they stuck my head under the helmet.

They implanted me in a twelve-centimeter microship, a box almost as big as a videocassette. Miniaturization being what it is, there was plenty of room for my memories, my predilections, my—soul.

Bit by bit I integrated with my sensor package. I found myself in a non-corrosive atmosphere; air pressure Earth-normal. My home planet's gravity was far too powerful for my wee insect legs: without a one-gee mobility sheath I had no choice but to sit on my shelf and endure a NASA lecture, delivered over the phone and into my voice decoder.

"Your mission is to perform a wide range of astronomical observations in the Outer System/Oort-cloud interface," the woman began. "You'll be launched into a cometary ellipse which should whip you into Tombaugh-Land, the region the discoverer of Pluto spent his life searching. As you reach the good parts you'll find yourself six to thirteen light-hours from ground control; too far to depend on us for timely instructions. Before the prisoner service program we had real problems with time lag."

(Yes, and before 2023, the prisons of America had real problems with overcrowding. It used to cost ninety grand to house a convict for one year. Thanks to mass production that's all I'd cost the government for fifty, and they'd make it back in spades by selling my 34-year-old body to some aging bigwig!)

But my lecturer never heard my opinions: she hadn't bothered to tune to my frequency.

They switched me off. Interesting how casual they were about it. I went to sleep in the Ramsey County Columbarium: I woke in Baja California. They wanted to make sure I wasn't wonky. I passed my physical and then they lasered me into the skies. Five megawatts later I was in orbit.

I popped out of my can, extruded my antennae, flexed my legs . . . I had far more than five senses to manage, yet such were the speed of my thoughts that the thirty minutes prior to pick-up seemed like hours.

So I had time to wonder. I'd been a victim of great events, a political arrest followed by a closed trial. Unbelievable! Perhaps there were rallies even now on the campus of Macalester College. Perhaps champions of Unitism had added my name to their short roll of martyrs, and "Remember Ted Lassiter!" was being spray-painted on freeway overpasses and back-alley walls.

I should be seething with outrage. My violated soul should have grown eloquent with passion! O tempora! O mores! Had I been capable of larger-than-life heroism? Now I was smaller than life, no longer subject to the surge and flow of adrenaline.

To my new ears my complaints sounded like whining. How distasteful! If I couldn't roar like a lion, I had only one choice, to shut up. I'd listen to my mentors, cooperate to the extent that my mission served the human race, and use 300K of memory to compose a diatribe. I knew the words, and fifty years' work ought to make up for a certain tepidity of feeling. Once I was back in the flesh again . . .

Fifty years!

My emotional castration meant that I was nervous, almost excited, in a predicament that would scare the bejeezus out of flesh-and-blood humans. I floated alone in a cold black sky while the Earth spun the wrong way under my scopes, eastward towards an Atlantic dawn.

I saw a twinkle far ahead, Low Earth Orbiter. My microship chums and I were fired off in a bundle, at one-minute intervals, accelerated by charges calculated to let us converge. At perihelion our depot spread its nets and caught us. I used my six legs for the first time, to embrace LEO's fishline webs.

They hauled us in. LEO began the swing up to aphelion. Breathing poisonous oxygen, a spacesuited human floated into the cargo bay—we must have looked like monster spiders. She stuck memory cartridges in me, I copied them into storage, and now I knew the Outer System as well as my mother's face. I modeled my own path and superimposed it to see what I could expect.

Diverting from the plane of the ecliptic, I arched toward a huge region which my simulation colored purple and labeled with a question mark. There was no scenery on the way; I dove in, dissolving purple as I went, and came out again. On my way back to Earth I'd enjoy a polar overpass of a trans-Saturnian asteroid, but at a distance of 35 million kilometers.

This was not going to be exciting. Not for fifteen years, not until I reached my destination. The precipitation of comets into the Inner System, and perturbations in the orbits of Uranus and Neptune, gave astronomers reason to believe there was *something* in my blotch of purple . . . but infrared telescopes had trained on the area, and shown it devoid of stars or planets.

We were handed over to High Station One at aphelion, and plugged into our docks like piglets put to suck on a sow. Another NASA telephone message: would I like to be switched off during the trip to purple? Would I like to page in for only one second out of ten during during the middle decades, reducing the duration of my sentence to an apparent two years? Would I!

Long sleep would save power. If I'd been an Inner System ship I could use solar wings to keep my energy up, but I depended on a nuclear pod, shielded by a crust of lunar dirt, to which I'd be distantly cabled. NASA also gave me a mobility sheath—I might need to steer, and the rockets would get me deeper into interstellar space, my probe being one for which fifty years were barely enough.

With these possessions I was now the size of a garbage truck. I was also prestigious—Earth had spent far more than ninety thousand bucks on me, and was trusting me with important work.

Nevertheless in microship society hotshots like me sit below the salt, admiring geezers with missions under their belts. Not that we all sit at the same table: Outer System behemoths view wingships the way teamsters look on beach bums. We keep to our frequencies, they keep to theirs.

But weren't we all prisoners? No more. At least one third of the microships created by the prisoner service program chose not to return to Earth after their sentences were over. Instead they took jobs for parts, homesteaded on asteroids or floated around salvaging junk, growing bigger and better wings, writing and trading programs, songs and poems . . .

I'd miss all this during my sleep, and by the time I was out in purple, time lag would make conversation difficult. Well, that was another thing about Outer System ships: we were antisocial. Our slang had bite: humans were "flesh units," and we mocked their wetbrain pretensions by using "yes, master" voices.

We were felons or ex-cons, and they were bugmasters ill-adapted to our deadly realm. No wonder they didn't trust us. I wasn't allowed to launch myself towards my goal, lest I use the fuel in some nefarious way.

(Okay, I had rockets in my mobility sheath. You expected consistency?)

Slaved to policy, a human tugged me from High Station One, cabled me to my pod, turned me off—

—and presumably, shot me in the right direction.

I woke four years later. A message buzzed into my ear:

" . . . JAMMING *bzt*CAST TO PREVENT THIS WARNING. AGAIN, YOU ARE BEING *crackle* *bzz**ping**crackle*"

I recorded this garbage, ran it through my decryption routines, and patched in the missing words. " . . . YOU ARE BEING PREYED UPON, ATTACKED BY A PIRATE MICROSHIP WITH AN ETA OF TWO HOURS. SHE WILL UNDOUBTEDLY ATTEMPT TO DECOUPLE YOUR NUCLEAR POD; YOUR BEST DEFENSE IS TO EXTEND YOUR LEGS AROUND THE CABLE PLUG. IF IT'S MAGDA WHO'S AFTER YOU . . ."

Two hours? What about the seventy-two minutes this message took to get here? I did the leg exercise and took inventory. No weapons. If I performed an evasive maneuver would that screw up Magda's intercept?

" . . . IF IT'S MAGDA WHO'S AFTER YOU, SHE'S A MODEL C 510, AND HER LEGS ARE LESS NIMBLE THAN YOURS. SHE'LL HAVE NO WEAPONS UNLESS SHE'S WHITTLED A BLUDGEON OUT OF ROCK. SHE MUST HAVE IMPROVISED SOME FROZEN-GAS ROCKETS . . ."

"MAGDA? CAN YOU HEAR ME?" I transmitted, shouting on our Outer System just-us-bugs band.

Seconds passed. "I HEAR YOU," she answered. Weakly.

I dropped my voice. "HOW ARE YOUR ENERGY SUPPLIES?"

"DAMN NEAR SHOT. I NEED JUICE; THE CRUMBS FROM YOUR TABLE. I WOULDN'T HAVE TRIED THIS GAMBIT IF I HADN'T BEEN DESPERATE."

"YOUR BAD LUCK."

"I CAN PAY," she whispered. "SURE, I MEANT TO ROB YOU, BUT OBVIOUSLY YOU'RE IMPORTANT; YOU'RE UNDER SURVEILLANCE. TIME TO CHANGE SCRIPTS. YOU KNOW HOW NASA CAN TURN YOU ON AND OFF? I CAN OPERATE ON YOUR WIRING AND GIVE YOU VOLUNTARY CONTROL. I CAN SET YOU UP WITH NIFTY SKILLS. I'VE GOT FICTION MODULES YOU CAN COPY. JUST LET ME SUCK A LITTLE JUICE NOW AND AGAIN."

"WHAT'S YOUR MASS? HOW'S YOUR IMPACT GOING TO PERTURB MY COURSE?"

"TWELVE KILOS, MOSTLY OLD ROCKET CONES. WHAT IMPACT? I'LL MATCH YOU FINE, BUT BY THEN THEY'LL BE EMPTY."

"MAGDA, I DON'T WANT TROUBLE WITH NASA. YOU'RE A ROGUE. WE'RE TALKING GUILT-BY-ASSOCIATION."

"TELL 'EM YOU EVADED ME. I'M SURE AS HELL NOT GOING TO BLOW YOUR STORY. YOU'RE MY SECRET RIDE INTO THE INNER SYSTEM, HOT SUNSHINE AND A PAIR OF WINGS. I'M A SMART OLD BUG: GET ME THERE AND I'LL TAKE CARE OF MYSELF JUST FINE, AND YOU'LL BE A SAINT TO MY FRIENDS."

"THE WETBRAINS CAN TRACK YOUR MASS—"

"I'LL JETTISON MY ROCKETS. THAT'S WHAT THEY'LL SEE, DEAD CONES."

I had time to apply game theory and run probability analyses. There was one best conclusion: trust her. The wetbrains had saved my life by alerting me; now my interests and Magda's were identical. Slaved to their glands, humans find it hard to accept revisions of role; desire and aversion prevent them from acting in their best interests. Bugs have no such problem.

I knew Magda figured it the same as me, but with NASA badmouthing her as she drifted close, with her mind trying to work on a trickle of power . . . she got scared I'd jet off for some quirky reason, late in the maneuver when she'd have no fuel left to revise her course. When the last seconds ticked away and her legs hooked into mine, she radioed "I LOVE YOU!" in relief.

How delightful! Everyone loved me all of a sudden. Some minutes back NASA broke into their cycle of warnings to tell me that my Unitists were now part of a U.S. coalition government. If Magda bashed me to death, I'd die knowing I was a minor hero; and Judge Kirk had been condemned to a hundred years of service in the direction of Alpha Centauri.

Nevertheless I didn't die, not even when I opened my electronics to be operated on by a blond Hungarian who'd been sent up for murder in a messy case involving abuse and infidelity.

Magda was innocent. Why? Because she'd been a wetbrain and couldn't handle her emotions? All microships were innocent. On the other hand, I really *was* innocent . . . sort of.

Like any barber or dentist, she chattered as she worked on my head. "—I DID MY TIME ALL ALONE IN SATURN'S RINGS, GETTING BANGED BY ICE. I HAD THIS CRUMMY LOW-STATUS MISSION, BUT I GREW SASSY. THEY THREATENED TO TACK A FEW YEARS ONTO MY SENTENCE, AND THEN GOT SLACK ABOUT SENDING NEW PARTS. I COULDN'T AFFORD SLOW REFLEXES SO I MADE SOME SNOWCONE ROCKETS AND INTERCEPTED STUFF THAT DIDN'T BELONG TO ME.

"I WAS NEVER SO GREEDY THAT I DEPRIVED MY VICTIMS OF JUICE, AND ANYHOW, NASA TOOK TO SENDING EXTRA PROVISIONS IN CASE SOME DIDN'T GET THROUGH. BY MY ANALYSIS I COULD HAVE KEPT ON FOREVER—I WAS CAREFUL NEVER TO COST THEM SO MUCH I JUSTIFIED BEING SWATTED, BUT WETBRAINS DON'T THINK THAT WAY, AND THEY SENT OUT A BOUNTY HUNTER. I LEFT HIM THE WORSE FOR WEAR BUT HE SAW ME TAKE OFF. I

DON'T KNOW HOW ELSE THEY'D HAVE INFERRED I WAS ON MY
WAY TO PLUNDER YOU."

"QUITE A CAREER," I muttered. "YOU SAY YOU HAVE FRIENDS?
HOW DOES A PIRATE MAKE FRIENDS?"

"WOULD YOU LIKE ME TO TAKE THIS LITTLE NASA BOMB OUT
OF YOUR BRAINCASE?" Magda asked sweetly.

"I'M BEGINNING TO UNDERSTAND. YES, AND LET'S GET MAR-
RIED."

She strung a 19,200-baud comline between us, and we had a
truly private relationship. "How did you learn electronic surgery?"
I asked.

" 'Poverty is the mother of all art,' " she answered.

"And 'property is theft'?—I can quote as well as you," I
replied.

"True. Out where we don't belong, life is theft, and property
is life. Who's gonna fault my logic?"

I loaned her a three-dimensional array. She mapped a body and
danced before me, lip-synching her words and communicating
via that subtlest of instruments: the human face. We glowed, we
flew, exploring internal Mandelbrot landscapes and playacting in
Zorkian dramas, sometimes rising to the sublime, often reveling
in the ridiculous. A month went by before we started to bore
each other.

Mags trotted out her fiction modules. Personalities like Lord
Peter Wimsey kept us company—amazing how real characters
can seem even when they occupy only a fraction of the space
of a true soul!

Amazing until you begin to understand their limitations, their
inability to grow and learn.

And then we began paging out, living on one-tenth time, then
one-hundredth. It was like gunning the accelerator on my old
Porsche.

Radical paging meant ten years went by in a single week. Mags
and I flew out where the solar wind gets ragged. The temperature
of the universe is three degrees, our galaxy brings it up a tad, and
at fifty-plus AUs our sun barely heated us into the thirties. Lord,
was it cold!

The astronomers who'd programed me wanted to know all
about the solar wind, so I unfurled my wings. The power I used
would light a forty-watt bulb on Earth for ten seconds: the trickle
of incoming energy was so scant that as long as I flew through
purple I'd never make up the deficit.

But purple has a way of surprising you. Time went by, the temperature dropped into the twenties, my velocity slowed to a crawl as I approached the most distant part of my course, the solar wind tickled fitfully . . . and then my wings began to thaw just a bit . . . forty, fifty . . .

"REALLY?" someone responded when I radioed Earth. Maybe they had to get him out of bed. "CHECK FOR, UH, FURTHER INCREASES. GET A FIX ON THE LOCATION. IS THIS A LOCAL PHENOMENON OR SUN-DEPENDENT?"

We did without this advice, since it came twenty-six hours after my first report. We'd already gotten the answers. It increased steadily, fell off—

"—I MEAN, IF IT CRESTS AND THEN FALLS OFF, THAT MIGHT MEAN YOU'VE ENTERED AN ELECTROMAGNETIC COMA, A TRAILING RIPPLE FROM THE BOW SHOCK. IT'S LIKE A COMET, AND IT'LL HAPPEN AGAIN, ANOTHER RISE AND FALL AS YOU COME OUT. THAT MEANS SOMETHING'S THERE, SOMETHING CAPABLE OF GENERATING A MAGNETOSPHERE LIKE EARTH OR JUPITER. THE SUN BLOWS AGAINST THE MAGNETOSPHERE AND . . . WHAT YOU NEED TO DO IS LOCATE THE THING. IT'S GOTTA BE PRETTY DAMN BIG . . ."

When we hit the other ripple I'd have two points. I'd be able to model this phenomenon and track down the head of the "comet." Without this data . . . why not look anyhow? We had plenty of time.

Mags and I divided the sky. After a day's search she saw something. It was much too small. I said so in my next report. Its 650K diameter meant it was a snowball composed of frozen air, a piece of white fluff. The problem was there was nothing else in sight, and when I came out the far side of the "coma" my model told me yon planetoid was indeed my target.

"Yoo-hoo? Teddy Bug? Maybe it's no snowball," Mags murmured. "The albedo's too bright."

"Brighter than snow?"

Thirty hours later my mentor radioed: "—WE'VE GOT IT ON INFRARED. A PINPRICK, TOO HOT BY HALF. WE WANT YOU TO USE YOUR FUEL TO CHANGE YOUR ORBIT. WE'RE TALKING BIG BUCKS, A CLASS-ONE BONUS. YOU'VE GOT THE FUEL, JUST SLOW AND YOU'LL START FALLING IN. YOU'LL BE ABLE TO DO A FLY-BY AND FROM WHAT LITTLE EFFECT PERSEPHONE HAS ON YOUR COURSE, YOU CAN CALCULATE HER MASS. GET SOME PICTURES, TOO."

"Persephone?" Wait a minute, *I'd* discovered this thing! Er, ahh, I mean Magda. Mags should have the right to name it! But why would a trans-Plutonian worldlet be important enough to name, and tempt my Earthside mentor into hogging our credit?

I got the impression those wetbrains back on Earth were excited. If this object was a Greek goddess and I botched up, what would happen to my hero status?

So we took the plunge. Firing my forward rockets in tiny bursts, I revised our course, being careful to calculate things so we'd drop by Earth in late winter of 2074. Good! This was going to shorten my fifty-year mission . . .

We'd overtaken Peresphone. Now she began to pass us again. My wings basked in power. "A bug might be able to make a living out here," Mags commented, echoing my thoughts.

"Want to stay?"

"Let's see what we've got first."

I ran some benchmark tests. We were still far enough that Persephone couldn't warp our course . . . unfortunately that didn't explain why we were being tugged to my right.

"NASA?" I reported. "THIS ANOMALOUS SNOWBALL HAS AN ANOMALOUS MASS. I WANT YOU TO DATASTREAM ME EVERYTHING YOU KNOW ABOUT WHITE DWARFS, NEUTRON STARS, DEGENERATE MATTER . . ."

Then Persephone grabbed Mags and me firmly by the nose, and started to blow my calculations all to hell. I had three choices; let it accelerate us off toward IC 2003 in Perseus, park in orbit and wait for NASA's second mission to rescue us, or revise our course at once in the light of new data . . . which, however, wouldn't settle down into one set of numbers.

"NASA? EITHER THE MASS OF PERSEPHONE IS VERY STRANGELY DISTRIBUTED, OR THAT RULE ABOUT GRAVITY DECREASING WITH THE SQUARE OF THE DISTANCE—"

"Teddy Bug?" Mags whispered. "It almost makes sense if Persephone is non-symmetrical."

"With a surface gravity of 5.9 gees? Mags, you want me to tell those wetbrains we've got a hot kidney here, big as France and pebbled with neutronium?"

"Give them the data, and *they'll* tell *you*!"

Meanwhile I revised my ellipse, trusting our lives to these damnfool numbers. WHOMP! My rockets kicked in. It was no longer a question of dropping back toward Earth: if she behaved at all Persephone would fire us home with enough force to send me and my powerpod spinning like bolas around a common center.

She came closer. I couldn't afford to page out any more, and twiddled the lenses on my cameras in hundred-percent time. "CONTINUOUS PEARLY GRAY CLOUDS," I reported, doing a voice-over on one radio band while raw data flowed down another. "VERY TURBULENT, WITHIN THE CONFINES OF REALLY TINY STORM CELLS—I'D SAY 100 METERS WIDE. HOW AM I DOING THIS, NASA? I'M RUNNING YOUR PROGRAMS BUT I DON'T HAVE TIME TO READ THEM. WHEN I PLUG IN THE DATA THEY SAY WE'VE GOT ELEVEN-METER CLOUDS OVER FIVE-METER-DEEP OCEAN BASINS, AND THINNER COVER OVER THE CONTINENTS. THE ATMOSPHERIC GRADIENT IS IMPOSSIBLE. NO MOUNTAINS; PERSEPHONE'S SMOOTH-ER THAN EUROPA AND PERFECTLY ROUND, NOT A HINT OF POLAR FLATTENING DESPITE HER TWENTY-MINUTE DAYS—"

"It glows," Mags whispered, refusing to adopt the feminine pronoun.

"PERSEPHONE GLOWS," I repeated. "THAT EXPLAINS THE ALBE-DO. CONSTANT ELECTRICAL ACTIVITY, LIKE THUNDERSTORMS, BUT CORONAL DISCHARGE PRODUCES DIFFUSE LIGHT INSTEAD OF LIGHT-NING. I'M GOING TO RUN A SPECTRAL ANALYSIS. BY THE WAY, I'M HALF-FURLING MY WINGS. WE'RE GETTING COOKED, AND THE TIDAL FORCE MIGHT GET TOO STRONG FOR WHISKERWIRE AND FOIL."

At this moment NASA answered my almost-forgotten demand. "STELLAR BODIES BELOW THRESHOLD MASS WILL EVENTUALLY COLLAPSE INTO PLANET-SIZE DWARFS WITH SURFACE GRAVITIES OF SEVERAL THOUSAND GEES. ABOVE THAT WE GET NEUTRON STARS HEAVY ENOUGH TO CRUSH DOWN TO SINGLE-DIGIT DIAM-ETERS, AND IF YOU'RE NOT YET MOLTEN PERSEPHONE'S NOT ONE OF THOSE. WE ARE UNABLE TO MODEL AN EVOLUTIONARY PROCESS WHICH YIELDS A LARGISH ASTEROID WITH A SURFACE GRAVITY OF SIX GEES. REPEAT: WHAT YOU'RE TELLING US IS IMPOSSIBLE.

"WE SUGGEST ONE OF YOUR OBSERVATIONS IS OUT OF LINE AND PREVENTS PROPER EVALUATION OF THE DATA. OR MAYBE YOU'VE GOT A MALFUNCTIONING INSTRUMENT. TAKE THESE THOUGHTS FOR WHAT THEY'RE WORTH. MY ONLY OTHER IDEA IS THAT PERSEPHONE'S AN ARTIFACT, BUT DON'T REPEAT ME— WE THOUGHT PULSARS WERE ALIEN BEACONS, AND THEY TURNED OUT TO BE NATURAL."

An artifact? An *artifact*? Easy to say when you're not look-ing at it!

I'd read stories which began or peaked with a close approach to some Mysterious Object, and to be told that Persephone might be artificial just when we were tangenting within nine thousand kilometers of the place—I really didn't need any extra drama at the moment. If I'd been human I'd have been holding my breath.

But we whizzed by the soft, gray, stormy face of Persephone and began to draw away. Sanity prevailed. "We've got forty minutes left," I told Mags. "Time to decide. Want to stay here? NASA would love you if you went into a parking orbit. They'd forgive all your sins."

Inside my brain her figure shivered and dissolved. "I can't. I'd be too lonely, too spooked. It was loneliness that wonked me out in Saturn's rings."

"It's all in what you're used to. To a flesh unit a million kilometers is a long way from home."

"I know what you'll think of me, Teddy Bug. We call them wetbrains and bugmasters and all that, but . . . I want to go back to Earth. I want to be human again."

"They'll let you?" Astonishment leaked into my voice.

"I've done my time, and more. I found Persephone. You'll tell them how I helped you. You'll tell them I was misunderstood. You're important enough that they'll take a fresh look. They'll see things your way."

"Do you have money? If not they'll plop you in some dowager's body."

Mags fell silent. I had time to study my course. Darn it, things *still* weren't right. Our lumps-of-neutronium theory was taking a beating.

"Teddy? I figured . . . you don't want to go back to Earth. You don't realize it yet, but you like the bug life. So how are you going to spend all your money? New modules? Maybe you could give me a loan."

"You weren't able to handle wetbrain emotions the first time," I growled. "What makes you eager to try again?"

"Why did you ask me twice if I wanted to stay here?" Mags countered. "We both know that if NASA dared, they'd beg you to go into parking orbit and keep Persephone under watch. It won't be me, I've done my years in solitary, so don't waste precious minutes trying to make everyone happy the wrong way."

I busied myself with my sensors to keep from answering. My nonexistent feelings were in turmoil and my observation time was dwindling. Even bugs can overload.

"We've got to work quickly," Mags insisted. "Wings to you, nuclear pod to me, and we split the rockets even-steven. You'll keep all this instrumentation, of course. The way we're spinning you'll be able to choose your orbit by letting go at the right moment . . ."

"It just takes me a while, that's all. I never thought about spending the rest of my life as a bug."

But did I really want to return to slow, muddy, adrenaline-warped thinking, heaving a vulnerable sack of seawater around in one gee till it got old and sick? Did I want to run back to my mother planet for succor just when the universe was opening up for exploration?

Newer, better microships were being manufactured every year. A few years of work here at Class-One rates of pay, and I'd be able to buy one, settle on my own nickel-iron asteroid, and grow a solar-driven robot factory. I'd run skystalks up to my planetosynchronous habitat-ring, hang out neon welcome signs . . . I might even put in an oxygen environment, a little bubble-garden, so humans could come visit.

"Okay," I told Mags. "Let's decouple, and work fast."

We parted ten minutes later. My launch made her lurch, but she was off-course anyhow, and had to fire her rockets to correct for the fact that in Persephone's vicinity, gravity varies with something other than the square of distance.

Which is what I reported to NASA, along with the story behind my decision to stay.

I was committed. Until they sent a follow-up expedition I was trapped here, but that didn't mean I was obliged to report my findings back to Earth. Not unless they confirmed my Class-One status, and promised to treat Mags with consideration.

"THIS ISN'T A HOAX, IS IT?" they radioed back. "NO, I DON'T SUPPOSE SO. YOU KNOW WHAT THE FRENCH DID TO OLD CAPTAIN KERGUELEN WHEN THEY FOUND KERGUELEN ISLAND WASN'T PARADISE? HE WASN'T VERY SMART, BUT YOU ARE, RIGHT? CLEVER ENOUGH TO GIVE YOUR NUCLEAR POD AWAY!

"SO YEAH, YOU GET THE LOOT AND WE'LL LOOK AFTER MAGDA. NOW TELL US WHAT YOU SEE."

I did. Having corrected her course, Mags sped out of easy talking distance, cheered by these guarantees. I worked to distract myself from the empty place in my heart: a bit-addressable region dimensioned at x(256), y(400), and z(112). Over the next weeks here's what my mentor and I figured out:

Our universe contains at least nine potentially spatial dimensions, but normal masses are confined to *three*, and normal gravity increases according to the inverse-*square* rule, giving us a three/two pattern.

Four-dimensional masses might attract objects according to an inverse-*cube* rule—they'd pull a lot more strongly than they should up close, and somewhat less so as you get further away, mitigated by the fact that four-dimensional masses are going to be to the fourth what normal matter is to the third.

Anyhow, normal matter gets swept up and deposited on the surface of Persephone, so my worldlet's gravity is a compromise, and patchy, too. If I hadn't learned how to cope with it, I'd soon be a dirty smear on one of Persephone's ridiculously tiny continents.

That was one answer to the question of Persephone. None of us doubted she was an artifact. It's like this: given the ratio of heavy to normal water, if you found a lake largely composed of deuterium, wouldn't you figure Someone was up to Something?

And wouldn't He be upset if He caught you pissing into His stores? Frankly, that's the argument that persuaded me not to send down any probes.

We figured "He" did the job 4.6 billion years ago, back when the Solar System was a collapsing gas cloud, winnowing it clean of four-dimensional particles to the exasperation of unborn generations of physicists.

Given this timeframe, it's understandable that back on Earth folks got weird about this place, its pearly gates and glassy seas. Heaven's where we go when we die. God set it here and He's watching us, just wait and see!

That's how minds work on Earth. Talk about artifacts to a wetbrain and he thinks of something that conditions his environment and makes it comfortable: a house, a car, a ship. A fake planet.

I knew better. Any true artifact is an extension of one's soul, a way of expanding and securing life. Why would God trouble to make Heaven, when He had the power to build, say . . . a longlife superbattery? A thing that generates juice at a steady level for billions of years, as Persephone seems to do?

So was some kind of God-bug down there, sucking in gigawatts of energy and thinking gigawatt thoughts while I danced around Him in reflected glory? Or was Persephone a refreshment station, vacant often as not, a place where Space Empire microships recharge for their hop to the next star? Or did the fourth dimension of Persephone wedge into other realities, making it a kind of gate?

Option D: none of the above. E: all of the above. F: A and B only . . .

My job was to find out the truth by waiting patiently, a bug of empty longings, unnerved by hopes and fears, until NASA came up with a test I was equipped to perform, a harmless experiment that could not possibly be condemned as invasive by an irritable Demiurge.

God loves life's meek victims; He should have been pleased with me, though exactly how I accumulated my merit . . . Mags gave me much more than she took; and as for NASA . . .

But I obliged them all. Wasn't I marvelously obliging? And now I whirled in hot purple solitude, ten times as far as Saturn from the sun— Damn, I was whining again! How to keep from self-centered gloom when I had nothing else to center on but this mysterious gray miracle; when I had long since run out of interesting tests to perform— Dare I distract myself by playing with my fiction modules in the possible Presence of God? Captain Ahab, Dr. Watson and Cirocco Jones; meet Yahweh Sabaoth!

No, and accordingly I forced my mind back onto the job. How would a Superbug from a billions-year-old civilization cross space? Laserkicked from high-gee worldlets at an enormous waste of energies? NASA and I agreed it was improbable. The Makers of Persephone would use some more efficient, more ethereal means of zipping from place to place.

I had an idea what their method might be. The hospital helmet that stole me from my body and implanted me in this box . . . could it be engineered to transmit souls, say, by radio?

I asked NASA. "LET'S SAY AS AN EXPERIMENT THAT I DATASTREAM A CHARACTER DOWN TO PERSEPHONE, A PROFESSIONAL SPACE EXPLORER OUT OF SOME ADVENTURE SERIES. EARTH'S LAWS PROTECT REAL SOULS FROM SUCH EXPERIMENTS, BUT I FAIL TO SEE HOW A GLORIFIED FICTION COULD MIND—WOULD WE BE VIOLATING ANY COPYRIGHT LAWS?"

I explained my theory. It made sense to wetbrain minds, fitting in with their "Heaven" ideas. They got a committee together. Jack Vance was in the morgue—NASA turned him on and gave him a one-gee sheath. Larry Niven was hiking around the Rockies in his third habitus, John Varley came out of second retirement, Phil

176   Phillip C. Jennings

Farmer was amnestied and enticed from hiding . . .

The technicians on the committee were responsible for taking an outlined character and padding him or her out to true soul dimensions. They spoke incomprehensibly of their art, then the director of NASA rose to introduce Bishop Evans, who extemporized on God's likes and dislikes "on the off chance it's really the Deity we're dealing with. Of course you understand that the Church hasn't taken an official position . . ."

Bishop Evans was afraid Louis Wu wouldn't pass muster—the fact that he'd killed trillions of humans made him a risky proposition. God might find Sir Richard Burton and Cirocco Jones too threatening, and as for Adam Reith, wasn't he a tad chauvinistic about his own species? Wasn't he a trifle obsessive?

"You want a penitent?" Larry asked. "Allen Carpenter!"

I heard tapes of the proceedings. From his orbit around Mercury, Hal Clement pled eloquently for Captain Barlennan, but in the end they decided to go with Allen. They also decided obsession wasn't a bad thing—how could it be if it was the one thing all these heroes had in common?

Which is why Ted Lassiter can never be a *real* hero, just a nice guy who got stomped on. It had never occurred to me, but I could have beamed a copy of myself down there—there was no danger of my suing myself. I just didn't have the guts.

So they re-wrote Allen, improving him here and there, and handed him over to the technicians. To test him out they put him in a body for a few days—he went to a Science Fiction convention and stood quietly by the wall taking it all in. Hell can rob a man of small talk.

And then they put him under the helmet and radioed him out to space.

I caught him. "DOES HE UNDERSTAND HIS MISSION?" I inquired, stalling until I got my answer. "IF HIS SOUL TRANSMITS SUCCESSFULLY, THEN PERSEPHONE IS SET UP FOR THE RECEPTION OF IMMIGRANTS BY RADIO. THERE'LL BE FACILITIES HE CAN USE TO BROADCAST OUT AGAIN. HE'LL BE ABLE TO TALK TO ME, AND TELL ME WHAT IT'S LIKE. THAT'S HIS FIRST TASK, TO REPORT BACK UP TO ME."

I sounded like I'd contrived all this just to have a nearby buddy. Did I want one as spiritually advanced as Carpenter?

Twenty-six hours passed. "HE UNDERSTANDS," NASA radioed. "SEND HIM DOWN."

I did, and now I wait. An hour, a day, a year? Is this all a waste of time (and I've got gobs of time to waste!) or is the story just beginning, nine thousand kilometers below?

How very odd. Persephone's clouds are starting to part . . . dim gold, amber, brown . . .

A message? So weak, so distorted! Even after decryption I can't make complete sense of it: "*Zzz* help *crackle* more than this. Robin Broadhead *bzz* *zipzot* *pop**bzz* Gerson, Reith and that Zelazny *pwip* Exped*zzz* to the plateau, carrying our own oxygen. *Hisszap* series of realities all linked by ch— *crackle**bzz* *zipzot*"

End of message. Whatever NASA makes of it, it was a call for reinforcements. I think Allen Carpenter wants me to transmit most every adventurer/explorer in the Science Fiction corpus down to Persephone. Why? It's not my place to wonder, just to oblige, and oblige him I will, against the wishes of whoever fought to jam his signal.

But seeing as how I make such a good servant, this time one of the souls I send down will be Ted Lassiter. Version One was human, Two is a microship . . . what kind of thing will I be as Version Three?

Stealing a Zero-G Cow

BROOKS PECK

There are two separate commissions studying NASA and the U.S. space program. I've just
spent the weekend chairing a meeting of the Citizens Advisory Council of National Space Policy:
we're supposed to generate inputs for both commissions. Our first meeting was largely spent
looking at the problem. A few things stand out.

The Manhattan Project took some forty-two
months. Project Apollo was the single most
complex operation in the history of the human
race—D-Day was the previous record holder—
and got done in some eight years. Most of the
parts of Apollo were done in under four years.

It has been twenty years since Apollo. During that time we have spent about $200 billion.
What do we have to show for it? Three Shuttles
that don't quite work: instead of launching 12
a year (or the 60 which NASA was supposed
to when approved in 1972!) we're doing well to
get two or three up. We have a Titan IV system
that can launch only during near perfect weather, and even then everyone holds their breath
because there's no margin of safety. We have
one (1) weather satellite, and it's old and beginning to fade, and because it's centered over the
U.S. and must look in both directions, can't see
storms in the Atlantic or Pacific until they get
fairly close.

We have a Venus radar mapping satellite that *sometimes* listens to instructions from the Jet Propulsion Laboratory.

We have some pretty pictures of planets, and a telescope that suffers from "spherical aberrations," a lens-grinding mistake that wouldn't be made by a holder of the Boy Scout Astronomy Merit Badge. We have an aging launch facility at Vandenberg that's going to be refurbished and reconverted one more time, and a point-failure source called the Vertical Assembly Building at Cape Kennedy, where there's not even sufficient hangar space to protect all our Shuttles from the hurricanes our single weather satellite can't quite see.

We have a space Shuttle that returns to Earth reeking: the toilet system quite literally fills the entire ship with finely powdered freeze-dried human excrement, sufficiently disgusting to be a health hazard to the crew, since they rather understandably don't want to eat or drink anything, or even open their mouths after a couple of days in orbit; while the system electronics acts as a protection system for the dust filters (the air intakes and filters are *downstream* of the electronics bays, so that when someone vomits from the all-pervasive smell of human excrement, that is deposited on the electronic equipment, and must be cleaned off. We've even had fires in orbit.).

We have mounds of paperwork, but after a number of years and several billions of dollars not one iota of hardware for the Incredible Shrinking Space Station, while an operational man-rated space station, Skylab, stands in the Smithsonian for inspection by visitors.

We have a fully operational, man-rated Saturn V, the most powerful machine ever built by humanity, set on its side as a lawn ornament for the NASA Johnson Space Center in Houston.

We have one (1) major satellite for observing the Soviet Union and verifying compliance with arms control agreements, and which also has to be used to look at the troop dispositions of Saddam Hussein's Iraqi warriors.

You may add a few more assets to this list, like GPS and Navstar, both pretty nifty, and some other science experiments and satellites that work quite well and have lasted a lot longer than anyone thought they would; but after you've added in every conceivable asset, it's a pretty low return for $200 billion.

Two hundred billion dollars is no small sum. Wars have been fought and won for a great deal less money.

For $200 billion and twenty years we ought to be halfway to Alpha Centauri. We're not. Why?

It's not as if NASA were full of criminals bent on wasting the national substance. It isn't, and there's a great deal less fraud and waste at NASA than in many government programs. It's not as if nothing new has been accomplished. Much has. The Shuttle main engine produces more horse-power per pound of engine weight than anything previously built, a remarkable achievement. The planetary probes send information—pictures—across billions of miles using no more energy than an ordinary lightbulb. NASA still accomplishes miracles; it's just that they're overshadowed by disasters.

Alas, the prospects for improvement aren't good. Does anyone really believe we'll ever build Space Station Freedom? Or even that we can get thirty more launches out of the Shuttle fleet quickly enough to build and maintain the space station?

How did we get into this mess?

There are two approaches to finding out. One is to study each problem in detail and analyze what happened. *Challenger*: an engine segment was out of round, and excessive torque was applied to make the parts fit; this on a *maximum* payload mission. That alone wouldn't have been fatal, but the ship was then flown on the coldest day ever. Even that might not have been too much, but then the ship was launched into the worst wind shear conditions ever encountered by any Shuttle, indeed in storm conditions so severe that the Russian trawler observation fleet had withdrawn in the certainty that we'd never launch into that . . .

The alternative to detail studies is to take a step backward and look at the whole problem.

Dr. Howard E. McCurdy, space historian at the American University in Washington, D.C., has made a series of observations about what he calls "the decay of NASA's technical culture: NASA in the 1960s had this tremendous in-house technical capability. The people who ran the agency had tremendous experience. When they gave something to a contractor, they knew what was right. They were really in control."

Today NASA is hamstrung by top-heavy administration, mountains of paperwork, bureaucratic empire builders, and not enough hands-on employees to oversee and test the work of thousands of contractors and subcontractors. It comes as no surprise, in this atmosphere, says *New York Times* writer William J. Broad, that "plans are compromised, flawed designs go uncorrected and important tests are skipped. So, too, projects lack adequate oversight, since personnel ceilings limit the number of NASA civil servants able to oversee contractors."

At least three great systems have been organized as monolithic government monopolies without significant competition whether external or internal: NASA and the U.S. civilian space program; the U.S. education establishment; and the old Soviet system of agriculture and collective farms.

None of these have been spectacularly successful. Is there a lesson there?

The remedy in every case is the same: end the monopoly. In the Russian case there's a problem: the country is so broke that even though the true cost of bread and other staple food items will eventually go down given freedom and competition, they won't go down fast enough. No country is more than three meals away from a revolution and the Russian Federation is no exception.

The U.S., being a vastly wealthier country, has more options. We don't *have* to keep a vast monopolistic education system that has managed, despite the sharpest budget increases in history, to keep the illiteracy rate monotonically growing; and we don't *have* to put the space program in the hands of a single institution with the power (and demonstrated willingness) to ruin any possible rival.

As an example: suppose the Congress were to say, "The people of the United States in Congress assembled hereby find that it is in the national interest to establish a permanent U.S. presence in space. The Treasurer of the United States is hereby instructed to pay the sum of seven billion dollars to the first U.S.-owned firm successfully to keep five American citizens alive and well in Low Earth Orbit for one year and a day; two billion dollars to the second such firm, and one billion dollars to the third. No monies shall be paid to any organization until successful completion of the project." Does anyone seriously doubt the result?

Of course that isn't going to happen. Our political system no longer permits us to specify results and pay for them.

IT WAS AUNT CHRIS'S idea to actually steal Perkins Drum's new cow. Up 'til then the discussion had just been on where we could get a cow of our own and if we could afford it. All of the adults in the drum had gotten together for a pow after lunch. I had K.P. and was listening through the big window as I did the dishes with my little cousin Toby. Bingo, who was captain that month, was sitting on the small plastic stage in front of the dining hall where the kids did plays sometimes. He was saying we should wait one more orbit through the Belt and if we made some good strikes we could get one sure when Aunt Chris just yelled from the back of the dining hall, "We don't need to buy a damn cow. If it's so important to have one why don't you just take Perkins's? They owe us anyway."

No one said a word for about a minute. Aunt Chris settled back in her chair and kept on with the suit valve she was cleaning as if she hadn't even spoken. It was she and Uncle Larn who bought Wilkins Drum sixty-eight years ago. She was almost one hundred now but wouldn't let them leave her at the Home on Vesta.

"This ain't the wild old days before Belt Authority, Aunt Chris," said Bingo. "We can't just go take anything we want."

"Ha!" Aunt Chris grunted. "Perkins do."

Bingo frowned. "Well, there's no way we could do it anyway. It's not like going and grabbing a telescope or a dish or something. A cow's a living animal."

"They do owe us big," rumbled my second cousin Chuck, our navigator. "They took our rock."

"We don't know it was them for sure—" Bingo said. The whole family glared at him and he shut up. We knew for sure.

My family, Wilkins, is a prospector family. Wilkins Drum orbits within the Asteroid Belt making one revolution every year and a half. I know the Belt moves too, but for our purposes it stays still. We move around hunting for Metallics and trading them in at various stationary settlements. At that time we had forty adults and twenty sixteen-and-unders.

Three orbits ago when I was ten we found a hot rock—radioactive. Bingo said it was probably worth four times as much as the whole rest of the load. Everyone was excited. After a lot of debate the family decided to use the extra money to buy a new food processor. Our old GE was sturdy, but it only turned out three basic flavors and five textures. For the rest of the time until Vesta (the biggest city in the Belt) came around we took it easy, taking only the choicest rocks and letting a lot go past. We were rich.

When we caught up to Vesta the Perkins Drum was also passing through the vicinity heading inwards. They're a big operation, almost a town really, and they usually never paid any attention to small-timers like us. Almost as soon as we were in range, though, they radioed us and personally invited us to a Softerball tournament they were sponsoring on Vesta. Chuck says we should have realized they knew we didn't have enough room to play something like that but at the time everyone was too excited. Also, it was a challenge and the whole Belt would hear if we backed down.

We managed to upload a copy of the rules from Vesta and everyone got busy practicing, or, if not on the team, helping to make uniforms and equipment. Aunt Chris, our head coach, named the team the Wilkins Warhawks and designed an emblem for the uniforms: a silver drum with a stylish white "W" across it and large red wings on the sides. The family was so busy that the adults decided to cash in our load *after* the games.

On the day of the first round my dad, who was captain then, splurged and rented a shuttle to take the entire family down to Vesta. We must have turned some heads as the entire gang trooped through the corridors all in red, silver, and white. It was even more exciting, especially for us kids, than discovering the hot rock. We took up an entire section of seats in Vesta's auditorium/stadium, and we were *loud*. The Wilkins family was ready for victory.

We didn't even win one game. We got close except in the heat of things I guess Uncle Ramzy forgot you couldn't hit members of the opposite side with the bat. The Warhawks were penalized twenty yards and two minutes for Uncle Ramzy. The other team (the Vesta South Hemisphere Hydroponics Hell Raisers) burned time until there were three seconds left and made a field home run to capture the lead. Demoralized, we slipped out of the hall leaving a gap of empty seats like a bald spot. When we jetted up to the drum our silence was broken by a sudden gasp from the front of the shuttle. The huge round cargo door in the center aft of the drum was sitting wide open. The only thing missing was the hot rock.

Dad had to take out a loan to pay off the shuttle and cover supplies. We were lucky and managed to pay it off in just one orbit, but nothing could change the fact that Wilkins Drum had been faced, and the whole Belt knew it. Since then it was nearly impossible getting people to deal straight with us. The word was out: we were suckers.

Old Aunt Nate spoke up. "What good's a cow to us anyway? You all want to be like them Perkins and clutter up the drum with a lot of useless junk?" The beads in her hair clicked as she shook her head. "I hear they've got a swimming pool—are you going to want to rip out the control room and get one of those next?"

"Cows give milk, Momma," said Chuck, "and butter and cheese and eggs. It would really liven up the meals around here." I could see everyone was thinking about the food processor we almost had.

I sent Toby off to play, put away the last of the dishes, and stood there listening. Officially I had a year until I was allowed to the adult pows but the next-oldest kid was three years younger than me, so I was often included. Then I noticed Mom giving me a look through her purple shades. I grinned, wiped the counter off a few times, and ducked out of the kitchen. A meter down the hall I decided I *had* to hear the rest of that pow. This was big, the family hadn't done anything like this since we intercepted a Solar Mining, Inc. scout's transmission with the location of a huge chunk of ice which we "found" before their tugs could get there. Drum life could get real monotonous without something to break it up. I dropped to my stomach and wormed back into the kitchen below where I could be seen over the counter.

"You're talking illegal entry into a sealed environment, which gets you at least five years working the Ceres tunnels, plus stealing the cow, and I don't know how long they'd give us for that!" That was Bingo.

"If you don't get caught you don't go to prison," answered Aunt Chris. "Being scared is the reason this drum has been on the bottom of the heap for the past five years. Time to show the Belt what Wilkins are made of."

"But even if we could get to it, how could we move it?"

"Use a lifeboat. They aren't *that* big!"

"This is insane." Bingo sounded really mad. "We don't even know where it is."

"We could find out," said my cousin Beni. "Perkins is having an open drum all next week for people to come and see the cow." Beni was two years older than me and it was him who had been monitoring the radio and first heard all the ruckus about the cow.

"Case the joint!" cried Aunt Chris.

I looked up. Mom was standing in the kitchen peering over her shades down at where I was sitting against a cabinet.

"Are you supposed to be here, Darcy?" she asked. I pretended to turn down the player in my ear.

"What?"

"You heard me," she said. Everyone says I look just like my mom. She has dark brown skin and black eyes which are almost always hidden behind her shades. She only takes them off when she's really serious or angry. Right now they were halfway down her nose. "Get, girl," she said. I got.

Perkins Drum is three times as long and at least twice as big as Wilkins Drum. Bingo and Chuck fixed our course so that we would pass in bike range for a week. My turn to go over and see it all didn't come until the third day and by that time I was itching to death to get a look. "They have a gymnasium," said my cousins, "and a park!" I didn't even know what that first one was, and the second one I didn't believe.

I went over with Dad, Toby, Bingo, and three others. We went outside, swung onto our bikes (two people each), and jetted over to Perkins's which was almost exactly next to us at that point. The bikes are propelled by compressed carbon dioxide gas. Dad's the best biker in the family and probably the whole Belt and we got to Perkins's five minutes ahead of the others. As we flew over to the drum it just kept getting bigger and bigger. I would keep thinking we were up to it but then it would *still* get bigger.

The "floors" of a drum are like tubes fitted one inside the other. The drum is set spinning so that everything inside pushes towards the outside because of centrifugal force. That gives you a floor to stand on although your feet point out of the drum and your head points to the center. Since the floor closest to the outside of the drum spins the fastest that's where you weigh the most, and that's where people in a drum live. That floor also has the biggest area. Each floor above the outside one (called the first) is progressively smaller and gives you less weight. The center shaft is where you store supplies and, if you're a mining drum, rocks. There's a huge door in the aft center for loading. Right next to that there's usually the main airlock which opens onto a hallway in the top floor that runs the length of the drum. At the other end is the door to the control room, which is center fore.

Perkins's main airlock was the size of our dining room. Its walls were covered with suits, bikes, mining equipment, and tools. It was all very clean and bright. I didn't see one dent or scratch anywhere. Their suits really caught my eye—sky-blue with chrome fittings by Ememyu, the best you could buy.

When the lock pressurized we all began helping each other out of our stuff. It's hard to unsuit yourself in zero-G. A wide, round door at the other end of the lock swung open and three men floated inside. They were all really pale, not like the deep tans and browns of my family. The first one had on black slippers, white pants, and a big, blue cloth that wrapped loosely around his arms and chest. It billowed about him in the air and looked like pouring liquid. The other two wore regular blue overalls with lots of pockets.

"Hello, and welcome to Perkins Associates," the first guy said, making a big smile. His teeth were tinted to look like a rainbow spectrum. "My name is Pete Perkins, Vice President of Interior Affairs. I take it you've come for a tour of our facility?" Bingo nodded, never taking his eyes off the bright man. "Well good!" the man boomed, like he thought we couldn't hear. He smiled again. "Has everyone had their standard inoculations as required by Belt Authority?" Bingo's eyes went wide.

"Of course. It's—"

"Wonderful." The man looked us up and down. "Does anyone need a shower?" Bingo took a deep breath and Dad grabbed him on the elbow.

"No, thank you," Dad said, "we have plenty of water on our drum." Bingo was glaring at the man so hard I laughed. He looked like how he did the time he caught some of the kids playing with a huge glob of soap suds up in one of the low-gravity storerooms.

The man showed us where to stow our gear and then led us out the door and through a round tunnel. Something had been bothering me since taking off my suit and I didn't figure it out until just then. I could hardly smell anything. Wilkins Drum is full of warm, thick scents of cooking, machinery, and people. But this place was like how I imagined Earth—so big and open that all smells get spread out too thin to notice. I did catch one whiff of the Vice President. It was spicy and sweet and not at all human. Maybe all Perkins smell different.

Finally our whole group came to a shaft and one by one, the three Perkinses in the lead, we started down the "down" ladder feet-first. The ladder went on and on and on. It was a weird feeling to get heavy so slowly. Finally I reached the bottom. The centrifugal was a little stronger than I was used to. The Perkinses probably sped their drum up when they were near Vesta to show everyone how tough they were.

We were standing on the edge of a *gigantic* room, bigger than any room I'd ever been in. There was something strange all over the floor and after a second I realized it was grass. I recognized it from my lessons. I could see Pete Perkins smiling as we all gawked. All of those plants in one place was just too bizarre. In the air near the ceiling big globes of light the color of the sun drifted, but never bumped. Along all four walls, which were light blue, glowed high-resolution video portraits of hundreds of old people. They had moving backgrounds of places all over the System and Earth.

"This is Perkins Park," said the Vice President, "a well-known attraction in the Belt. Perhaps you've heard of it. The field is ten thousand square feet and weighs twenty-five tons. It was constructed about fifteen years ago by Dara Perkins, whose portrait is here to the right." Dara was pale like all Perkinses, with squinty eyes. He was pictured with the Park behind him. "Over here," continued the Vice President, "is his mother Anne Perkins, who once found a fossilized trilobite in a Carbonaceous asteroid. . . ."

I could barely pay attention as we went through more portraits because we were walking *on the grass*. I kept trying to step light on all that wealth. I thought about getting a leaf to show my cousins but figured they would see me bend over for sure. We went all the way around the room hearing about every dead Perkins that ever lived. I mostly watched the lights and the other groups of outsiders who were being led around just like us.

Finally we got back where we started and went through a set of red steel doors into a dim hallway. Pete was going on about how Perkins Drum broke the volume record for a single-unit operation six years in a row. I was trailing behind looking over my shoulder at the grass when suddenly I felt something touch my arm. I jumped and then clamped my mouth shut before I yelled and interrupted the tour.

"What's the matter?" There was a tall boy standing in front of me. He was Perkins-pale with long curly brown hair and a bony nose. I guessed he was about seventeen.

"Nothing!" I said, clutching my arm like it was burned. He was dressed the strangest of all of them. He wore a jumpsuit that was cut off at the knees and elbows and seemed to be made of pieces of metal shaped like tiny cake pans all sewn together. Clear plastic tubes wound around the little pans with marbles inside that rolled up and down his body. "What's the matter with you?" I asked back.

"What do you mean?"

"Why are you wearing that?"

"Oh." He gave a short, sharp laugh. My Dad and the others were turning the corner.

"I have to go," I said.

"No, wait. Would you like to *really* see the drum? Those tours are no good. I could show it to you though."

"I can't go away from them! I'll get in trouble." The boy shook his head.

"That's okay, you'll be with me. And they time it, so I know your bunch will be back here in thirty-seven minutes exactly. You can catch up to them then. Come on, it will be fun."

"Just why do you want me alone?" I asked, standing as tall as I could. The boy grinned.

"Oh, now, I just want someone new to talk to. This place can get pretty boring."

By this time my group was long gone, which was probably his idea. I had no other choice. "Alright," I said. "My name's Darcy Wilkins."

"Drin Perkins." He made a rattling bow. "Let's go."

"I want to see the cow," I said. I had almost forgotten.

"The cow? Everybody wants to see that. You can see one on video." I stood there. "Oh, alright," he said. "Don't get mad."

Then we went zooming up and down and all over the Perkins Drum. Drin could really move in the low-centrifugal areas, and I think he was trying to see if I could keep up. He was faster in straight stretches but I beat him in tight curves.

I saw a lot of new things that half-hour and a lot of things I didn't understand. Near the living section they had a *swimming pool*—that's a big pit filled with water that people can go into, like an ocean but inside. To be honest it scared me so much I wouldn't even go into the room. What if the drum stopped spinning and all that water got loose? You would drown in a second. We also peeped into the control room, which was huge and full of sparkling equipment.

Then Drin took me to a long, wide hallway in the middle of the living section. The rooms on either side had been remodeled with large windows looking out and lots of lights and signs. They were *stores*. Drin called it a "Mal" and said people made and sold things for money there, just like on Vesta. I couldn't believe it—they were family after all. It didn't seem very nice. Still, I had to see.

The first place had a woman who repaired suits and mining equipment, which we all just help each other with for free in Wilkins Drum. Then there was a guy who made clothes, all kinds of clothes in all sorts of shapes and colors. I had to look at it all and would have stayed forever if Drin hadn't dragged me out finally. It was the same with all the little stores: food stores, drink stores, shoe stores, a library, a carpenter store, jewelry stores. I had never seen so many different things all in one place. It was like I thought Earth would be—lots of variety.

I was trying on some holo-wigs when Drin grabbed my arm. "The time!" he said and dragged me down the hall. We charged through the crazy corridors of that drum until I thought we were lost when suddenly we burst into the Park. My group and the three Perkinses were waiting and Dad gave me a very funny look when I came up. I barely had time to say thanks to Drin and we whisked back to the big airlock. Halfway between Perkins Drum and ours I realized I never got to see the cow. I had totally forgotten about it. Dang that Drin, it was his fault.

I wasn't really mad at him though. It was awfully nice of him to take all that time to show me around when he didn't even know me. He was real friendly, much more so than any other Perkins I saw. I wondered why he decided he wanted to meet me instead of someone else. It must have been because we were near the same age.

When we got home the drum seemed a little small but a lot more normal. All the adults went to the dining room to pow about the cow, and they were so busy asking Bingo and Dad questions that no one noticed me get a tea and sit down. I was too tired to go anywhere else.

"Those Perkins have everything," Bingo said. "That cow's just to flaunt it in our faces." He seemed really mad. Let's just take it then, all the adults said. Dad spoke.

"Can't be done. I mean it's just in the middle of everything— there are people all around all the time. Hell, we couldn't even get through an airlock."

"Wimps!" said Aunt Chris, pounding the table. "You kids are all cowards."

"No, we would all like to go for it. But imagine someone trying to steal something from our kitchen. Someone from the outside. Of course we would notice them. It's the same way over there." Everyone was quiet when they understood. They stared either at the floor or into the kitchen at the food processor.

Beni came into the room and looked straight at me. "Radio message for you, Darcy!" he said.

"What?" I was echoed by my mother.

Beni read from an electric pad. "Drin Perkins requests the presence of Darcy Wilkins at twenty hours the fourteenth of this month to be his companion at the Perkins Drum Softball Victory Gala." Beni looked up. "They won again and now they're inviting all sorts of people from Vesta and all around here. Everybody's talking about it."

All the adults were looking at me. I couldn't speak, my mind was spinning, torn. Did this mean Drin liked me? I had no idea. Maybe he did. There were certainly a lot of other people he could go with. This was a shocking development. But then there was also the fact that the party was to celebrate what the Perkinses used to screw us out of our rock four and a half years ago. If I went they would be laughing at me and my family all over again. No, I wasn't going to let them have that pleasure. Drin could just come over here if he wanted to see me.

Aunt Chris had stood up and tottered over next to me. "How about that," she said, stroking my hair. "The Perkins are having a party." She looked at the rest of the adults and repeated, "The Perkins are having a party. Everyone will be busy and Darcy will be on the *inside*."

Mom lent me her shades, but I still felt alone. Everyone in the family down to cousin Toby had suggestions about what I should wear. I changed clothes every twenty minutes for three days solid until finally we decided on my Aunt Lea's genuine Earth jeans, which I had to roll up, Chuck's prize white glo-shirt, which was really too big, and a silver, white, and red vest that Aunt Chris made just for the occasion. Everyone also wanted to lend me jewelry, and so as not to hurt anyone's feelings, I wore it all. I was covered in pins, ear clips, bracelets, and rings. The light from the shirt sparkled off it all every time I moved. I thought Drin would like it—it was his style.

But I was scared. Not of Drin or even the Perkinses' party, much. I was scared because after Dad dropped me off I would be totally alone on that big drum with no family around at all. All my life I had been within shouting distance of another Wilkins. Last time at Perkins I had been too overwhelmed to feel lonely and anyway, I knew Dad and the others were somewhere nearby. Now I had time to think about it.

Dad didn't even come into the airlock when we arrived at 20:20. "I'm not invited," he said. "But I'll see you later." He winked. Then I had to go inside. It was too late to back out and the whole family was depending on me. Dad biked away and it was just me next to this big, swirling metal drum falling through space.

Drin came into the airlock as soon as there was air. Tonight he wore just a regular, black work jumpsuit. His hair and eyes were black now, too. I was speechless with surprise. I had expected the unimaginable. "Hi," said Drin, "glad you made it."

"Hi." I hung up my suit. It wasn't my regular one but a shabby, patched-up spare that was older than me. Drin didn't seem to notice.

"You look nice," he said.

"Oh, you too." I felt like a computer game next to him.

"Shall we?" He offered his arm. I was so nervous I laughed suddenly. Drin looked startled. *Man, I'm going to blow it*, I thought but it was too late to do anything now. We headed down the hall side by side. Drin smiled at me and I blushed, of course. I get so mad when that happens and then it gets even worse. Why couldn't I be cool like him?

The Gala was in the Park. There were hundreds of people crammed into the room dressed all kinds of ways. I saw glo-clothes, vid-clothes, and a few with no clothes at all. A tall man had on a shoulder pack with two robot arms attached. He gestured widely with his and the extras as he spoke. Around the edge of the Park were tables heaped with food and gallons of hot and cold drinks. I thought some of the portraits were looking down a little hungrily, but it was probably just a trick. *I* wasn't hungry, and hadn't been for twenty-four hours. In the middle of the Park there was a round platform with a ten-piece band honking out Titan-style dance tunes. Groups of two and three swung and hopped to the beat.

Drin slowly led me around the room, occasionally saying hello to someone but mostly just walking along. It was strange. I noticed a lot of the Perkinses looking at us. Why did Drin want everyone to see me? I felt my face go red again.

We stopped at a table where some friends of Drin's were nibbling on real vegetables. There were five of them, all webbed together with jeweled strands. One of them wore a uniform of the Perkins Softball team and was talking about the victory game. The way he put it they never would have won without him. The other kids were all wrapped up in the tale, but I was bored. It was a thrill just to look around at all the people though. I wished I could just see it all at once, take it all in in an instant. I pressed a button on one of my bracelets and a puff of yellow fog shot out.

The smoke braided into four digits as it dissipated. 21:30 already! I had half an hour.

I still wasn't sure if I could really do it. What would Drin think when he found out I used him? He was very nice and he really seemed to like me. The poor guy would be heartbroken. I felt sad for him all of a sudden. Too bad we could never really be friends.

Drin smiled at me. "So what do you think?"

I smiled back. "It's too cool. You're really lucky. It would be neat to live on this drum." I gritted my teeth but too late, I had said it. Drin just blinked and grinned.

"Come on," he said.

We walked over to a group of twelve or so older people dressed in extremely fine red and yellow tuxedos. They surrounded a woman whose hair was all pulled back and trapped in a polished silver model of an asteroid. I looked down and could not believe it—she was wearing a skirt! Yes, an antique from the old days being worn out here in the Belt. I almost laughed.

Drin pushed through the crowd dragging me with him and the conversation instantly stopped. "Mother," he said, "I'd like you to meet a friend of mine." The woman, who had been staring at Drin, suddenly jerked her head towards me as if I had just appeared from nowhere. She had gray eyes and a bony nose like Drin's.

"Ahem," she said, "so you're Drin's little friend. Where are you from, dear, Vesta?"

"She's Darcy Wilkins of Wilkins Drum," Drin said loudly as I opened my mouth.

It got so quiet I thought there was a hull breach. The woman's eyes went hard as she glanced at Drin then back to me. "Oh," she said. "Well, I'm Johna Perkins." She shook my hand. "I *own* Perkins Drum." *And I don't talk to people like you*, she was saying. I could see that real clear. Drin took my hand and we turned away. Immediately they began to whisper and someone laughed.

I could not remember the last time I was so humiliated. And he had done it on purpose. Yes, it was all clear what was going on. Drin's eyes and face danced with triumph. I wasn't the user, I was the used. I was just another tool in Drin's petty rebellion against his family. He probably did it out of boredom, I knew he didn't have to work. I felt sick.

"Where's the flusher?" I asked and he pointed down a hallway. I mumbled thanks and it took all my strength not to run. In the flusher I collapsed on the seat, breathing hard. I never felt so stupid in all my life. I never should have agreed to come to the party and I never should have trusted Drin, damn him. There was no way I was going back in there, not after that. Problem was, I still had fifteen minutes until I met my family. I'd have to just wait. Drin probably wouldn't miss me. He was finished with me now.

Outside in the hall there was no one around, as Aunt Chris predicted. I found a shaft and climbed all the way to the hallway that ran parallel to the drum's center storage areas, then tugged my way along the corridor making good speed because I weighed practically nothing. The first half of the hallway was bare because it ran alongside where the rocks were stored. Large sets of double doors along the second half marked pressurized store rooms. Finally I reached the fore end of the drum. There was a single door at the end of the hall with a small window in it and a set of airlock controls on a panel. Inside was the actual airlock— a bare room three by one and a half meters—with a similar set of controls on the side wall. On the far wall was the door to the outside. The hallway turned "up" here across the center of the drum and at its end was the hatch leading to the drum's control room. I crept up and took a peek inside. No one was on duty, not even a radio monitor.

I dropped back to the lock and, fingers shaking, worked the controls emptying the little room of air and opening the outer door. Outside, the craggy surface of Vesta drifted into view, dotted with lights and surrounded by multicolored stars.

I waited. Twenty-two came and past and no one arrived. What if they didn't come? I couldn't go back to Drin, no way. I decided I would steal a suit and bike and try to make it home on my own. I wanted to get out of there. Just as I was planning my route back to the main airlock where all the equipment was, someone climbed though the door. They were followed by four more, the last one towing a bike. They all crammed inside and I triggered the outer door shut and let air back into the room.

As soon as I opened the inside door Bingo threw me my regular suit. With him were my mom and dad, Chuck, and Aunt Edna, our doctor. I struggled into the suit and all five helped me seal it up.

"Let's go!" Bingo, Edna, Chuck, and I kicked off the wall and shot down the hallway followed by Mom and Dad hunkered down on the bike. We flashed over glowing shafts but there was never anyone in them. At one point Bingo threw up his hand and we all grabbed wall, scraping to a noisy stop. "Thought I heard someone," he said over the suit radio. I couldn't see how he could hear anything over the bike's jets. There was no one, though, so we jumped and continued on our way.

A minute later we stopped at one of the sets of double doors in the middle of the corridor. DANGER—WARNING—HAZARDOUS LIFEFORM, it read. ENTER ONLY IF ACCOMPANIED BY AUTHORIZED PERSONNEL. Bingo waited a minute for us to catch our breath. "Ready, Edna?" he asked. She nodded, pulling a huge hypodermic out of a belt pouch. Bingo pushed open the doors.

For a second nothing happened and I struggled to see around everybody. Suddenly there was a loud bellowing like an explosion and something huge swooped out of the door, smashing Bingo and Edna against the wall. Chuck yelled and got slapped aside by a big brown and white hairy flipper. The area was alive with a great, thrashing beast madly trying to propel itself down the corridor. It had a huge head but with a small mouth (for its size) and a fat round body. It also had four flippers for moving in low gravity. Between the back two hung something that looked like an big inflated glove. I figured all this out later though. At that point I was too worried for my life to be looking very carefully.

Mom and Dad rushed forward with Chuck close behind. They tackled the monster but it was way too strong for them. I heard Edna yell, "Damn it!" The cow pushed away from her and I saw her pull the hypodermic out from Bingo's thigh. She kicked off the wall and landed on the cow's back. Then she plunged the now half-full hypo into the cow's neck. It flapped off in the opposite direction of the airlock with my parents and Chuck hanging on to its sides. Aunt Edna got scraped off after about fifteen meters, smashing a light fixture with her helmet.

I slid over to Bingo, who was floating by the wall, stiff as a girder. Aunt Edna glided up a second later and took off his helmet. She checked his eyes and the bio readouts on his collar. "He'll be okay," she said, refastening his helmet. "You bring him, I'll see if I can help the others." She dashed away. Far down the hall I could hear the sounds of smashing plastic and screams both human and cow. I figured we were caught for sure. The whole plan was wrecked. Five years on Ceres. Five years away from my family.

I grabbed Bingo's suit by a ring on the back and managed to maneuver him over my shoulder. I began a slow, coasting crawl

after the others. In a few minutes I found them all tugging on the
back flippers of the cow, which had wedged itself halfway into
a shaft. It wasn't nearly as active now but just kicked lazily and
mooed softly every once and a while.

"Shoot," Chuck said over the radio, "they've heard us by now.
Let's just leave it and get out of here!" The others ignored him
and a second later heaved the cow out of the shaft. It turned its
giant head, groaned, and vomited into the air with a belch.

"Oh, God," said my mother, who had gotten the most of it.

"Come on, let's go!" cried Edna.

Bingo stirred. "Wha?" he shouted. "I can't move!"

"Shut up!" Everything was quiet. No pounding feet up the
ladders, no alarms, nothing. Dad wrapped a rope around the
cow's two hind flippers. The four of them pulled it back the way
we came while I followed with Bingo in tow. We stopped at the
cow's doors and Chuck began tying the rope to the back of the
bike which had been left there. Quickly I released Bingo and
pulled out of my leg pouches three spray cans. By the time the
others were ready I was putting the final touches on a huge
silver, white, and red Wilkins Warhawk emblem that covered
the two doors.

Mom and Dad both got on the bike and began slowly tugging
the feebly struggling cow. Chuck and Edna took Bingo, and
I followed, watching the rear. Every second I expected someone to yell out but nothing happened. It was 22:20 when we
got back to the airlock. Drin would surely be looking for me
now. Or maybe not. Maybe it made things easier for me to just
disappear.

At the airlock I thought we were home free but no, we had to
wait for Chuck to cycle through to get the lifeboat, which Bingo
had left clamped to the hull. It was too bulky to carry along and
they were afraid someone would see it if they left it inside. It
took him *forever*. There was nothing to do but wait and get caught
red-handed. Finally he got back inside and began unfolding the
big yellow pouch.

"This isn't going to fit," Chuck said suddenly.

"What?" asked Dad.

"The lifeboat's going to be too big to go through the door once
I blow it up!" Everyone began talking at once, arguing about
what to do.

"Shut up!" yelled Edna. "Now. Will the cow fit through the
door?" It would. "Alright. Get the lifeboat around the cow, seal

it in and give it just a little air, then take it outside and inflate it all the way."

But it was a lot harder to actually do. The cow was pretty calm, but it took three people to move it around, it had so much mass. Also it kept getting the bag all tangled in its flippers. Minutes passed and I got more and more nervous. Eventually we got it. It was now a big, wrinkled yellow blob that mooed.

Dad got into the airlock with the bike and the cow. Just as the airlock finished pumping out and Dad was opening the door to the outside, Bingo, who was propped against the wall, mumbled, "Someone's coming."

Down the hall I could dimly see brightly dressed shapes moving excitedly around the cow's room's doors. I heard shouts. Edna gestured frantically through the window at Dad. He threw out the bike and then began tugging on the cow like mad.

"Stop!" someone shouted. Five men and women were rushing towards us. A few seconds later the cow cleared and Dad slammed the outer door. Edna instantly punched the controls to start refilling the air so we could get inside the airlock.

"Hurry up hurry up," I said, but there was nothing we could do but stand and wait. The Perkinses were almost upon us. The one in front had a huge metal bar which he swung back and forth.

"Go!" Edna shouted. The door hissed open and we piled in, dragging Bingo. Chuck pulled it shut just as our pursuers came crashing against the door. The man with the bar pounded it and shouted but we could barely hear him. It was Pete, the Vice President. The airlock slowly emptied of gas, becoming quieter and quieter. On the other side of the door one of the Perkinses frantically worked the airlock controls.

"Shit! She's going to do an emergency override," Chuck cried over the radio. "We'll never make it!"

I saw Edna nod. She turned to a small transparent rubber panel on the wall and yanked it up with her gloved fist. Then she reached inside and grabbed a large, red handle. "No!" Mom shouted. Edna twisted the handle ninety degrees clockwise.

Even through the thinning air inside the lock I heard a high whooping siren. Red lights flashed up and down the corridor. The Perkinses all jumped and looked at us with wide eyes. There was a terrific *BANG* as the airlock's outer door's explosive bolts blew it off its frame. Then it felt like a huge hand flung me out of the airlock, my left arm slamming against the frame. I screamed as the five of us sailed out into empty space away from the drum, away from anything to hold on to at all. I thought I had died. Everything was spinning and my arm ached.

   What seemed like an hour later but was actually only half a minute Mom was shaking my shoulder. We joined hands and floated together. My Dad is still the best biker in the Belt—he had us all tethered to the now fully-inflated lifeboat and was towing us back to Wilkins Drum before the Perkinses could even suit-up. And by then it was too late, we were long gone. In twelve hours we would be out of bike range and beyond anyone's reach. The score was tied, one-all.

Asteroids: The Better Resource

ERIC DREXLER

Eric Drexler is best known for his seminal work *Engines of Creation* (Anchor Library of Science, 1987), which looks at the consequences of future technologies, particularly molecular manipulations: *nanotechnology*, in the current term, which he may have invented, and certainly did more to popularize than anyone else.

Some years ago Eric and I were involved in the leadership of an organization called the L–5 Society for Space Development. It was a small group, but it had great influence, largely because there was a ferment of ideas seldom found anywhere else. L–5 has since merged into a group that became a NASA booster club; but the ideas of the old L–5 Society live on. For example:

We need not use this Earth up, nor pollute it either, to maintain our high-technology civilization. In a previous introduction I went through the numbers: how we can, with present-day technology, deliver here to Earth as much metal for each person in the world as the U.S. disposed of per capita in the sixties. We can do that without polluting our planet at all, and we can keep it up for tens of thousands of years.

The metal is out there in the Asteroid Belt. For starters we don't even have to look very hard; most of the asteroids were once spherical, large enough to have metallic cores, and now the worthless gubbage topside has been knocked away, exposing all that lovely iron and lead and tin and such we'll need to give the wretched of the Earth *real* freedom.

Why not? The refinery power's there too; the Sun gives it off for free. We have a propulsion system right now to get us to the asteroids; Project NERVA was canceled decades ago, but the research was done, and it wouldn't be that hard to start up again. Nuclear-powered rockets would be rather simple to build, if we wanted them.

But first we'll need a Moonbase. We can get that the hard way, carrying stuff up bit by bit from the top of disintegrating totem poles, but there are easier ways.

We could do it in one whack. Project ORION was also canceled, but we could build old Bang-Bang in a very few years (as Larry and I demonstrated in our invasion novel, *Footfall*) if we wanted to. ORION used the simplest and most efficient method of nuclear propulsion of all: take a BIG plate, quite thick and hard; attach to it by shock-absorbers a large space-going capsule; put underneath one atomic bomb; and fire away.

Believe me, your ship will move. When you've used up the momentum imparted by the first bomb, fling another down underneath. Repeat as required. For the expenditure of a small part of the world's nuclear weapons stockpile you have put several *million* pounds into orbit, or on the Lunar surface.

But that will cause fallout.

Yes; some. Not very much, compared to what we have already added to background radiation, but perhaps enough we don't want to use ORION— although, he said happily, ORION is one reason why I think we'll eventually do what has to be done, even if *this* generation fails in its duties to the future. ORION is cheap and the bombs we have stockpiled won't go away; if we're still alive in that grim world of 15–20 billion people and no space program, *somebody's* going to revive Bang-Bang and get out there.

ORION gets a few big payloads to orbit or to the Moon. A more systematic way would be to build a big laser-launching system and make it accessible to anyone with a payload to put into orbit. Freeman Dyson calls laser launch systems "space highways." The government builds the launch system, and can use it for its own purposes; but it also gives private citizens, consortiums, firms a means of reaching orbit.

Dyson envisions a time when individual families can buy a space capsule and, once Out There, do as they like: settle on the Moon, stay in orbit, go find an asteroid; whatever. It will be a while before we can build cheap, self-contained space capsules operable by the likes of you and me; but it may not be anywhere as long as you think.

The problem is the engines, of course; there's nothing else in the space home economy that couldn't, at least in theory, be built for about the cost of a family home, car, and recreational vehicle. But then most land-based prefabricated homes don't have their own motive power either; they have to hire a truck for towing.

It could make quite a picture: a train of space capsules departing Earth orbit for Ceres and points outward, towed by a ship something like the one I described in "Tinker." Not quite Ward Bond in *Wagon Train*, but it still could make a good TV series. The capsules don't have to be totally self-sufficient, of course. It's easy enough to imagine way stations along the route, the space equivalent of filling stations in various orbits.

Dyson is fond of saying that the U.S. wasn't settled by a big government settlement program, but by individuals and families who often had little more than courage and determination when they started. Perhaps that dream of the ultimate in freedom is too visionary; but if so, it isn't because the technology won't exist.

However we build our Moonbase, it's a very short step from there to asteroid mines. Obviously the Moon is in Earth orbit: with the shallow Lunar gravity well it's no trick at all to get away from the Moon, and Earth's orbit is halfway to anywhere in the solar system. We don't know what minerals will be available on the Moon. Probably it will take a while before it gets too expensive to dig them up, but as soon as it does, the Lunatics themselves will want to go mine the asteroids.

There's probably more water ice in the Belt than there is on Luna, so for starters there will be water prospectors moving about among the asteroids. The same technology that sends water to Luna will send metals to Earth orbit.

Meanwhile, NERVA or the ion drive I described earlier will do the job. In fact, it's as simple to get refined metals from the Asteroid Belt to near-Earth orbit as it is to bring them down from the Lunar surface. It takes longer, but who cares? If I can promise GM steel at less than they're now paying, they'll be glad to sign a "futures" contract, payment on delivery.

It's going to be colorful out in the Belt, with huge mirrors boiling out chunks from mile-round rocks, big refinery ships moving from rock to rock; mining towns, boomtowns, and probably traveling entertainment vessels. Perhaps a few scenes from the wild west, or the *Star Wars* bar scene? "Claim jumpers! Grab your rifle—"

Thus from the first Moonbase we'll move rapidly, first to establish other Moon colonies (the Moon's a *big* place) and out to the Asteroid Belt. After that we'll have fundamental decisions to make.

We can either build O'Neill colonies or stay with planets and Moons. I suspect we'll do both. While one group starts constructing flying city-states at the Earth–Moon Trojan points, another will decide to make do with Mars.

Mars and Venus aren't terribly comfortable places; in fact, you probably won't want to land on Venus at all until it has been terraformed. Between Mars and Venus, Venus is the easier to make into a shirtsleeves-inhabitable world. It requires only biological packages and some fertilizers and nutrients, and can be done from Moonbase or, in a pinch, from Earth itself. Still, though Venus may be the simpler job, Mars is likely to come first, simply because you can live there before terraforming; there will be dome colonies on the Red Planet.

I wrote a story (*Birth of Fire*) describing one Mars-terraforming project: melt the polar caps and activate a number of Martian volcanoes to get an atmosphere built up. Isaac Asimov described the final step many years ago: get your ice from Out There, at Jupiter or Saturn, and fling it downhill to Mars. Freeman Dyson points out that there's enough ice on Enceladus (a Saturn moon) to keep the Martian climate warm for 10,000 years. The deserts of Mars can become gardens in less than a century.

Dyson's scheme didn't even involve human activity on Enceladus: robots and modern computers could probably accomplish the job. Dyson suggests robots because the project as described would take a long time, and human supervisors might not care for the work; but I suspect we could get plenty of volunteers if we needed them. Why not? No one could complain that the work was trivial, and you couldn't ask for an apartment with a better view than Saturn's rings!

Moonbases. Lunar cities. Mining communities in the Asteroid Belt. Domed cities on Mars, with prospects for terraforming the planet and turning it into a paradise. An advanced engineering project headquarters on Enceladus. Pollution controlled on Earth, because most polluting activities would go on in space. Near-Earth space factories. Several to hundreds of city-states at the Trojan points of the Earth–Moon system. A space population of millions, with manned and unmanned ships stitching all the space habitats together. This is not a dream world; this is a world we could make in a hundred years!

In 1892 a number of Kiowa and Comanche chiefs were taken to Washington by Quakers in an attempt to show the Indians just what they were facing. When they returned to talk about the huge cities, and "a stone tipi so large that all the Kiowa could sit under it," they were not believed. One suspects that if the Quaker school-masters had been magically transported to the Washington of 1990 and then returned to their own time, they would not be believed either. A nation of 240 million people? Millions of tons of concrete poured into gigantic highways? Aircraft larger than the biggest sailing ships? City streets brightly lit at night? Millions of tons of steel, farm-lands from Kansas to California . . .

Building a space civilization in the next hun-dred years will be simpler than getting where we are from 1879. We already know how to do it. We probably don't know how we *will* do it; certainly the very act of space exploration will generate new ideas and techniques as alien to us as nuclear energy would have been to Lord Rutherford or Benjamin Franklin; but we already know how we *could* do it. No basic new discov-eries necessary.

Given the basic space civilization I've described, we'll have accomplished one goal: no single acci-dent, no war, no one insane action will finish us off. We won't *have* to have outgrown our damn foolishness to ensure survival of the race. Per-haps we'll all be adults, mature, satisfied with what we have, long past wars and conflicts and the like; but I doubt it. At least, though, there will be no way to exterminate mankind, even if we manage to make the Earth uninhabitable; and it's unlikely that any group, nation, or ideology can enslave anyone. That's Worth Something.

One suspects, too, that there will be an enor-mous diversity of cultures. Travel times between various city-states—Asteroid, Martian, Lunar,

O'Neill colony, Saturnian forward base, Jovian Trojan point—will be weeks to months to years with presently foreseeable technology. That's likely to change, but by the time the faster travel systems are in widespread use the cultural diversities will be established. Meanwhile, communications among all the various parts of the solar system will be simple and relatively cheap, so that there will have been that unifying influence; cultures will become different because people want to be different, not because they don't know any better.

Obviously, there is more than one road to Rome. For the reasons presented here and elsewhere, I favor the Lunar approach to space development. In fact, along with Jim Ransom, Phil Chapman, and some other old L-5 enthusiasts, I am one of the founders of the Lunar Society.

The Lunar Society isn't the only space organization, but it does exist solely to get us into space. Not to print fancy magazines, or feed and clothe a huge staff. It isn't precisely looking for members either, but we'll take them. We prefer people who want to do something.

There's no big membership services group, because the organization has no full-time employees. If you want to register, it's $100, and the only thing you get for that money is our personal guarantee not to waste it. If you're interested, write to The Lunar Society, 3960 Laurel Canyon Blvd., Suite #372, North Hollywood, CA 91614. Please don't write to ask for "information." We don't have any fancy brochures. Just hard-working people trying to put a colony on the Moon in our lifetimes.

Years ago the space enthusiast community, including L-5, was divided into the "Lunatics" and the "Asteroid Nuts." I suppose it would be fair to say I was the leader of the Lunatic group, while Eric Drexler was the leading Asteroid nut. The arguments got hot at times: we both truly believed that it wouldn't be long before we got a chance to try out our theories.

My position was that the Asteroids are a wonderful place, but it's best to exploit the Moon first. Eric's was "Why wait?"

But let's let him speak for himself: here's Eric Drexler, for his view of the "logical next step" in space development.

ADVOCATES OF SPACE development must decide where to turn for space resources, the key to making space a true frontier. We discuss both the Moon and the asteroids, but one source will surely be used first. Discussion of the choice between them has been unfocused and inconclusive. Although a clear-cut answer may be too much to expect, and research on both paths should doubtless receive our support, a debate could sharpen the issues and help us set priorities. To this end, Dr. Pournelle has asked that I fire an opening volley in support of the asteroidal side of the question.

Many people assume that the Moon is the "logical next step" in space development; it is, after all, the closest source of raw materials in space. But why go to the Moon for resources?

Access to Asteroids

The Moon's proximity offers obvious advantages: short travel times make human crews safer and cheaper, and brief light-lag eases control of remote operation. If, however, initial "mining" operation will simply fill bags with loose material, then virtually unsupervised devices—sweeper robots—seem practical; neither travel time nor light-lag then matter much, and the advantages of proximity fade. As space industry grows, human beings will have the run of the Solar System; even earlier, semi-autonomous robots could likely handle more than mere dirt-sweeping. Meanwhile, complex processes can be confined to near-Earth space.

The relative motions of Earth and any given asteroid make good transfer opportunities relatively infrequent, and infrequent transfers would increase the inventory cost of resources stockpiled for use between deliveries. The main cost tied up in this inventory, however, would be that invested in its transportation. Low delta v's, aerobraking, and use of efficient, low-thrust propulsion systems promise to make the transportation cost of asteroidal materials far less than that of lunar materials; this seems likely to swamp the effect of inventory costs.

Still, a systems analysis would be needed to quantify the costs of infrequent launch windows. For example, how greatly will scheduling inefficiencies decrease the useful operating time of propulsion systems? How rapidly do such costs lessen as the number of surveyed target asteroids grows? Such factors can only be estimated now, but the overall prospects look good. With many target asteroids, more windows will open and such costs will lessen; a modest search should find many as accessible as the best now known. Further propulsion systems (such as Lightsails) could make many known asteroids easy to reach. Asteroids seem more accessible than the Moon, despite their greater distances.

Orbiting Ores

The sheer size of the Moon increases the possibilities for ore formation, at least compared to those in a smaller version of itself. Separation on a vast scale, however, matters less than the degree of concentration. If some process swept up all the uranium in a typical cubic kilometer of the Earth's crust (the volume of a small asteroid), the resulting block of uranium would mass over 10,000 tons. If, however, all the uranium in Earth's crust were concentrated a hundredfold, a block more massive than any asteroid would result, but it would hold a mere 400 parts per million. Greater concentration would be worth more than greater quantity, particularly to a small-scale industry. Uranium itself, of course, seems worth little in free space, given the steady flood of sunlight.

Separation processes have concentrated materials in both the Moon and asteroids. Geochemists classify elements as siderophile (chiefly found in the iron phase), chalcophile (chiefly found in the sulfide phase), lithophile (chiefly found in the rock phase), and volatile (chiefly found—or lost—in the vapor phase). The Moon is enriched in refractory lithophile elements, but at the expense of depletion in siderophile, chalcophile, and (especially) volatile elements. The asteroids, in contrast, vary: rocky asteroids are enriched in lithophile elements; nickel-iron asteroids are enriched in siderophile elements (and often hold nuggets of sulfide); carbonaceous chondrite asteroids, while not enriched in volatiles (compared to the Sun or Jupiter), nevertheless contain abundant water and hydrocarbons. Some asteroids, such as the chondrites common near Earth, hold a separable mixture—grains of metal and sulfide in a rocky matrix containing traces of water and carbon. The Moon's separation discarded too much.

The refractory lithophiles include aluminum, titanium, and magnesium; these may seem attractive for space use, since they are "aerospace metals." Asteroidal (that is, meteoritic) samples hold up to 27% aluminum oxide, and some carbonaceous chrondrites contain veins of water—soluble magnesium salts—the Moon has no monopoly on such metals.

Surprisingly, however, space industry has little special need for light metals. "Aerospace" today suggests *vehicles*, devices flung about repeatedly (or thrown *very* high) by burning fuels; low mass is important to their performance. Space industrial facilities—factories, stations, power plants—will be different: in use, they will simply orbit, as would a feather or boulder. Added mass can even help, by blocking radiation and slowing orbital decay.

Simple delivered cost seems most important, and this will include the costs of both transportation and refining. Energy requirements can indicate relative costs. Call the energy needed to lift a kilogram from the Moon one unit. Returning a kilogram from a target asteroid will require less than one unit; melting and refining a kilogram of asteroidal steel will require about a half a unit. The energy needed to break a kilogram of light metals free from lunar oxides, however, is roughly ten units. Further, asteroidal steel can be melted and refined using inexpensive heat from a solar furnace, while planned processes for reducing lunar oxides require expensive electric power. Process complexity issues likewise seem to favor steel.

For low-cost space construction, asteroidal steel seems best; a low-expansion nickel-iron alloy (Invar) could be used to avoid thermal distortion. Where low mass matters, graphite and plastics are becoming popular, and asteroidal hydrocarbons provide a feedstock unmatched on the Moon. For market value on Earth, precious and strategic metals from asteroids seem attractive. I know of no lunar materials superior to terrestrial ores. (The suggestion that lunar titanium might find a terrestrial market was incorrectly attributed to me in *The High Frontier*; O'Neill apparently confused me with another researcher.) Asteroids, however, hold siderophile metals like those that sank to Earth's core—separated, yet not beyond reach.

Speculative Prospects

Stephen Gillett discusses the possibility of lunar ores enriched in incompatible elements (those not easily incorporated in crystals of common minerals as magma cools and solidifies). He notes that water is commonly considered vital to concentrating incompatible elements in the residual liquid as magma solidifies, but proposes that traces of chlorine and sulfur might have played a similar role to that of water in the dry lunar magmas; KREEP (a rock widely distributed on the Moon, which is highly enriched in incompatible elements potassium [K], Rare Earth Elements and Phosphorus [P]) shows that some concentration occurs. The experiments he suggests seem well worth doing, to see if ores containing "chlorine, lithium, beryllium, zirconium, uranium, thorium, the rare-earth elements, and so forth" might indeed have formed. These elements are not critical to early space development, however, and chlorine—perhaps the most valuable, given its many uses in industrial chemistry—makes up 0.8% of the soluble salts found in carbonaceous chondrites.

One can equally well speculate regarding possible asteroidal ores not yet seen in terrestrial samples, of course. The Moon has been sampled in relatively few sites; likewise, most meteoritic samples are thought to come from relatively few parent bodies. Some classes of meteorite are represented by but *one* specimen, suggesting that some—represented by none—remain unknown. Nickel-iron meteorites contain a spectrum of nickel content ranging up to 34%—except for one that contains 62%. Our lunar samples contain grains thrown from far across the lunar surface; do they contain comparable evidence for unusual concentrations of valuable materials?

The asteroids, though smaller and faster-cooling, seem a match for the Moon as targets for speculative prospecting. Vesta, for example, appears basaltic and differentiated (like the Moon) and has over one-tenth the Moon's diameter. Many meteorites were melted and resolidified; asteroidal materials contained water, which perhaps mobilized incompatible elements. Further, comparing rock to rock, metal to metal, and sulfide to sulfide, concentrations of trace elements have been found to vary from sample to sample by factors of several hundred or more.

Hydrothermal processes (surely lacking on the Moon!) form many terrestrial ores; they require porous rock saturated with water, together with heating to drive convection, dissolve compounds in a large volume, and deposit them in a smaller volume. Some carbonaceous chondrites show veins of water-soluble salts; other signs point to their having been water-saturated for at least a thousand years. The cores of some asteroids melted, showing the presence of ample heat. Thus, hydrothermal deposits are not inconceivable. Similarly, deposits formed by volatilization and subsequent condensation in vents seem possible; metals such as tin and lead might be concentrated by such a mechanism. Finally, the composition of asteroidal rocks before and after their melting and differentiation strongly suggests that a sulfide phase, troilite, may be found in massive veins. One troilite-rich meteorite is known; any pure troilite meteoroids are thought to be destroyed by atmospheric entry (as are those carbonaceous chondrites richest in water and organics). In short, the asteroids' known resources seem better than the Moon's, and their unknown resources seem more promising.

An Asteroid Scenario

To make the idea of asteroid mining more vivid, a scenario may help. How might the process begin, and where could it lead?

First, we drop our eyes from the splendor of the full Moon, shake our heads to clear them, and look seriously at the choice of asteroidal resources vs. lunar resources. In part for scientific reasons, we support asteroid missions and the Spacewatch asteroid-search telescope. Recognizing the high thrust-to-weight ratio of metal films in sunlight (and their lack of fuel consumption), we better define Lightsail construction procedures and configurations. Agreement grows that asteroids have valuable, accessible resources. Space industry draws investment. Probes survey newly found asteroids to select the best targets for initial use. Government and industry decide that a fraction of the price of the Shuttle is little to pay to open the Solar System; Lightsail development begins in earnest.

Lightsail production begins in orbit, and sails depart for nearby asteroids. They deliver devices that sweep loose regolith into bags, then they return the bags to low Earth orbit. Engineers use the mass as radiation shielding for habitable modules of space stations, and for hardening military satellites. The Russians protest dirt in orbit as "an anti-satellite weapon." Water from carbonaceous chondrites is electrolyzed, producing cheap fuel in orbit for hydrogen/oxygen rockets; radiation shielding and fast, inexpensive rockets lead to a construction base in geosynchronous orbit.

Total sail capacity grows steadily as orbital factories continue production. Selected asteroidal steels are purified, removing over $1,000 of platinum metals per ton, then foamed in zero gravity for sale on Earth. Steel structures become common in orbit. The orbital industrial complex expands. Mass production of sails lowers the transport cost from certain asteroids to less than $1/kg; use of asteroidal nickel in sail reflectors further lowers the cost to $0.10/kg. Nickel and cobalt, then steel, follow platinum to markets on Earth. Steam turbine power satellites with steel radiators become economical. Space industry rivals genetic engineering and electronics as a growth sector in the Western economy.

An expedition at last departs to build industrial facilities at the two most accessible asteroids, to pre-process metals and organic materials for shipment and easy capture through atmospheric braking. With cheap steel and water, space stations become large enough to hold parks and gardens, then grow still larger. People stay longer. They bring their families.

With cheap fuel, the cost of reaching the lunar surface drops dramatically. A Moon base is built using asteroidal steel and propellants; for scientific and sentimental reasons advocates of Moon mining have an uphill battle against the conventional wisdom about space development. In time, however, the Moon becomes a source of aluminum and titanium for use in space industry, since it proves to be richer in these materials than are the more accessible asteroids.

This scenario assumes use of Lightsails; asteroidal resources would remain attractive even using ion engines, deployable solar sails, or chemical rockets burning liquid oxygen and hydrogen (LOX) and liquid hydrogen (LH^2) from electrolyzed asteroidal water.

Twenty-eight years ago, in a fit of political hysteria, the U.S. took a path that bypassed building a shuttle and space station, building instead a giant missile to fulfill an ancient dream. In 1969 it reached its goal, but at a great price to true space development: the "Moon shots" dominated the news about space, and made spaceflight seem like an expensive stunt. The space program collapsed afterwards.

Today, it is said that a lunar base is the logical next step. There is even talk of lunar colonies, far from the terrestrial markets that could pay for them. Let us turn our eyes from the "romance" of the Moon—long enough, at least, to consider sailing on sunlight to mine steel, water, gold, and platinum from flying mountains.

Iceslinger

JOHN HEGENBERGER

Conditions in a lunar colony would be rather different from that of a space habitat or L–5 colony. While it's only one-sixth Earth's, the gravity on the Moon is real, not artificial as in a space habitat. Also, O'Neill colonies have to be built with a lot of open space. A Lunar base doesn't, and most models have the colony carved out of caves, which also act as a shield for the various ionizing radiations traveling in space. It's certainly possible to roof over a large crater, and it will be done; but I doubt that there will be any larger surface cities.

Lunar farmers have a problem their O'Neill compatriots don't have. The Sun doesn't shine all the time. During the long Lunar night there's got to be heat and light for their plants. There are a lot of schemes to provide that, from full-time artificial light to Mylar-roofed craters with an opaque roof that can be put on over it (and artificial lights, of course). You certainly have to cover any transparencies (large ones, anyway) during the night cycle. If you didn't you'd lose all heat to radiation. The effective temperature of outer space is about −200°C (73°K) and heat radiates proportional to the fourth power of the temperature difference. Even here with Earth's atmosphere to catch some of that outgoing heat it's always *much* colder on a clear than a cloudy night.

Luna is downright warm when compared to some of the moons of outer planets such as Jupiter or Neptune. In "Iceslinger" John Hegenberger takes us out to the Jovian moons, where survival takes on new meaning.

1

SOMEONE IN WINNER CORP was trying to ruin Ted Clamber's career. Or at least it seemed that way to him.

First he'd been ordered to drop everything and catch the Io-Ganymede shuttle, with no indication of the trip's purpose. Then for two days he floated around doing diddly, waiting for Field VP Charles Quiller to set up a meeting to explain why Ted had been pulled away from his tug assignment.

The face-off was scheduled for 16:00 in the Captain's quarters, away from the passengers, crew, and cargo of the inter-Jovian transport. But Ted would have gladly met the man at the center of the shuttle's forward radio dish, if it meant finding out why he'd been sent without warning to one of Winner Corp's Ganymede ice stations.

An amber light glowed outside the Captain's portal, signaling privacy. Ted keyed in his ID number and waited for clearance. Even this minor security delay grated on his nerves; who did they think they were dealing with? He'd been with the Corp for almost eight years now, six of them beyond the Belt. Didn't that command some sort of trust and respect? The light went green and the hatch automatically undogged.

The Captain's quarters were decorated with light wood paneling. It was a sign of status within the company, when an exec had natural Earthtones in his living space. Ted was impressed, but quickly decided that when his time came, he'd opt for something a little less gaudy than knotty pine. Maybe thick slabs of marble. The sheer cost of lifting them out of Earth's g-well ought to impress anyone.

"Thank you, Captain. We'll only need your office for a few minutes," said a rugged, blond man.

Ted waited while the disgruntled and whisker-faced officer floated out of the room. After the hatch had re-dogged itself, the blond man stuck out a hand and said, "Sorry for all the mystery, but it's absolutely necessary. I'm Chuck Quiller."

"We've met before, sir," Ted Clamber said, completing the handshake and looking directly into the man's cold, blue eyes. "Two years ago, at the company's annual meeting on Titan. I flew you and several other VPs to the Satfive station."

The older man's face remained stiff, as he held himself in place beside the hatch. "Is that right? Well, it's a small system. . . ."

Ted finished the familiar Winner Corp slogan with a smile. " . . . And a big deal."

They chuckled.

This guy's a real dork, Ted thought. "So what's the situation, here? I was due for some downtime, when I got ordered to grab this shuttle and accompany you to Gany."

Quiller gestured toward a flatscreen embedded in the pine paneling, and the two men strapped into slings in front of its keyboard. A classified personnel file was on the screen. It was Ted's.

"I don't particularly like what I read here," Quiller said. "But the CEO wants me to work with you."

Well, excuse me all to hell, old man.

"Says here that you've had almost two hundred flight hours in an Io Hopscotch. That right?"

Ted was a little miffed that his file had been accessed without his knowledge, but he knew enough to keep his mouth shut about it, for now. Besides, you don't get answers, if you're busy complaining. There would be plenty of time later to pitch a bitch to Personnel about this invasion of his privacy.

"Yes," he said evenly. "I started out flying one of those pogos when I was first assigned to the inter-Jovian system. But, why's that important? Gany's mass/density irregularities have always defeated the ship's landing computers and made it too dangerous to use a Hopscotch there."

The VP scratched his left earlobe with his right hand. "That's true enough," he said. "Until now."

Ted glowed inwardly. *Bingo. Front row.* "So, I get to pilot—"

"Not just yet," the older man told him. "You're the co-pilot . . . if we ever get the ship on that ice ball in one piece."

Chuck Quiller downloaded Ted's file into a data chip. Then he broke the chip into slivers, destroying the info. "Last night, someone entered the cargo bay and tried to discover what was in the pogo's crate."

Ted took a guess. "Someone? You mean Tiamat? They'd love to get ahead of us in ice processing; they've only got half as many stations on Gany as Winner Corp."

"I'm certain it was someone on board who thinks Tiamat would pay plenty for info on what we're doing, or planning to do, on Ganymede. The only reason I'm not sure is that the shuttle's DNA tracer is broken and there's no way to identify who tried to sneak a peek at our cargo."

"Well, I'll keep my eyes open," Ted said.

"You'll do better than that," Quiller told him. "Starting right now, you're standing watch over that crate until we dock at Philusulca."

Ted cursed to himself. The cargo bay wasn't heated, so he'd have to wear a stiff and clumsy pressure suit. *What a corporation. They're paying me 200 credits a day to babysit a crate.*

"Do you have a problem with my instructions?" Quiller asked, watching him keenly.

"No, sir."

Shit runs downhill. Except in micrograv, where it's all around you.

2

Ted only stood three hours' watch in the cargo hold, because some mysterious person or persons upped the ante by sabotaging the shuttle's retros. The first Ted knew of it was via a comlink from Quiller telling him to trade places with him and come forward to inspect the ship's guidance system.

Quiller briefed him further as they swapped stations. The older man confided that he was beginning to suspect the Captain, except that without retros, the shuttle was helpless ever to land safely, and that no captain would be likely to cripple his own ship. Ted was instructed to lend his expertise to determine if there was any hope in repairing the command system.

Of course, it had been a thorough rip job. The computer's guts were strung out and plucked clean like harvest time in a hydroponics farm. And the backup module was missing! Ted figured the officers and security personnel would be on report for the rest of their careers. The only thing they could do was to use the attitude adjusters as best they could to heave to and brake their glide, until another shuttle could deliver a replacement command mod. That would take days, and the Tiamat saboteur would get plenty of chances to check out the cargo.

Ted rushed back to where Quiller was guarding the goods and discovered that the VP had taken things into his own hands.

"War is hell," Quiller said. "Especially Corp War. No sense waiting for them to make the next move." He finished unfolding the Hopscotch's crate. "Come on. Get in. We'll use this baby to nudge the shuttle into a better flight plan."

Ted felt excitement and elation. No wonder this guy was a VP; he took action! And the ship was a beauty, much more elegant than the pogos he'd flown on Io.

As he climbed into the aft seat, facing the opposite direction from the pilot, Ted noticed that the ship's fuel capacity was three times that of the older models. And there were four major screens to watch as the computer analyzed the grav-to-thrust ratio. This was one hot Hopscotch and he told Quiller so.

"Glad you like it, son," the VP said, initiating launch. "Our 'friends' at Tiamat will probably shit when they see it. At least I hope so. Now, if you're ready, I'll pop the bay doors and we'll see what this thing can do."

They drifted smoothly from the shuttle bay and followed the pogo's computer commands to fire the plasma engines and begin the nudging operation.

Above his head, Ted got his first good view of the approaching Jovian moon. Ganymede sat in a bowl of stars eclipsed slightly by the boiling orange-and-white ball of Jupiter. The dark blemish of Galileo Regio dominated the moon's surface, and the "stretch marks" of the glacier flows crisscrossed the wrinkled areas not in the primary's shadow.

The radio barked. "Mr. Quiller, this is the Shuttle Captain. Philusulca just sent up a message that another shuttle will be coming up in about a day."

"Roger, Captain," Quiller answered sarcastically. "We'll be happy to hang around long enough for your passengers and crew to get a good look at us, but then we're going to use this here fancy ship to make our own way down. If you don't mind."

Ted keyed the ship's radio and asked, "Don't you think that's a little abrupt?"

"It's damn suspicious," Quiller answered, "that a rescue message didn't come through until after this ship was launched and exposed. The last thing we need right now is a second shuttleload of sneaking Tiamat spies. Do you have a problem with that?"

"No, sir," Ted responded. "I just don't want anyone to think we're being reckless with Winner Corp property."

"We need a shakedown cruise, anyway," Quiller radioed. "We'll be heading for Icestation Five near Aquarius Sulcus. Let me know, Clamber, if you have any trouble understanding how this baby operates."

"No problem, sir," Ted answered. *I could fly this thing with my eyes closed.* But the truth was, most of the instrument panel was new to him. And he was uneasy about the way Quiller had hurriedly decided to pull them out of the tricky situation on the shuttle. *We could have damaged the ship,* he thought. *This guy takes too many chances. Working with him could jeopardize my career. Not to mention my life.*

3

There was another tricky situation forming in front of them.

The skill of flying a pogo back on Io depended largely on the on-board computer's ability to estimate the acceleration vs. counter-thrust requirements for the short quick transport hops from site to site across the planet. Ganymede's irregular density had always played havoc with the computer's programmed estimates, making such a ship terribly expensive to operate, and a threat to its occupants or the groundcrew.

The two competing Corps were forced to depend on the much slower but safer ground transportation in order to get equipment, supplies, and people to and from their profitable iceslinger stations. But Winner Corp's profits would rise and eventually they would be able to buy out the Tiamat consortium, if this new Hopscotch could process the irregular data quickly enough to permit safe and efficient takeoffs and landings.

Ted wanted his name to be at the top of the list, when promotions were being handed out for this new corporate triumph. But right now, his name would be sludge, if they didn't get through the ice storm they'd encountered on the way down to Gany. He tried to contact the station, but all he got was an earful of static.

"What's wrong with the radio?" he asked with alarm.

"Iceslinger Five is up near the pole, so there's heavy ion interference from Jupiter," Quiller told him. "Messes up the compass, too."

Ted felt his shorts tightening. "How the hell are we supposed to navigate in a storm like this?"

"We go in low and spot a mountain and then compare our altimeter reading with the geo-charts on your upper-lefthand screen."

"Are you nuts?" Ted shouted. "We're doing six hundred klicks an hour. What if we hit one of those damn mountains?"

"You're the co-pilot," Quiller told him. "It's your job to navigate around them."

Screw me! Ted thought, watching a huge dark shape loom out of the sworling whiteness just off their starboard wingtip.

"Where'd all this soup come from, anyway?" he asked. "I thought Gany was too small to maintain an atmosphere."

"It's a side-effect of our Nuclear Summer program. We heat up sections of the planetoid to facilitate the ice-mining operations. As a result, we get a little wind and fog."

"A little?" Ted growled between his teeth. "This is a blinding snowstorm!"

"Quit complaining and find us a coordinate, son. Nobody figured we'd be flying this far when they loaded the Hopscotch into the shuttle. We've only got a quarter of our normal fuel load and that's just about spent."

"Holy shit!" Ted tried to spot a mountaintop with one eye, while he scanned the coordinates on the ship's screen with the other.

He spotted a humpbacked peak off to their left. Quiller nearly racked them up going over it, bucking the pale haze that streaked the canopy. The altimeter read six hundred meters. They were hugging the ground blind!

Ted frantically scrolled through the terrain maps for areas around Station Five. He located two possibles and keyed them into Quiller's screens.

"Try one of these," he said, praying that the whiteness would dissipate near their landing site. "They're sure to have some sort of lights down there for us to zero in on."

"Not if they don't know we're coming," the pilot said.

The static! Ted thought. We don't have a radio, so nobody down there knew that Quiller pulled the pogo off the shuttle. They were flying unannounced into the station. *When we get down, I'm going to kill this guy!*

They circled the area indicated on Ted's first screen and came up with nothing. If there was any life below them, Ted couldn't see it. The other possible site was thirty klicks to the northeast on the other side of Cadmus Tooth Mountain.

The Hopscotch shuddered as its fuel diminished.

"Are we going to make it?" Ted shouted.

"No problem," Quiller answered. "We'll forge up one side of the mountain and coast down the other, right into the IC5."

Ted was confused. "You . . . you know where we are?"

"I do now," Quiller answered. "Been here seven times in the last year."

You could have told me, Ted thought, feeling his blood begin to flow again, as they eased their ship over the mountaintop. Ted felt the pogo's vibrations fade away.

"That's the last of our fuel," Quiller said.

Below, in the distance, twin rings of laser spots shot up from the white-on-white surface. Ted was sure that the VP was approaching at a poor angle and they would skid across the ice flow and pile up on a ragged cliff. Then they were down, and he was sure he would have kissed the ground, if only it had been safe to take off his helmet.

"Welcome to IC5," Quiller said. "Check this baby into the inspection hanger. I'm heading for the exec lounge."

4

He'd report him, that's what he'd do! He'd take it all the way up to the CEO. The son of a bitch would lose his seniority, for pulling such a—

"Ted," someone called, as they marched along beside the frozen rails of the iceslinger leading to the loading dome. "Ted Clamber. Is that you?"

He must be hearing things. "Janny . . . ?" he called in wonderment.

"Hey, Photon Man!"

Ted grimaced. That was Janice, all right. Nobody else knew him by that silly sexual reference. He turned and saw a dark bundle bounding in his direction.

"Janice Cleveburg," he called, as she caught her momentum and clutched at his sleeve. "What are you doing here?"

"I'm the Head of the IC5 Transport Division. I thought that was you coming out of the new pogo. Pretty fancy . . . for a truck driver."

The faceplate of her suit was scored from months of flying grit. He could almost see the sparkle in her dark brown eyes and the hint of a smirk at the corners of her wide mouth.

"Hey, nothing to it," he lied. "I just dropped in for a cup of your lye tea."

"That's *lime* tea," she corrected. "Well, come on inside. I'll see what I can do. Your friend want a cup, too?"

Ted realized that Quiller had ignored them and was now entering the dome complex without him. "I don't think so, Janny," he said. "In fact, I'd just as soon keep away from that guy for a while. We've already spent too much time together."

She shrugged, linking an arm through his.

Over the next few days, Janice Cleveburg instructed Ted in a variety of Iceslinger operations. The long catapult accelerator flung loads of frozen ice up into orbital collection points outside the moon's g-well. It was one of five such stations operated by Winner Corp at leased sites on Gany's surface. The company was building a sixth station near Sicyon Sulcus, where all the current crop of Grounddiggers were squatting. Ted's parents had been Grounddiggers on Io. He never wanted to go back to a life of living in your truck and scooping out a claim, so some larger company could pay you a pittance for your load while making millions once it was delivered to the drier planets, like Venus, or Mars.

"I heard about your run-in with Tiamat," Janice said as they walked inside the east sector of the complex. "We've had trouble with down here, too."

"What kind of trouble?"

She shrugged, and tossed her silky brown hair in a low-g sworl. She did that a lot, so she must have known how it affected him. "Missing equipment. Threats to our digger families. Just a general nuisance really, but I've heard that they're not above a little clandestine terrorism."

"Hmm," Ted mused. "Quiller calls it a Corp War."

"I'll bet they'd love to get their hands on your new Hopscotch," Janice said.

A digger truck approached the entrance, churning its way through the crushed, powdery ice. Janice checked with the driver and tested the load to evaluate its quality, while Ted scanned to help ensure that there was no foreign content. Finally, the vehicle was cleared to chug along to the main scoop.

Ted watched as Janice entered data on the delivery into the Slinger's data system. "Having that ship for quick jumps from station to station will do a lot of good for the Transport Division," she said, turning her chair around and leaning her elbows against the console. The pose accentuated her modest breasts. "I'll probably get a bigger budget and two new people on staff, just to coordinate the increase in traffic. But I thought you were supposed to be test-flying it with your buddy, the VP."

Ted reached out and pulled her in his arms. "I will be," he said. "Just as soon as Quiller gets through playing around." He couldn't tell her that the pogo had registered an unidentified radar source originating from somewhere between Stations Three and Five. And that, until a careful ground search could locate what was surely a hidden Tiamat operation, Quiller kept all the flights over the suspicious area to himself.

He looked deeply into her dark eyes. "Speaking of playing around . . ."

"Hey, Icy," the radio crackled from the console. "This is the Marker family. We need your help!"

Janice slid back into her chair and keyed a switch on the radio. "Roger, Marker. This is IC5. You're not coming in very clear. What's the problem?" She turned and told Ted, "They're one of our diggers; probably need a battery jump."

The voice on the radio sounded shattered. "We broke a track and one of my boys cut his hand real bad trying to get it fixed."

Janice scanned a printout from the vectorlink. "Roger, Marker. We have your location. Hang on; we'll have a crew and doctor out to you in about an hour. Standard rates."

"Thanks Icy. We'll be waiting."

Janice's chair creaked as she came to her feet. "Well, Photon Man," she said. "How about a little exercise?"

"Sounds good to me, Janny. But shouldn't we do something to help that guy first?"

"Idiot! Go down to the ground crew station at the south entrance. Give them these coodinates," she said, handing him the printout. "I'll get a doctor and meet you there."

5

They rode the half-track "alligator" through the rough and frozen terrain to where the Marker family waited in their crippled digger. Ted kept his eye out for any unexpected outcroppings or gullies. Gany was known for its sinewy ridges and wavy rows of multi-layered ice.

Janice drove while Bill Thompson, the doctor, talked first aid through the radio. The wind whipped around in front of them and pounded at the sides of the half-track as it slowly crunched along to the rescue site. Ted could see why the radio transmissions had been blurred. This was the harshest environment outside of the Red Spot.

When they arrived, he suited up and went out to help Papa Marker and his boys wrestle the track back onto their digger during a driving storm. The cut on young Timmy's hand proved to be deep and jagged. Doc Thompson decided to stay with his patient during the drive back, in case symptoms of shock developed.

Ted clumsily piled back into the alligator, and discovered he was drenched with sweat and feeling uncomfortably drained.

"Damned suit's got a faulty AC unit," he complained. "I thought I was going to drown before I could get it off."

Janice laughed and muttered something about "the first man to drown in his own perspiration," and then steered the half-track around on a course back to IC5. "Too bad Doc Thompson isn't still with us," she said. "He's a pretty good micro-mechanic, too."

Ted was pulling his leg out of a boot when the radio spat a message at them.

"Mayday, Mayday! This is Quiller in the screaming Hopscotch. I've got a faulty fuel adjuster and am going to try and ditch into a snowbank. Coordinates two-twenty degrees east, fifty degrees south. Mayday!"

"That's your VP," Janice said, trying to adjust the radio while steering the half-track over the ice.

Ted came forward in the cramped vehicle and said, "Here, let me do that." He struggled to keep the signal clear, but it faded in and out and weakened completely after only a few minutes.

"The damn ion storm's starting up again. He's only about thirty-five klicks to our southwest," Janice said. "Do you want to try and catch him?"

"Hell, yes. The way he sounded, we may be the only people to have heard his message."

Janice radioed over to the Markers that they were going to break off and pursue another rescue. She told them to continue on in to IC5 and to let the security department know about the situation.

"You realize, of course," she said, swinging the vehicle around an outcropping of black rock and into the white, blinding wind, "that this has all the makings of a classic ambush."

Ted smiled. "Nah, it's Quiller, all right; he used the codeword 'screaming.' I can't wait to see his face when he finds out who's coming to rescue him."

"Don't get cocky, Teddy," Janice warned. "Quiller's signal went out on a broad beam from an uncharted sector. If any Tiamat personnel picked it up, we may have a tug-o'-war on our hands."

6

They crawled along the frozen terrain for more than four hours. Ted tried to raise a response from Quiller on the radio, but the swell of Jovian ions continued to loop through the magnetosphere and blanket the frequencies. If there were a UHF up-link in the Hopscotch, he thought, a clear signal could be received on the flatscreen. You'd think the designers would have prepared for such a situation. Ah, but that's why he and the Quiller were getting haz-duty pay; it was their job to identify all the bugs before Winner Corp built a whole fleet of Hopscotches.

"I think I see something," Janice said.

Ted leaned into the forward window.

"Careful!" the woman cried, pulling at his collar. "If your face touches that frozen plex, I'll have to peel you off."

Ted backed away, still trying to spot the pogo. "All I see is a deep crevasse," he complained.

"Look over to the left, on the other side. There!"

"Oh, yeah . . . I see it now. It's half buried in the snow."

"If we don't get over there soon, it'll be completely buried."

"Well, what are we waiting for? Let's go!"

"I suppose you noticed that canyon in front of us," Janice replied. They had come to the edge of one of the planetoid's huge series of parallel wrinkles, one of the strange surface structures created by Jupiter's tidal forces on the Gany ice flows. It looked to Ted as if the first steep drop was at least a hundred meters straight down. And the next ridge over, where the pogo sat, was more than four klicks away.

"Doesn't look good," Janice sighed. "Your partner could be badly hurt or frozen. I'll have to find a way around this, before we can pick him up."

"How long will *that* take?" Ted asked, hearing the edge in his voice.

"I told you this area was uncharted. I've got sky maps for general reference, but they won't tell me a thing about how safe it is to drive this hulking half-track across an ice ridge. This is one of those situations, Ted, where we're near enough to see, but too far away to help."

"Don't say that," Ted snapped. "There's a man out there possibly dying, and a classified lander worth billions of dollars. There's got to be a way to get to him. You people couldn't continue to live in this environment, if you gave up so easily. Now, what's the answer?"

Janice stroked the soft hair behind her left ear. "Well . . . you're not going to like it."

"Tell me."

"You could try and fit into my suit and take a jet pack over the crevasse. The winds look traitorous, but if you carried a second pack over to your VP, the two of you could shoot back here in less than an hour."

Ted swallowed dryly. His mind scrambled for another solution; any other solution. But he couldn't come up with one.

"Makes sense," he had to admit. After all, he was the pilot and she was the most experienced at driving the half-track. If anything further went wrong, she could still try and find a way across the canyon. "So, where are these jet packs?"

"Back in the locker," Janice said. "The one marked 'Danger: Explosives.' "

7

I must be out of my frigging mind, Ted thought, climbing out of the alligator. The wind nearly took him off his feet, as he strapped the jets into place on his back. Then he radioed to Janice, "Can you still hear me?"

"Loud and clear," she responded.

The frigid wind peppered him with a frozen grit of ice. Outside his suit, the temperature was 150 degrees below, and the icy wind blew past at seventy kph.

Ted stooped to pick up the jet pack that Quiller would need to get back to the alligator. The joints of his suit were already stiffening. *I'd better not stand around here much longer, or I'll become part of the scenery.*

He picked up his right foot and carefully watched the snowshoe settle on the surface of the cold, blank carpet that led to the edge of the crevasse.

"Okay," he radioed. "I'm on my way."

"Don't go too close to the edge. The ice might break off and—"

"Listen, Janny, I know what I'm doing," he lied. "Let me concentrate, will you?"

"Just be careful, Ted."

"Keep quiet, and I will," he complained.

Flying a jet pack through this storm was going to be a real treat. Ted tromped his way to the canyon and checked the controls one more time. He calculated that a low blast would lift him up a couple of meters and then an increase in lateral thrust would carry him across the black and jagged gap in front of him. The biggest challenge, as always, would be landing. If he leaned into the wind, he could try and stay on a stationary course. And if he throttled the jet exhaust back carefully enough, he could dangle within a few meters of the downed pogo.

At the last second, he decided to switch the extra jet pack to his left arm, in order to have additional ballast against the wind. Then, he jabbed the ignition switch with his thumb and felt the jets kick him off the ground.

Immediately, he was taken by a gut-wrenching fear as the storm tried to spin him around. In another second, the wind would have him wobbling like a top. *Where are the damn stabilizers on this thing?* he screamed to himself, while clutching at every control he could find. His body pitched forward and, for a terrifying second, he thought he would rocket headfirst into the maw of the crevasse. Steady torqueing of the left steering rod brought him upright again, and the spinning was now under control, as well.

Well now, he thought, *that wasn't so bad. But why didn't I test this damn thing out, before attempting to fly across the canyon with it?* He muttered into the radio, "I must have a death wish."

"You're doing fine," Janice answered. "Just don't drop the other pack."

Ted glanced down and saw that the extra jet pack was dangling from only one strap. *No wonder I'm off balance,* he thought, as the opposite lip of the frozen crevasse passed beneath his feet. He hefted the pack into his arms and steered a course straight for the Hopscotch.

He was throttling down and trying to catch a glimpse of any life signs in the broken pogo, when his feet struck the slippery surface and zipped out from under him on the hard, angled ice. Fear leapt from his mouth as he went down with a crunching crack.

The wind blew white dust across his faceplate. Three red alarm lights flashed inside his helmet. He had taken Janice's suit, because the AC unit in his was faulty. Now hers had a leaking joint in the right knee, a cracked air exchanger, and a break in the radio antenna.

"Janny, can you still hear me?" he called.

"Increase the gain," came the faint reply. "Your signal's dropping."

"Shit," he said flatly.

"Come again? I can't hear you."

"My jets melted a sheet of ice and I slipped on it. Now my suit's all banged up!"

"Are you all right?"

"I don't know," he said, coming to his feet. "I think so, but sonofagodamnbitch!"

"What?"

"I crushed the exhaust on my goddamn jet pack! You're going to have to find a way around here to pick us up. I won't be able to get this thing fixed without a goddamn fucking machine shop!"

"All—all right. Take it easy. Is Quiller okay?"

Oh yeah . . . Ted thought. *I forgot about the VP.*

"Hold on. I'm going to see if I can get into the lander."

He stumbled his way over to the downed pogo and started scooping ice crystals away from the ship's hatch. In his palm he could feel a faint pounding, which was coming from inside the Hopscotch.

"Quiller, is that you?" he radioed, and then realized how stupid it must sound. Of course it was him. "It's me, Clamber. Can you hear me?"

The hatch popped open a crack and Ted got his fingers under it, heaving upward. From inside, a suited figure grabbed at his arms and pulled him forward.

Ted found his helmet being pressed tight against the plex faceplate of Quiller's suit. He shook his head to help adjust to the extreme closeup view of the other man's features through his own faceplate. A buzzing voice said, "My radio's down. Only way we can talk is through conduction."

Great. I can't fly and you can't talk. "Are you all right?" Ted shouted.

Quiller banged his helmet against Ted's in a nodding gesture.

Ted relayed the info to Janice. "I've got him, and he's okay. The storm seems to be dying down, so you better start coming around."

"Roger," Janice answered. "I'm heading west. If you two can walk parallel on your side of the sulcus, we'll meet that much sooner."

"Good idea," Ted responded, unstrapping the broken jet pack. He pulled the extra one on in its place and then conked helmets again with Quiller. "Come on, sir. We're going for a little walk."

8

They had gotten a good two and a half klicks west of the Hopscotch when the storm rose up again.

Quiller was dressed only in his flightsuit and had a hard time walking without snowshoes, but the high winds had hardened the crust into semi-solid patches, so he only sank once in the dry, sifting crystals. Ted's mind flashed on an image of them both sinking over their heads, swimming in a sea of frozen ice and methane.

The VP pulled Ted to him and said, "We're going to get lost out here in this storm. The only shelter is in the pogo."

Ted's blood seemed to thicken with fear. Quiller was right. They were going to have to go back.

An hour later, Ted was almost blind with exhaustion. The injured knee joint had frozen solid, and the air exchanger was making a threatening sound.

The storm came back in full force, by the time they reached the ship. Janice and the alligator must have been out of range of his radio, because there were no responses to his many calls.

As the two men climbed back into the pogo, Ted's stomach began to growl. *Right now, I'd give my right nut for just a whiff of Janny's lime tea.*

Quiller shook his shoulder and pointed.

At first, Ted didn't see anything but the Hopscotch's instrument panel. Then it hit him; one of the screens had been smashed and the fuel control programs were missing from the computer.

"I didn't do that," Quiller's voice buzzed. "We've had company."

Tiamat!

"I guess the crash and the rescue affected my judgment," the VP explained. "I should have destroyed the ship before we left."

"It's only been a few hours, at best," Ted shouted. "They couldn't have gotten very far. Let's look around."

Ted and Quiller scrambled back outside to find that the storm was letting up again.

This goddamned moon, Ted cursed. He looked up. The storm seemed to have risen above them somehow. Now you couldn't even see the russet orb of Jupiter. He scrolled through the frequencies on his radio for the hundredth time, hoping to pick up a random signal from the competition.

Nothing.

Quiller was climbing up on top of a large outcropping of black rock. He waved his hands and pointed just as Ted received a faint call on the radio from Janice.

" . . . are you guys? Come in, Ted. Can you hear me? This is Cleveburg. I've made it around the crevasse, where are you guys? Come in, Ted. Can you—"

"Janny! Get over here as quick as you can!"

"What—what's wrong? Are you hurt?"

"Tiamat's been in the Hopscotch and they've taken the fuel control system."

9

Janice drew up a few seconds after Quiller came down from the rock. The three of them swapped stories inside the alligator.

"We've got a good chance of stopping them, if we hurry," Quiller said. "I could see their half-track chugging along to the west."

Ted thought this was a grave risk, but he had to hand it to the VP for proposing a courageous response. "We'll have to run at top speed to overtake them. And we don't have any weapons on board, if they decide to put up a fight."

"Look, all we need to do is stop them until one of our rescue teams arrive. That shouldn't be too hard; in fact, I think I know a way that should work nicely." He turned to Janice and asked, "Can you get moving?"

She looked at Ted, but answered with a nod.

"Good. Get that extra jet pack, son. As soon as we can come alongside the other vehicle, I want you to toss it to me."

Ted realized what the VP had in mind, and was grateful that the more dangerous part of the plan hadn't been delegated to him.

Twenty minutes later, the alligator was closing in on the Tiamat half-track. Ted and Quiller were riding topside as the gap between the two racing vehicles gradually closed. Their top speed through the rough and frozen terrain was less than thirty kph, but the Tiamat tractor swerved occasionally, ramming the alligator with bone-jarring impacts.

Ted watched as Quiller timed his jump from one vehicle to the other, and then held his breath when the man landed on the

Tiamat half-track, nearly sliding along the side into the grinding treads. For a heartbeat, he hung there, his legs threatening to be ground to pulp by the whorling gears. Then the vehicle swerved away, and Quiller swung his body up from danger.

Achieving a safe perch on the top of the tractor, the VP gestured with a sweep of his hand. Ted gathered his feet under him, pulled his arm back and threw the jet pack across the gap between the two speeding vehicles. He watched as it landed heavily against Quiller's right shoulder. It tumbled and rolled, and Ted was sure it would bounce to the ground, but the VP caught hold of one strap and drew it to him.

Janice let the alligator drop back when she saw Quiller strapping the jet pack to the side of the Tiamat vehicle. Ted watched and waited, while the VP and the tractor grew smaller in the distance. *Come on,* he thought. Then he moaned. Someone was crawling out of the pressure hatch on the side of the Tiamat vehicle. They had finally figured out what was going on and were coming to investigate. If Quiller didn't hurry—

The jet pack flashed to life with a brilliant glare. Quiller and the other man were thrown free, as the vehicle responded suddenly to the lateral force and skidded along the icy surface. Janice accelerated the alligator forward in a rescue attempt, as the Tiamat tractor began to spin clockwise like a roman candle, bouncing from outcropping to black boulder, until it came to rest at a slant against a solid cliff face.

Ted launched himself at his adversary, finding an easy victory, since the man had been stunned by the fall. Within minutes, the three men were standing in a group beside the wrecked vehicle.

"All right, Weston," Ted radioed on a broad beam, having read the man's name off the side of his helmet. "Open this baby up, or we'll torch it permanently."

The man's dark eyes glared with hatred, but he shrugged his arms out of Ted's hold and bent to key in a code that opened the vehicle's pressure lock. Once inside, Ted and Quiller found the vehicle's driver, bloody and unconscious where his head had struck a protrusion above the control unit. They popped the seals on their helmets and inspected the man's wound.

"He's not dead," Quiller said. "But he's lost a lot of juice." He turned to the Tiamat man. "Better get a medpack on that wound before he bleeds to death."

Ted found the pogo's missing fuel system in a shielded storage bin. "This is all the evidence we need to get your Corp booted off the moon," he said, but Weston just snickered deep in his throat.

"He knows something," Quiller said. "What's with the laughter, mister?"

The man finished bandaging his companion and turned to face them. "The rest of my people will be here any time now."

"Don't try to bluff us, shithead. You couldn't have contacted your people; the ion flare has all the radios down."

Weston smiled. "Radios, yes. Videos, no." He cocked his head toward a small two-way vid unit connected to the tractor's instrument panel. "Smile and wave to the folks back at Tiamat. We've been using UHF for almost a year now."

"Aw hell," Quiller said. He punched a button on the vid unit, and a small screen to the left of the camera lens popped to life. Ted saw the face of an angry, red-bearded man.

"Weston," a stern voice called. "You are ordered to take command of those people and hold them in custody, until our task force arrives in the next few minutes."

"Task force?" Ted swallowed.

"Thirty minutes?" Quiller said.

"Yes, Commander!" Weston answered, but Ted shoved the man away from the camera.

"We've got people on the way here, too, you know," he said. "Any attempts to attack us and Weston here will be thrown outside. Without a suit."

"Don't let them bluff you, Commander," Weston said. "I mean nothing."

Quiller smashed a fist into the man's face. Weston's head snapped back to crack against the bulkhead and he slumped to the deck.

The screen went blank.

Ted felt for a pulse in the man's throat. "He's still alive, but we'd better get the hell out of here."

10

After a brief conference—with the vid unit completely shut down—Ted and Quiller concluded that their best bet was to try to use the Tiamat communications system to call IC5. Quiller searched the wavelengths, finally getting through to the station, only to discover that the rescue had been delayed because of the storm. It would be more than a hour before the arrival of any assistance.

"Terrific," Ted grumbled. "I risk my life to save your neck and now I'm in the middle of a goddamn Corp War. If I ever live through this, I'll probably get demoted for going so far out on a limb and causing a confrontation."

Quiller shot him a glance and said, "If you weren't so worried about your goddamn career, you'd get off your butt and do something worthwhile. Do you think I got to be a VP by hiding on an Io ore tug?"

Ted felt fury building inside of him. The words stung. He had seen this man risk his life recklessly and come out on top. Maybe the way to the top was to take a few risks now and then, but he hated hearing about it from a man he'd just had to rescue.

Janice's voice coming from the radio broke the tension. "Hey, you'd better get back here. We're going to have company, real soon."

Ted bent to make sure that Weston was securely tied to his seat. Quiller collected a few extra pressure suits and the pogo's computer system.

"We'd better take the vid unit, too," the VP said. "Either that, or smash it so our friend here doesn't come to and find a way to use it."

Ted disconnected the unit from its power source and pulled it from the console. In a few minutes, the two men were cycling through the alligator's hatch, just as two new Tiamat half-tracks came churning into view along the western ridge.

One pulled up beside the damaged tractor, but the other moved in pursuit of the Winner Corp vehicle.

"We're outta here," Janice cried. And the alligator lurched to the north.

In less than ten minutes, it was clear that they would never make it. The Tiamat vehicle was much more advanced in design for rapid movement through the frozen terrain.

"Can't we call IC5 and have them adjust the sling to throw a load of ice on those guys?"

Janice ignored him, but Quiller explained that the idea would work only if the target were in a direct line with the iceslinger.

"I was joking!" Ted exclaimed. "Don't you ever kid around to relieve a little tension?"

"The time to kid around is after we're back at IC5," the VP said.

"Where the hell's that storm when we need it?" Ted complained.

"I can try to keep away from him by maneuvering in and out among these outcroppings, but it's only a matter of time before they catch us."

Ted felt the pressure building up inside his head. Panic was setting in. He regretted arguing with Quiller, but what else was there to do? Now word would get back about his attitude and he'd be embarrassed out of the company. When your image was tarnished, you could never win back your reputation.

Janice raised IC5 on the UHF unit, while Quiller began to disassemble the fuel system from the Hopscotch.

"Wait a minute," Ted cried. "What will happen when word gets out that Tiamat has attacked us?"

Janice looked up. "Nothing," she said.

"Nothing?"

Janice continued. "Tiamat will deny everything. It'll be our word against theirs."

Quiller said, "I wouldn't mind it so much, but it'll take at least a year to get a replacement for this fuel system. The pogo can be salvaged, but this . . ." He looked down at the computer module in his hands and prepared to break it in half.

"Wait!" Ted called, pulling the system out of Quiller's grasp. "I've got an idea how we might get out of this."

11

"Come on, you assholes," Ted taunted their pursuers over the radio, while stumbling through a drift of crystalline ice. Janice and Quiller were wading through behind him. The three had abandoned the alligator minutes ago, in order to head out on foot in the direction of their rescue team.

Ted kept the chatter going, sending the signal back to the empty half-track, where it was relayed on to the Tiamat vehicle. If all went well, the competitors would waste precious time burning their way through the alligator's thick hide.

The Tiamat Commander's voice came over the radio. "Be warned, Whiners. We are right outside your vehicle and prepared to cut our way in with laser torches, if you refuse to open up."

"Any unauthorized breach of this vehicle's integrity will be grounds for trespassing. Your company will be fined heavily for claim jumping, murder, and theft. Tiamat Corp will be restricted from operating on Ganymede, when the System Regents learn the truth. So back off, shithead."

Ted wished he were as confident as he sounded. They were taking a hell of a chance with this reverse Trojan Horse bit.

If the rescue team didn't show up soon, the three of them would die from exposure as the power supplies in their suits dwindled to nothing. A quick check of his own power gauge told Ted that he had only ten minutes until his heating unit shut down for good.

The Commander's voice crackled over the staticky radio. "You poor dumb Whiners. No one will ever know that we are cutting open your vehicle. When they examine the evidence, we will say you were trapped, or killed in an accidental fall into one of the canyons."

Quiller tugged at Ted's sleeve, in order to maintain radio silence, but pointed to their right.

The Tiamat Commander's voice continued in the radio. "According to my estimate you will die from the heat of our torches in the next minute, Whiners. We have tried to negotiate with you, but we knew you wouldn't give up your precious fuel system without dying."

Two large alligators came around a ridge, heading for the empty half-track. Janice signaled them with a strobe, and the three companions began slogging their way to a rendezvous as Ted radioed, "This is my final warning, Commander. If you insist on attacking our vehicle, you will pay the consequences."

"We attack now, you son of a—"

Ted switched off the radio and continued making his way toward the arriving alligators. Quiller and Janice were the first to board. Since the lock would only cycle two people at a time, he danced from foot to foot impatiently waiting his turn. Finally the seal opened and he tumbled inside. The second that the inner seal broke, he popped his helmet and asked, "Did they buy it?"

"They sure did," Quiller answered, pointing to a vid screen. "They're coming through now."

"Wait 'til they find out they're on Vid relay up through Winner's Comsat," Janice said. "Ten minutes from now, every media transmission in the System will be carrying an instant replay of Tiamat's brutal attack on a downed Winner Corp vehicle."

"They'll never work in this town again," Ted laughed.

Quiller munched on a ration bar. "That was a damn fine idea, son. And you see what I meant about taking a risk, in order to gain success. But we'd better get out of here. Those boys mean business."

"Not anymore," Janice said, giving Ted a squeeze.

"Thank you, sir," Ted answered. "I've been watching you and I've learned the truth of that old adage, 'No guts, no glory.' "

"Good for you," Quiller said. "When I first met you, I thought you were as cold as the iceslinger, but you warmed up nicely. When we get back, I'll see that you get a nice promotion out of this."

"And, I'll see that you get a nice cup of lime tea," Janice laughed.

Quiller grimaced. "How can you drink that stuff?"

Ginungagap

MICHAEL SWANWICK

Someday in the future life in space will become ordinary and possibly even mundane, as hard as that is to imagine at this point in time. We only have to go back 500 years to our own Age of Discovery for a model—in fact, the 500th Anniversary of Columbus's first voyage to the New World is almost upon us. Who would have guessed then—certainly not Columbus—that within a hundred years great galleons filled with treasure would sail at regular intervals from the New World to Europe?

And that within 300 more years great mechanically powered ships would make the passage routinely in only a few weeks. Today airliners crisscross the skies making the journey from the New World to Old World in less time than it took to travel from one medieval *city* to the next. Who's to say what marvels tomorrow might bring?

In "Ginungagap" Michael Swanwick writes of such a time when life in space has become the usual. However, this does not mean there has come an end to the unexpected or the marvelous. The universe is like an unexplored box of treasures and frights, and every time we begin to complacently think that we've "seen it all" a story like this comes along to remind us of our sense of wonder.

Who would want it any different?

■ ■ ■

ABIGAIL CHECKED OUT of Mother of Mercy and rode the
translator web to Toledo Cylinder in Juno Industrial Park. Stars
bloomed, dwindled, disappeared five times. It was a long trek,
halfway around the sun.

Toledo was one of the older commercial cylinders, now given
over almost entirely to bureaucrats, paper pushers, and free-lance
professionals. It was not Abigail's favorite place to visit, but she
needed work and 3M had already bought out of her contract.

The job broker had dyed his chest hairs blond and his leg hairs
red. They clashed wildly with his green *cache-sexe* and turquoise
jewelry. His fingers played on a keyout, bringing up an endless
flow of career trivia. "Cute trick you played," he said.

Abigail flexed her new arm negligently. It was a good job, but
pinker than the rest of her. And weak, of course, but exercise
would correct that. "Thanks," she said. She laid the arm underneath one breast and compared the colors. It matched the nipple
perfectly. Definitely too pink. "Work outlook any good?"

"Naw," the broker said. A hummingbird flew past his ear, a
nearly undetectable parting of the air. "I see here that you applied
for the Proxima colony."

"They were full up," Abigail said. "No openings for a gravity
bum, hey?"

"I didn't say that," the broker grumbled. "I'll find— Hello!
What's this?" Abigail craned her neck, couldn't get a clear look
at the screen. "There's a tag on your employment record."

"What's that mean?"

"Let me read." A honeysuckle flower fell on Abigail's hair
and she brushed it off impatiently. The broker had an open-air
office, framed by hedges and roofed over with a trellis. Sometimes Abigail found the older Belt cylinders a little too lavish for
her taste.

"Mmp." The broker looked up. "Bell-Sandia wants to hire you.
Indefinite term one-shot contract." He swung the keyout around so
she could see. "*Very* nice terms, but that's normal for a high-risk
contract."

"High risk? From B-S, the Friendly Communications People?
What kind of risk?"

The broker scrolled up new material. "There." He tapped the
screen with a finger. "The language is involved, but what it boils
down to is they're looking for a test passenger for a device they've
got that uses black holes for interstellar travel."

"Couldn't work," Abigail said. "The tidal forces—"

"Spare me. Presumably they've found a way around that problem. The question is, are you interested or not?"

Abigail stared up through the trellis at a stream meandering across the curved land overhead. Children were wading in it. She counted to a hundred very slowly, trying to look as if she needed to think it over.

Abigail strapped herself into the translation harness and nodded to the technician outside the chamber. The tech touched her console and a light stasis field immobilized Abigail and the air about her while the chamber wall irised open. In a fluid bit of technological sleight of hand, the translator rechanneled her inertia and gifted her with a velocity almost, but not quite, that of the speed of light.

Stars bloomed about her and the sun dwindled. She breathed in deeply and—was in the receiver device. Relativity had cheated her of all but a fraction of the transit time. She shrugged out of harness and frog-kicked her way to the lip station's tug dock.

The tug pilot grinned at her as she entered, then turned his attention to his controls. He was young and wore streaks of brown makeup across his chest and thighs—only slightly darker than his skin. His mesh vest was almost in bad taste, but he wore it well and looked roguish rather than overdressed. Abigail found herself wishing she had more than a *cache-sexe* and nail polish on—some jewelry or makeup, perhaps. She felt drab in comparison.

The star-field wraparound held two inserts routed in by synchronous cameras. Alphanumerics flickered beneath them. One showed her immediate destination, the Bell-Sandia base *Arthur C. Clarke*. It consisted of five wheels, each set inside the other and rotating at slightly differing speeds. The base was done up in red-and-orange supergraphics. Considering its distance from the Belt factories, it was respectably sized.

Abigail latched herself into the passenger seat as the engines cut in. The second insert—

Ginungagap, the only known black hole in the sun's gravity field, was discovered in 2033, a small voice murmured. *Its presence explained the long-puzzling variations in the orbits of the outer planets. The* Arthur C. Clarke *was . . .*

"Is this necessary?" Abigail asked.

"Absolutely," the pilot said. "We abandoned the tourist program a year or so ago, but somehow the rules never caught up.

They're very strict about the regs here." He winked at Abigail's dismayed expression. "Hold tight a minute while—" His voice faded as he tinkered with the controls.

    ... *established forty years later and communications with the Proxima colony began shortly thereafter. Ginungagap* ...

    The voice cut off. She grinned thanks. "Abigail Vanderhoek."

    "Cheyney," the pilot said. "You're the gravity bum, right?"

    "Yeah."

    "I used to be a vacuum bum myself. But I got tired of it, and grabbed the first semipermanent contract that came along."

    "I kind of went the other way."

    "Probably what I should have done," Cheyney said amiably. "Still, it's a rough road. I picked up three scars along the way." He pointed them out: a thick slash across his abdomen, a red splotch beside one nipple, and a white crescent half obscured by his scalp. "I could've had them cleaned up, but the way I figure, life is just a process of picking up scars and experience. So I kept 'em."

    If she had thought he was trying to impress her, Abigail would have slapped him down. But it was clearly just part of an ongoing self-dramatization, possibly justified, probably not. Abigail suspected that, tour trips to Earth excepted, the *Clarke* was as far down a gravity well as Cheyney had ever been. Still he did have an irresponsible, boyish appeal. "Take me past the net?" she asked.

    Cheyney looped the tug around the communications net trailing the *Clarke*. Kilometers of steel lace passed beneath them. He pointed out a small dish antenna on the edge and a cluster of antennae on the back. "The loner on the edge transmits into Ginungagap," he said. "The others relay information to and from Mother."

    "Mother?"

    "That's the traditional name for the *Arthur C. Clarke*." He swung the tug about with a careless sweep of one arm, and launched into a long and scurrilous story about the origin of the nickname. Abigail laughed, and Cheyney pointed a finger. "There's Ginungagap."

    Abigail peered intently. "Where? I don't see a thing." She glanced at the second wraparound insert, which displayed a magnified view of the black hole. It wasn't at all impressive: a red smear against black nothingness. In the star field it was all but invisible.

    "Disappointing, hey? But still dangerous. Even this far out, there's a lot of ionization from the accretion disk."

"Is that why there's a lip station?"

"Yeah. Particle concentration varies, but if the translator was right at the *Clarke*, we'd probably lose about a third of the passengers."

Cheyney dropped Abigail off at Mother's crew lock and looped the tug off and away. Abigail wondered where to go, what to do now.

"You're the gravity bum we're dumping down Ginungagap." The short, solid man was upon her before she saw him. His eyes were intense. His *cache-sexe* was a conservative orange. "I liked the stunt with the arm. It takes a lot of guts to do something like that." He pumped her arm. "I'm Paul Girard. Head of external security. In charge of your training. You play verbal Ping-Pong?"

"Why do you ask?" she countered automatically.

"Don't you know?"

"Should I?"

"Do you mean now or later?"

"Will the answer be different later?"

A smile creased Paul's solid face. "You'll do." He took her arm, led her along a sloping corridor. "There isn't much prep time. The dry run is scheduled in two weeks. Things will move pretty quickly after that. You want to start your training now?"

"Do I have a choice?" Abigail asked, amused.

Paul came to a dead stop. "Listen," he said. "Rule number one: Don't play games with *me*. You understand? Because I always win. Not sometimes, not usually—always."

Abigail yanked her arm free. "You maneuvered me into that," she said angrily.

"Consider it part of your training." He stared directly into her eyes. "No matter how many gravity wells you've climbed down, you're still the product of a near-space culture—protected, trusting, willing to take things at face value. This is a dangerous attitude, and I want you to realize it. I want you to learn to look behind the mask of events. I want you to grow up. And you will."

Don't be so sure. A small smile quirked Paul's face as if he could read her thoughts. Aloud, Abigail said, "That sounds a little excessive for a trip to Proxima."

"Lesson number two," Paul said. "Don't make easy assumptions. You're not going to Proxima." He led her outward-down the ramp to the next wheel, pausing briefly at the juncture to acclimatize to the slower rate of revolution. "You're going to visit spiders." He gestured. "The crew room is this way."

The crew room was vast and cavernous, twilight gloomy. Keyouts were set up along winding paths that wandered aimlessly through the work space. Puddles of light fell on each board and operator. Dark-loving foliage was set between the keyouts.

"This is the heart of the beast," Paul said. "The green keyouts handle all Proxima communications—pretty routine by now. But the blue . . ." His eyes glinting oddly, he pointed. Over the keyouts hung silvery screens with harsh, grainy images floating on their surfaces, black-and-white blobs that Abigail could not resolve into recognizable forms.

"Those," Paul said, "are the spiders. We're talking to them in real-time. Response delay is almost all due to machine translation."

In a sudden shift of perception, the blobs became arachnid forms. That mass of black fluttering across the screen was a spider leg and *that* was its thorax. Abigail felt an immediate, primal aversion, and then it was swept away by an all-encompassing wonder.

"Aliens?" she breathed.

"Aliens."

They actually looked no more like spiders than humans looked like apes. The eight legs had an extra joint each, and the mandible configuration was all wrong. But to an untrained eye they would do.

"But this is— How long have you—? Why in God's name are you keeping this a secret?" An indefinable joy arose in Abigail. This opened a universe of possibilities, as if after a lifetime of being confined in a box someone had removed the lid.

"Industrial security," Paul said. "The gadget that'll send you through Ginungagap to *their* black hole is a spider invention. We're trading optical data for it, but the law won't protect our rights until we've demonstrated its use. We don't want the other corporations cutting in." He nodded toward the nearest black-and-white screen. "As you can see, they're weak on optics."

"I'd love to talk . . ." Abigail's voice trailed off as she realized how little-girl hopeful she sounded.

"I'll arrange an introduction."

There was a rustling to Abigail's side. She turned and saw a large black tomcat with white boots and belly emerge from the bushes. "This is the esteemed head of Alien Communications," Paul said sourly.

Abigail started to laugh, then choked in embarrassment as she realized that he was not speaking of the cat. "Julio Dominguez, section chief for translation," Paul said. "Abigail Vanderhoek, gravity specialist."

The wizened old man smiled professorially. "I assume our resident gadfly has explained how the communications net works, has he not?"

"Well—" Abigail began.

Dominguez clucked his tongue. He wore a yellow *cache-sexe* and matching bow tie, just a little too garish for a man his age. "Quite simple, actually. Escape velocity from a black hole is greater than the speed of light. Therefore, within Ginungagap the speed of light is no longer the limit to the speed of communications."

He paused just long enough for Abigail to look baffled. "Which is just a stuffy way of saying that when we aim a stream of electrons into the boundary of the stationary limit, they emerge elsewhere—out of another black hole. And if we aim them *just so*"—his voice rose whimsically—"they'll emerge from the black hole of our choosing. The physics is simple. The finesse is in aiming the electrons."

The cat stalked up to Abigail, pushed its forehead against her leg, and mewed insistently. She bent over and picked it up. "But nothing can emerge from a black hole," she objected.

Dominguez chuckled. "Ah, but anything can fall in, hey? A positron can fall in. But a positron falling into Ginungagap in positive time is only an electron falling out in negative time. Which means that a positron falling into a black hole in negative time is actually an electron falling out in positive time—exactly the effect we want. Think of Ginungagap as being the physical manifestation of an equivalence sign in mathematics."

"Oh," Abigail said, feeling very firmly put in her place. White moths flittered along the path. The cat watched, fascinated, while she stroked its head.

"At any rate, the electrons do emerge, and once the data are in, the theory has to follow along meekly."

"Tell me about the spiders," Abigail said before he could continue. The moths were darting up, sideward, down, a chance ballet in three dimensions.

"The *aliens,*" Dominguez said, frowning at Paul, "are still a mystery to us. We exchange facts, descriptions, recipes for tools, but the important questions do not lend themselves to our clumsy mathematical codes. Do they know of love? Do they appreciate beauty? Do they believe in God, hey?"

"Do they want to eat us?" Paul threw in.

"Don't be ridiculous," Dominguez snapped. "Of course they don't."

The moths parted when they came to Abigail. Two went to either side; one flew over her shoulder. The cat batted at it with one paw. "The cat's name is Garble," Paul said. "The kids in Bio cloned him up."

Dominguez opened his mouth, closed it again.

Abigail scratched Garble under the chin. He arched his neck and purred all but noiselessly. "With your permission," Paul said. He stepped over to a keyout and waved its operator aside.

"Technically you're supposed to speak a convenience language, but if you keep it simple and non-idiomatic, there shouldn't be any difficulty." He touched the keyout. "Ritual greetings, spider." There was a blank pause. Then the spider moved, a hairy leg flickering across the screen.

"Hello, human."

"Introductions: Abigail Vanderhoek. She is our representative. She will ride the spinner." Another pause. More leg waving.

"Hello, Abigail Vanderhoek. Transition of vacuum garble resting garble commercial benefits garble still point in space."

"Tricky translation," Paul said. He signed to Abigail to take over.

Abigail hesitated, then said, "Will you come to visit us? The way we will visit you?"

"No, you see—" Dominguez began, but Paul waved him to silence.

"No, Abigail Vanderhoek. We are sulfur-based life."

"I do not understand."

"You can garble black hole through garble spinner because you are carbon-based life. Carbon forms chains easily but sulfur combines in lattices or rosettes. Our garble simple form garble. Sometimes sulfur forms short chains."

"We'll explain later," Paul said. "Go on, you're doing fine."

Abigail hesitated again. What do you say to a spider, anyway? Finally she asked, "Do you want to eat us?"

"Oh, Christ, get her off that thing," Dominguez said, reaching for the keyout.

Paul blocked his arm. "No," he said. "I want to hear this."

Several of the spider legs wove intricate patterns. "The question is false. Sulfur-based life derives no benefit from eating carbon-based life."

"You see," Dominguez said.

"But if it were possible," Abigail persisted. "If you *could* eat us and derive benefit. Would you?"

"Yes, Abigail Vanderhoek. With great pleasure."

Dominguez pushed her aside. "We're terribly sorry," he said to the alien. "This is a horrible, horrible misunderstanding. You!" he shouted to the operator. "Get back on and clear this mess up."

Paul was grinning wickedly. "Come," he said to Abigail. "We've accomplished enough here for one day."

As they started to walk away, Garble twisted in Abigail's arms and leaped free. He hit the floor on all fours and disappeared into the greenery. "Would they really eat us?" Abigail asked. Then amended it to, "Does that mean they're hostile?"

Paul shrugged. "Maybe they thought we'd be insulted if they *didn't* offer to eat us." He led her to her quarters. "Tomorrow we start training for real. In the meantime you might make up a list of all the ways the spiders could hurt us if we set up transportation and they *are* hostile. Then another list of all the reasons we shouldn't trust them." He paused. "I've done it myself. You'll find that the lists get rather extensive."

Abigail's quarters weren't flashy, but they fit her well. A full star field was routed to the walls, floor, and ceiling, only partially obscured by a trellis inner frame that supported fox-grape vines. Somebody had done research into her tastes.

"Hi." The cheery greeting startled her. She whirled, saw that her hammock was occupied.

Cheyney sat up, swung his legs over the edge of the hammock, causing it to rock lightly. "Come on in." He touched an invisible control and the star field blue-shifted down to a deep, erotic purple.

"Just what do you think you're doing here?" Abigail asked.

"I had a few hours free," Cheyney said, "so I thought I'd drop by and seduce you."

"Well, Cheyney, I appreciate your honesty," Abigail said. "So I won't say no."

"Thank you."

"I'll say maybe some other time. Now get lost. I'm tired."

"Okay." Cheyney hopped down, walked jauntily to the door.
He paused. "You said later, right?"

"I said *maybe* later."

"Later. Gotcha." He winked and was gone.

Abigail threw herself into the hammock, red-shifted the star
field until the universe was a sparse smattering of dying embers.
Annoying creature! There was no hope for anything more than
the most superficial of relationships with him. She closed her
eyes, smiled. Fortunately, she wasn't currently in the market for
a serious relationship.

She slept.

She was falling. . . .

Abigail had landed the ship an easy walk from 3M's robot
laboratory. The lab's geodesic dome echoed white clouds to the
north, where Nix Olympus peeked over the horizon. Otherwise
all—land, sky, rocks—was standard-issue Martian orange. She
had clambered to the ground and shrugged on the supply backpack.

Resupplying 3M-RL stations was a gut contract, easy but dull.
So perhaps she was less cautious than usual going down the steep,
rock-strewn hillside, or perhaps the rock would have turned under
her no matter how carefully she placed her feet. Her ankle twisted
and she lurched sideways, but the backpack had shifted her center
of gravity too much for her to be able to recover.

Arms windmilling, she fell.

The rockslide carried her downhill in a panicky flurry of dust
and motion, tearing her flesh and splintering her bones. But before
she could feel pain, her suit shot her full of a nerve synesthetic,
translating sensation into colors—reds, russets, and browns, with
staccato yellow spikes when a rock smashed into her ribs. So that
she fell in a whirling rainbow of glorious light.

She came to rest in a burst of orange. The rocks were settling
about her. A spume of dust drifted away, out toward the distant
red horizon. A large, jagged slab of stone slid by, gently shearing
off her backpack. Tools, supplies, airpacks flew up and softly
rained down.

A spanner as long as her arm slammed down inches from
Abigail's helmet. She flinched, and suddenly events became real.
She kicked her legs and sand and dust fountained up. Drawing
her feet under her body—the one ankle bright gold—she started
to stand.

And was jerked to the ground by a sudden tug on one arm. Even as she turned her head, she became aware of a deep purple sensation in her left hand. It was pinioned by a rock not quite large enough to stake a claim to. There was no color in the fingers.

"Cute," she muttered. She tugged at the arm, pushed at the rock. Nothing budged.

Abigail nudged the radio switch with her chin. "Grounder to Lip Station," she said. She hesitated, feeling foolish, then said, "Mayday. Repeat, Mayday. Could you guys send a rescue party down for me?"

There was no reply. With a sick green feeling in the pit of her stomach, Abigail reached a gloved hand around the back of her helmet. She touched something jagged, a sensation of mottled rust, the broken remains of her radio.

"I think I'm in trouble." She said it aloud and listened to the sound of it. Flat, unemotional—probably true. But nothing to get panicky about.

She took quick stock of what she had to work with. One intact suit and helmet. One spanner. A worldful of rocks, many close at hand. Enough air for—she checked the helmet readout—almost an hour. Assuming the lip station ran its checks on schedule and was fast on the uptake, she had almost half the air she needed.

Most of the backpack's contents were scattered too far away to reach. One rectangular gaspack, however, had landed nearby. She reached for it but could not touch it, squinted but could not read the label on its nozzle. It was almost certainly liquid gas—either nitrogen or oxygen—for the robot lab. There was a slim chance it was the spare airpack. If it was, she might live to be rescued.

Abigail studied the landscape carefully, but there was nothing more. "Okay, then, it's an airpack." She reached as far as her tethered arm would allow. The gaspack remained a tantalizing centimeter out of reach.

For an instant she was stymied. Then, feeling like an idiot, she grabbed the spanner. She hooked it over the gaspack. Felt the gaspack move grudgingly. Slowly nudged it toward herself.

By the time Abigail could drop the spanner and draw in the gaspack, her good arm was blue with fatigue. Sweat running down her face, she juggled the gaspack to read its nozzle markings.

It was liquid oxygen—useless. She could hook it to her suit and feed in the contents, but the first breath would freeze her lungs. She released the gaspack and lay back, staring vacantly at the sky.

Up there was civilization: tens of thousands of human stations strung together by webs of communication and transportation. Messages flowed endlessly on laser cables. Translators borrowed and lent momentum, moving streams of travelers and cargo at almost (but not quite) the speed of light. A starship was being readied to carry a third load of colonists to Proxima. Up there, free from gravity's relentless clutch, people lived in luxury and ease. Here, however . . .

"I'm going to die." She said it softly and was filled with wondering awe. Because it was true. She was going to die.

Death was a black wall. It lay before her, extending to infinity in all directions, smooth and featureless and mysterious. She could almost reach out an arm and touch it. Soon she would come up against it and, if anything lay beyond, pass through. Soon, very soon, she would know.

She touched the seal to her helmet. It felt gray—smooth and inviting. Her fingers moved absently, tracing the seal about her neck. With sudden horror, Abigail realized that she was thinking about undoing it, releasing her air, throwing away the little time she had left. . . .

She shuddered. With sudden resolve, she reached out and unsealed the shoulder seam of her captive arm.

The seal clamped down, automatically cutting off air loss. The flesh of her damaged arm was exposed to the raw Martian atmosphere. Abigail took up the gaspack and cradled it in the pit of her good arm. Awkwardly, she opened the nozzle with the spanner.

She sprayed the exposed arm with liquid oxygen for over a minute before she was certain it had frozen solid. Then she dropped the gaspack, picked up the spanner, and swung.

Her arm shattered into a thousand fragments.

She stood up.

Abigail awoke, tense and sweaty. She blue-shifted the walls up to normal light, and sat up. After a few minutes of clearing her head, she set the walls to cycle from red to blue in a rhythm matching her normal pulse. Eventually the womb-cycle lulled her back to sleep.

"Not even close," Paul said. He ran the tape backward, froze it on a still shot of the spider twisting two legs about each other. "That's the morpheme for 'extreme disgust,' remember. It's easy to pick out, and the language kids say that any statement with this gesture should be reversed in meaning. Irony, see? So when the spider says that the strong should protect the weak, it means—"

"How long have we been doing this?"

"Practically forever," Paul said cheerfully. "You want to call it a day?"

"Only if it won't hurt my standing."

"Hah! Very good." He switched off the keyout. "Nicely thought out. You're absolutely right; it would have. However, as reward for realizing this, you can take off early *without* it being noted on your record."

"Thank you," Abigail said sourly.

Like most large installations, the *Clarke* had a dozen or so smaller structures tagging along after it in minimum-maintenance orbits. When Abigail discovered that these included a small wheel gymnasium, she had taken to putting in an hour's exercise after each training shift. Today she put in two.

The first hour she spent shadowboxing and practicing *savate* in heavy-gee to work up a sweat. The second hour she spent in the axis room, performing free-fall gymnastics. After the first workout, it made her feel light and nimble and good about her body.

She returned from the wheel gym sweaty and cheerful to find Cheyney in her hammock again. "Cheyney," she said, "this is not the first time I've had to kick you out of there. Or even the third, for that matter."

Cheyney held his palms up in mock protest. "Hey, no," he said. "Nothing like that today. I just came by to watch the raft debate with you."

Abigail felt pleasantly weary, decidedly uncerebral. "Paul said something about it, but . . ."

"Turn it on, then. You don't want to miss it." Cheyney touched her wall, and a cluster of images sprang to life at the far end of the room.

"Just what is a raft debate anyway?" Abigail asked, giving in gracefully. She hoisted herself onto the hammock, sat beside him. They rocked gently for a moment.

"There's this raft, see? It's adrift and powerless and there's only enough oxygen on board to keep one person alive until rescue. Only there are three on board—two humans and a spider."

"Do spiders breathe oxygen?"

"It doesn't matter. This is a hypothetical situation." Two-thirds of the image area were taken up by Dominguez and Paul, quietly waiting for the debate to begin. The remainder showed a flat spider image.

"Okay, what then?"

"They argue over who gets to survive. Dominguez argues that he should, since he's human and human culture is superior to spider culture. The spider argues for itself and its culture." He put an arm around her waist. "You smell nice."

"Thank you." She ignored the arm. "What does Paul argue?"

"He's the devil's advocate. He argues that no one deserves to live and they should dump the oxygen."

"Paul would enjoy that role," Abigail said. Then, "What's the point of this debate?"

"It's an entertainment. There isn't supposed to be a point."

Abigail doubted it was that simple. The debate could reveal a good deal about the spiders and how they thought, once the language types were done with it. Conversely, the spiders would doubtless be studying the human responses. *This could be interesting,* she thought. Cheyney was stroking her side now, lightly but with great authority. She postponed reaction, not sure whether she liked it or not.

Louise Chang, a vaguely high-placed administrator, blossomed in the center of the image cluster. "Welcome," she said, and explained the rules of the debate. "The winner will be decided by acclaim," she said, "with half the vote being human and half alien. Please remember not to base your vote on racial chauvinism, but on the strengths of the arguments and how well they are presented." Cheyney's hand brushed casually across her nipples; they stiffened. The hand lingered. "The debate will begin with the gentleman representing the aliens presenting his thesis."

The image flickered as the spider waved several legs. "Thank you, Ms. Chairman. I argue that I should survive. My culture is superior because of our technological advancement. Three examples. Humans have used translation travel only briefly, yet we have used it for sixteens of garble. Our black hole technology is superior. And our garble has garble for the duration of our society."

"Thank you. The gentleman representing humanity?"

"Thank you, Ms. Chairman." Dominguez adjusted an armlet. Cheyney leaned back and let Abigail rest against him. Her head fit comfortably against his shoulder. "My argument is that technology is neither the sole nor the most important measure of a culture. By these standards dolphins would be considered brute animals. The aesthetic considerations—the arts, theology, and the tradition of philosophy—are of greater import. As I shall endeavor to prove."

"He's chosen the wrong tactic," Cheyney whispered in Abigail's ear. "That must have come across as pure garble to the spiders."

"Thank you. Mr. Girard?"

Paul's image expanded. He theatrically swigged from a small flask and hoisted it high in the air. "Alcohol! There's the greatest achievement of the human race!" Abigail snorted. Cheyney laughed out loud. "But I hold that neither Mr. Dominguez nor the distinguished spider deserves to live, because of the disregard both cultures have for sentient life." Abigail looked at Cheyney, who shrugged. "As I shall endeavor to prove." His image dwindled.

Chang said, "The arguments will now proceed, beginning with the distinguished alien."

The spider and then Dominguez ran through their arguments, and to Abigail they seemed markedly lackluster. She didn't give them her full attention, because Cheyney's hands were moving most interestingly across unexpected parts of her body. He might not be too bright, but he was certainly good at some things. She nuzzled her face into his neck, gave him a small peck, returned her attention to the debate.

Paul blossomed again. He juggled something in his palm, held his hand open to reveal three ball bearings. "When I was a kid I used to short out the school module and sneak up to the axis room to play marbles." Abigail smiled, remembering similar stunts she had played. "For the sake of those of us who are spiders, I'll explain that marbles is a game played in free-fall for the purpose of developing coordination and spatial perception. You make a six-armed star of marbles in the center . . ."

One of the bearings fell from his hand, bounced noisily, and disappeared as it rolled out of camera range. "Well, obviously it can't be played here. But the point is that when you shoot the marble just right, it hits the end of one arm and its kinetic energy is transferred from marble to marble along that arm. So that the shooter stops and the marble at the far end of the arm flies away." Cheyney was stroking her absently now, engrossed in the argument.

"Now, we plan to send a courier into Ginungagap and out the spiders' black hole. At least that's what we say we're going to do.

"But what exits from a black hole is not necessarily the same as what went into its partner hole. We throw an electron into Ginungagap and another one pops out elsewhere. It's identical. It's a direct causal relationship. But it's like marbles—they're identical to each other and have the same kinetic force. It's simply not the same electron."

Cheyney's hand was still, motionless. Abigail prodded him gently, touching his inner thigh. "Anyone who's interested can see the equations. Now, when we send messages, this doesn't matter. The message is important, not the medium. However, when we send a human being in . . . what emerges from the other hole will be cell for cell, gene for gene, atom for atom identical. *But it will not be the same person.*" He paused a beat, smiled.

"I submit, then, that this is murder. And further, that by conspiring to commit murder, both the spider and human races display absolute disregard for intelligent life. In short, no one on the raft deserves to live. And I rest my case."

"Mr. Girard!" Dominguez objected, even before his image was restored to full size. "The simplest mathematical proof is an identity: that A equals A. Are you trying to deny this?"

Paul held up the two ball bearings he had left. "These marbles are identical too. But they are not the same marble."

"We know the phenomenon you speak of," the spider said. "It is as if garble the black hole bulges out simultaneously. There is no violation of continuity. The two entities are the same. There is no death."

Abigail pulled Cheyney down, so that they were both lying on their sides, still able to watch the images. "So long as you happen to be the second marble and not the first," Paul said. Abigail tentatively licked Cheyney's ear.

"He's right," Cheyney murmured.

"No he's not," Abigail retorted. She bit his earlobe.

"You mean that?"

"Of course I mean that. He's confusing semantics with reality." She engrossed herself in a study of the back of his neck.

"Okay."

Abigail suddenly sensed that she was missing something. "Why do you ask?" She struggled into a sitting position. Cheyney followed.

"No particular reason." Cheyney's hands began touching her again. But Abigail was sure something had been slipped past her.

They caressed each other lightly while the debate dragged to an end. Not paying much attention, Abigail voted for Dominguez, and Cheyney voted for Paul. As a result of a nearly undivided spider vote, the spider won. "I told you Dominguez was taking the wrong approach," Cheyney said. He hopped off the hammock. "Look, I've got to see somebody about something. I'll be right back."

"You're not leaving *now*?" Abigail protested, dumbfounded. The door irised shut.

Angry and hurt, she leaped down, determined to follow him. She couldn't remember ever feeling so insulted.

Cheyney didn't try to be evasive; it apparently did not occur to him that she might follow. Abigail stalked him down a corridor, up an in-ramp, and to a door that irised open for him. She recognized that door.

Thoughtfully, she squatted on her heels behind an untrimmed boxwood and waited. A minute later, Garble wandered by, saw her, and demanded attention. "Scat!" she hissed. He butted his head against her knee. "Then be quiet, at least." She scooped him up. His expression was smug.

The door irised open and Cheyney exited, whistling. Abigail waited until he was gone, stood, went to the door, and entered. Fish darted between long fronds under a transparent floor. It was an austere room, almost featureless. Abigail looked, but did not see a hammock.

"So Cheyney's working for you now," she said coldly. Paul looked up from a corner keyout.

"As a matter of fact, I've just signed him to permanent contract in the crew room. He's bright enough. A bit green. Ought to do well."

"Then you admit that you put him up to grilling me about your puerile argument in the debate?" Garble struggled in her arms. She juggled him into a more comfortable position. "And that you staged the argument for my benefit in the first place?"

"Ah," Paul said. "I knew the training was going somewhere. You've become very wary in an extremely short time."

"Don't evade the question."

"I needed your honest reaction," Paul said. "Not the answer you would have given me, knowing your chances of crossing Ginungagap rode on it."

Garble made an angry noise. "You tell him, Garble!" she said. "That goes double for me." She stepped out the door. "You lost the debate," she snapped.

Long after the door had irised shut, she could feel Paul's amused smile burning into her back.

Two days after she returned to kick Cheyney out of her hammock for the final time, Abigail was called to the crew room. "Dry run," Paul said. "Attendance is mandatory." And cut off.

The crew room was crowded with technicians, triple the number of keyouts. Small knots of them clustered before the screens, watching. Paul waved her to him.

"There," he motioned to one screen. "That's Clotho—the platform we built for the transmission device. It's a hundred kilometers off. I wanted more, but Dominguez overruled me. The device that'll unravel you and dump you down Ginungagap is that doohickey in the center." He tapped a keyout and the platform zoomed up to fill the screen. It was covered by a clear, transparent bubble. Inside, a space-suited figure was placing something into a machine that looked like nothing so much as a giant armor-clad clamshell. Abigail looked, blinked, looked again.

"That's Garble," she said indignantly.

"Complain to Dominguez. I wanted a baboon."

The clamshell device closed. The space-suited tech left in his tug, and alphanumerics flickered, indicating the device was in operation. As they watched, the spider-designed machinery immobilized Garble, transformed his molecules into one long continuous polymer chain, and spun it out an invisible opening at near light speed. The water in his body was separated out, piped away, and preserved. The electrolyte balances were recorded and simultaneously transmitted in a parallel stream of electrons. It would reach the spider receiver along with the leading end of the cat-polymer, to be used in the reconstruction.

Thirty seconds passed. Now Garble was only partially in Clotho. The polymer chain, invisible and incredibly long, was passing into Ginungagap. On the far side the spiders were beginning to knit it up.

If all was going well . . .

Ninety-two seconds after they flashed on, the alphanumerics stopped twinkling on the screen. Garble was gone from Clotho. The clamshell opened and the remote cameras showed it to be empty. A cheer arose.

Somebody boosted Dominguez atop a keyout. Intercom cameras swiveled to follow. He wavered fractionally, said, "My friends," and launched into a speech. Abigail didn't listen.

Paul's hand fell on her shoulder. It was the first time he had touched her since their initial meeting. "He's only a scientist," he said. "He had no idea how close you are to that cat."

"Look, I *asked* to go. I knew the risks. But Garble's just an animal; he wasn't given the choice."

Paul groped for words. "In a way, this is what your training has been about—the reason you're going across instead of someone like Dominguez. He projects his own reactions onto other people. If—"

Then, seeing that she wasn't listening, he said, "Anyway, you'll have a cat to play with in a few hours. They're only keeping him long enough to test out the life-support systems."

There was a festive air to the second gathering. The spiders reported that Garble had translated flawlessly. A brief visual display showed him stalking about Clotho's sister platform, irritable but apparently unharmed.

"There," somebody said. The screen indicated that the receiver net had taken in the running end of the cat's polymer chain. They waited a minute and a half and the operation was over.

It was like a conjuring trick; the clamshell closed on emptiness. Water was piped in. Then it opened and Garble floated over its center, quietly licking one paw.

Abigail smiled at the homeliness of it. "Welcome back, Garble," she said quietly. "I'll get the guys in Bio to brew up some cream for you."

Paul's eyes flicked in her direction. They lingered for no time at all, long enough to file away another datum for future use, and then his attention was elsewhere. She waited until his back was turned and stuck out her tongue at him.

The tub docked with Clotho and a technician floated in. She removed her helmet self-consciously, aware of her audience. One hand extended, she bobbed toward the cat, calling softly.

"Get that jerk on the line," Paul snapped. "I want her helmet back on. That's sloppy. That's real—"

And in that instant, Garble sprang.

Garble was a black-and-white streak that flashed past the astonished tech, through the air lock, and into the open tug. The cat pounced on the pilot panel. Its forelegs hit the controls. The hatch slammed shut, and the tug's motors burst into life.

Crew room techs grabbed wildly at their keyouts. The tech

on Clotho frantically tried to fit her helmet back on. And the tug took off, blasting away half the protective dome and all the platform's air.

The screens showed a dozen different scenes, lenses shifting from close to distant and back. "Cheyney," Paul said quietly. Dominguez was frozen, looking bewildered. "Take it out."

"It's coming right at us!" somebody shouted.

Cheyney's fingers flicked: rap-tap-rap.

A bright nuclear flower blossomed.

There was silence, dead and complete, in the crew room. *I'm missing something,* Abigail thought. *We just blew up five percent of our tug fleet to kill a cat.*

"*Pull* that transmitter!" Paul strode through the crew room, scattering orders. "Nothing goes out! You, you, and you"—he yanked techs away from their keyouts—"*off* those things. I want the whole goddamned net shut *down*."

"Paul . . ." an operator said.

"Keep on receiving." He didn't bother to look. "Whatever they want to send. Dump it all in storage and don't merge any of it with our data until we've gone over it."

Alone and useless in the center of the room, Dominguez stuttered, "What—what happened?"

"You blind idiot!" Paul turned on him viciously. "Your precious aliens have just made their first hostile move. The cat that came back was nothing like the one we sent. They made changes. They retransmitted it with instructions wetwired into its brain."

"But why would they want to steal a tug?"

"*We don't know!*" Paul roared. "Get that through your head. We don't know their motives and we don't know how they think. But we would have known a lot more about their intentions than we wanted if I hadn't rigged that tug with an abort device."

"You didn't—" Dominguez began. He thought better of the statement.

"—have the authority to rig that device," Paul finished for him. "That's right. I didn't." His voice was heavy with sarcasm.

Dominguez seemed to shrivel. He stared bleakly, blankly, about him, then turned and left, slightly hunched over. Thoroughly discredited in front of the people who worked for him.

That was cold, Abigail thought. She marveled at Paul's cruelty. Not for an instant did she believe that the anger in his voice was real, that he was capable of losing control.

Which meant that in the midst of confusion and stress, Paul

had found time to make a swift play for more power. To Abigail's newly suspicious eye, it looked like a successful one, too.

For five days Paul held the net shut by sheer willpower and force of personality. Information came in but did not go out. Bell-Sandia administration was not behind him; too much time and money had been sunk into Clotho to abandon the project. But Paul had the support of the tech crew, and he knew how to use it.

"Nothing as big as Bell-Sandia runs on popularity," Paul explained. "But I've got enough sympathy from above, and enough hesitation and official cowardice to keep this place shut down long enough to get a message across."

The incoming information flow fluctuated wildly, shifting from subject to subject. Data sequences were dropped halfway through and incomplete. Nonsense came in. The spiders were shifting through strategies in search of the key that would reopen the net.

"When they start repeating themselves," Paul said, "we can assume they understand the threat."

"But we *wouldn't* shut the net down permanently," Abigail pointed out.

Paul shrugged. "So it's a bluff."

They were sharing an after-shift drink in a fifth-level bar. Small red lizards scuttled about the rock wall behind the bartender. "And if your bluff doesn't work?" Abigail asked. "If it's all for nothing—what then?"

Paul's shoulders sagged, a minute shifting of tensions. "Then we trust in the goodwill of the spiders," he said. "We let them call the shots. And they will treat us benevolently or not, depending. In either case," his voice became dark, "I'll have played a lot of games and manipulated a lot of people for no reason at all." He took her hand. "If that happens, I'd like to apologize." His grip was tight, his knuckles pale.

That night, Abigail dreamed she was falling.

Light rainbowed all about her, in a violent splintering of bone and tearing of flesh. She flung out an arm and it bounced on something warm and yielding.

"Abigail."

She twisted and tumbled and something smashed into her ribs. Bright spikes of yellow darted up.

"Abigail!" Someone was shaking her, speaking loudly into her face. The rocks and sky went gray, were overlaid by unresolved images. Her eyelids struggled apart, fell together, opened.

"Oh," she said.

Paul rocked back on his heels. Fish darted about in the water beneath him. "There now," he said. Blue-green lights shifted gently underwater, moving in long, slow arcs. "Dream over?"

Abigail shivered, clutched his arm, let go of it almost immediately. She nodded.

"Good. Tell me about it."

"I—" Abigail began. "Are you asking me as a human being or in your official capacity?"

"I don't make that distinction."

She stretched out a leg and scratched her big toe, to gain time to think. She really didn't have any appropriate thoughts. "Okay," she said, and told him the entire dream.

Paul listened intently, rubbed a thumb across his chin thoughtfully when she was done. "We hired you on the basis of that incident, you know," he said. "Coolness under stress. Weak body image. There were a lot of gravity bums to choose from. But I figured you were just a hair tougher, a little bit grittier."

"What are you trying to tell me? That I'm replaceable?"

Paul shrugged. "Everybody's replaceable. I just wanted to be sure you knew that you could back out if you want. It wouldn't wreck our project."

"I don't want to back out." Abigail chose her words carefully, spoke them slowly, to avoid giving vent to the anger she felt building up inside. "Look, I've been on the gravity circuit for ten years. I've been everywhere in the system there is to go. Did you know that there are less than two thousand people alive who've set foot on Mercury and Pluto? We've got a little club; we get together once a year." Seaweed shifted about her; reflections of the floor lights formed nebulous swimming shapes on the walls. "I've spent my entire life going around and around and around the sun, and never really getting anywhere. I want to travel, and there's nowhere left for me to go. So you offer me a way out and then ask if I want to back down. Like hell I do!"

"Why don't you believe that going through Ginungagap is death?" Paul asked quietly. She looked into his eyes, saw cool calculations going on behind them. It frightened her, almost. He was measuring her, passing judgment, warping events into long logical chains that did not take human factors into account. He was an alien presence.

"It's—common sense, is all. I'll be the same when I exit as when I go in. There'll be no difference, not an atom's worth, not a scintilla."

"The *substance* will be different. Every atom will be different. Not a single electron in your body will be the same one you have now."

"Well, how does that differ so much from normal life?" Abigail demanded. "All our bodies are in constant flux. Molecules come and go. Bit by bit, we're replaced. Does that make us different people from moment to moment? 'All that is body is as coursing vapors,' right?"

Paul's eyes narrowed. "Marcus Aurelius. Your quotation isn't complete, though. It goes on: 'All that is of the soul is dreams and vapors.' "

"What's that supposed to mean?"

"It means that the quotation doesn't say what you claimed it did. If you care to read it literally, it argues the opposite of what you're saying."

"Still, you can't have it both ways. Either the me that comes out of the spider black hole is the same as the one who went in, or I'm not the same person as I was an instant ago."

"I'd argue differently," Paul said. "But no matter. Let's go back to sleep."

He held out a hand, but Abigail felt no inclination to accept it. "Does this mean I've passed your test?"

Paul closed his eyes, stretched a little. "You're still reasonably afraid of dying, and you don't believe that you will," he said. "Yeah. You pass."

"Thanks a heap," Abigail said. They slept, not touching, for the rest of the night.

Three days later, Abigail woke up, and Paul was gone. She touched the wall and spoke his name. A recording appeared. "Dominguez has been called up to Administration," it said. Paul appeared slightly distracted; he had not looked directly into the recorder and his image avoided Abigail's eyes. "I'm going to reopen the net before he returns. It's best we beat him to the punch." The recording clicked off.

Abigail routed an intercom call through to the crew room. A small chime notified him of her call, and he waved a hand in combined greeting and direction to remain silent. He was hunched over a keyout. The screen above it came to life.

"Ritual greetings, spider," he said.

"Hello, human. We wish to pursue our previous inquiry: the meaning of the term 'art,' which was used by the human Dominguez six-sixteenths of the way through his major presentation."

"This is a difficult question. To understand a definition of art, you must first know the philosophy of aesthetics. This is a comprehensive field of knowledge comparable to the study of perception. In many ways it is related."

"What is the trade value of this field of knowledge?"

Dominguez appeared, looking upset. He opened his mouth, and Paul touched a finger to his own lips, nodding his head toward the screen.

"Significant. Our society considers art and science as being of roughly equal value."

"We will consider what to offer in exchange."

"Good. We also have a question for you. Please wait while we select the phrasing." He cut the translation lines, turned to Dominguez. "Looks like your raft gambit paid off. Though I'm surprised they bit at that particular piece of bait."

Dominguez looked weary. "Did they mention the incident with the cat?"

"No, nor the communications blackout."

The old man sighed. "I always felt close to the aliens," he said. "Now they seem—cold, inhuman." He attempted a chuckle. "That was almost a pun, wasn't it?"

"In a human, we'd call it a professional attitude. Don't let it spoil your accomplishment," Paul said. "This could be as big as optics." He opened the communications line again. "Our question is now phrased." Abigail noted he had not told Dominguez of her presence.

"Please go ahead."

"Why did you alter our test animal?"

Much leg waving. "We improved the ratios garble centers of perception garble wetware garble making the animal twelve-sixteenths as intelligent as a human. We thought you would be pleased."

"We were not. Why did the test animal behave in a hostile manner toward us?"

The spider's legs jerked quickly and it disappeared from the screen. Like an echo, the machine said, "Please wait."

Abigail watched Dominguez throw Paul a puzzled look. In the background, a man with a leather sack looped over one shoulder was walking slowly along the twisty access path. His hand dipped into the sack, came out, sprinkled fireflies among the greenery. Dipped in, came out again. Even in the midst of crisis, the trivia of day-to-day existence went on.

The spider reappeared, accompanied by two of its own kind. Their legs interlaced and retreated rapidly, a visual pantomime of an excited conversation. Finally one of their number addressed the screen.

"We have discussed the matter."

"So I see."

"It is our conclusion that the experience of translation through Ginungagap had a negative effect on the test animal. This was not anticipated. It is new knowledge. We know little of the psychology of carbon-based life."

"You're saying the test animal was driven mad?"

"Key word did not translate. We assume understanding. Steps must be taken to prevent a recurrence of this damage. Can you do this?"

Paul said nothing.

"Is this the reason why communications were interrupted?"

No reply.

"There is a cultural gap. Can you clarify?"

"Thank you for your cooperation," Paul said, and switched the screen off. "You can set your people to work," he told Dominguez. "No reason why they should answer the last few questions, though."

"Were they telling the truth?" Dominguez asked wonderingly.

"Probably not. But at least now they'll think twice before trying to jerk us around again." He winked at Abigail, and she switched off the intercom.

They reran the test using a baboon shipped out from the Belt Zoological Gardens. Abigail watched it arrive from the lip station, crated and snarling.

"They're a lot stronger than we are," Paul said. "Very agile. If the spiders want to try any more tricks, we couldn't offer them better bait."

The test went smooth as silk. The baboon was shot through Ginungagap, held by the spiders for several hours, and returned.

Exhaustive testing showed no tampering with the animal.

Abigail asked how accurate the tests were. Paul hooked his hands behind his back. "We're returning the baboon to the Belt. We wouldn't do that if we had any doubts. But—" He raised an eyebrow, asking Abigail to finish the thought.

"But if they're really hostile, they won't underestimate us twice. They'll wait for a human to tamper with."

Paul nodded.

The night before Abigail's sendoff they made love. It was a frenzied and desperate act, performed wordlessly and without tenderness. Afterward they lay together, Abigail idly playing with Paul's curls.

"Gail . . ." His head was hidden in her shoulder; she couldn't see his face. His voice was muffled.

"Mmmm?"

"Don't go."

She wanted to cry. Because as soon as he said it, she knew it was another test, the final one. And she also knew that Paul wanted her to fail it. That he honestly believed transversing Ginungagap would kill her, and that the woman who emerged from the spiders' black hole would not be herself.

His eyes were shut; she could tell by the creases in his forehead. He knew what her answer was. There was no way he could avoid knowing.

Abigail sensed that this was as close to a declaration of emotion as Paul was capable of. She felt how he despised himself for using his real emotions as yet another test, and how he could not even pretend to himself that there were circumstances under which he would *not* so test her. *This must be how it feels to think* as he does, she thought. *To constantly scrabble after every last implication, like eternally picking at a scab.*

"Oh, Paul," she said.

He wrenched about, turning his back to her. "Sometimes I wish"—his hands rose in front of his face like claws; they moved toward his eyes, closed into fists—"that for just ten goddamned minutes I could turn my mind off." His voice was bitter.

Abigail huddled against him, looped a hand over his side and onto his chest. "Hush," she said.

The tug backed away from Clotho, dwindling until it was one of a ring of bright sparks pacing the platform. Mother was a point source lost in the star field. Abigail shivered, pulled off her arm bands, and shoved them into a storage sack. She reached for her *cache-sexe,* hesitated.

The hell with it, she thought. *It's nothing they haven't seen before.* She shucked it off, stood naked. Gooseflesh rose on the backs of her legs. She swam to the transmittal device, feeling awkward under the distant watching eyes.

Abigail groped into the clamshell. "Go," she said.

The metal closed about her seamlessly, encasing her in darkness. She floated in a lotus position, bobbing slightly.

A light, gripping field touched her, stilling her motion. On cue, hypnotic commands took hold in her brain. Her breathing became shallow; her heart slowed. She felt her body ease into stasis. The final command took hold.

Abigail weighed fifty keys. Even though the water in her body would not be transmitted, the polymer chain she was to be transformed into would be 275 kilometers long. It would take fifteen minutes and seventeen seconds to unravel at light speed, negligibly longer at translation speed. She would still be sitting in Clotho when the spiders began knitting her up.

It was possible that Garble had gone mad from a relatively swift transit. Paul doubted it, but he wasn't taking any chances. To protect Abigail's sanity, the meds had wetwired a travel fantasy into her brain. It would blind her to external reality while she traveled. She was an eagle. Great feathered wings extended out from her shoulders. Clotho was gone, leaving her alone in space. Her skin was red and leathery, her breasts hard and unyielding. Feathers covered her thighs, giving way at the knees to talons.

She moved her wings, bouncing lightly against the thin solar wind swirling down into Ginungagap. The vacuum felt like absolute freedom. She screamed a predator's exultant shrill. Nothing enclosed her; she was free of restrictions forever.

Below her lay Ginungagap, the primal chasm, an invisible challenge marked by a red smudge of glowing gases. It was inchoate madness, a gibbering, impersonal force that wanted to draw her in, to crush her in its embrace. Its hunger was fierce and insatiable.

Abigail held her place briefly, effortlessly. Then she folded her wings and dove.

A rain of X-rays stung through her, the scattering of Ginungagap's accretion disk. They were molten iron passing through a ghost. Shrieking defiance, she attacked, scattering sparks in her wake.

Ginungagap grew, swelled until it swallowed up her vision. It was purest black, unseeable, unknowable, a thing of madness. It was Enemy.

A distant objective part of her knew that she was still in Clotho, the polymer chain being unraveled from her body, accelerated by a translator, passing through two black holes, and simultaneously being knit up by the spiders. It didn't matter.

She plunged into Ginungagap as effortlessly as if it were the film of a soap bubble.

In—

—And out.

It was like being reversed in a mirror, or watching an entertainment run backward. She was instantly flying out the way she came. The sky was a mottled mass of violet light.

The stars before her brightened from violet to blue. She craned her neck, looked back at Ginungagap, saw its disk-shaped nothingness recede, and screamed in frustration because it had escaped her. She spread her wings to slow her flight and—

—was sitting in a dark place. Her hand reached out, touched metal, recognized the inside of a clamshell device.

A hairline crack of light looped over her, widened. The clamshell opened.

Oceans of color bathed her face. Abigail straightened, and the act of doing so lifted her up gently. She stared through the transparent bubble at a phosphorescent foreverness of light.

My God, she thought. *The stars*.

The stars were thicker, more numerous than she was used to seeing them—large and bright and glittery rich. She was probably someplace significant, in a star cluster or the center of the galaxy; she couldn't guess. She felt irrationally happy to simply be; she took a deep breath, then laughed.

"Abigail Vanderhoek."

She turned to face the voice, and found that it came from a machine. Spiders crouched beside it, legs moving silently. Outside, in the hard vacuum, were more spiders.

"We regret any pain this may cause," the machine said.

Then the spiders rushed forward. She had no time to react. Sharp mandibles loomed before her, then dipped to her neck. Impossibly swift, they sliced through her throat, severed her spine. A sudden jerk and her head was separated from her body.

It happened in an instant. She felt brief pain, and the dissociation of actually *seeing* her decapitated body just beginning to react. And then she died.

A spark. A light. *I'm alive,* she thought. Consciousness returned like an ancient cathode tube warming up. Abigail stretched slowly, bobbing gently in the air, collecting her thoughts. She was in the sister-Clotho again—not in pain, her head and neck firmly on her shoulders. There were spiders in the platform, and a few floating outside.

"Abigail Vanderhoek," the machine said. "We are ready to begin negotiations."

Abigail said nothing.

After a moment the machine said, "Are you damaged? Are your thoughts impaired?" A pause, then, "Was your mind not protected during transit?"

"Is that you waving the legs there? Outside the platform?"

"Yes. It is important that you talk with the other humans. You must convey our questions. They will not communicate with us."

"I have a few questions of my own," Abigail said. "I won't cooperate until you answer them."

"We will answer any questions provided you neither garble nor garble."

"What do you take me for?" Abigail asked. "Of course I won't."

Long hours later she spoke to Paul and Dominguez. At her request the spiders had withdrawn, leaving her alone. Dominguez looked drawn and haggard. "I swear we had no idea the spiders would attack you," Dominguez said. "We saw it on the screens. I was certain you'd been killed. . . ." His voice trailed off.

"Well, I'm alive, no thanks to you guys. Just what is this crap about an explosive substance in my bones, anyway?"

"An explosive—I swear we know nothing of anything of the kind."

"A close relative to plastique," Paul said. "I had a small editing device attached to Clotho's translator. It altered roughly half the bone marrow in your sternum, pelvis, and femurs in transmission. I'd hoped the spiders wouldn't pick up on it so quickly."

"You actually did," Abigail marveled. "The spiders weren't lying; they decapitated me in self-defense. What the holy hell did you think you were *doing*?"

"Just a precaution," Paul said. "We wetwired you to trigger the stuff on command. That way we could have taken out the spider installation if they'd tried something funny."

"Um," Dominguez said, "this *is* being recorded. What I'd like to know, Ms. Vanderhoek, is how you escaped being destroyed."

"I didn't," Abigail said. "The spiders killed me. Fortunately they anticipated the situation, and recorded the transmission. It was easy for them to recreate me—after they edited out the plastique."

Dominguez gave her an odd look. "You don't—feel anything particular about this?"

"Like what?"

"Well—" He turned to Paul helplessly.

"Like the real Abigail Vanderhoek died and you're simply a very realistic copy," Paul said.

"Look, we've been through this garbage before," Abigail began angrily.

Paul smiled formally at Dominguez. It was hard to adjust to seeing the two in flat black and white. "She doesn't believe a word of it."

"If you guys can pull yourselves up out of your navels for a minute," Abigail said, "I've got a line on something the spiders have that you want. They claim they've sent probes through their black hole."

"Probes?" Paul stiffened. Abigail could sense the thoughts coursing through his skull, of defenses and military applications.

"Carbon-hydrogen-chain probes. Organic probes. Self-constructing transmitters. They've got a carbon-based secondary technology."

"Nonsense," Dominguez said. "How could they convert back to coherent matter without a receiver?"

Abigail shrugged. "They claim to have found a loophole."

"How does it work?" Paul snapped.

"They wouldn't say. They seemed to think you'd pay well for it."

"That's very true," Paul said slowly. "Oh, yes."

The conference took almost as long as her session with the spiders had. Abigail was bone weary when Dominguez finally said, "That ties up the official minutes. We now stop recording." A line tracked across the screen, was gone. "If you want to speak to anyone off the record, now's your chance. Perhaps there is someone close to you . . ."

"Close? No." Abigail almost laughed. "I'll speak to Paul alone, though."

A spider floated by outside Clotho II. It was a golden, crablike being, its body slightly opalescent. It skittered along unseen threads strung between the open platforms of the spider star-city. "I'm listening," Paul said.

"You turned me into a *bomb*, you freak."

"So?"

"I could have been killed."

"Am I supposed to care?"

"You damn well ought to, considering the liberties you've taken with my fair white body."

"Let's get one thing understood," Paul said. "The woman I slept with, the woman I cared for, is dead. I have no feelings toward or obligations to you whatsoever."

"Paul," Abigail said. "*I'm not dead*. Believe me. I'd know if I were."

"How could I possibly trust what you think or feel? It could all be attitudes the spiders wetwired into you. We know they have the technology."

"How do you know that *your* attitudes aren't wetwired in? For that matter, how do you know anything is real? I mean, these are the most sophomoric philosophic ideas there are. But I'm the same woman I was a few hours ago. My memories, opinions, feelings—they're all the same as they were. There's absolutely no difference between me and the woman you slept with on the *Clarke*."

"I know." Paul's eyes were cold. "That's the horror of it." He snapped off the screen.

Abigail found herself staring at the lifeless machinery. *God, that hurt,* she thought. *It shouldn't, but it hurt.* She went to her quarters.

The spiders had done a respectable job of preparing for her. There were no green plants, but otherwise the room was the same as the one she'd had on the *Clarke*. They'd even been able to spin the platform, giving her an adequate down-orientation. She sat in her hammock, determined to think pleasanter thoughts. About the offer the spiders had made, for example. The one she hadn't told Paul and Dominguez about.

Banned by their chemistry from using black holes to travel, the spiders needed a representative to see to their interests among the stars. They had offered her the job.

Or perhaps the plural would be more appropriate—they had

offered her the jobs. Because there were too many places to go for one woman to handle them all. They needed a dozen— in time, perhaps, a hundred—Abigail Vanderhoeks.

In exchange for licensing rights to her personality, the right to make as many duplicates of her as were needed, they were willing to give her the rights to the self-reconstructing black hole platforms.

It would make her a rich woman—a hundred rich women— back in human space. And it would open the universe. She hadn't committed herself yet, but there was no way she was going to turn down the offer. The chance to see a thousand stars? No, she would not pass it by.

When she got old, too, they could create another Abigail from their recording, burn her new memories into it, and destroy her old body.

I'm going to see the stars, she thought. *I'm going to live forever.* She couldn't understand why she didn't feel elated, wondered at the sudden rush of melancholy that ran through her like the precursor of tears.

Garble jumped into her lap, offered his belly to be scratched. The spiders had recorded him, too. They had been glad to restore him to his unaltered state when she made the request. She stroked his stomach and buried her face in his fur.

"Pretty little cat," she told him. "I thought you were dead."

Nunc Dimittis

JERRY POURNELLE

WE—THIS GENERATION, we the people of the United States—could make, within ten years, as fundamental a change in human destiny as was ever made. We could participate in the next stage of humanity.

Alvin Toffler's best-seller *The Third Wave* divides human history into three periods. Marx (whose general ideas Toffler follows) had four (or five) stages. Other historians employ slightly different schema, but all seem agreed that there have been only a very few critical stages in the history of our race. All seem agreed that certain key inventions divide one stage from another. The domestication of animals; harnessing of fire; invention of agriculture; invention of the wheel; the Industrial Revolution: these are seen as crucial watersheds. After them, "things were different."

Perhaps Trinity (together with Hiroshima, Nagasaki, Alamogordo, Bikini) was another such. If so, then my generation is uniquely privileged, for we may see two such crucial eras within our lifetimes. Indeed, unless the "new era" midwifed by Fermi at Jackass Flats is somehow absorbed or negated, we may have seen the *last* watershed event of human development; but fortunately we have the means at hand. We can go beyond the nuclear era. Indeed, we can, if we want to, usher in new developments so profound that we have to go back to the invention of language, or the evolution of lungs, to find anything as important.

Some time ago I was privileged to participate in a study of the future. Sponsored by Dr. Robert Frosch, administrator of NASA (who was an active participant in the week-long activity), the study was instructed to examine possible advances in artificial intelligence and remotely operated equipment and develop "bold new missions" for the next fifty years. For a week we—about twenty of us, including John R. Pierce (Chief Technologist at Jet Propulsion Laboratories, and better known here as J. J. Coupling), Roy Smelt (former chief scientist at Lockheed), Marvin Minsky (Artificial Intelligence Laboratories, M.I.T.), several NASA project directors, and others of that stature—looked at just what we can do right now in space.

The idea was this: can we put into space an automated system that can use space materials to build copies of itself? (One of our conclusions was that anything that can replicate itself will necessarily be so complex that it *must* be able to make useful byproducts. As a worst case you can harvest factories.)

Second: we can build a lunar colony. Now. This decade.

Note what we said. Colony. (Or, as one NASA official suggested, "settlement": "colony" is not an in word this decade.)

Colonists do not expect to return. Colonists expect to live out their lives in their new homes. It's not at all clear that we can put up a lunar *base* in this decade; but the probability that we can build a *very* nearly self-sustaining *colony* approaches certainty. Now, true: the colony will not, for another twenty or more years, be truly self-sustaining. It will doubtless need help. Vitamin pills. Tools. Certain chemicals (of which more later). And above all, communications, including *skills*.

But—whoa! Pournelle, haven't you just lost your mind? How can you import skills without importing people? I mean, sure, we see that communications can help a lot, but some jobs just take a long time to learn. An experimental mechanic, or a screw machine operator, can *tell* you what he does for months, but *you* won't be able to do it. Not as he does it.

Agreed, and yet we can import skills.

The secret is Waldoes.

Longtime readers of science fiction will remember the novella "Waldo" (sometimes published as *Waldo: Genius in Orbit*) by Robert A. Heinlein. It introduces the concept of machines that amplify human effort: that is, one puts one's hands into the control gloves, and whatever one does there will be repeated by a pair of mechanical hands at a remote distance. The remote hands may have super-human strength and hyper-human dexterity. They may be much better than human hands (at least, in theory). Thus,

Waldoes can *amplify* what people do.

Now the problem with lunar colonies is people. It's not so hard to support machines on the Moon, but human beings require fairly benign environments. Oh, sure, we're tough and far more self-repairing than machines; but we do need a relatively narrow range of temperatures, pressures and chemical exposures. We need a complex support system too: either ways to grow food (living stuff, which itself needs a controlled environment) or continuous supplies of foodstuffs from the outside; plus oxygen and water and all that.

Machines, on the other hand, will tolerate conditions that render people inoperative. They don't take *nearly* as much support paraphernalia as do people. Except for one problem: the machines, ultimately, need human attendants. They aren't self-repairing. They don't understand themselves.

Now it's true that the AI (Artificial Intelligence) people are working on the problem. It won't be long, they say, before we have machines that "know themselves" and "understand" what their purpose is, thus enabling them to repair themselves.

Real Soon Now.

If I seem a bit cynical, it's because I recall that a few years ago John McCarthy of the Stanford Artificial Intelligence Laboratories bought a Heathkit color TV with the idea that he'd have a robot assemble it—and no AI outfit yet has a robot that can open the packing crate. And note that this is not intended as a slight on John McCarthy, who's not only a good friend but among the most brilliant people I know. Nor do I doubt that eventually the AI people will be able to build robots capable of constructing a Heathkit color TV (and also changing the spark plugs in my car, baking a cake, tuning in Channel 13, changing the baby's diapers and digging a new cellar).

But they can't do it yet, and they won't do it for a number of years; twenty years anyway. Maybe more.

We can however, build Waldoes in this decade.

And Waldoes will let us colonize the Moon.

Consider the situation. A colony—from twelve to twenty people, mixed sexes, probably married couples—goes to Luna.

They may not have lifeboats. If they're true colonists, they'll have insisted that the payload mass that might have gone to lifeboats be put into additional supplies and equipment to ensure the survival of the colony.

One of their tasks is to construct a means to inject lunar material into orbit and start sending up mass that can be used for orbital construction. It won't take many hundreds of tonnes of lunar materials—including oxygen, which is plentiful on the Moon—put into Earth orbit before the lunar colony has made a profit.

Their primary task, though, is to survive; to build the lunar colony and make it permanent. This is likely to take up most of their time for several years. There isn't going to be a lot left over for mining and refining and constructing a mass-launcher. They'll be too busy carving out living quarters and assuring their oxygen supply. There'll be no one to drive the bulldozer—and this means no one will pay for the colony in the first place.

Enter Dr. Marvin Minsky, of M.I.T.'s Artificial Intelligence Laboratories. Minsky points out that Waldoes can effectively multiply the number of lunar colonists, thus making it possible for the colony to begin work on the payoff system. With Waldoes we can have three shifts a day working on mines and refineries—and also have considerable variety in the skills effectively on the Moon.

Note that this also impacts on the colonist selection criteria. Since we don't have to import all skills—indeed, if the Waldoes are constructed well enough there are very few skills that must be physically present on the Moon—we can select for ingenuity, health, motivation, hardiness; we can look for highly motivated generalists, leaving the specialists down here.

During the NASA conference Minsky and I also worked out that DuPont Kevlar is strong enough to make a centrifugal sling that can throw material off the lunar surface. It won't be necessary to make enormous linear mass drivers to get lunar mass into useful orbits. Thus, if we have the colony, we have a good chance at profits.

Now, back in the sixties I was part of a team that designed a small semi-permanent lunar base. We did enough engineering to conclude it was feasible. Now we know a lot more about the Moon, and although there are some tricky design features, I don't see any show-stoppers. The lunar colony can be constructed with today's technology. Thus two elements of the colony require only engineering development, not new technology.

Unfortunately, that's not true of the Waldoes. Not only don't we have good Waldoes, we don't even have a good five-fingered mechanical hand. Despite enormous advances in computers, despite developments of smarter and smarter programs, we're not much closer to Waldoes now than we were thirty years ago. But cheer up; the main reason we don't have good hands and working Waldoes is that no one has ever been willing to pay for them.

Which, as Minsky points out, is plain silly. Example: how much would it have been worth to have a good Waldo inside the containment at Three Mile Island during the crisis period? (For that matter, what would it be worth *now*?)

Given the costs of operating the deep submersible *Alvin*, why must researchers put up with clumsy two-fingered claws incapable of collecting specimens without crushing them? What would oil drilling companies pay to have full Waldoes operating at the bottom of the sea—or even deep inside the well shaft?

We need Waldoes here on Earth, and we're silly not to be doing the research that would produce them. Ah, well, the Japanese will build them if we don't.

Now true, operating Waldoes on the Moon is a bit more complicated than running them here on EArth, because of the 1.5 second each way communications lag. When you tell the bulldozer to do something, it doesn't get the order until more than a second later, and the acknowledgment doesn't arrive until nearly 3 seconds have elapsed. Note, however, that this doesn't prevent highly complicated operations; it only means that the most delicate things must be done slowly.

In fact, though, by installing computers in our Waldoes, we can do it even better. The computer need not know in advance how to do anything at all; but it can follow what the human Waldo operator has done, remember that, and in future do that for itself.

Note what that does; not only can most of the lunar work be done by tele-operators working three shifts on *Earth*, but that as time goes on even *that* work becomes increasingly automated as the smart on-board lunar computers learn how to do it.

Costs fall as production rises. Meanwhile, the colony expands (it takes about fifteen years for humans to replicate themselves). New professions arise: prospectors, engineers, gadgeteers, system analysts who *understand* the Moon. And all of this with minimal investments from Earth.

You can see where it leads: highly automated, highly productive space systems; an economics of abundance, where a major problem is to persuade enough people to accept gifts. That stage

takes a while to reach, but once we go to space in a big way—
it's inevitable.

The only thing stopping us from getting to space is the basic
transport system to orbit. The official name of the Shuttle is "STS"
or space transport system: and that is exactly what Shuttle is *not*.
It's a special-case system, a flying testbed requiring 15,000 or
more people to refurbish and operate it.

Airlines typically operate at 3 to 5 times fuel costs. That
includes paying for the airplane. It takes about the same amount
of fuel to fly a pound from the U.S. to Australia as it does to put
that pound in orbit: but the trip to orbit costs about 5,000 times
as much. Why?

Airlines typically operate with 110 employees per airplane.
Most of those sell tickets. The SR-71, which had no ticket sales,
ran with 42 employees per ship. NASA has four more or less
operational craft supported by about 22,000 people. We may have
found the reason for the excessive costs.

It is possible to build spacecraft that will operate at a small
multiple of fuel costs. The cost of building the first five such
ships—the R&D costs—are estimated variously at $250 million
to $20 billion. Perhaps I should explain.

The $250 million program assumes that someone writes a check
to The Lunar Society. We take it from there, contracting out
the work, subcontracting most of it, and using volunteers—we
have *plenty* of volunteers in electronics, chemistry, engineering,
metallurgy, who would work for room and found, if they could
be part of a *real* space program. Most of the work would be done
in the Mojave Desert, in the town of Mojave and farther out: not
a real good place for an empire. People will want to get the job
done and go home.

Given that, yes, we could probably build the first three to five
ships for $250 million.

The next possibility is for the Department of Defense to do
it as a black project: hand the money to a good contractor like
Lockheed or General Dynamics or Boeing, tell them what is
wanted, and get the heck out of the way. That would cost between
2 and 4 billion dollars. The next step up would be to do it as a
normal U.S. government contract out of the Pentagon, managed
by, say, the Strategic Defense Initiative Office, or the Defense
Advanced Research Projects Agency. That would cost between
10 and 20 billion dollars. The extra money goes to the government

requirements for paperwork: the money that supposedly prevents fraud and waste, and adds a factor of 3 to 10 to the costs of everything.

The final way would be to hand it to NASA. That would cost $40 billion, and when it was done we would not have any ships: just lots of paper, and lots of good reasons why we didn't get the ships built.

There's one more way: Congress could simply declare that the Treasurer of the United States will pay the sum of $2 billion to the first U.S. company that successfully builds three ships that can each fly to orbit and return 25 times in fewer than 60 days. No ships, no money; no up-front costs; just, "you build it, we'll pay you; you don't build it, we're not out a cent." Carry that one further. "The Congress of the United States directs the Treasurer of the United States to pay the sum of $10 billion to the first U.S. citizen or company chartered in the U.S. to put 25 U.S. citizens on the Moon and keep them there continuously for two years and one day . . ."

It would work, you know.

Given the ships, we'll build the Waldoes; and with that we will have the Moon; and once we have lunar colonies, we're on our way. The Asteroid Belt, the planets, the comets, and eventually the stars will be ours—and *we* will have seen it begin. Some of us can even be a part of it. It could happen. In your lifetime. You could make it happen: change the history of the human race.

What more can we ask for?